A TOUCH
UNEXPECTED

A.L. RIVERS

ISBN # 979-8-9922115-2-8

www.alriverswrites.com

Selfishly, for myself—for actually seeing this through. And for those like me, who tend to let insecurity and perfectionism get the best of them.

1

FIFTEEN YEARS EARLIER

A HEAVY LAYER OF morning mist blanketed the shabby, weather-worn wooden platform on which Rosalind and her father stood quietly. The somber eeriness that enveloped them had Rosalind shuffling a little closer to the comforting presence beside her.

"Rosalind, my love, let me have a good look at you," said her father as he knelt down to level his gaze with hers. His movements were slow and strained, and Rosalind didn't miss the grimace that flashed across his face as he settled into an unsteady crouch.

For a long moment, he said nothing. He simply regarded her with glassy eyes and a smile that was equal parts tender and sorrowful.

Rosalind's eyes traced the lines of her father's face, which had grown sharper in recent weeks. There was a grayish hue to his skin that she wanted to believe was attributed to their drab surroundings. But his hollowed cheeks and labored breath indicated otherwise.

"Do you remember what I told you? You're to get off at a station called Denault Proper, about five hours from here. *Denault Proper,*" he repeated slowly for emphasis. "It's the largest town in the region. That's where my cousin Maria and her husband, Louis, will meet you. She is the housekeeper of Brighthall Manor, and her husband is the steward there. They'll be taking you to the manor, and I am told it's grander than anything we've ever seen around here. Much more impressive than the rickety old place we've been holed up in."

Our home, Rosalind wanted to say. She had lived in the little one-room house her whole life and she liked it there. It was where they spent their days tending to their garden of vegetables and chasing ladybugs. And in the evenings, they sat beside the hearth, reading stories of pirates, princesses, and far-off lands. They had spent more and more time inside as of late, but Rosalind didn't mind. At home, nobody gave her odd or wary looks. No one whispered about her.

"Just imagine all the advent—" her father began, but he was cut short by a bout of strangled coughs. "Adventures you're going to go on there," he rasped out once he'd caught his breath.

"I don't want to go," Rosalind said quietly. She stared down at her hands, tugging and twisting at the fabric of her linen dress. "What if I get lost?"

"Maria will take good care of you, my love," he reassured her. "She'll make sure you always find your way. She and Louis have a little cottage on the estate grounds. That's where I imagine you'll spend most of your days. Not too big to get lost in." Her father offered her an encouraging smile.

Rosalind's vision blurred as hot tears surfaced. They streamed down her cheeks as she looked at him. "But I want to stay here with you, Papa," she whispered.

"I know," her father said hoarsely, sadness in his eyes. "I know."

He moved a hand toward her, but it never reached Rosalind's face. Instead, he drew back as sparks of gold light erupted from where his fingers met invisible resistance just inches away. The sparks soon faded into nothingness between them.

Rosalind wiped at her tears. "I'm sorry," she murmured.

Her father shook his head. "You never need to apologize to me, my love. It isn't your fault," he said gently. "None of it is your fault."

Rosalind sniffled. "Then why are you sending me away?"

His shoulders sagged. "You know why," he answered softly.

And she did. It had never been voiced aloud, but the signs were there. She could see it on his face. Smell it on his clothes. Not unlike the wounded dove she and her father once cared for.

Her father spoke again. "I have done the best I can since your mother left this world, but you deserve more. You need someone who can take your hand when you're scared, hold you when you're hurt, embrace you when you're sad." He wore a wistful smile as he added, "Someone who will be by your side for years to come."

As if on cue, a horn sounded in the distance, and the tracks beyond them began to rattle.

"It's time, my love." Her father carefully pushed himself off the ground and turned to face the approaching train. "Now, remind me. Which station are you to get off at again?"

"Denault Proper," Rosalind replied but her answer was drowned out by the train's horn as it announced its arrival.

Her father put a hand to his ear and hollered, "What's that?"

"Denault Proper!" she shouted at the top of her lungs. She knew he'd heard her by the approving grin he wore.

The wooden platform shuddered beneath their feet as the train slowed to a halt in front of them. The pair stood silently next to one another until an attendant slid open a door and stuck her head out. "Headed for the inner cities?"

"Ah, perfect. A woman," her father exclaimed, to which the attendant gave him an odd look.

Rosalind looked up at her father one last time. He offered her a reassuring nod and guided her to the steps of the train door. "Up you go, little one."

Hesitantly, Rosalind reached out to meet the attendant's outstretched hand and was promptly pulled up onto the train. Once on, the attendant patted gently at her shoulder.

"It's alright, my dear. You'll see him again soon. Now, feel free to take any available seat. Perhaps one by the window?"

Though the attendant meant well, her words brought fresh tears. Rosalind jumped as the train horn sounded and rushed to the nearest window seat. Her breath fogged up the windowpane as she held her face close to it, her eyes glued to her father's.

Soon, the train began to move. Rosalind watched her father keep pace alongside the train as it slowly picked up speed. He mouthed the same words over and over again.

I love you. I love you. I love you.

As the train pulled farther and farther away from the station, she could only sit and watch as his figure faded into the mist.

Rosalind followed her father's instructions and departed the train at Denault Proper. Not knowing what to do next, she weaved her way through the stream of bodies that strolled along the platform, careful not to run into anyone. She then tucked herself into a corner and waited. It wasn't long before a stout woman with kind eyes approached her, accompanied by a wiry man with prominent sideburns.

"You must be Rosalind," said the woman with a soft smile. "My name is Maria, and this is my husband, Louis. We are here to take you to Brighthall." She held out her hand.

Rosalind didn't move. Instead, her gaze drifted from the hand in front of her to the train she had arrived on. If she got back on it, would it take her back to her father? A pang of longing burned in her chest. Then she recalled his words. *She'll take good care of you.* And she knew this was what he wanted for her.

With slight trepidation, Rosalind reached out and took hold of the woman's hand.

"Stay close to me," Maria said, drawing Rosalind into her. "I'll make sure no one gets near you, my dear."

The three of them exited the station and stopped in front of a large black carriage. Emblazoned on the side was a circular emblem the color of deep violet. The letter D was etched in gold, enveloped by sprigs of wheat. It was like something out of a fairytale, or so Rosalind thought.

"The lady of the manor let us borrow it. Impressive, isn't it?"

Rosalind looked up at Louis, the man who had spoken. He was smiling at her. So overwhelmed by everything she'd seen and heard since departing the train, she could only nod in response.

Louis opened the carriage door and Maria helped Rosalind inside. She took the seat across from her as Louis shut the door behind them and took his place at the front. Rosalind felt the carriage shift under her as it began to move.

"It's about an hour's ride to the manor," Maria remarked. "Are you hungry at all? I packed a few sweets with me." She rummaged through her bag.

Rosalind had been too nervous to order anything on the five-hour train ride, but now the thought of food had her stomach grumbling. She watched as Maria untied the cloth pouch in her lap, revealing three scones.

"Do you like blueberries?" Maria asked, offering one to Rosalind.

Rosalind nodded as she reached for the scone. She brought it to her nose; it was the loveliest scent she had ever smelled in her life. She took a bite, and then another. And then another.

"There's two more waiting for you," Maria said with a chuckle. "Blueberry scones are Jonathan's favorite. You'll meet him later today, I suspect."

Rosalind watched in awe as they rode alongside luscious green rolling hills, spanning as far as the eye could see. Eventually, the landscape beyond the window changed from spacious meadows to tall cypress trees, all tidy and in a line. Soon after passing a large stone fountain, the carriage came to a halt and Maria helped Rosalind out.

Brighthall Manor was indeed grand—grander than anything Rosalind could have imagined. Stone steps led up to two massive wooden doors, which stood ajar. Tall windows adorned the front of the building and Rosalind had to turn her head far to the left and then to the right to see where the wall started and ended.

"I'll take the carriage to the stables while you head in to see her ladyship," Louis said to Maria.

Rosalind scrambled for Maria's hand, not wanting to be left alone. Maria squeezed it reassuringly as they started toward the double doors. Once inside, Rosalind was again met with a sight unlike anything she had seen before. A vaulted ceiling loomed above her while black and white marble squares lay at her feet. In front of her stood an ebony staircase, leading up to a balcony, which overlooked the sprawling entryway. Rosalind could just make out the row of doors that sat far back from the balcony's edge.

Maria guided Rosalind past the staircase to a short hallway under the balcony. Dark mahogany lined the bottom half of the walls, while paintings of landscapes, mountaintops, and ships at sea hung on burgundy damask wallpaper. They stopped in front of a door, the same mahogany as the walls. Maria knocked, and a muffled voice sounded from the other side. She opened it and led Rosalind inside.

Rosalind's gaze was immediately drawn to the vast wall of books that lined the left side of the room. She hadn't thought it possible for anyone to own so many. How different it was to the small stack of books her father would choose from in the evenings. She bit at her lip to keep it from quivering, desperate not to cry.

"My lady, I would like to introduce you to Miss Rosalind Carver. This is the young girl I told you about." She patted Rosalind's back, encouraging her to step forward.

Rosalind gazed up at the older woman who approached her. She was tall and narrow-framed, and she seemed to glide across the floor, the hem of her pleated, cream-colored dress skimming along the carpet. A black ribbon adorned the dress's high collar, emphasizing her long neck. The coal black and silver strands of her hair were swept into a tidy updo, revealing a sharp jawline and prominent cheekbones. She looked exceedingly stern, Rosalind decided. But once the woman knelt in front of her, it was impossible to miss the softness in her eyes and the slight quirk of her lips.

"My name is Lady Tildawan Rashford and this is my home. It's a pleasure to make your acquaintance." The woman dipped her head slightly.

Rosalind's eyes widened at the gesture. She wasn't a lady; she didn't know how to respond. No one had ever greeted her that way before. Unsure of what to do, she simply mimicked the gesture.

The woman, Lady Rashford, chuckled. "Very good, thank you. I saw you eyeing the bookshelf earlier. Do you like books?"

Rosalind nodded.

"Not chatty, this one," said Maria from behind her. "Been mum since she arrived."

"Hmm." A moment later, Lady Rashford inquired, "How would you like to meet my grandchildren? You've been around adults all day. I suspect it'd be rather nice to be around those your own age for a change."

Rosalind chewed her lip. On rare occasions, she played with children from the village nearby, but the fun was often short-lived. Once they learned about her *affliction*, they tended to steer clear of her. The fact that it had no effect on girls meant nothing. She was considered by many to be a bad omen. A relic of the Old Laws that no one truly understood. If it could happen to her, what's to say it couldn't happen to them? To associate with her was to tempt fate, or so they believed. It seemed unlikely her grandchildren would be any different.

"It'll be alright, my dear," Maria said, reassuringly. "I promise."

"They're in the drawing room, I believe," said Lady Rashford as she led Maria and Rosalind out of the study. They made their way past the grand staircase to a large room filled with warm afternoon light.

Rosalind peered around. A pianoforte sat in one corner of the room, a small desk in another. In the center was a seating area with a sizeable striped settee and two paisley armchairs. The wall behind them housed a large hearth with a carved stone mantelpiece. A boy and a girl sat at its base with cards, colored pencils, and papers strewn about them.

"Children," Lady Rashford announced, "there is someone I would like you both to meet. This here is Miss Rosalind Carver. She has traveled over five hours to join us today. Impressive, yes? Now, how about you two introduce yourselves."

The young girl with plaited hair, dark as obsidian, shot to her feet.

"My name is Valentina," she said with a shallow bow of her head, "but most call me Val. Well actually, only those I like can call me that. I am seven years and nine months old. I know, you probably thought I was older because I'm quite tall for my age. But truly, my birthday is in three months—ninety-two days to be exact." She beamed. "How old are you?"

"Six," Rosalind said quietly. "And a half," she added quickly.

"We're only a year apart, you and I. Well, more like fifteen months. If you have any questions about turning seven, you can ask me." She proceeded to jab a finger into the arm of the boy next to her. "Oh, and this is my brother, Jon—"

"Val," the boy groaned as he batted her hand away. "I can do my own introductions, thank you very much." He cleared his throat and bowed his head. "My name is Jonathan and I'm ten years old. In case you're wondering, I'm the average height for my age. Even so, Grandmum says the men in my family are late bloomers so I will be as well."

Rosalind's eyes darted between the siblings. They were nearly the same height, with Jonathan winning out by mere inches. Had she not known their ages, she might have thought they were twins. Like Valentina, Jonathan had dark hair. And they had the same eyes. They reminded her of the sea—not for their color, but for their profound depth, akin to staring into deep waters on a starless night.

Valentina snorted. "She just says that to make you feel better."

Jonathan shot her a narrow look and opened his mouth to speak. He closed it and turned back to Rosalind. "Ignoring her is the best way to annoy her. Anyway, it's nice to meet you." He held out his hand.

Rosalind felt her stomach drop as she stared helplessly at the hand outstretched in front of her. She looked over at Maria, terrified and uncertain of what to do next.

"Oh, I'm sorry about that, love," Maria called out to Jonathan. "She won't be able to shake your hand, I'm afraid."

"Why not?" Valentina asked. "Is she missing a hand?" She peered over to see Rosalind wringing her hands. "Oh, no, she has both," she murmured, a hint of disappointment in her voice.

"Well..." It was Lady Rashford who spoke this time. "I guess one could say Rosalind here is special. She has"—she paused briefly—"a condition, if you will. One that makes it so men can't touch her."

"But Jonathan isn't a man. Quite far from it," Valentina said with a smirk.

"Valentina," Lady Rashford warned before continuing. "Miss Rosalind is from a small village in the borderlands of Denault." She turned to Jonathan. "Remember your studies. What can you tell me about that area?"

Jonathan furrowed his brow in consideration. His eyes lit up when the answer came to him. "The borderlands are located in the westernmost part of our region. It extends into Meridian, the region next to us. There aren't any big cities like Denault Proper, but plenty of villages. And just beyond the borderlands is a large forest, which divides Sauvign from Erdesay."

"Very good," said Lady Rashford. "Now, what is the most significant difference between our country and Erdesay?"

Jonathan squinted in thought, absentmindedly rubbing at his chin. "Erdesay," he began slowly, "abides by the Old Laws whereas we abide by the New Laws. Magic is forbidden under the New Laws so we can't use magic, but Erdesians can."

"That is very nearly correct, my dear."

Valentina snickered. "She means you got it wrong."

Lady Rashford leveled a reproving eye on her granddaughter. "Tell me, Valentina, since you were so quick to mock your brother, what was inaccurate about what he said?"

Valentina fell silent. Averting her gaze, she murmured, "I don't know."

Lady Rashford sighed. "Magic itself is not forbidden under the New Laws. If that were the case, we wouldn't be allowed to possess magical items as we do. Take your pencil, for example, Valentina. It will never break nor will it expire because it has been imbued with magic for precisely that purpose."

"It is the practice of *wielding* magic that is against the law," she explained. "Under no circumstances may someone with the ability to manipulate magic to their will be permitted to do so."

Lady Rashford turned to Jonathan. "Do you understand the distinction?"

He nodded.

Rosalind watched the entire exchange with a mix of terror and awe. She was amazed at how knowledgeable Jonathan was and how easily he seemed to comprehend what Lady Rashford had said. At the same time, she was terrified to think she might be expected to know all of this as well.

"Don't worry if you didn't catch all that," Valentina whispered as she shuffled to where Rosalind stood.

"Jonathan needs to know these things because he's going to be Chancellor of Denault one day, like our father was. He takes special lessons with Grandmum while I sew and paint and do whatever it is polite ladies are supposed to do." She rolled her eyes at the last part.

"Valentina, do you have something you would like to add?" Lady Rashford asked with a critical brow.

The young girl in question straightened and shook her head.

"Pay attention, please. There's a reason why I want both you and Jonathan to know the difference. While wielding magic is illegal, simply possessing something of magic is not unlawful. Most often, such magic will come in the form of an imbued tincture or artifact, but occasionally it can manifest in other ways."

Lady Rashford moved to stand behind Rosalind and gently rested her hands atop her shoulders. "In Rosalind's case, the magic she possesses comes in the form of an enchantment, one she has no control over."

"An enchantment? You mean like something out of a fairytale?" Valentina's eyes widened and more questions spilled out in quick succession. "Can you fly? Do you have a tail? Can you turn into a dragon?"

Rosalind chewed the inside of her lip. "No, nothing like that," she said quietly.

Not knowing how best to explain it, she decided it would be easiest to recite the proverb aloud.

"A young girl's life
Taken too soon by man's foolish strife.
Wielded in heartbreak,

An enchantment a grieving mother did make.
So to all men, Beware
All around, there is fervid magic in her air.
Kept safe from all of he,
Until two and twenty, a border born shall be."

Rosalind stared down at the ground, hands wringing together as she waited for someone to say something. Anything. Now that they had heard it, would they think her a bad omen? Most others did. What if they didn't want to be around her? Or worse, what if Maria changed her mind and no longer wanted to care for her? She felt tears prick the corner of her eyes.

"So what would happen if I tried to shake your hand? Would I die?" Jonathan inquired cautiously.

Rosalind shook her head wildly back and forth. "No!" she said hurriedly. "No, but it might..." She hesitated. "It might hurt a little. My father says it feels like putting your hand too close to the flame."

Jonathan seemed to consider her answer before asking, "Does it hurt you?"

The question took Rosalind by surprise. No one besides her father had ever asked her that.

"N-no," she stammered, "I don't feel anything at all."

Without warning, Jonathan stepped toward Rosalind and reached out a hand. Moments later, she heard him yelp as sparks of golden light crackled in the air where his hand had ventured.

"Jonathan," Lady Rashford admonished.

"Sorry," he said sheepishly. "I just wanted to see for myself."

"And?" Valentina asked eagerly.

Jonathan shrugged. "It happened so quickly, but..." He paused as if to consider. "I touched *something*. It was like a wall I couldn't see. And for a second, it felt cold like ice, and then—well, then it burned. Kind of like when you accidentally pick up a hot poker."

"That's unfortunate for you," said Valentina unsympathetically as she took Rosalind's hand in hers. "Doesn't bother me in the slightest." She grinned triumphantly.

Rosalind stared at Valentina incredulously. Even after everything she had learned, she still wanted to associate with her?

Jonathan rolled his eyes. "I'm not sure which is worse. Her enchantment"—he nodded his head at Rosalind—"or having *you* as a sister."

Rosalind couldn't believe her ears. Instead of taunting her, they were taunting one another. She peered around and found Lady Rashford was watching her grandchildren with a contemplative expression.

"Maria, may I have a word?" Lady Rashford ushered the housekeeper to the corner of the room, and the two spoke in hushed conversation.

Rosalind observed the women, attempting to decipher what they were talking about based on their expressions. Lady Rashford maintained a calm demeanor as she spoke. Maria's expression, however, shifted from what looked like worry to disbelief to elation. Rosalind watched Maria wipe a tear from her eye.

"Are you quite certain, my lady?"

It was the only snippet of conversation Rosalind could make out. Her palms began to sweat. They were talking about her; she just knew it. Were they going to send her away? To where? There was nowhere else, no one else. She thought of her father and her heart ached.

The women rejoined the children and Lady Rashford cleared her throat, silencing the Rashford siblings.

"Jonathan, Valentina, starting today, Miss Rosalind will be staying with us. She is to settle into the room neighboring yours, Valentina."

Rosalind couldn't have heard her correctly. Wasn't she supposed to stay in the cottage with Maria and Louis? She glanced over at the housekeeper, who nodded and offered her a reassuring smile.

Valentina clapped her hands together. "How wonderful! But what of your mother and father? Will they be joining us as well?"

"No, my dears," Maria chimed in. "It'll just be Miss Rosalind." The softness in her voice was comforting even as Rosalind's heart tightened in her chest. She thought of her father's face and couldn't hold back the tears that welled up in her eyes.

"It's alright," said Valentina gently as she once again took hold of Rosalind's hand. "Jonathan and I lost our parents two years ago to the Serral Sea. Sometimes, we like to imagine they're still out there. Sailing around as pirates, going wherever the wind takes them."

Rosalind envisioned her father hoisting the sail of a large ship, dressed in all black like one of the pirates from the fairytales. He could breathe in the fresh, salty air and never have to worry about another coughing fit. The thought of him happy and healthy helped ease the longing in her heart.

Valentina leaned in close. "I have a feeling you and I are going to be great friends so you can call me Val."

For the first time all day, Rosalind smiled. Perhaps this would be the adventure her father had promised.

2

HOMECOMING

BRIGHTHALL MANOR WAS ABUZZ with commotion, and the excitement in the air was palpable. Fresh flowers in varying shades of violet, lavender, and lilac lined the entryway and banisters. The scent of freshly baked pastries and the delightful aromas of the extravagant feast to come wafted throughout the house. Housemaids bobbed in and out of each room, dusters in hand, drawing open curtains and fluffing pillows on every bed, settee, and armchair in sight. In the fifteen years Rosalind had resided in the manor, she had never known it to look as primed and pristine as it did today.

"Did I mention how he dressed when I went to visit him at the capital last autumn? In the most finely crafted suits I've ever seen. Each and every one tailored to perfection."

Rosalind glanced up from her book to where Valentina sat in front of a large oak vanity, running a soft horsehair brush through her luxurious, black hair.

"You did. Mentioned something about his hair as well if I recall," Rosalind remarked as she closed the book and set it beside her on the bed.

"Oh yes, styled within an inch of its life. It's what everyone is doing over there," Valentina said with a wave of her hand. "I suggested he move his part a smidge to the left and he dared to say I wouldn't understand because I didn't know what was fashionable." She scoffed. "Me? Not know fashion? Ridiculous. I most certainly know more than he does on the matter."

Rosalind chuckled. "He isn't even here yet and already he's managed to vex you."

Valentina interlocked her fingers and stretched her arms out in front of her. "Just airing out last-minute grievances now so I can play the doting sister when he arrives."

Rosalind raised her brows. "And how long do you think that will last?"

"Minutes," Valentina remarked. "If we're lucky," she added with a wink.

The pair burst into laughter.

"Pardon me, Lady Valentina, Miss Rosalind," came a sheepish voice from the doorway. Sylvia, one of the young housemaids who'd joined the manor a few months back poked her head into the room. "I'm sorry to interrupt, but Louis wanted me to inform you both that his lordship's carriage is approaching the estate."

Rosalind shot a surprised look at Valentina, who bolted upright and rushed over to the wardrobe.

"That bastard," she murmured. "Of course he would arrive early."

Rosalind was the last to join the welcome party lined up beyond the manor's double doors; her breaths were short from hurrying down the stairs. She sidled up next to Valentina and threw Maria an apologetic look. The housekeeper sighed and gave a small, disapproving shake before tapping the side of her head. Rosalind lifted her hand to where Maria had indicated and felt an unruly patch of hair.

"Here, let me get that for you," Valentina said as she tamed the stray hairs and brushed them behind Rosalind's ear.

Valentina looked elegant as usual. She wore an emerald dress with a tiered skirt, made from a rich silk brocade with floral embroidery. Her hair was drawn up into a low twist, held together by a delicate gold hairpin comb. A light dusting of rouge sat atop her high cheekbones.

Rosalind looked down at her outfit of choice. She wore a terracotta-colored linen dress that bunched high on one side, revealing matching billowing slacks underneath. Valentina had tried desperately to dress Rosalind in clothes similar to her own, but Rosalind didn't like the attention it drew from certain members of high society, who thought she was taking advantage of the Rashfords' hospitality. So she opted for simpler, more subdued clothing, though Valentina made certain they were impeccably tailored.

Everyone's attention shifted to the gravel drive as the sound of hoofbeats slowed and a carriage adorned with a familiar violet-and-gold emblem came to a halt. Franklin, the Rashfords' white-haired coachman, moved to open the door, and a figure seemingly twice Franklin's size emerged. The two shared a warm exchange and then the man of the hour was bounding up the stone steps.

The Jonathan Rashford who stepped into the entryway was not the one Rosalind had been expecting. The Jonathan she remembered had a sort of unkempt look about him. His dark hair was long and tousled and fell in front of his eyes. He had a rather spindly physique, having grown nearly a foot and a half within a year, and his weight hadn't caught up. And he dressed in plain clothes, often not bothering to darn his boots or tuck in his shirts.

This Jonathan was something else entirely. He remained tall and slim—a Rashford trait—but there was a leanness to his figure now that Rosalind hadn't noticed before. He wore a navy suit, tailored to accentuate the long lines of his body. A silver brooch and chain was pinned neatly atop one of his black peaked lapels. His hair was slicked back and styled into a sleek pompadour.

Valentina had told her as much, but Rosalind hadn't thought anything of it. Now she saw it for herself, she found she couldn't look away.

"Louis, my good man, I've missed you," Jonathan said with a smile, his voice deep and melodic. He held out a hand.

"It's good to have you back," Louis replied as he shook it.

Jonathan pulled the steward in for an embrace. "It's good to be back."

Turning to Maria, Jonathan smiled again. The housekeeper threw her arms open, and Jonathan drew her into him. When they parted, she cupped his face in her hands. "Your grandmother would be so proud of you."

Rosalind could tell by the hitch in Maria's voice that she was close to tears, happy ones. Jonathan was like their own child to Maria and Louis, who helped raise him, Rosalind, and Valentina alongside the late Lady Rashford. And she was right; his grandmother would undoubtedly be proud of him.

At twenty-six, Jonathan was the youngest to assume the Chancellorship under the New Laws established a century ago. He was one of four Chancellors who comprised the country's High Council, each responsible for a designated region. Denault was Jonathan's jurisdiction, which he would govern alongside a regional council of five members. If Rosalind did her math correctly, he was set to serve as Chancellor for the next twenty-four years.

Legislation preceding the New Laws dictated that the Chancellorship transfer to a different member of the regional council as determined by the public every seventy-seven years. During that time, the position could be assumed by any next of kin should the need arise. A little more than half a century into the era of the New Laws, the Chancellorship transferred from the DuPonts to the Rashfords. Lord Thomas Rashford, husband of the dearly beloved late Lady Rashford, held the role for twenty-one years before his son,

Lord Arthur Rashford, succeeded him. Jonathan and Valentina's father was fourteen years into his tenure when both he and his wife perished at sea. Because Jonathan was only eight years old at the time, his grandmother stepped in as Chancellor Regent in his stead. When she passed away, Jonathan chose to defer his induction until he had completed his schooling, leaving the governing of Denault in the hands of the regional council.

Jonathan continued down the line, taking his time to greet every member of the household. He clapped a hand on the shoulder of Groundskeeper Kemba, who, like Louis and Maria, had attended the family for more than two decades. He proceeded to introduce himself to the newer staff members who had joined in recent years. First was Colby, a young footman who'd arrived at the estate two years ago. Next were Maria's two housemaids, Charlene and Sylvia. Both were young and had only joined the household a few months back.

Though Jonathan was only four years her senior, Rosalind felt it could have been so much more at that moment. It was the way he carried himself, with confidence beyond his years. He exuded an almost palpable charisma that captivated those around him, apparent in the way the housemaids looked at him in awe and fawned over him as soon as he turned away.

His eyes briefly caught on her as he made his way over to where she and Valentina stood. He cocked his head slightly, and Rosalind wasn't sure whether it was out of intrigue, surprise, or something else. Whatever the reason, it made her heart skip a beat.

Jonathan approached Valentina, brow arched. "Glad to see you haven't burned the place down."

Valentina raised her chin and brought a hand to her hip. "Perhaps I should have. Then we could have built a place large enough to house your undoubtedly inflated ego, *Chancellor Rashford*," she drawled.

"If it's been able to weather yours for the past few years, I suspect it'll do just fine as it stands," he said wryly.

Valentina scoffed, but before she could dole out a retort, Jonathan pulled her in for a hug. She groaned for a moment before relenting and wrapping her arms around him.

"Maddening as ever," she grumbled as she pulled away from him, but Rosalind spied the slight upward curve at the edge of Valentina's mouth.

Rosalind huffed a laugh at her friend's poor attempt at feigning annoyance. Sensing his gaze on her, Rosalind turned to Jonathan, who eyed her curiously.

"Rosalind, it's been a while."

She swallowed the lump that had formed in her throat. "Yes, it has," she breathed. Words seemed challenging to come by as she peered up at the man before her. She recognized the eyes looking back at her, but the fine lines between his brows and lines at the corners of his eyes were less familiar. He was handsome but not exceedingly so. Individually, his features were quite sharp and pronounced, but together, they seemed to soften each other out somehow. And his lips appeared fuller, though she didn't think she had paid them any mind before.

"You look quite well." The sound of his voice brought Rosalind's attention back to the moment, and she felt her cheeks warm. How long had she been staring at him?

"Th-thank you," she stammered. "And you look..." She paused, trying to drum up some semblance of coherent thought. Impressive seemed fitting, but the idea of saying it aloud unnerved her, so she said the only other word that came to mind. "Different."

Valentina snorted. "Different is one way to put it," she interjected.

"In a good way, I hope," Jonathan mused, ignoring his sister's retort.

Rosalind felt gooseflesh prickle at the back of her neck as his gaze roamed her face, pausing fleetingly at her mouth. His eyes returned to hers and lingered for a moment longer before he turned and grinned at Maria.

"Any chance there's a blueberry scone in my near future?"

Jonathan insisted everyone take the rest of the evening off to join him in the drawing room. Maria brought in a delightful selection of treats and refreshments—freshly baked rye topped with red wine and shallot-infused butter, cucumber sandwiches, warm blueberry scones with homemade apricot jam, and white wine and champagne.

For the next hour, Jonathan regaled the group with stories of his time at Sauvign's capital, where he had spent the past three and a half years, studying law and observing High Council meetings. He spoke of the people he'd met, those he'd befriended, and others he recommended they steer clear of. He fielded questions from Charlene and Sylvia about the extravagant dinner parties and balls he'd attended. He described what it was like to walk through the halls of the oldest university in the country, its corridors adorned with paintings and sculptures designed by some of the country's most illustrious artists.

In return, Valentina caught him up on happenings at the estate, which were few and far between—life at the manor had run smoothly while he was away, thanks largely to Maria and Louis. Valentina had managed estate affairs and ensured all accounts remained in good standing. She assured him she had returned the study to the way he liked it—dark and drab, she teased.

Charlene and Sylvia, giddy from the champagne, filled him in on the most lurid scandals and rumors that plagued high society. Not even Maria's critical eye could keep them from divulging the latest gossip they'd heard from fellow housemaids at neighboring estates.

Rosalind smiled and laughed along with the rest of the group. It warmed her to see everyone she cared about in the same room, happy and relaxed. Any fears or reservations she'd held about Jonathan returning from the capital, cold and imperious, like so many others in high society, quickly dissipated. In its place, however, rose a new sort of uncertainty. One that questioned the way her heart fluttered whenever their gazes met.

3

SPARKS FLY

OVER THE LAST FEW years, Rosalind had grown accustomed to waking in the quiet hours of the morning. At first, she would read in bed until the clock struck a more reasonable hour, but it wasn't long before restlessness set in. Certain her time could be put to better use, she began venturing downstairs in search of something to do. Eventually, she succeeded in persuading Maria to let her help out in the kitchen, preparing breakfast for the household. In recent months, Maria had even gone so far as to teach her how to bake.

Now, Rosalind stood at the large stone counter in the center of the kitchen, her hair tucked into a loose bun and a determined look on her face. She pulled at the dough in front of her, stretching each end until her arms protested. With the weight of her body, she pressed into the dough, kneading it into submission slowly and deliberately. While she hadn't yet developed the strength or confidence Maria had when baking, Rosalind was proud she was capable enough to prepare the bread on her own.

"You're not who I was expecting to find in here."

Rosalind jumped at the voice. She looked up to find Jonathan leaning against the kitchen doorway, watching her. Three days had passed since his return to Brighthall, and she had scarcely seen him. He spent the majority of his time in the study, emerging late at night after the rest of the house had retired to their rooms.

Since he kept to himself in the study during the day, she thought he'd have worn more casual attire, as he had in the past, but such was not the case. Today he wore a suit the color of storm clouds. Underneath his double-breasted jacket, he donned a crisp white shirt with black buttons, and a gold brooch was pinned at his collar.

Rosalind, on the other hand, had put little effort into her attire. Knowing she was going to bake today, she'd opted for a plain cotton dress that, to its credit, was once a lovely shade of turquoise. Now it was a very pale blue, having faded over time. True, she wore an apron, but still knew she would manage to get flour all over her dress.

"Good morning," she greeted him. "If you're looking for Maria, I can go get her. I suspect she's in the laundry room."

"No need." Jonathan pushed himself off the doorframe and walked over to the stove. "I can help myself." He poured himself a cup of freshly brewed coffee and approached the counter idly. "I didn't know you baked," he commented, taking a sip from his steaming cup.

"It's a rather recent skill I've picked up," she admitted sheepishly, eyeing the mess she had made on the counter. "Thought I might as well help out if I'm up at this hour."

Jonathan nodded. "Early riser as well then? Have you always been that way? I don't recall..." He trailed off.

"No, I suppose it's been a while," Rosalind said quietly.

It had been almost eight years since they were around one another for any real length of time. They had grown up spending much of their days in each other's company—playing games, sharing meals, studying together. With Valentina, too, of course. Then Jonathan went off to university, the same year Lady Rashford passed away. He would return for the holidays and over long breaks, but his visits grew fewer and farther between as time went on. Afterward, he left for the capital to further his studies and now here they were, three and a half years later.

It wasn't that he'd forgotten about them; she knew that. He sent letters regularly and gifts for every special occasion. Valentina even made it out to the capital to visit him several times. Rosalind stayed behind because the thought of entering the most affluent city in Sauvign terrified her. High society in Denault Proper wasn't particularly accepting of her, how much more in the capital?

Rosalind shook away the thoughts and turned her attention back to Jonathan. "Are you enjoying being back at Brighthall?" Or would he rather be back in the capital, she wondered.

Jonathan sighed. "Well, so far I have spent most of my time combing through decades of council meeting transcripts and notes my father and grandmother left behind. It's dreadfully dull and a bit depressing, so I can't say that has been all that enjoyable," he said sardonically. "But," he added, voice softening, "it's been nice seeing everyone again." He paused. "It's odd, how some things change while others stay the same." He peered around the room. "The house, for instance, looks and feels largely the same as it did when I was last here. But you"—Rosalind felt the weight of his gaze on her—"are not as I remembered."

She let out a shaky laugh. "I could say the same of you."

Their eyes held one another's for a moment before Rosalind looked away, her nerves getting the best of her.

"For one thing," she went on, her fingers drumming restlessly against the countertop, "you're Chancellor now. That's no small feat." She hesitated. "I suppose I should refer to you as such from here on out?" She chided herself, not having meant to pose it as a question.

Jonathan set his cup down and trailed the counter's edge until he stood before her. "You may call me whatever you like," he said gently, "though I must admit I'd prefer that you call me by my name, seeing as we're old friends, are we not?"

Rosalind looked up at him, nodded, and smiled. "Yes, of course."

Jonathan's gaze fell to her lips and lingered ever so briefly before drawing up to meet her eyes again. Warmth crept up the back of Rosalind's neck and bloomed in her cheeks. She absentmindedly drew a hand to her face as if to wipe away the blush.

Jonathan cleared his throat. "You have a bit of flour on your face." He tapped his left cheek. "Right there," he added, lips quirking upward.

Realizing the flour had likely come from her hand, Rosalind wiped at her face with the back of her forearm.

Jonathan chuckled. "I'm afraid there's even more now."

Rosalind wrinkled her nose in frustration and looked down at her hands and arms, coated in flour.

Jonathan stepped closer. "Here," he said softly as he reached out a hand, "let me help you with—"

Sparks of gold light erupted in front of Rosalind's face, and in their wake, she saw Jonathan shaking out his hand, mumbling profanities.

Rosalind winced. "Sorry about that..."

Jonathan let out a dry laugh. "No, it isn't your fault. I'm the one who should apologize. For the cursing, for one. And because I seem to have forgotten myself."

He straightened and glanced around the kitchen. He picked up a washcloth from the sink and held it out to her.

"Thank you." She took the washcloth and began to wipe her face.

"I suppose this won't be an issue for much longer."

Rosalind tilted her head in question.

"The enchantment," he clarified. "What with your birthday only about a month away now."

"Oh, yes," Rosalind said with a half-smile.

If the proverb is true, she thought. Growing up, she'd clung to every word of it, whispering it into existence every night like a wish or a prayer. She told herself everything would be alright in the end because the enchantment had an expiration date. She just had to be patient.

Kept safe from all of he, until two and twenty, a border born shall be.

But in recent months, doubt began to weasel its way into her consciousness. What if the proverb was wrong? What if the enchantment didn't lift on her twenty-second birthday? Or worse. *What if it never does?* It would be utterly devastating to hope with abandon after all these years, only for it not to happen. And so, she decided to temper her expectations and protect her heart as best she could by embracing the doubt. To let it eclipse whatever hopes she had of being normal, of being like everybody else.

"A man's touch isn't so different from a woman's if that's what concerns you," Jonathan explained, seeming to sense her apprehension. "Should you like to see for yourself, I humbly offer my services." He rested a hand on his chest. "Because as Chancellor, I am, above all else, a servant to the people." He lowered himself into a deep bow.

Rosalind stared at him wide-eyed, and her breath caught in her throat. She couldn't have heard him correctly. That, or she must have misunderstood him because, if her ears were to be believed, he was implying something altogether indecent. For a second time that morning, her cheeks burned so hot she feared they might ignite.

She got her answer as Jonathan returned to full height and revealed a mischievous grin. He had spoken in jest, she realized, to allay her nerves. Feelings of gratitude and relief—and something else she couldn't quite decipher—washed over her culminating in a bubble of nervous laughter.

"How noble of you," she quipped.

Their eyes met and Rosalind knew then what that *something else* had been. How ridiculous, she thought, to feel a tinge of disappointment at it only being in jest.

The rear door to the kitchen swung open and Rosalind turned to see Maria shuffling into the room with a basket full of crisp linens.

"Jonathan," she exclaimed with a warm smile. "Oh good, looks like you've found the coffee."

"That I have," Jonathan replied, lifting his cup to her. "Stumbled upon Ros here as well."

Rosalind bit back a smile at the affectionate way he referred to her. She hadn't heard him call her that in quite some time.

"I had hoped to speak to you about hosting a dinner next week for the council," Jonathan remarked as he maneuvered his way over to Maria and relieved her of the linen basket. The pair chatted amiably as they headed for the hallway beyond the kitchen. Just before disappearing through the doorway, Jonathan threw a last glance at Rosalind and smiled.

She dusted her hands in a fresh coat of flour and returned to the task at hand, attempting to ignore the butterflies in her stomach.

4

An Invitation

Rosalind leaned back in her chair, feet resting atop the seat beside her. She nibbled at a piece of bread smothered in butter and jam and stared absentmindedly out the dining room window.

Valentina sat at the head of the table reading aloud from *The Great Vine*, the local newspaper that collated the top stories of the past week from each of Sauvign's four regions.

"*Chancellor Rashford mum upon return to Denault,*" Valentina recited dryly. "*Nearly a fortnight into his return to the region, there has yet to be a public sighting of the newly inaugurated Chancellor. An unnamed source claims 'the young man has cold feet.*'" Valentina scoffed. "What absolute poppycock."

She peered over the paper at Rosalind. "How much do you want to bet the 'unnamed source' is that loathsome creature who haunts the halls of Harcourt Manor?"

"Not to mention our nightmares," mumbled Rosalind. "But yes, I wouldn't put it past DuPont to say as much," she said grimly. "That or perhaps he commissioned Armory to do so."

"Pitiful," Valentina muttered as she rolled her eyes. "They're bitter, old men who can't stand the idea of reporting to someone half their age. Jonathan better not let them walk all over him tomorrow evening. If he doesn't put them in their place, I will."

Tomorrow would be Jonathan's first time convening with the regional council as Chancellor of Denault. To commemorate the occasion, Brighthall Manor was hosting a dinner for the council members and their partners. While Valentina would accompany Jonathan as his guest, Rosalind intended to retreat to her bedroom for the evening to avoid encountering Lord DuPont and his bootlicking colleague, Lord Armory.

Both had been unkind to her over the years, Lord DuPont especially so. According to him, Rosalind wasn't befitting of high society. Not only was she a low-born from the borderlands, but she was also, as he so aptly put it, *tainted* by magic. She was a constant reminder that, while wielding magic was banned under the New Laws, magic itself still existed. And to him, anyone associated with magic was either evil or weak. Evil because magic was inherently corruptive, and no one person should be able to wield it while another could not. Weak because to have been affected by it meant a person lacked the mental, physical, or emotional fortitude to stop it. Rosalind knew he believed this because he was not quiet about his opinions.

He was largely responsible for why most of high society viewed her unfavorably. The only reason more did not voice their contempt was because of her association with the Rashfords.

"You two look like you've just tasted something bitter. Better not have been anything I made."

Rosalind glanced over her shoulder to see Maria standing with a tray in her hands, her brows raised in question.

"Never," she said, pressing a hand to her chest. "We were just speaking about DuPont."

"The embodiment of distasteful," remarked Valentina.

"Ah." Maria nodded. "I would tell you two to be more respectful, but that man doesn't deserve it."

The two younger women glanced at one another and snickered.

"Like children, the pair of you," Maria said with a shake of her head. "I had come in here hoping to find a young lady to help me with something."

Valentina set down her newspaper. "How may we be of service?"

The housekeeper peered down at the tray in her hand. "I would appreciate it if one of you could take Jonathan his breakfast this morning."

"Why?" Valentina asked Maria skeptically. "Is he in a foul mood?"

Maria laughed. "No, darling. I'm hoping you two will have more luck getting that boy to eat. Every morning I serve him his breakfast and every afternoon, I come to collect it only to find hardly a thing has been touched. Perhaps one of you could convince him to take a short break and eat a proper meal."

Valentina reached for the newspaper again and fanned it out in front of her. She sat back idly in her chair, speaking from behind the paper. "Unless you'd like me to waltz in there and shove it down his throat, which I would do with glee, I suggest Ros do the honors. She has far more patience than I."

Sighing, Rosalind turned to Maria and nodded. "I'll give it a try."

Rosalind hovered outside the study. Nearly every day since their reunion in the kitchen the week prior, Jonathan had stopped in to pour himself a cup of coffee. They exchanged pleasantries about the weather and what they had planned for the day. Sometimes he would ask about something he'd noticed in the manor, like a new vase or painting. Each time they spoke, she found herself growing more and more at ease in his presence. His manner and appearance were so refined that he had intimidated her. But underneath it all, she caught glimpses of the Jonathan she was familiar with.

Their interactions were brief, each having things to attend to. Still, Rosalind found herself spending a few extra minutes getting ready in the morning in anticipation. For pragmatic reasons, of course. She should always strive to show her best around someone in such an eminent position as he, should she not?

She carefully balanced the tray between her hand and hip and lightly tapped the door. On hearing his invitation to enter, she slipped inside and approached the desk with muted steps.

Jonathan didn't look up. An elbow was propped up on the desk and he rubbed at his temple as he read through what looked to be a large stack of handwritten notes. To Rosalind's surprise, he was wearing glasses.

"Thank you," he murmured as she sat the tray near him.

Wordlessly, Rosalind prepared a slice of bread for him. If she recalled correctly, he liked a hefty drizzle of honey and a dash of cinnamon on his toast. She set the plate down and slid it toward him.

Jonathan's head tilted slightly as his attention shifted to the plate. He peered up, clearly surprised to see Rosalind.

"Good morning," she said softly. "Do you still favor honey on your toast?"

The corner of his lips quirked up. "I do, though it's been some time since I've enjoyed it." He lifted the toast to his mouth and took a bite.

Rosalind watched as he licked at a small bead of honey that clung to his lips. She dropped her head to conceal the fierce blush that swept across her cheeks, making quick work of tidying the tray in front of her.

It was only natural to find him attractive. He was clever, confident, and charming. And there was something about his face, or perhaps his eyes, that drew one's gaze to him and made it hard to look away.

Even when he was younger and hadn't quite grown into his long, lean limbs and sharp features, many men and women clamored for his attention. Now it seemed everyone did—evidenced by the frequency of his name in the society papers.

The sound of her name pulled Rosalind out of her thoughts. "Pardon?"

"I was just thanking you for bringing me my breakfast," Jonathan said, motioning to the tray. He was standing now, eyeing her curiously.

"Oh, you're welcome," Rosalind answered bashfully, embarrassed at not having heard him the first time. She paused. "Maria worries about you, you know. Says you haven't been eating properly."

"I don't do it purposefully." Jonathan rubbed at the back of his neck. "I merely get caught up in things and forget. I'll make a more concerted effort from here on out."

"Good," Rosalind replied cheerily. "Maria will be pleased."

Silence fell over the pair. Rosalind contemplated leaving, but instead, for some inane reason, she blurted out, "I didn't know you wore glasses."

"Ah, yes. These," Jonathan said as he went to remove his spectacles. He leaned against the desk and examined them. "I can go without them, but they help stave off the headaches when I read for long periods. Though I've been advised not to wear them in public."

"Why?"

Jonathan shrugged. "Apparently, it's a sign of weakness. No self-respecting man would put himself in such a vulnerable position," he said in a low, affected voice that sounded oddly familiar.

Rosalind's eyes widened in realization. "*He* said that to you?"

Jonathan nodded. "He did, during one of his visits to the capital. Never misses a chance to offer unsolicited advice."

"Speaking of DuPont..." He set the glasses on the table and slipped his hands into his pockets. "There's something I wanted to ask you. It's about the welcome dinner tomorrow evening."

"What about it?"

"I was hoping you would accompany me as my guest."

Rosalind blinked. "You... want me to attend your dinner with the Denaultian council?"

"I do," he said. "Everyone will be accompanied by a guest if that makes it any more enticing."

"But I thought Valentina was acting as your guest for the evening?"

"She was, but Lady Condry's guest had to cancel on short notice. She intended to bring her niece but recently received word that she had fallen under the weather. Not wanting Lady Condry to be unaccompanied, Valentina offered to accompany her in her niece's stead. That leaves my guest's seat unattended."

Rosalind chewed the inside of her lip. "There isn't another you wish to ask? I'm certain most anyone in Proper would be delighted to accompany you."

"I could, but I thought it might be a good opportunity for us to become better acquainted."

"Oh," she breathed. It was nice to know he was also interested in rekindling their friendship after so many years.

"I should mention," he added hesitantly, "there is another reason I'm hoping you will accompany me."

Rosalind eyed him warily. "And that is..."

"As you know, DuPont and Armory have each served as council members for nearly three decades. In that time, they have never shied away from making their opinions known. As such, I am well aware of their stances on nearly every issue, wielding and otherwise.

"Then there's Lady Condry," he went on. "She inherited the role a little over a decade ago following the passing of her husband.

Council records show she tends to vote in line with DuPont and Armory.

"It is the final two members, Lord Sene and Lord Aston, I'm less certain about. They are relatively new to the council, both having been inducted within the last five years. This is where I'm hoping you might be of help."

Rosalind hazarded a guess. "You want to see how they behave around me." If they treated her well enough, he would know they were not yet wholly under Lord DuPont's thumb.

Jonathan nodded. "I know this isn't an easy ask of you, and were you to accept, I'd ensure everyone is on their best behavior. If you choose to decline, please rest assured there will be no hard feelings on my part. I swear it."

"I... will attend," she replied tenuously. Before she could change her mind, she bid him farewell and hurried out of the room. As soon as the door closed behind her, she leaned against it and let out a long breath.

Spending an entire evening sharing a room with Lord DuPont and his wife sounded absolutely dreadful. She could already imagine the contemptuous looks they'd level at her. As for what they might say about her... best not to think about it. Why, then, had she agreed?

The answer was simple—because he had asked.

5

WELCOME DINNER

ROSALIND STOOD BEHIND VALENTINA at the vanity, weaving strands of her friend's long, dark hair into delicate plaits and pinning them one over the other in a cascade atop her head. Valentina dusted rouge across her cheeks.

"I think we'll use a softer pigment on you, love," Valentina commented as she dabbed red crepe paper against her lips. "One that complements your dress."

Rosalind gave a reluctant smile and continued busying herself with Valentina's hair. She pulled a spool of golden thread from her pocket and carefully interlaced it through the intricate layers of plaits, securing them in place and adding a subtle glimmer to the elegant coiffure. It was a welcome distraction that kept her from fretting over the fact that she too had to get ready for the evening. Then she would be drinking and dining alongside the most powerful and influential people in Denaultian society. The thought made her stomach churn.

"Everything will be alright, you know," Valentina offered reassuringly. She shifted around in her seat and took hold of Rosalind's hands. "Jonathan won't stand for any of DuPont's antics, and neither will I. One of us shall be beside you at all times."

But what of everyone else, Rosalind wondered. She knew what to expect from Lord and Lady DuPont as well as Lord Armory and his wife, but she wasn't as familiar with the other members of the council. She had managed to avoid most society events in the past few years, with the exception of a rare ball or two that Valentina had dragged her to. Even then, she was able to stay largely unnoticed, settling against a back wall and fading into the background. She couldn't do that as easily tonight.

"Now, now, there you go again," Valentina said. "Getting lost in your own thoughts and worries. I won't stand for it." She pushed herself off the chair and made her way over to the wardrobe in the corner of the room, pulling Rosalind along with her.

"But I haven't finished with your hair," Rosalind groaned.

Valentina ignored her as she rifled through the wardrobe and pulled out a lilac gown. "This one." She beamed and held it up for Rosalind to see. She thrust it into Rosalind's hands and returned to the wardrobe, rustling around until she pulled out a silk dress in a deep violet. "Can't attend an event hosted by my brother and not don the Rashford shade, now can I?"

The pair took turns helping each other dress, then stood side by side in front of a massive, ornate mirror that hung in the room.

Rosalind looked over at Valentina, whose striking gown clasped around her long neck and hugged the length of her lithe figure. Draped across her shoulders was a delicately crafted beaded bolero she had commissioned after seeing something similar in an Erdesian magazine. Tall and elegant with sharp features and even sharper wit, she was an enviable force to be reckoned with.

Leveling her gaze on herself, Rosalind was pleasantly surprised by her reflection, unkempt hair aside. Last year, Valentina had taken her to the modiste in town to have a set of outfits made to accommodate her fluctuating figure. This luscious gossamer gown was one of the finished pieces she had yet to wear. Enveloping the length of her arms were sheer, voluminous sleeves that cinched at her wrists. The dress's stiff bodice laced behind her back like a corset, which allowed for some much-appreciated flexibility, though Valentina showed no mercy this evening. From her waist, the fabric loosened, resting gently against her hips before cascading to the floor.

Valentina sighed. "I wouldn't have minded a few inches on my chest," she remarked as she eyed Rosalind in the mirror. "But apparently, I only grew up, not out."

Rosalind snorted. Her friend was being generous. True, she had a bit more on top, but not by much. In recent years, her once scrawny frame had filled out, gaining several inches all around, and then some at her hips and thighs. However, she had not grown much in height since early adolescence, making her a head shorter than Valentina.

"And I wouldn't mind the ability to breathe," Rosalind lamented wryly, tugging at her bodice.

"Overrated if you ask me." Valentina gave a careless shrug. "Now, let's have you put the finishing touches on my hair so we can focus on you." She rubbed her hands together excitedly. "I have something fabulous in mind."

The sun was low in the sky as guests began to arrive at Brighthall, and the time had come for Rosalind and Valentina to join in. They stood just beyond sight of the drawing room, and Rosalind felt her heart race so fast that she feared it might burst from her chest and leave her a heap on the floor.

A hand squeezed hers. "Are you ready?"

Valentina must have sensed her inner turmoil because when Rosalind looked up, she was met with a soft and encouraging smile.

"As I'll ever be," Rosalind said with a breathy laugh.

Valentina winked at her, turned, and drew her shoulders back. She raised her chin high and let a polite smile settle over her lips. In the gentle evening light, the beads of the bolero gleamed like armor, and a relaxed and easy confidence emanated from her, reminiscent of the self-assured air Jonathan exuded. As soon as she stepped into the room, conversation stilled, everyone's attention drawn to her like moths to a flame.

"Lady Valentina," came a cheery voice from across the room.

"Lord Aston," crooned Valentina as she swept over to where the handsome blond man and his partner stood.

In Valentina's wake, Rosalind slipped quietly into the room. She peered around and let out a tentative breath upon noticing the DuPonts were nowhere to be seen.

The back of her neck prickled when she sensed someone was watching her. She peered up and her eyes met Jonathan's. He stood with his arm resting against the wooden mantel of the hearth across the other side of the room, a glass of amber liquid in his hand. His eyes never left hers as he murmured something to a white-haired man with an impeccable mustache. Rosalind bit back a grimace as recognition sparked—Lord Armory.

Jonathan rested his drink on the mantel and pushed off the wall.

"You look positively divine," he said as he approached.

Heat bloomed in Rosalind's cheeks, and she silently thanked the dim light for concealing her deep blush.

"Th-thank you," she stammered. "You look quite handsome yourself." She congratulated herself on voicing the words aloud, as quiet as they were.

Jonathan wore a dark gray tailcoat, with breeches tucked into long black boots. Underneath he wore a white shirt with pearlescent buttons. Violet jewels adorned his cufflinks, and a matching pendant adorned the front of his tightly knotted cravat.

"Can I interest you in a drink?"

"Yes, please," she replied a little too enthusiastically, but she needed a drink or two if she were to survive the evening.

Jonathan chuckled. He held out a hand in the direction of the bar cart. "After you."

Their path was soon interrupted by the mustachioed menace and his wife.

"Chancellor Rashford, this must be your lovely guest for the evening," Lord Armory exclaimed after a passing glance at Rosalind. "I don't believe we're acquainted."

"On the contrary, Lord Armory," Jonathan remarked. "Both you and Lady Armory have had the pleasure of meeting my guest several times over the last fifteen years. This is none other than Miss Rosalind Carver."

The older man stiffened. "Ah, yes." The corner of his mouth twitched as he offered her a curt bow. His wife mimicked the cursory movement. "I do believe it has been some time since we last shared a room, Miss Carver. I did not recognize you."

They had both attended a charity ball last year, but Rosalind ensured they didn't cross paths. She had no intention of mentioning that now, of course.

"We thought you'd found living arrangements elsewhere; perhaps someplace more suitable for someone in your predicament." The last words were uttered in a tone dripping with such mock sympathy it took everything in Rosalind's power not to roll her eyes.

There were rumors of discreet locations where those affected by magic were, for lack of a better word, housed. That was the preference of most in high society: not to be burdened with the presence of *tainted* individuals. Out of sight, out of mind as they say.

"This is as much her home as it is mine, Lord Armory," Jonathan was quick to say. "I daresay more so being as I've been away for several years. As she is a dear friend of mine, I appreciate your concern for her wellbeing." He placed a hand on his chest. "I should like to allay your worries by affirming that Miss Rosalind shall continue to reside in Brighthall for as long as she so desires. Please do feel free to relay this to anyone who shares your concerns, as I wouldn't wish to cause undue distress." His mouth drew into a charming smile.

Both Lord and Lady Armory smiled too, though their smiles were exceedingly tight-lipped.

"Now if you'll both excuse us"—Jonathan inclined his head—"I promised my guest here a drink. I do hope you two enjoy the evening; Maria has prepared an exquisite feast for us." He bowed, and Rosalind reluctantly followed suit. Before parting with their company, he added, "I haven't forgotten our earlier conversation, Lord Armory. I look forward to continuing it after dinner."

The pair reached the bar, and Jonathan poured Rosalind a glass of Bordeaux.

"You didn't have to do that," Rosalind murmured as she took a sip.

"Oh, but I did," Jonathan countered as he guided her to the spot near the hearth where he'd been standing earlier. He picked up his glass and downed the remnants. "Both he and DuPont have spent the past eight years with what was essentially carte blanche over Denaultian law. No Chancellor to answer to and no real opposition to contend with." His voice was just loud enough so only she could hear. "Suffice it to say, they won't be keen to relinquish control simply because I've been inducted," he continued. "To gain the upper hand and restore balance to the council, I need to play my cards right. If I don't assert myself early on, they may see fit to walk all over me. That won't do if I'm to be at all effective at my duties."

Rosalind watched as he raised his glass and smiled at someone across the room. Even as he divulged the precariousness of his situation, he maintained an air of easy confidence.

Aware of how duplicitous Lord DuPont and Lord Armory could be, she asked, "How does one play their cards right when their opponents do not play fair?"

Jonathan met her gaze, a sly glint in his eye. He leaned toward her and murmured, "By beating them at their own game."

Half an hour after dinner was intended to begin, the DuPonts' carriage finally came to rest in front of Brighthall. Louis informed Jonathan, who encouraged everyone to make their way into the dining room.

Rosalind was last to exit the drawing room, not wanting to chance triggering the enchantment by getting too close to any of the gentlemen. She was partway through the foyer when a familiar voice stopped her in her tracks.

"Jonathan," bellowed Lord DuPont as he strode casually through the entryway doors. "It is so good to see the golden boy back in Denault. My apologies for the late arrival—I was in an important meeting and couldn't break away earlier. It was with the Chancellor of Meridian, Lord Mason. An old friend of mine—great business-man, very successful. I presume you two are vaguely acquainted?"

Jonathan's back was to Rosalind as he welcomed the DuPonts. His hands were clasped behind him, flexing open and closed in silent agitation.

"Lord and Lady DuPont," he said as he lowered into a courteous bow. "How good of you both to make it in the midst of what sounds like a very involved day. And to your question, Lord DuPont, I am indeed acquainted with Chancellor Mason, having attended mul-tiple gatherings of the High Council during my time at the capital. I also studied alongside his son, Lord Padraic Mason, and consider him to be a close friend."

"Ah yes, Padraic. Eccentric, that one," Lord DuPont comment-ed disparagingly. "Quite prone to whimsy, is he not? Difficult to imagine someone so young and untested assuming one of the most prominent positions in the country. At least he'll have his father to provide him with sage counsel. Lessons in a book can't compare to years of experience, I always say.

"Between you and I," he said in a conspiratorial tone, "Lord Mason would be better off seeing the chancellorship through until the end. He's got, what, six years left? Things are running well as they are. I see no need to force such responsibility on the boy when he's not ready. In six years, Padraic will be older and wiser and better prepared to assume his father's seat on the regional council."

Though he never once mentioned Jonathan directly, the implication was acutely apparent. There was something deeply insidious about the manner with which Lord DuPont spoke. It was practiced and deliberate, the way he would say one thing and mean another.

"I am inclined to agree with you," Jonathan replied to Rosalind's surprise. "Lord Mason should remain as Chancellor. That would allow Padraic to dedicate more time to learning the family business, where his true interest lies."

Jonathan tilted his head in thought. "You know," he started again, the words leaving his mouth slow and steady as if an idea were coming to fruition as he spoke, "I think a tutelage under a prominent figure in Sauvign's trade industry, like yourself, could prove quite valuable to someone like him. I understand the Masons are sea traders and you deal primarily with land routes, but surely there is common ground. And now that I'm here, you'll have fewer council matters to attend to and more time to dedicate toward such endeavors."

Her head downcast, Rosalind smiled to herself. Jonathan had said he planned to beat Lord DuPont at his own game. In this instance, with sweet words that concealed thorned intimations. When she looked up, she found Lady DuPont watching her. The older woman leaned over to whisper something into her husband's ear.

Rosalind felt Lord DuPont's icy gaze land on her. He said nothing, but the curl of his upper lip spoke volumes. Turning his attention back to Jonathan, he voiced his disdain. "Really now, Jonathan, please tell me you don't intend to pollute such pleasant and upstanding company with her presence. How are we to enjoy dinner in the presence of something so distasteful?"

The words stung, but they were hardly the worst she had heard him say. Evidently, he didn't feel the need to disguise his slights when they were directed at her.

"Lord DuPont," Jonathan warned, but before he could continue, the older man pressed on.

"I had hoped you would come to your senses during your time away. But alas, it appears she still has her claws in you. Your sister as well, though I suppose it can't be helped, seeing as you left her alone with"—Lord DuPont waved a hand in Rosalind's direction—"for all these years. If we had known she was to attend this evening, perhaps my wife and I would have made different arrangements. The Chancellor did ask us to stay..." He trailed off.

Jonathan straightened and let out a measured breath. "I am sorry to hear that," he began. "As you have not yet greeted the others, you're free to part company, though I'd hoped to discuss a few pressing matters with the council later this evening. Perhaps I can have someone take notes and share them with you at a later time?"

A tight smile formed. "No, that will not be necessary," Lord DuPont said through gritted teeth. "The others have surely heard us arrive and we wouldn't want to disappoint them. No doubt Lady Armory is very much looking forward to my Mary's company." He patted his wife's arm. "We shall stomach the evening with your guest as best we can," he added grimly.

Without affording Rosalind another glance, he and Lady DuPont turned and made their way toward the formal dining room.

Jonathan stared ahead quietly for a moment before turning to Rosalind, flashing her a smile that didn't quite reach his eyes. "Shall we?"

Rosalind followed Jonathan to the head of the table and settled into the seat on his left. Though she had expected as much, she was still relieved to feel Valentina's comforting presence at her other side. Once seated, Valentina introduced her to Lady Condry, and though the widow greeted her politely enough, Rosalind could sense she was eager to get it over with.

Seated across from Rosalind was the handsome blond man Valentina had spoken with earlier. Jonathan introduced him as Lord Thomas Aston, who was relatively new to the council, having inherited the role only two years ago. To his right sat his partner, Dr. Benjamin Tremblay, a recent graduate of Sauvign's prestigious Orion College. Both regarded her warmly and engaged her in pleasant conversation. They were so cordial, she wondered if perhaps they didn't know of her enchantment.

She leaned over to Valentina and murmured, "Are Lord Aston and Dr. Tremblay aware of my enchantment?"

"Oh yes," Valentina replied under her breath. "In fact, I was supposed to ask if you'd be willing to spare them a few moments later this evening. Dr. Tremblay is quite keen to witness the enchantment in person. For scientific purposes, of course." A sly smile tugged at her lips. "Can't say I would be all that bothered if he wanted to poke and prod at me all day for the sake of science."

Rosalind bit back her laugh long enough to bring her napkin to her mouth in a poor attempt to conceal her amusement.

Soon, dinner began in earnest, with Maria, Charlene, and Sylvia taking turns serving guests course after course of delectable dishes—oysters, leek soup, pheasant, potatoes, and green beans, to name a few. Louis made the rounds with bottles of wine in hand, ensuring no one found themselves without a drink.

As expected, Rosalind caught Lord DuPont, Lord Armory, and their wives throwing disdainful looks her way from the opposite end of the table. Seated between their lot and Dr. Tremblay were Lord Sene and his guest. The pair spoke little with their tablemates, seemingly content with conversing amongst themselves. Only once did Rosalind feel their gazes linger in her direction but they looked away before she could glean their sentiment toward her.

Rosalind savored the last bite of apple tart. Not only did the dessert taste fantastic, it also marked the end of dinner. It had been a daunting affair, but she had survived it without incident. And what's more, she'd actually found it rather enjoyable, unkind words and nasty glares aside.

Following dinner, members of the council were escorted to the drawing room while the remaining guests were to make their way to the adjoining conservatory. Rosalind jumped at the opportunity to be the first one to settle into the other room, itching to leave her seat. She expected the others would join shortly, but she hoped to give herself a brief moment of respite.

Her jaw dropped as she entered the room. Candles of all shapes and sizes adorned the windowsills, tables, and shelves, basking the room in a warm glow. Panels of delicate chiffon fabric draped from the ceiling, adding to the ethereal ambiance of the space. Maria and the rest of the household had really outdone themselves tonight, Rosalind mused. She would be sure to sing their praises in the morning.

"It must be difficult," remarked a cool voice from behind her. Rosalind whirled around to find Lady DuPont eyeing her from the doorway. "To be the only pebble in a room full of gems."

The older woman took a sip from her glass and then proceeded toward Rosalind, hips swaying with each languid step. Every muscle in Rosalind's body protested as she dug her heels into the ground, fighting the urge to step back in silent retreat. She refused to give the other woman the satisfaction. Rosalind even went as far as to incline her head.

"Lady DuPont," she muttered under her breath.

It didn't surprise her to receive no such acknowledgment in return.

"What is it about you that has the Rashfords so thoroughly wrapped around your finger?" Lady DuPont wrinkled her nose as she looked Rosalind up and down. "My husband wonders if perhaps you have bewitched them. That the magic from your pathetic curse has ensnared them in some way. But I think there is a much simpler answer."

Rosalind braced herself for whatever biting words were to come next.

"Pity." The older woman let the word hang heavy in the air before continuing. "Do us all a favor and relieve them of this burden. Wouldn't it be nice to find a quaint little pond full of pebbles just like yourself? Somewhere you fit in; somewhere you belong. How might they shine without you there to muddy their waters?"

Her words weighed heavily on Rosalind's chest, and she found it growing harder and harder to breathe.

"Take, for instance, this evening. Had another been in your place, we may have all been able to enjoy ourselves a little more—the Chancellor included. Yet instead, we must all be on guard lest you get too near any of the men and hurt and humiliate them.

"And were it not for you, I'm certain we would have been seated closer to the Chancellor. Without his father around, the poor boy is in need of guidance, and my husband can offer that to him. But you complicate things because you are the one *thing* they don't see eye to eye on."

Rosalind bit back her protest. Somehow she doubted her existence was the only thing they disagreed on.

"Perhaps they're having fruitful discussions as we speak, now you're not there to test the Chancellor's compassion. If only I could be free of you as well," lamented the older woman. "I am certain I am not the only guest who feels that way. But what can be done?"

Lady DuPont gave a small shrug. Out of the corner of her eye, Rosalind glimpsed the careless tilt of her glass, but by then, it was already too late. She looked down at the front of her dress, which was drenched in wine so dark that it appeared nearly black under the candlelight.

"Oh, clumsy me," Lady DuPont remarked with feigned remorse.

Rosalind felt tears prick the corners of her eyes and she wasn't sure whether she wanted to shout or cry. Then she remembered something the late Lady Rashford had once said to her.

There are those who thrive on the sorrow of others. To react to their barbs is to grant them power over you. Better to give them nothing and to soothe your wounds in private.

With measured breaths, Rosalind blinked back the tears and rose to meet the other woman's gaze. She forced her lips into a tight smile.

"If you'll excuse me," she muttered and rushed out of the room.

Not watching where she was going, Rosalind bumped into Louis. "Is something the matter, my dear?"

"It's nothing," she muttered. "I just need to grab something from the kitchen." She continued past him, not waiting for his response.

Relieved to find the kitchen empty, she quickly sought out a washcloth and began to scrub vigorously at her wine-soaked dress, knowing full well it was pointless. A stain like this would require a good long soak and Maria's special touch. Even then, there was a chance it wouldn't be enough.

She should have listened to her instincts and left the room as soon as Lady DuPont entered. The very first words out of the woman's mouth were cruel, so why did she continue to stand there and let the vindictive woman berate her further? It was foolish of her; *she* was foolish. She shouldn't have been there—in the conservatory, at the dinner, all of it. It was as Lady DuPont said. Had someone else been in Rosalind's place, everyone would have enjoyed themselves more. Rosalind herself would have much preferred to spend the evening tucked into bed with a good book.

"Ros." The sound of her name pulled her out of her thoughts. She turned to see Jonathan standing across the room.

"Louis mentioned you seemed upset. Said I might find you here," he said as he approached her.

Rosalind frowned. "He shouldn't have bothered you. I'm fine." She found she couldn't quite meet his gaze.

"You don't seem fine."

"Well, I am fine," she reiterated. "Spilled a bit of wine, that's all."

"Seems a bit clumsy, even for you."

Rosalind shot him an indignant look. Jonathan simply arched a brow.

She sighed, her frustration waning. "It doesn't matter *who* spilled the wine, only what I'm to do about it now," she said despondently. She let her hands fall to her sides, revealing the stain.

Jonathan's brows narrowed. "Is it who I think it is?"

Rosalind shifted uncomfortably as she tried to decide the best way to respond.

"Right," he muttered, straightening his jacket. "Well, I'll just have to give her a piece of my mind."

"No!" Rosalind blurted. "Please," she added hurriedly, "I would rather you not."

"Why not?"

"I..." She hesitated. "I don't wish to cause a scene."

"But you wouldn't be causing a scene," he answered. "I would."

Rosalind shook her head. "I don't think it wise, Jonathan. If you go out there upset, imagine how they might use it to their advantage. Claim you are young and reckless or something. This is your first night hosting the council as Chancellor; first impressions are crucial. Please," she implored. "It isn't worth it."

He held her gaze for a long moment and then let out a small huff. "If that's what you wish, I won't speak of it."

"Thank you," she replied softly.

"At least, let me lend you my coat." He shrugged off his jacket and held it out.

Rosalind nodded her thanks as she carefully plucked it from his grasp. She slid one arm into the jacket and then the other. As she did, the scent of Jonathan's cologne, a subtle blend of amber and orange citrus, wafted over her. "I can have someone return it to you after I've escaped upstairs."

"No need," Jonathan said as he worked to undo his cufflinks. "I can retrieve it from you tomorrow." He proceeded to roll his shirtsleeve to his elbow and then repeated the same on the other side. The entire time, Rosalind watched as the muscles in his forearms flexed with every twist and fold.

When she looked up, her eyes met Jonathan's and the ghost of a smile flitted across his lips. Rosalind straightened and brushed wisps of hair behind her ear in a poor attempt to detract from her blush.

"I should probably be off," she said. "I wouldn't want to take up any more of your time. They will surely be missing you in the drawing room." She opened her mouth to speak again but closed it after a second thought.

"What is it?" Jonathan inquired.

Rosalind hesitated, unsure of whether or not to repeat what Lady DuPont had mentioned to her. "You may already be aware of this, but DuPont has hopes to advise you. He seems to be under the impression you two share similar views in... just about everything."

Jonathan scoffed. "He would hope that. And perhaps I'll hear him out. Find something we do agree on and let him have at it. Distract him so I can attend to other matters that'll require a bit more finesse." Just as it looked like she might lose him to thought, he added, "Did she say anything else to you?"

"Oh." Rosalind racked her brain for something else Lady DuPont said that wasn't merely an insult. "Just something about pebbles," she said with a dismissive wave of her hand. It wasn't a lie—the woman had indeed mentioned something about pebbles. Multiple times, in fact.

"Ros," he said gently, "whatever she said, it isn't true."

Rosalind flashed him a half-smile and looked away so he couldn't see the doubt in her eyes.

"I'm sorry, but this just won't do," Jonathan said. "I know you don't want to cause a scene, but perhaps I could just have a few words with her..." His voice trailed off as he turned toward the doorway.

"No, please don't!" In a panic, Rosalind reached out a hand to stop him. It might burn him a little, but at least it'd draw his attention back to her.

Jonathan stilled. Rosalind was ready to apologize profusely when the words caught in her throat. She flexed her fingers and felt the resistance of something warm. Slowly, she shifted her gaze to her outstretched hand and was surprised to see it firmly clasped around Jonathan's wrist. Eyes wide, she glanced up at Jonathan who stared back at her unblinking.

Dumbfounded, Rosalind let go of his wrist and pressed her hand to her chest. After a moment, she lifted it up in front of her face, turning it back and forth as if expecting to see something. Failing to find anything new or different, she looked to Jonathan. He, too, was examining his wrist.

How could this be? Her twenty-second birthday wasn't for another three weeks, and even then, she doubted whether the enchantment would truly lift. But if what she had felt was real, then there was reason to hope. And she had felt something, or rather, someone. Right? She had felt him, hadn't she?

Again, she looked over to Jonathan, hoping for some kind of answer. When their gazes met, she read the same question in his eyes. He said nothing, only held out a hand between them.

Rosalind's hand shook as she slowly raised it until it hovered only inches above his. Just as she was about to graze his palm with her fingers, Valentina burst into the room.

"There you are," she exclaimed. "Are you alright? You look like you might be sick. Are you going to be sick?"

Rosalind pulled her hand away from Jonathan's as Valentina neared. "No, no, I'm alright. Just a little shaken up."

Valentina sidled up next to Jonathan. She glanced between the pair with a skeptical eye. She opened her mouth as if to ask something, but closed it again.

"I'm not an idiot," Valentina muttered after a moment, and the statement made Rosalind's eyes widen.

"I didn't think—" She began hurriedly but was cut short.

"No, not you," Valentina said dismissively, "Lady DuPont. She acted as if she had no idea why you ran off. Funny thing, her glass was empty and here you are with your gown drenched in red."

"Val, please. I asked Jonathan not to say anything. And now, I ask the same of you."

Valentina rolled her eyes and grumbled something inaudibly.

"Please," Rosalind insisted, taking Valentina's hands in hers and gently squeezing them.

"Fine," she huffed. "But you absolutely cannot keep me from silently berating her *with my eyes*."

Rosalind chuckled. "No, I suppose I can't."

Valentina smiled triumphantly and turned to Jonathan. "If anyone asks, Rosalind felt a headache coming on and thought it best to retire early." She linked arms with Rosalind and shuffled her out of the kitchen before she could spare Jonathan another look.

6

QUITE CURIOUS

ROSALIND GRUMBLED AS SHE tossed in bed, turning onto her side for what felt like the hundredth time. She hadn't been able to sleep well, given what had happened the night before. The moment repeated in her head again and again, her hand clasped around Jonathan's wrist. A tiny sliver of doubt made her question whether the memory was simply a fever dream brought about by too much wine and not enough sleep.

She opened one eye; light from the rising sun peeked through the curtains. It was early, but she knew Maria would be awake, so she slipped out of bed and tugged on a linen blouse, tucking it into an olive split skirt. When she looked in the mirror, she couldn't help but frown. There were dark circles under her eyes and her hair was a tangled mess. Most nights she abided by a routine that included brushing and plaiting her hair. Last night, however, she had been too distracted for any of it. With a sigh, Rosalind wrangled her hair into a loose bun and pinched at her cheeks, hoping to put a little color back in her face.

⁂

"Maria, now I know it isn't my day to bake," she announced as she strolled into the kitchen, "but I couldn't sleep, and I would really like something—"

Rosalind had barely entered the room when she stopped in her tracks. As expected, Maria was at the counter getting a head start on the day's meal preparations. What surprised her was the familiar figure standing across from her.

"Jonathan," she breathed. "What are you doing awake so early?" Realizing she sounded almost accusatory, she quickly added, "I mean, I didn't expect you to be up at this hour after such a long evening."

She had hoped to run into him today but didn't imagine it would be so soon. She hadn't yet thought of what to say to him or built up the courage to do so.

"Also couldn't sleep," Jonathan replied. He eyed her curiously as he sipped from his mug.

"Sounds like the sandman skipped you both last night," Maria remarked, tilting her head toward the stove. "There's a pot of freshly brewed coffee ready for you if Jonathan here hasn't finished it all already."

"Plenty to go around," Jonathan commented. "Let me pour you one."

The rich, earthy scent of coffee bloomed around them as he poured her a cup. He made his way over to her and held the cup out in front of him. Ribbons of steam wafted into the air as Rosalind eyed it, unmoving.

Her eyes trailed up to meet Jonathan's, and she held his gaze for a long moment. She searched his eyes for any trace of hesitation but found only what seemed to be curiosity and anticipation. Tentatively, she reached out a hand. Out of the corner of her eye, she glimpsed Maria and stilled, suddenly aware they were not alone. She saw Jonathan's gaze track hers to where the housekeeper stood. Just as he turned back to her, a voice called out from beyond the kitchen's back entrance.

"Ma'am, I've come to drop off your produce for the week. Anyone there?"

"That'll be Albert," said Maria. "Go on and help the boy out for me, will you, Rosalind dear? I'm sure he'll be pleased to see you."

"Yes, of course. Happy to be of assistance." She threw Jonathan a quick glance before making her way out the door.

"Good morning, Albert," she called out, greeting a broad-shouldered young man who stood beside a large wooden cart.

"G-good morning, Miss Rosalind," he stammered in return, quickly pulling off his flat cap and running a hand through his auburn hair.

She gave a small smile and walked up to the rear of the cart to peek inside. "Oh, are those courgettes? Maria prepares a lovely dish with them."

Albert nodded as he fiddled with the cap in his hands. "And if you open up the small pouch on top there, you'll find some raspberries. I know they're your favorite," he added timidly.

Rosalind picked up the linen pouch and carefully untied its knot, revealing a large handful of ripe red raspberries. With the persistent dry weather that plagued Sauvign, they were hard to come by nowadays.

"These look lovely! But how did you..."

"Traded with another farmer traveling through the area," he said proudly.

Rosalind grinned. "Thank you, Albert. It's so kind of you to share some with me." She popped one into her mouth, savoring the burst of sweet and tangy juice that danced on her tongue.

Albert looked at her as though he wished to speak but couldn't. The silence soon began to drag.

Unable to take it any longer, Rosalind said, "Well, I'd best be off; things to do and all that. I'm certain Maria will be thrilled to see what you've brought us this week." She reached back into the cart and picked up a crate overflowing with local fruits and vegetables.

"You look nice today," Albert blurted out.

Rosalind's eyes widened in surprise. "Oh." It was all she could manage at first. "Thank you," she added hurriedly. "Y-you look nice as well." She offered him a sheepish smile, unsure of what else to say.

She didn't have much personal experience in flirting or courtship, but she had read enough romance novels to recognize Albert's intentions. That, and she had seen quite a few suitors attempt to court Valentina—unsuccessfully.

Although those outside high society didn't often view her with contempt, many were afraid to consort with her should their employers hear of it. Others considered her a harbinger of misfortune, seeing as she had encountered misfortune herself. But Albert had never expressed such notions in the two years he had delivered produce to Brighthall. In fact, he had never shown her anything but kindness. It was only in the last few months that he appeared more nervous in her presence and had gone out of his way to bring her little tokens of affection, like the raspberries.

"This is quite full," she commented when he didn't reply, indicating the heavy crate in her arms. "It was good seeing you, Albert. Please do give your father our regards."

Albert bowed. "I hope to see you again soon, Miss Rosalind."

Rosalind blew at a lock of hair that had fallen in front of her face as she entered the kitchen, and she lugged the crate to a nearby table.

"Seems you have an admirer."

She glanced over at Jonathan who leaned idly against the counter. "Oh, it's nothing really. Friendly is all."

"Friendly." Maria huffed a laugh. "Asks about her every time he visits, he does."

Rosalind felt her cheeks warm.

"Oh, courgettes," the housekeeper exclaimed as she dug through the crate. "My! Are these what I think they are?"

Rosalind nodded. "Raspberries."

"And you think he's only friendly." Maria leveled her a knowing look.

"I half thought the poor man might keel over when you returned his compliment," Jonathan chimed in. "Though I did find it surprising he didn't carry the crate in for you."

"Oh, I rather prefer to do so myself to avoid any accidental, you know..." She trailed off, waggling her fingers in the air to get her point across.

"Speaking of," Jonathan said. "I'd like to borrow you for a moment if I may. Fancy a stroll through the courtyard this fine morning?"

The morning fog had lifted, though the sky remained gray, as the pair followed a narrow flagstone path to the hidden courtyard. They walked quietly side by side until they approached a wall of massive green hedges. Hard to distinguish from afar was an opening between the hedges that marked the entrance of a maze. Jonathan broke the silence as they ventured inside.

"Couldn't sleep, hmm? If I had to guess, I'd say it might have something to do with last night's surprise in the kitchen."

Rosalind peered up at him, hope unfurling in her chest. "So it was real then? A part of me wondered if I had imagined it..."

"Sure felt real to me."

Her pulse raced as they continued to weave their way through the maze, the sound of their footfalls along the gravel path echoing around them. It wasn't long before the hedges gave way to an enclosed courtyard. Tall stone planters filled with flowers of all different colors and varieties encircled the hidden space, a marble compass medallion marking its center. A bistro table with intricate openwork floral details and two coordinating chairs stood off to one side.

"If you were at all curious, we could find out for certain," Jonathan suggested.

Rosalind's heart leaped at the proposal. "Quite curious," she said as she rocked back and forth on her heels.

Jonathan moved to stand in front of her and held out a hand, his palm facing toward her. "Whenever you're ready."

She slowly lifted her hand until it was level with his. With a shaky breath, Rosalind guided it forward until their hands were only a hair's breadth apart. She was close enough to have prompted the enchantment, yet nothing happened. Feeling emboldened, she stretched out trembling fingers until they met his.

Jonathan didn't pull back, nor did the familiar golden sparks erupt between them. An astonished laugh escaped from Rosalind's mouth as she pressed her palm against his.

Slowly and gently, as if afraid she might disturb the enchantment from its slumber, she brushed her fingertips down the length of his fingers and then across the small calluses that lined the top of his palm. She lifted her gaze to Jonathan in silent question.

He answered by turning his palm away from her, granting her permission to explore the back of his hand. The skin was cooler to the touch and smoother than his palm had been. She let her thumb lightly trace over the hills and grooves of his knuckles, and her brows shot up in surprise when she noticed how the size of his thumb dwarfed hers. Finally, her fingers grazed the dusting of delicate dark hairs that disappeared under the cuff of his shirt. Her eyes darted from his silver cufflink to the matching brooch pinned to the lapel of his jacket.

"Go on."

Rosalind glanced up at Jonathan who stared back at her with a hint of amusement in his eyes.

She reached out and ran her fingers over the brooch, noting the letter R etched neatly into the silver. Tempted by the luxe fabric of his jacket, Rosalind swept a light touch along his lapel, its fine wool tickling her fingertips. She paused when she reached the edge of his collar, though her eyes continued to trail the length of his neck and follow the line of his sharp jaw. He showed the barest hint of a shadow, and she couldn't help but wonder what he might look like with facial hair.

Her thoughts must have been evident because, wordlessly, Jonathan took her hand gently and brought it to rest against his cheek. Rosalind wondered if he could feel the slight tremble of her thumb as she lightly caressed the side of his face. It was soft, not at all coarse like she had imagined, then again, he'd likely shaved that morning. Her thumb stilled at the edge of his lips and a little voice in her head implored her to go on.

She blinked away the thought and looked up to find Jonathan watching her intently. Heat crawled up the back of her neck, and the sensation made her pull her hand away from him. The sound of her heart pounding in her chest reverberated in her ears and she was almost certain he could hear it.

"I didn't dream it then," she whispered.

"Am I often in your dreams?"

"No," Rosalind exclaimed in a voice higher than intended.

Jonathan let out a low chuckle.

"D-do you think it has fully lifted?" Rosalind asked, attempting to distract from the blush that dusted her cheeks. "The enchantment, I mean."

"I don't know," he said with a shrug, "but we could find out."

Rosalind nodded.

Jonathan took a step toward her, narrowing the gap between them. "Well, we know I can touch your hand," he explained. "Shall we try a little higher?"

He let his hand hover above her forearm for a moment before cautiously lowering it. Rosalind huffed a small laugh when his hand rested against her with not a spark in sight. Jonathan, too, let out a relieved breath.

Again, he let his hand hover inches away from her, this time at her shoulder. And once again, he lowered it slowly. To Rosalind's dismay, sparks of golden light shot out.

Jonathan swore as he shook out his hand. "Not quite all the way," he admitted ruefully.

Frustration knitted her brow; she bit the inside of her lip, willing herself to keep the disappointment at bay.

"We're still three weeks away from your birthday," Jonathan reminded her. His voice was soft as he spoke. "Perhaps it's lessening by the day?"

With slight reluctance, Rosalind glanced at Jonathan and was met with an encouraging smile. Then his attention shifted to something over her shoulder.

"I believe our time is up."

Rosalind followed his gaze to the entrance of the courtyard, and moments later, Louis appeared.

"Jonathan, Lord Aston is here to see you. I have escorted him into the study."

Jonathan sighed and rubbed at his temple. "Ah, yes. He did mention last night that he hoped to speak with me privately. Tell him I'll be with him soon, will you?"

Louis lowered his head. "Of course." He lifted his head and greeted Rosalind. "Good morning, my dear."

"Good morning, Louis." Rosalind smiled.

"Seeing you two in here brings back old memories," he said wistfully. "How time has flown by."

7

THIRTEEN YEARS EARLIER

THE AIR WAS WARM and dry as the summer sun blanketed Brighthall's lush green grounds in dazzling light.

Rosalind sat in the shade, her back against the cool stone wall of the stately house she had lived in for the past two years. Beside her sat Valentina, who was scribbling furiously in her notebook. Craning her neck to see what she was drawing, Rosalind spied what looked to be someone riding a horse. On closer inspection, she realized it wasn't a person on the horse, but a cat.

"Done!" Valentina exclaimed as she triumphantly held out her drawing. Noting Rosalind's quizzical look, she shrugged. "I didn't feel like sketching a person. Animals are much more fun to draw."

"Now," Valentina continued, setting her notebook aside and turning to the lawn ahead of them. "I could do with a stretch of my legs. What say we convince them to play a game with us?"

Rosalind looked over at the "them" in question—Jonathan and a small group of boys and girls around his age. She hesitated. "I don't know…"

"It'll be fun." Valentina grinned. "Pleeease," she said, dragging out the word.

Rosalind sighed, but before she could answer, Valentina pulled at her hand and dragged her off her feet.

"Fancy losing a game of tig?" Valentina asked as they approached the group of children. She placed a hand on her hip and raised a challenging brow at Jonathan.

Jonathan shrugged. "Haven't lost a game today and don't plan to now. Question is, do *you* fancy losing a game of tig, Val?"

Some of the children snickered behind him.

Valentina rolled her eyes. "All I'm hearing is that your friends don't pose much of a challenge."

Though she was three years younger than Jonathan, Valentina had never let him or any of the other children intimidate her. It was something Rosalind greatly admired about her friend.

"You've got to be joking," someone called out from behind Jonathan. "You can't expect us to play with Cursed Carver over there."

Rosalind flinched. She didn't have to look up to know who'd said it—Marcus Trainor, nephew of Lord DuPont.

"It isn't fair," he groaned. "None of us can even touch her." He crossed his arms over his chest and sneered. "Wouldn't want to if I could."

Valentina scowled at him. "Scared of a little competition, Marcus? This is my house as well as Jonathan's and I say what goes. Rosalind is playing," she said in a determined voice.

Marcus turned to Jonathan, brows raised. "You know it's true."

Rosalind stared down at her shoes throughout the exchange, not wanting to catch Marcus's eyes. She also wasn't sure how Jonathan would react around his friends. If he joined in their mockery, she didn't want to witness it.

"How about this," Jonathan began. "It will count as a touch if you get within one step of her. Ros will gladly concede if it happens, won't you?"

Rosalind lifted her head to face him and nodded. A small smile tugged at the corner of her lips.

"Fine," Marcus grumbled.

"Excellent." Valentina beamed. "Last one standing gets the largest slice of lemon loaf."

She took one step backward and then another before shouting, "Jonathan is it first!" Then she turned and darted away, Rosalind and the other children quickly following suit.

Jonathan sighed but covered his eyes and counted aloud.

Rosalind ran toward the towering hedges of the maze that enveloped the courtyard garden. She weaved along the gravel path and soon stumbled into the hidden space.

Valentina argued the courtyard was a terrible place to hide, but Rosalind disagreed. The planters abutting the hedges provided ample hiding spots to choose from and there were two ways to enter and exit, which allowed for a daring escape.

She settled behind a planter seated partway between both entrances and kept her ears peeled for frenzied footsteps atop the gravel. For minutes, only the chatter of birds echoed around her. Then suddenly, she heard someone racing along the winding path.

Rosalind peered around the planter to see Marcus bounding into the courtyard. She held her breath to keep quiet and eyed him cautiously. Had he come to look for a place to hide or was he on the chase, having been caught by Jonathan?

"I know you're in here, Cursed Carver," he said between huffs of breath. "You're always in here. So predictable."

Definitely not here to hide, Rosalind bemoaned. She tracked Marcus's movements as he made his way around the courtyard, peering around each and every planter.

As he crept closer, she considered her plan of action. Marcus was much larger than her, but he was also slower. Her best bet was to make for the exit furthest away from him.

She took a deep breath and darted out from behind the planter. As she sprinted for the gap in the hedges, she heard him shout her name. Her heart leaped as she drew nearer to the opening of the maze, knowing she was closing in on her escape.

Suddenly, something hard struck her back, and Rosalind found herself tumbling forward. Her knees were the first to hit the ground, followed by her hands and then her chin. For a moment, it felt as if she had plunged headfirst into icy waters, but soon the sensation morphed into searing hot pain.

Rosalind slowly peeled herself off the ground and sat back, only to find Marcus looming over her, a smug expression on his face. Through bleary eyes, she noticed he stood there with a shoe on one foot and a torn sock on the other. Marcus leaned down to pick up his missing shoe before cupping both hands around his mouth and hollering, "I got Cursed Carver!" He laughed and ran out of the courtyard.

Stretching her legs out in front of her, Rosalind groaned at the tear in the leg of her trousers. Lady Rashford had let her wear an old pair of Jonathan's and she had gone and ripped them.

Her fingers shook as she pulled back the torn fabric to reveal the broken skin on her knee. She let out a soft sob, unable to hold back the tears that now streamed down her cheeks in earnest. The bottom of her chin burned as she cried, reminding her she had scratches there as well.

"Ros?"

Rosalind peered up to see Jonathan rushing over to her. He knelt down beside her and took stock of her injuries. "It's alright. It'll be alright," he soothed. He then patted his trouser pockets and pulled out a handkerchief, holding it out carefully in front of her. "Here. I'm going to get Grandmum or Maria to come help you. I won't be long, I promise."

Rosalind blew into the handkerchief and nodded. Jonathan scrambled up and made for the exit. Just before rounding the hedges, he paused and turned back to her. "Marcus told us he got you, and I came to find you to check he really had. He didn't mention you were hurt."

Jonathan's brows drew together and Rosalind thought he might say something more. Instead, he simply offered her a reassuring smile and disappeared around the corner.

Rosalind sat on a dark green tartan settee in the study as Lady Rashford tended to her injuries. She bunched and pulled at the handkerchief Jonathan had given her as the older woman piped a few drops of a blue shimmering liquid over the scrape on her knee. Tears pricked Rosalind's eyes as she struggled to remain still.

"Shh," Lady Rashford soothed. "I know it hurts, dear, but we need to make certain it doesn't get infected. I'm nearly finished." She reached for a strip of cloth and carefully wrapped it around Rosalind's knee, tying the ends together in a snug knot.

"What a brave girl you are." She leaned over and lifted her thumb to wipe at a tear that streaked down Rosalind's face. Then she sat back and considered her for a moment. "Sometimes people fear what they do not understand," she explained. "And that fear can manifest in all sorts of ways—panic, ignorance, mistrust, and on occasion, cruelty.

"Jonathan and Valentina are lucky, you see. They have had the wonderful opportunity to live with you and to grow alongside you. They have come to know of your gentle and kind nature. To them, the enchantment is but a small part of you. The Trainor boy, on the other hand, does not share in their experience. He's only come to know of you and all that pertains to magic through the words of others."

"Like his uncle?" Rosalind asked as she drew her knees to her chest and wrapped her arms around her shins.

Lady Rashford wore a sad, knowing smile as she nodded. "Like Lord DuPont, yes."

Rosalind could still recall the glower Lord DuPont had cast her way when she first encountered him. It was frightening, to say the least. As such, she made a habit of retreating to the courtyard with Valentina whenever he visited Brighthall.

Lady Rashford gently patted Rosalind's hand. "Now we've patched you up, how about we see if there is anything left of Maria's famous lavender lemon loaf? If that doesn't perk you right up, I don't know what will."

8

SPOT OF WHISKEY

IT WAS WELL AFTER dusk and Brighthall was quiet, with most everyone having retired to their rooms for the evening. Not yet ready to call it a night, Rosalind found herself in the kitchen seated across from Valentina at a small wooden table lit by the wavering glow of an ostentatious candelabra. Clutter was pushed to the side to make room for two bottles of wine Valentina had pilfered from the cellar, one nearly emptied, and a plate of freshly baked sweet bread.

Valentina had just finished divulging the latest gossip from a ladies' luncheon she had attended earlier that day when a question popped into Rosalind's head.

Rosalind stared into her glass of wine and traced a finger along its rim as she voiced her query aloud. "Val, what might you do in my position? If you were coming up to a particularly significant birthday and could suddenly do something you had never been able to before."

"Fuck."

Rosalind nearly choked on her wine. "P-pardon?"

"I think I broke a nail," Valentina grumbled as she looked down at her hand. Then she drew her gaze back up to Rosalind. "Sorry, back to your question..." She trailed off, rubbing her chin in consideration. "For starters, I would have a close friend organize a fabulous soiree under the guise of a musical exhibition or charity function or what have you. I would then curate a very particular guest list composed only of eligible bachelors who met my strict criteria, and acquaintances whom I could trust to sing my praises."

Rosalind eyed her friend skeptically. "Why not simply host it on behalf of your birthday?"

"No, no, that won't do," Valentina remarked as she reached for the other bottle of wine and uncorked it. "Hosting my own birthday would have me appear vain. It would also cast too much attention on me. How am I to intimately acquaint myself with anyone when I'm constantly under watch?" She beckoned Rosalind to hold out her glass.

"The entire point of the soiree is to provide me the opportunity to determine which men, if any, are worthy of more of my time," she explained as she topped off Rosalind's glass and refilled her own. "Look, Ros, I don't possess your level of patience. Never have. If I had to wait twenty-two years to touch a man, you'd better believe I'm going to sort that out rather quickly. Find out what all the fuss is about." She paused briefly before adding, "Aren't you the least bit curious?"

Rosalind chewed the inside of her lip as she mulled over the question. She was curious, certainly, but to what extent was something she hadn't fully considered yet.

"How many days left until the big day?" Valentina asked when Rosalind didn't respond. "Nine, yes?" she said after counting the days on her fingers. "You know, it isn't too late if you'd like me to organize something..."

Rosalind snorted. "It'd be an enormous waste of time. You'd be hard-pressed to find men willing to give me the time of day regardless of the status of my enchantment. Social pariah, remember?"

"What about that fidgety boy, Anton or Alfred or whatever?"

"So close." Rosalind gave a little chuckle. "Albert is his name."

"Yes, that one. He's plenty interested in you, is he not? Perhaps we need to seek out more men like him, those not under DuPont's influence."

"That rules out all of Proper high society then," Rosalind mumbled into her glass.

"If there were anyone, I would've slept with them already and could tell you if any were worth their salt. Alas, I've only had the terrible misfortune of bedding incomprehensible pricks—and I mean that in every sense."

"Come now. What about Charles?"

"Ah, yes, charitable Charlie," Valentina said wistfully. "Good chap, that one. Such a shame he inherited an estate away in the salt marshes. He waxed on and on about the endless blue sea and vibrant sunrises I could wake up to every morning, as if living by the ocean would entice me. Can you imagine the havoc salty air would wreak on my hair? Not to mention my skin. Absolutely not." She grimaced.

Rosalind bit her lip in a poor attempt at hiding her amusement. As soon as their eyes met, the pair burst into uncontrollable laughter.

"What are you two on about?"

Wiping away the tears from her eyes, Rosalind looked to where Jonathan had appeared in the doorway. She had only caught glimpses of him in recent days. According to Louis, he was busy visiting with farmers, factory workers, and tradespeople in the area. He would slip out of the house early in the morning and return well after dark.

Her heart fluttered at the sight of him. The last time they were together, he'd helped her confirm her enchantment truly was lifting—and ahead of schedule at that. To say she was eager to uncover whether any more of the enchantment had lifted would be an understatement, and now, here he was. Rosalind's gaze flicked to Valentina, and the flutter abruptly petered out when she remembered she hadn't yet confided the revelation to her dearest friend.

"Wouldn't you like to know," Valentina said smugly as she peered at him over her shoulder.

Jonathan huffed a laugh. "Fair enough. I'll leave you two to your secrets then. I only came to check that Death hadn't come to collect the pair of you. It's difficult to discern the sounds of your drunken gaiety from those of agonizing terror."

"How quaint of you to think you could do anything about it if it had," Valentina retorted. "Now, come and have a seat. You look like you need a glass." She turned to Rosalind. "Pour him one, will you?"

Rosalind opened the large cabinet behind her and plucked a glass from it. She poured with a heavy hand and held it out for Jonathan to collect. A sudden wave of panic rushed over her as he approached. She locked eyes with him and implored him to heed her unspoken plea.

Jonathan squinted slightly, and his gaze darted briefly to Valentina before returning to hers. Slowly he reached for the wine glass and grabbed hold of the stem, careful to maintain a safe distance from Rosalind's hand. She sighed, releasing the breath she hadn't realized she was holding.

"You've looked better, dear brother," Valentina said as she sat back and sipped her wine, eyeing Jonathan curiously. "Something on your mind?"

Rosalind looked at Jonathan. He wasn't wearing a jacket, only a white shirt with the top few buttons undone and the sleeves rolled up to just below his elbows. No pins or brooches or tightly knotted cravats adorned his person. And in the dim glow of candlelight, the circles under his eyes looked more pronounced than usual. Perhaps most surprising was his hair, which was not held in its typical rigid coiffure. Instead, tousled obsidian curls frayed above his ears and along his neck. Wavy locks sat atop his head, and a few strays tumbled loosely onto his forehead.

Jonathan ran a hand through his hair. "I'd rather not spoil your fun with my vexations."

"And I'd rather you not take us for such fickle creatures," Valentina countered. "I shall sleep soundly regardless of whether or not you confide in us, but I must admit I'm intrigued to know why you look as if you've just returned from a bender at the card room."

"I wish," he murmured into his drink. He took a sip, which turned into him finishing the glass. Valentina was quick to refill his cup as he spoke. "Frankly, I'm exhausted and it's been—what, not yet a month since I was inducted? Already I feel as if I am *this* close"—he brought his thumb and forefinger together—"to tearing out all of my hair."

"Is that possible? I hadn't thought so given all the pomade you use."

Jonathan chuckled. "For the sake of my vanity, let's hope you're right. But if you must know, I have come to realize things are far worse than they're made out to be."

"Do tell," Valentina entreated.

He was quiet for a moment as if unsure of where to begin. "Denault can't sustain its population independently. Hasn't been able to for more than a century due to dwindling crop yields. Over the years, our harvests have suffered from all sorts of calamities, be it too little rain, too much rain, frost, soil degradation, pests, diseases—you name it. To account for the deficit, we've invested heavily in imported commodities from elsewhere in Sauvign and overseas."

Last year marked the centennial of the New Laws' establishment in Sauvign. It was doubtless no coincidence that the laws came into effect shortly after regions like Denault began to suffer agricultural setbacks.

"In theory, it's a viable solution," Jonathan went on. "Trouble is, it's an expensive one. On top of the price of the commodities themselves, there are labor and transportation costs to account for. Ends up being quite lucrative for those who've invested in the trade industry. Quite costly for most everyone else."

"How fortuitous for our old pal, DuPont," Valentina remarked dryly.

"Isn't it just?"

Rosalind was vaguely familiar with the struggles local farmers faced through passing conversations with Albert and his father. Maria, too, had often lamented how expensive produce had become over the years. If Brighthall could feel the effects, how much more for households not of high society?

Jonathan rubbed at his forehead. "What's frustrating is learning what little the council has done to curb costs and explore other more economical solutions. Reports compiled for the capital over the years hardly mention the issue. I wouldn't have known it was so dire had I not met with nearby townkeepers and union leaders in the city.

"It took a bit of convincing to get them to speak candidly with me," he added. "They found it difficult to believe I had come to inquire about their well-being. I don't blame them. Care to guess how long it's been since the council last held an audience with members of the public? Nearly *thirty years*."

Rosalind didn't miss how his leg bounced as he spoke. For a fleeting moment, she considered reaching out to try and settle his nerves, but her nerves swiftly rejected the notion.

"Can you change that?" She asked instead. It was the weight of past thoughts—things beyond his control—that seemed to agitate him. Perhaps shifting his focus to the present, where he could make a difference, might help ease his restlessness.

"I intend to, yes. I can reinstate public audiences with the council. I can also report my findings to the capital so that we may be held accountable for presenting an alternative solution. I know it can be done, I just haven't figured it out yet…"

Jonathan swirled the dregs of wine in his glass, appearing lost in thought. He seemed so far away, and Rosalind wasn't sure he could be pulled out of it. However, evidently not everyone agreed. Out of the corner of her eye, she saw Valentina tear off a piece of the leftover bread. Then, to Rosalind's surprise, she flung it at Jonathan.

He shot her an incredulous look. "What was that for?"

"To get you out of your own head." Valentina tilted her head as she considered her brother. "You're not going to solve anything tonight, so you might as well give your mind a rest. Wake up refreshed, and perhaps you'll be able to assess it in a different light, hmm?" There was a softness in her eyes as she spoke. If confronted, she would undoubtedly attribute it to a trick of the light. But Rosalind knew her friend well enough to recognize the sympathy seeping through the cracks of her cavalier facade.

As if sensing she had been found out, Valentina sat back and crossed her arms. "It's as I said, you need it. Just look at the state of you," she scoffed.

Jonathan rubbed a hand down his face. "I can't believe I'm saying this, but you have a point. Is there any more wine?"

Valentina picked up the bottle and gave it a slight shake. "Sadly, no."

Jonathan stood. "I'll be back."

Moments later, he returned with a decanter of whiskey. "Will this do?"

"Oh yes," Valentina said with a clap of her hands. "Give it here."

She poured some into her empty wine glass, then glanced over at Rosalind. "Good times, eh?" she said with a wink.

Rosalind wrinkled her nose as she eyed the liquor sloshing in the decanter.

"Not a fan?" Jonathan asked as he settled back onto his chair.

"Not particularly," she mumbled.

"There's a reason for that," Valentina chimed in. "Want to hear it?"

Rosalind groaned into her hands. "Val..."

"I convinced her to sneak out with me one night to visit a nearby tavern," Valentina began, ignoring Rosalind's protestations. "One at the edge of Proper. It had a name to do with an animal, like a boar or sheep or something."

"Ram's Head?" Jonathan suggested.

"Yes, that's the one," Valentina said with a snap of her fingers.

She proceeded to regale him with a colorful account of the evening, some of which Rosalind had no recollection of. She explained how they had struck up a conversation with a few locals who recommended they try the homemade whiskey. One drink turned into a few. The whiskey continued to flow as the locals showed them how to play darts. They lost track of time and found themselves still at the tavern when dawn arrived. In order to make it back before Maria and the rest of the household awoke, they had to hurry back. Valentina reminisced about the brisk ride and recounted Rosalind's experience.

"Ros here abhors horseback riding," Valentina reminded Jonathan. "It terrifies her. Honestly, I don't know how I convinced her to come with me in the first place. Well, anyway, I suppose the combination of sheer terror and whiskey made for a very uncomfortable ride home."

She patted Rosalind's hand. "I applaud her for making it until we got to the stable. Got sick in a nearby bush and refused to head up to bed with me. If I recall correctly, Colby found her passed out in a pile of hay."

Jonathan threw his head back and laughed. The sound of his warm laughter almost made the humiliating story worth it. Almost. At least Valentina had omitted a few other details from the evening to save her from abject mortification.

"The more I come to learn about you, the more curious I become."

Rosalind felt his eyes on her, and when she lifted her gaze to him, it fixed on the small dimple in his cheek that accompanied his broad smile. Her fingers itched to acquaint themselves with it. Worried her impulses might get the best of her, she tucked her free hand under the crook of her knee.

Another hour passed as the trio chatted idly about anything and everything that came to mind, including a scandal Rosalind and Valentina recounted from a few years back, about a nude painting of one of Proper's most prominent goldsmiths mysteriously appearing on a bench in the town square one morning.

Valentina tipped her head back and drained the remainder of the whiskey. She then wiped a hand across her mouth. "Well, ladies and gentlemen, I do believe it's time for me to take my leave."

She pushed herself off her chair and brushed stray crumbs off her dress. "I'm hoping to get a few more chapters in before I sleep. I'm halfway through an exquisite little novel about a love-deprived young maiden who finds herself in the arms of a war-hardened blacksmith with a giant—"

"I think we get the premise," Jonathan interjected. "I can't think of anything I want to hear less than the rest of that sentence."

Valentina shrugged. "Suit yourself. I'll let you borrow it when I'm finished, Ros." She gave her a wink.

Without another word, Valentina strolled out of the kitchen, leaving Rosalind and Jonathan alone.

"So I take it you haven't told Val about the enchantment?"

"Not yet," Rosalind said, shifting in her seat. "I've been meaning to, I just..." The words died on her tongue.

Why she hadn't yet told her dearest friend was a question she was struggling to answer, even to herself. At first, she didn't say anything because she wanted to wait until she had confirmation. Then, after she and Jonathan had met in the courtyard, she told herself she needed time to process it. But that was nearly a week ago, and she still hadn't confided in Valentina, though there had been ample opportunities to do so. Tonight, for instance.

"Well, fear not. I won't say anything."

"Thank you," she said quietly.

She was grateful Jonathan hadn't pushed for an answer, but with that thread of conversation at an end, silence settled over the pair. Rosalind scrambled to think of something to say but struggled to concentrate. Her attention was drawn to the gentle drumming of Jonathan's fingers against his glass. She tried to formulate a coherent thought but was met with only flashes of memories. Her fingertips skimming along the ridges and troughs of his knuckles. The small calluses that dotted the palm of his hand. The dusting of dark hairs at his wrists that disappeared under his shirt cuff. She had taken the time to study his hand, but what would it feel like for his hand to study her?

Rosalind hadn't realized she was staring until Jonathan's fingers stilled against the glass. Her gaze shot up to find Jonathan watching her. Warmth flooded her cheeks as soon as she caught the hint of his smile.

Feeling dreadfully exposed, retreating was all she could think to do. She stood abruptly from her chair. "It's getting quite late, isn't it?" she said, in a voice much too high. "I-I should probably take my leave now as well."

Jonathan drew himself up and his close proximity had Rosalind's instincts telling her to move away so as not to set off the enchantment. She stumbled backward only to bump into the cupboard that towered behind her.

"Aren't you curious?" He asked.

He stood close enough that his height forced her head back to look up at him. "Yes, of course. Very much so," she admitted earnestly. "But I wouldn't wish to trouble you with..." She trailed off, forgetting what she was going to say.

Her focus shifted to Jonathan's hand, which now hovered in her eyeline. She watched as his outstretched fingers captured a lock of hair that had fallen in front of her face. Ever so gently, he tucked the loose hair behind her ear. His fingers never left her skin as they continued their exploration, delicately tracing the line of her jaw until coming to rest on her chin. She closed her eyes as the pad of his thumb swept upward and lingered briefly at the corner of her mouth before venturing along her bottom lip.

"Ros..."

Her eyes fluttered open at the sound of her name on his lips, so enticing it made her pulse quicken. "Yes?" she breathed.

She was vaguely aware that Jonathan had placed a hand on the cupboard beside her head, steadying himself as he leaned in. Slowly, he lowered his head until their faces were mere inches apart, his presence closing in around her in a way that felt impossibly intimate. "What say you to a spot of whiskey now?"

Her momentary bewilderment dissipated as soon as his warm breath ghosted across her lips, and she inhaled the faint scent of whiskey. She bit back a smile.

"Perhaps just a taste," she whispered into the small space between them.

The words had barely left her when Jonathan leaned in and captured her lips with his. The kiss was soft and tentative and, to Rosalind's dismay, achingly brief.

Jonathan drew his head back and she choked down the protests that rose in her throat. His eyes roamed her face as if he were searching for something.

He must have found what he was looking for because the next thing she knew, his mouth was on hers again. The tentativeness from earlier was gone this time around. His lips pressed more firmly against hers, and she could almost taste his burgeoning hunger. It made her crave more in return. She parted her lips in invitation and Jonathan swiftly obliged. The kiss deepened, and Rosalind reached out to grasp the fabric of Jonathan's shirt, fearing her knees might buckle at any moment.

Without warning, Jonathan broke the kiss. "This isn't your first kiss," he murmured against her lips. Then he drew back warily. "It wasn't my sister, was it?"

Rosalind let out a shaky laugh. "No, it's not. And no, it was not."

Evidently, that was all Jonathan needed to hear. He dove in for another kiss, and they took their time exploring one another's mouths with lips and tongues and teeth. Just as Rosalind contemplated the necessity of air, Jonathan's lips parted from hers to pepper kisses along her jaw. Rosalind inhaled deeply, only to gasp out seconds later as Jonathan nipped at her earlobe before lowering his mouth to kiss her neck.

The hairs on her skin stood on end as his fingertips trailed up the length of her arm. They continued their exploration, tracing along her collarbone before venturing down her décolletage toward the low neckline of her dress. Just then, sparks of golden light erupted, and Jonathan's hand drew back. He let out a soft, frustrated hum against Rosalind's neck before slowly pulling himself upright.

For a brief moment, the room was filled with only the sound of their quick, heavy breaths. Then Jonathan cleared his throat. "Shall we?"

Rosalind nodded and led their silent retreat upstairs. When they reached her door, she turned to bid him goodnight. The muscle in his jaw ticked and there was a stiffness to his stance as he offered her a hasty bow in return. His hand clenched open and closed at his side as his figure disappeared down the hall.

Once inside, she leaned against her door and smiled. That was one way to measure the progress of the dwindling enchantment. What might have happened had it been fully lifted? She shook her head. It would do her no good to wonder, to ask, what if? At best, such musings could inspire pleasant dreams. At worst, they could ignite something dreadfully foolish—hope. No, it was better to take it for what it was: a new experience for her and a welcome distraction for him. Curiosity combined with alcohol did tend to lower inhibitions.

Not wanting to bother with every arduous step of her typical nighttime routine, Rosalind hastily pulled off her dress and slipped on her nightgown. She was halfway through a perfunctory attempt at plaiting her hair when a disconcerting realization weaseled its way to the forefront of her mind. The reason she hadn't confided in Valentina was rather apparent now, wasn't it? She'd enjoyed her clandestine rendezvous with Jonathan and, had she told Valentina, tonight wouldn't have happened as it did. Her friend would have had other more outlandish ideas as to how and with whom to test the boundaries of the enchantment.

Rosalind slipped under the thick, warm sheets of her bed to hide from the guilt that began to niggle at her. She shut her eyes and tried to still her whirring mind. Instead, the thought of Jonathan's lips warm and wanting against hers surfaced. She touched her fingers to her lips before letting them trail languidly down the length of her body, dipping between her breasts and over her belly, skimming lightly across the thin fabric of her nightgown.

Shamelessly, she licked her lips, seeking any lingering taste of him. She recalled the low hums and uneven breaths that escaped his mouth as he kissed her neck, and she pulled at the hem of her gown and slid her hand between her thighs.

As vivid memories flooded her mind and she beckoned bliss to consume her, she couldn't help but wonder if he was doing the same.

9

A Favor

ROSALIND STOOD OVER A pot of boiling water and added slices of peeled pumpkin, careful not to let the bubbles spill over the brim. Though she kept a watchful eye on the pot, her mind was elsewhere.

In just four days, she would be twenty-two. She had spent her entire life anticipating this day and it was finally on the horizon. Somewhere along the way, doubt had crept in and tempered her hopes, and she'd embraced it, fearing the heartbreak that would befall her if the proverb turned out to be untrue.

But her unexpected encounter with Jonathan the night of the council dinner put an end to that fear and loosened the thread of doubt that had wound its way around her heart. The proverb held true, and she would soon be free of her enchantment. She could walk through a crowded room without concern for proximity—propriety aside, of course. She could pass dishes at the dinner table without fear of hurting anyone, or accept a man's hand for help into a carriage. She could partake in country dances or even waltz with a gentleman.

For all intents and purposes, she would be like everybody else. But would they accept her as such? It was naive to think high society would forget so easily. And what of those who perceived her as an omen of misfortune? Would she continue to bear that burden in their eyes?

Rosalind jabbed at a slice of pumpkin and felt it give way. She removed the pot from the stove and transferred the boiled pumpkin onto a thin layer of cheesecloth. After it had cooled for a few minutes, she tied the cloth taut and squeezed the soft pumpkin, emptying the steaming liquid into a large bowl.

Once finished, she sought out the coachman, Franklin, with pumpkin puree in hand. While she may not be partial to horseback riding, horses themselves were quite majestic and kind. They would appreciate the sweet treat and she enjoyed observing them from afar.

Rosalind was on her way back to the kitchen when a familiar voice called out to her from behind. "Good morning, Miss Rosalind."

She turned to see Albert approaching her, wheeling a cart behind him. "Albert, how lovely to see you."

"I have this week's produce for Maria," he said as he brought the cart to a stop in front of her. "Though I don't have anything special for you this time around, I'm afraid."

Rosalind gave a small chuckle. "I shan't take offense."

"I'm only teasing, miss." He pulled a small bouquet of purple wildflowers from the breast pocket of his vest. "These are for you. Well, I hoped to give these to you if I saw you. If not, I would have likely given them to my mum." He brought a hand to rub at the back of his neck, a lopsided smile on his lips.

"Oh my." Rosalind stared wide-eyed at the flowers in his hand. "Th-that is very kind of you," she stammered.

She started to reach for them but reflexively retreated when her hand neared his. "I'm sorry, I don't wish to accidentally..." She let her fingers do the rest of the talking, wiggling them in the air.

"Ah, right. How about I set them here on the cart and you can take them from there?" Albert settled the bouquet gently atop the cart.

Rosalind flashed him a reluctant smile and moved to pick up the flowers. "Thank you, Albert."

"They reminded me of you." He slid his hands into his trouser pockets and rocked back and forth on the heels of his feet. "Delicate and pretty," he added quietly.

Her mouth went dry. "That's very kind of you." She found herself repeating her words in the absence of coherent thought.

"Miss Rosalind," Albert started again, his eyes not meeting hers. "I wish to ask you something."

"Oh?" she said, voice cracking. She placed her arms behind her back and straightened her spine in an attempt to maintain a calm demeanor.

"If I recall correctly, your upcoming birthday is a significant one." He kicked at the dirt as he spoke. "And I was wondering if you would do me the honor of joining me for dinner. I could prepare us something or—or if you felt it too forward, perhaps I could accompany you on a stroll through town?"

Rosalind's heartbeat rang in her ears. She had sensed this was coming and yet, she was still surprised by it. She twisted her hands behind her as she contemplated how to respond. Never had she been asked anything like this before.

"I..." she started. When nothing followed, she shut her mouth and forced her nerves back down her throat. Then she took a few steadying breaths and tried again. "I—"

Her attempt was cut short by a stammering, wide-eyed Albert. "Oh, L-Lord Rashford, good day to you, sir." He removed his cap and ran a hand through his hair.

Rosalind followed Albert's eyeline past her shoulder to find Jonathan leaning against the kitchen doorway. Her heart skipped a beat at the sight of him. He wore a burgundy double-breasted suit, the jacket cut at his waist in front and tapering out behind him. Peeking out underneath was a white shirt with black buttons. A gold bar and matching chain adorned his collar. As usual, his dark hair was swept up in a neat coiffure with not a hair out of place.

"Have we been acquainted before?" Jonathan asked as he made his way toward them. His casual stride and affable smile softened what would otherwise be a rather intimidating appearance.

"No, sir," Albert replied, straightening himself. "The name's Albert, Albert Burrows. You may recall my father, Andrew Burrows? He's been delivering to your family for decades. I've taken over a few of his routes, you see. Yours being one of them, sir. Been coming here for the last two years now."

"It is a pleasure to meet you, Albert." Jonathan held out his hand.

Albert's gaze flicked from Jonathan's outstretched hand to his face and back again. "It's an honor to make your acquaintance, Lord Rashford." He eagerly shook Jonathan's hand. "Chancellor Rashford, that is," he added hurriedly.

"You do us a great service, bringing us our produce each week. That makes us fast friends, so you should feel free to call me Jonathan if you're so inclined. Since my return, I have thoroughly enjoyed every meal Maria has prepared, thanks in large part, I suspect, to the fresh foods you deliver. Between you and I"—Jonathan leaned forward conspiratorially—"everything here is more delicious than anything I had back at the capital."

Jonathan glanced at Rosalind briefly, igniting a trail of gooseflesh along her spine, before returning his attention to Albert.

Albert beamed at the compliment. "Thank you, sir. Means a lot to me, and my pops will be thrilled to hear it."

Jonathan smiled. "Well, I suppose I should be off. Have an appointment in town later today that I really must prepare for." He reached between Rosalind and Albert to lift the crate marked *Rashford* from the cart.

Albert darted forward. "Oh no, sir, I can take—"

"Not a bother, Albert. It's the least I can do. Granted, I will need to steal Rosalind here so she can instruct me where best to put this. I hope you don't mind."

"Oh yes, of course," Albert replied. A frantic expression suddenly crossed his face. "I mean, no! W-what I mean to say is yes, I understand, and no, I don't mind." He finished with a sheepish chuckle.

Jonathan flashed him a smile. "Again, it has been a true pleasure, Albert. Until next time." He bowed his head at Albert, then turned to Rosalind. "Shall we?"

Rosalind looked from Jonathan to Albert and back again. She considered him for a moment, then nodded slowly. Turning her attention back to Albert, she smiled. "Thank you again for the flowers."

Her eyes darted briefly to where Jonathan stood before she lowered her voice and added, "If it's alright with you, might I give you my answer next week?"

"Certainly, miss. I shall look forward to seeing you then," Albert said with a hopeful grin. He bowed, and she returned it with one of her own before heading for the kitchen with Jonathan in tow.

"You can set it here," she said, indicating the table they had sat at five nights ago. Her gaze lingered briefly on the large cabinet beside it before she made her way to the counter where she had been preparing the pumpkin bread earlier.

She was trying to recall the recipe when Jonathan slid a glass of water in front of her. She looked up at him with a quizzical brow.

"For the flowers."

Rosalind let out a small gasp and peered down at the forgotten bundle of purple wildflowers, held firmly in her hand. Reluctantly, she unwound her fingers, revealing their crumpled stems. "Thank you," she muttered as she hastily placed them in the water. Unsurprisingly, their pretty petaled heads drooped listlessly over the rim of the glass.

It had been such a thoughtful gesture from Albert. Why hadn't she held onto them with more care? So much for being delicate.

"Do you plan to accept his invitation?"

Rosalind glanced over at Jonathan, whose back was to her. He appeared to be rummaging through the produce crate.

"Yes, I suppose so," she answered quietly. "I mean, I should... shouldn't I?"

Albert had been kind to her. He was polite and patient and seemed to like her regardless of the enchantment. And it wasn't as if she had a line of suitors waiting for her.

"Do you think Maria would be upset if I ate this?" Jonathan asked, holding up an apple. Before Rosalind could answer, he rubbed it against his sleeve and took a bite. Then he pulled a chair out from under the table and swung a leg over the seat so he sat facing backward. He rested an arm atop the back of the chair and regarded Rosalind.

"If you want to, I don't see why not," he said, shrugging. "He seems like a good enough lad. A bit naive perhaps, but I wouldn't hold that against him."

"I hadn't planned to," she muttered under her breath, a slight furrow forming between her brows. She had half a thought to point out that Albert was only two years younger than him when Jonathan spoke again.

"He isn't wasting any time, is he? Makes me wonder how long he intends to court you before proposing."

Rosalind made a strangled noise. "Come again?"

"He doesn't strike me as someone who takes these things lightly. And if I recall Maria correctly, he's harbored affections for you for some time now. Given what I witnessed today," Jonathan explained with raised brows, "he hasn't much practice in making such advances. That leads me to believe he's been biding his time to ask you. I don't know of many men who wait unless their intentions are serious."

"But he hardly knows me," Rosalind insisted.

"He's delivered to our estate for two years now, yes? So he knows you some. Others have married knowing far less," Jonathan pointed out.

Until a month ago, she had barely let herself imagine a life free of the enchantment. To be able to touch a man—to feel him, to kiss him, to hold him, and to be held by him—was something she was only now beginning to envision, admittedly in vivid detail. She hadn't yet allowed thoughts of love and companionship, let alone marriage, to take up residence in her mind.

Agitation flickered across her brow again. "Why are you telling me this?" she pressed, not bothering to hide the irritation in her voice.

Jonathan didn't answer right away. Instead, he set his half-eaten apple down on the table behind him and pushed off the chair. He strolled around the stone counter until he stood catercorner from her. Leaning against the counter's edge, he said simply, "I figured you'd want to know."

"How can you be so confident in your assertions about someone you've known for mere minutes?"

A smirk tugged at his lips. "What can I say? I'm good at first impressions. It's a useful skill in my line of work, you know."

Rosalind snorted. "And you are never wrong, I take it?"

"Rarely."

"So you're saying there's a chance…"

Jonathan huffed a laugh. "Fine, I will admit there is a tiny, minuscule, almost imperceptible possibility I'm wrong and he doesn't have his sights set on marriage just yet. Perhaps his motivations are more carnal in nature." He crossed his arms. "Is that what you want to hear?"

Rosalind drew back. "What? No, I—"

"Good, because frankly, I don't think he knows how to make head or tail of another's body."

"There you go again, making assumptions based on a brief acquaintance," she shot back. His flippant remarks fueled her irritation, which in turn hampered her ability to think straight. "And for your information, I am plenty familiar with my own body for the both of us."

"Are you now?"

A blush crept over Rosalind's cheeks. The retort had sounded cleverer in her head. She knew better than to attempt to match wits with a Rashford, yet she couldn't stop herself from rising to the bait.

"Oh, please," she scoffed. "Simply because he isn't as handsome or charming or refined as you doesn't give you the right to disparage him so."

"Handsome, charming, *and* refined," he drawled. "You flatter me."

Rosalind leveled him an icy glare, and he raised his hands in mock surrender. "Your words, not mine."

She huffed. "Why are you so intent on sullying my perception of him?"

"I'm not," Jonathan countered. "I'm just being honest—"

"Judgmental," she interjected. "Suffice it to say, you know your way around another's body."

"I do," he admitted.

"Quite practiced, are you?"

"Who is being judgmental now, hmm?" Jonathan asked pointedly. "I think you overestimate how much free time I've enjoyed in the last decade. That said, I've been with enough to know I am more than competent."

Ashamed of her earlier sentiments, Rosalind looked away. She wrung her hands as she spoke. "I apologize. I didn't mean to pry."

"It's alright. I'm quite the man about town if the gossip columns are to be believed," he remarked sardonically. "Apparently, the allure of one's name in the papers proves too tempting to some, regardless of what may or may not have actually happened."

How awful. She would never do such a thing if they were to…

"I know."

She stiffened. Slowly, she raised her gaze to meet Jonathan's. His eyes searched hers as if to uncover the dregs of her thoughts. So it was as she feared—she had voiced it aloud.

As they bickered, an indecent idea had taken root in the farthest corner of her mind. Born of her own curiosity and desire and sustained by Jonathan's allusions to intimacy, its tendrils sprouted and quickly weaved their way into her consciousness. They tangled with her every thought and emotion, and she couldn't ignore it any longer.

"What if—" she started, then stopped as the air in her lungs left her. She sucked in a shaky breath and tried again. "Would you—" Again, the words abandoned her. It was too absurd to voice aloud.

Jonathan leaned forward. "Go on," he coaxed. "Would I what, Ros?"

Rosalind's heart was racing so fast that she glanced down to reassure herself it hadn't burned a hole in her chest. She looked back up to find Jonathan watching her intently. It was a miracle her legs didn't give way. Mustering up every ounce of courage in her body, she opened her mouth to try again.

"If I wanted to know what it was like, would you"—she swallowed—"sh-show me?" Her breath stilled as she waited for his response.

Jonathan held her stare for a moment longer before straightening himself and smoothing out the front of his jacket.

"Huh, I rather thought you were going to ask me to grab you something from the top shelf of the pantry before I left. It seems I was wrong."

The color drained from her face as he spoke. It wasn't until his lips curved into a sly smile that she realized he was teasing her. Conflicting emotions rushed in, and she wasn't sure whether to laugh, shout, or cry. Ultimately, she resorted to her preferred course of action—retreat. She pushed away from the counter and started for the doorway.

She had only made it a few steps when Jonathan caught her hand. "Ros, wait. Please."

It was their first touch of the day. Their first since their lips had met in this very room. She couldn't very well ignore it. Sighing, Rosalind turned to face him.

"I was only teasing, but I shouldn't have," he admitted. "Forgive me."

He stepped forward, narrowing the gap between them. "My answer is yes. That is if the request still stands."

She eyed her hand, still clasped in his, then raised her eyes to meet his. "It does," she said quietly.

"If you change your mind at any point, I won't take offense. And I'll leave it to you to decide when—"

"The night of my birthday." The words tumbled out before she could gather her wits.

Jonathan gave a soft chuckle. "And so it shall be. Funny thing, I was wrestling with what to give you this year. I suppose I have my answer now."

"Good luck finding a ribbon large enough for such a gift," she quipped.

He rubbed a hand behind his neck. "Well," he drawled, "I think you'll find a modest-sized ribbon will do the trick just as well."

Rosalind bit back a smile, but it wasn't long before a pang of worry sobered her thoughts. There was one more thing she needed to say to him, needed him to understand. Her hand slipped from Jonathan's and into her own as she readied herself. Hands wringing, she cleared her throat.

"Jonathan," she began, her voice wavering, "I want you to know that you needn't worry about me. I won't make anything more of this than what it is—a favor or a gift or what have you—from one friend to another. I value our history and friendship far too much to allow myself to jeopardize it. One night is all it shall be, I swear it. I won't ask for anything more. I won't want for anything more. And it'll just be between us, of course."

Having been too nervous to meet his gaze earlier, Rosalind now risked a glance at him. He was regarding her with a look she couldn't decipher, though she could see the gears at work behind his eyes. It felt as though there was an eternity of silence. For a brief moment, she worried he might reconsider and her heart sank a little at the thought, but then his features slackened and one corner of his lips drew up into a half-smile.

"That makes the two of us, then, as I would also not wish to tarnish our friendship especially when we are only just becoming reacquainted. So, as you so delicately put it, but a favor it will be."

At this, they both smiled at one another. Rosalind felt hers falter slightly as her eyes swept across his face, only to find that his smile did not yield the small dimple she sought.

"Well, I probably should get back to it or Maria will have my head," she said, injecting levity into her voice. She pointed to the ingredients on the counter.

"Ah, yes, the, uh..." He gestured aimlessly around as if attempting to pull the word from the air.

"Pumpkin bread," she chimed in.

"Oh? That sounds lovely."

Rosalind nodded. "And thank you again"—she hesitated briefly—"for doing me this favor." She nervously brushed at a non-existent piece of lint from her skirt.

To her surprise, Jonathan stepped close and leaned down so that his mouth settled beside her ear. He held his arms behind his back as if to ensure he did not incite the enchantment.

"I mean this in more ways than one, Ros. It will be my pleasure. And yours as well, if I can help it."

And with that, he left her near breathless in the kitchen. His words echoed in her ear as she absentmindedly returned to her preparations. It would undoubtedly be her worst attempt at pumpkin bread yet.

10

TWENTY-TWO

ROSALIND WOKE UP TO an endless gray morning, the faint chattering of birds drifting into her room on a bed of cool, crisp air. She sat in bed, blankets drawn up to shield her from the cold, her eyes on the sky, and her head in the clouds. Quietly, she recited the proverb.

"A young girl's life

Taken too soon by man's foolish strife.

Wielded in heartbreak,

An enchantment a grieving mother did make.

So to all men, Beware

All around, there is fervid magic in her air.

Kept safe from all of he,

Until two and twenty, a border born shall be."

Such words had held so much power over her; as of today, they would be but a memory. Would she ever look back and wonder if any of it had been true in the first place? She threw the blankets over her head at the silly question. Slow down, Rosalind, she thought. She shouldn't be thinking so far ahead when the day hadn't yet begun, not really.

A little at a time, she mused, and then draped the top blanket around her shoulders and slipped out of bed. The thick fabric dragged along the floor as she made her way over to her vanity. Rosalind brushed absentmindedly at her hair while she considered her reflection. She didn't appear or feel any different, and yet there was no denying that something had changed. For the past month, the enchantment had slowly been relinquishing the rights to her body, a fact that only she and Jonathan were privy to.

She smiled to herself. Then, she recalled her last encounter with him just days before. A rush of heat flooded her face and ignited a trail of gooseflesh that prickled down the length of her back. She had asked him for a favor. But not just any favor; one that surpassed the boundaries of platonic friendship. How she had arrived at such a ridiculous idea and then proceeded to have the gall to voice it was incomprehensible.

It was likely for the best that Rosalind hadn't seen much of him since. He continued spending most days elsewhere, in the town or a nearby village, conversing with local farmers and tradespeople. Perhaps he was so preoccupied with his duties as Chancellor that he had forgotten the entire conversation.

She groaned and covered her face in her hands. It was foolish enough to keep the truth about the enchantment a secret. Even more foolish to have kissed. To ask this of him was beyond foolish; it was idiotic. The worst part was that she knew all of this to be true, but had no intention of denying herself if tonight went as planned. She would be selfish and deal with the repercussions as they came.

Deciding she was not quite ready to start the day, Rosalind hopped back into bed and curled up under the warm embrace of her sheets with no one, not even her own reflection, to level a critical eye in her direction. It was another hour before she made her way down the stairs.

Rosalind had asked that her birthday be a simple affair so there were no concrete plans until dinner that evening. She had until then to acquaint herself with her newfound freedom without everyone's gazes fixed upon her. The thought made her stomach lurch a little. Who better to begin with than the one person who always put her at ease?

The steward was in the common room that lay beyond the kitchen. It was where he and Maria, along with the rest of the household staff, would often dine and decompress once the estate had wound down for the evening. He wore glasses and looked to be scribbling arithmetic on a loose sheet of paper before jotting down numbers in a small black notebook. Sensing her presence, he looked up and beamed.

"Well, aren't you a sight for sore eyes," Louis said as he took off his glasses and stood. "To what do I owe the pleasure? Should you not be enjoying a lazy morning with a fresh pot of tea and a tray full of sweets as one is expected to do on their birthday?"

Rosalind huffed a small laugh. "I do intend to indulge, but first I..." She hesitated, rubbing a hand on the back of her neck. "I was wondering if perhaps you would try something with me?"

Seemingly understanding her intent, his expression softened even further as he replied. "Of course, my dear. What do you have in mind?" He brought his hands behind his back and straightened, waiting for her instructions.

Tentatively, Rosalind held out her hand. Even though she knew it would be alright, she couldn't quell the quick patter of her heart as she waited for him to respond. If Louis had any reservations, he didn't make them known. He simply clasped her hand in his and shook it.

A grin spread across Rosalind's face. With more than a little enthusiasm, she shook his hand in return, which prompted Louis to clear his throat.

"That's quite a grip you've got there. Might I suggest a lighter touch lest you wish to rid me of all feeling in my fingers, dear."

She drew her hand away and offered him a rueful smile. Louis chuckled.

"Fear not, these hands have weathered far worse in the last sixty-some years. Broken multiple fingers, I have. That's why this one never stands quite straight," he said, wriggling his pinky. "Now, how about we set you up real nice in the conservatory? If we're lucky, the clouds will clear in the next couple of hours." He crooked an elbow out toward her.

Rosalind nodded and bit back a smile before gingerly slipping her arm into his. It was such a simple act, linking arms and walking alongside one another. She had seen countless men and women do so as they approached the dancefloor or perused shops along bustling streets. She had done so herself with Valentina many a time, often leaning in to hear her friend whisper something conspiratorially.

"Alright, you settle here, and I'll see what the missus has cooked up for you this morning," Louis said when they arrived in the room that gave Brighthall Manor its name. He smiled softly at her. "Happy birthday, my love."

My love. A sudden wistfulness washed over her and settled heavily in her heart. Many years had passed, and still, she could envision the deep pools of adoration in her father's eyes when he called her such. A similar look now swam in Louis's eyes. Right as he was about to turn and leave, Rosalind threw her arms around him. Without hesitation, he wrapped her in a warm embrace. She held on to him as she imagined she would her father, and though no words were spoken, she hoped he felt her love and her appreciation. He'd cared for her as if she were his own and she would be forever grateful.

Rosalind lounged on the cushioned seat of the conservatory's bay window. Beyond her sat a tray of half-eaten pastries and a pot of tepid rose tea. Around her, sheer blue curtains, which ran the length of the glass walls, were drawn open, welcoming in the cool, gray light from a partly cloudy sky. She was thumbing through pages of her book when movement in the doorway caught her attention.

"Chapter nineteen."

"What?"

"The chapter you're looking for," Valentina explained as she waltzed into the room, nibbling on a piece of leftover scone. "The scene I mentioned where he takes care of her; it's in chapter nineteen."

Rosalind wrinkled her nose. "That's not what I..." she began to protest but the words died on her tongue when she met Valentina's arched brow. "Fine." She snapped the book shut.

Valentina smirked. "Doing a bit of research are you? Have someone in mind?"

Rosalind's eyes widened. "No," she said a little too emphatically.

Valentina laughed. "I promised myself I wouldn't tease you today, so I suppose I'll let that one slide. Now, have you tested out your enchantment? Is it truly done with?"

A pang of guilt niggled at Rosalind's conscience. "Oh, yes. I, ah, sought Louis out earlier this morning. Shook his hand and then surprised the both of us by embracing him. No sparks, no shocks. It appears the proverb holds true," she said with a strained smile.

"Oh, splendid! Though I must admit, I'm curious to see it myself." Valentina tapped a finger on her chin as she considered aloud. "I believe Jonathan has buggered off to town already so who else can we bother?"

Her face lit up, but before Rosalind could ask, Valentina grabbed her by the hand and dragged her out of the room. They ventured to the stables and found Colby. With Franklin's approval, the young footman accompanied them in their search for Charlene and Sylvia. After a bit of badgering, Maria agreed to let the housemaids take an extended break. The five of them then returned to the conservatory and settled onto cushions on the floor like children. For the next hour, shouts and laughter emanated from the room as they played round after round of Slaps.

Admittedly, it had taken a bit of convincing to get Colby to participate. Somewhat recently, Rosalind had bumped into him as she turned a blind corner. The shock from her enchantment made him drop a tray of tea and biscuits intended for Jonathan. Since then, the footman had gone out of his way to avoid her. The possibility of their hands frantically meeting atop a pile of cards didn't seem particularly enticing to him. But as usual, Valentina's persuasion proved too powerful, and she soon coaxed him into playing.

It was past midday when Colby, Charlene, and Sylvia were called back to work. After grazing on a light lunch, Rosalind and Valentina made their way upstairs to bathe. The sweet scent of violet filled the air as Rosalind took her time to scrub each and every inch of her body. Her face, already red from the heat of the water, flushed a deeper crimson when her thoughts drifted to why she cared to wash herself so thoroughly.

Rosalind was deliberating over the contents of her wardrobe when Valentina entered the room.

"I have a gift for you," she said giddily, setting a large, ribboned box atop Rosalind's bed.

"Val," she drawled, eyeing the present. "You needn't have gotten me anything so... massive."

"Oh, hush now. I can get you whatever I please. Now, go on and open it."

Rosalind approached the box and pulled apart the purple silk ribbon wrapped around it. She lifted the lid off, revealing a sage-colored dress folded neatly inside. "Oh my," she breathed.

"I had the modiste make it according to your measurements, though it's been more than a year since you last visited her. To be safe, I requested that she fashion it to be somewhat adjustable. We landed on this little number, which you can tighten by taking the strands at your waist and tying them behind your back."

Rosalind freed the dress from the box and held it out in front of her. Delicate floral eyelet details adorned the cotton fabric. It had what appeared to be a generous square neckline, slightly puffed half sleeves, and shimmering shell buttons that trailed down the length of her dress.

"It's beautiful," she murmured in awe.

"I thought it perfect for tonight. And that's not all," Valentina added with a playful grin.

Reluctantly, Rosalind set down the dress and peered into the box again. Something the color of pale pink peonies caught her eye. She reached in and held up what looked to be a half stay made of silk jacquard. Small, gold clasps trailed down the front, while strands of silk crossed over one another at the back.

"Isn't it pretty?" Valentina asked. "And functional, which I know you'll appreciate. The clasps allow you to take it on and off without having to do up the laces every time." She clapped her hands. "Now, let's look at the undergarments that go with it. They're the most interesting part, I think."

Again, Rosalind reached into the box and pulled out a silk chemise. The fabric was a similar color to the stay, but it lacked the jacquard print and was so thin it was nearly sheer. Delicate Leavers lace adorned the top and bottom hems.

She eyed it skeptically. "It looks a little on the short side..."

"It's meant to be." Valentina pointed at the box. "There are matching drawers to go with it."

Rosalind picked up said drawers, though that didn't seem like quite the right word for them. They were incredibly short, shorter than any drawers she'd ever seen. She couldn't help but question whether they'd be large enough to cover her backside.

"The entire set was modeled after a design I saw in an Erdesian fashion magazine. They're so much more innovative over there.

"I had a set made for myself as well," Valentina admitted. "And I must say, it feels absolutely lovely against the skin. No rough fabric or stiff boning; the structure is held in place with cording instead. Much less cumbersome than what we typically wear. Give it a go, will you? I think it'll fit nicely under your new dress."

Rosalind swallowed. "Y-you mean for me to wear it tonight?"

"I don't see why not."

Heat crept up the back of Rosalind's neck. What if it didn't fit right? What if he didn't like it?

"Here," Valentina said as she swiped the garments from Rosalind's hand. "I'll help you. We might as well start getting ready."

Rosalind considered herself in the mirror. Valentina had spared no effort in beautifying her this evening. And she truly did feel beautiful. Her thick, brown locks cascaded over her shoulders in luscious curls. It had been a painstaking process, taking nearly two hours to perfect, using hot tongs, paper, and a keen sense of smell so as to prevent scorching. Magenta stained her lips and cheeks, which Valentina made by blending a particular ratio of crushed blueberries, raspberries, and grapes. The reddish-purple color superbly complemented the sage green of her dress.

As suspected, the décolletage left little to the imagination, aided in part by the silk stay she wore underneath. When Rosalind first slipped on the undergarments, she was scandalized; the pieces barely covered her bits. However, she couldn't deny how luxurious the material felt. What's more, she had to admit she looked rather good and felt good too. So, she didn't protest; instead, she left her room with a smile.

The pair made their way downstairs for dinner and settled into their seats at the formal dining table. The men of the house soon joined them, all dressed in their finest raiments. Louis wore a black suit and a white bow tie, while Franklin and Kemba donned brown and plaid morning coats, respectively. Rosalind was surprised to see Colby in a paisley waistcoat and figured he likely borrowed it from Louis. But the empty seat at the head of the table drew her eyes immediately.

Maria swept into the room with wine bottles in hand, and Charlene and Sylvia followed close behind, carting an assortment of lavish dishes. "Jonathan sent word that he will miss dinner. But he promised he would return as soon as he is able. I'm sorry, my dear."

Rosalind tried not to let her dismay show. She knew his duties came first and he wouldn't neglect them to attend her birthday dinner. She hadn't expected him to, wouldn't dream of it. But that knowledge didn't assuage the pang of disappointment in her chest. Perhaps he wouldn't be able to attend any of tonight's festivities. Perhaps he had changed his mind, and this was his way of letting her down gently. It was better than him saying it to her face, she supposed. Just the thought of such a mortifying conversation made her shiver.

"He'll show," Valentina whispered, leaning toward her. "If he doesn't, he'd better sleep with one eye open lest he wishes to relive his worst nightmare."

Rosalind cocked her head in silent question.

"Do you remember when I brought that garden snake into the conservatory during one of our lessons? I have yet to see Jonathan move as fast as he did when he bolted out of that room."

Rosalind smiled at the memory and her shoulders relaxed a little. Valentina always knew how to pull her from her spiraling thoughts. Intent on setting her worries aside, she turned her attention to the rest of the table. Her one request for the evening had been for the entire household to join in on the festivities.

Once all the food had been brought out, Maria removed her apron and settled into the seat beside Louis. Charlene and Sylvia quickly followed suit with giddy expressions on their faces. It wasn't often Rosalind saw them out of their liveries, and it was apparent the women had jumped at the chance to dress up. Charlene's hair was fashioned into an intricate updo and adorned with a large, handwoven flower piece. Sylvia, on the other hand, wore her hair in a simple chignon. It was her lace-frilled sleeves that caught one's eye.

Valentina lifted her glass and offered a small toast that had the whole table laughing by the end. Glasses clinked, and dinner began. For the next hour, everyone enjoyed their fill of some of Rosalind's favorite dishes: red wine braised duck, steamed fish with ginger, sweet bread, apple dumplings, pickled artichokes, and fried oysters.

An ease fell over the table, and conversation flowed as plentiful as the wine. It didn't take much for Charlene to divulge the latest gossip she had heard from housemaids at other estates. Word was that Emilia Grant had broken her engagement to Lord DuPont's nephew, Marcus Trainor, due to an indiscretion on his part. The news wasn't surprising given his proclivity for indulgence likely spurred by his over-inflated ego. A family trait, Rosalind mused.

After dinner, Maria herded everyone into the drawing room. Moments later, she wheeled in a cart topped with a chestnut tea cake, strawberries and cream, and champagne on ice. Maria lit candles on the cake and ushered Rosalind over.

"Make a wish, love."

Rosalind shut her eyes, wished, and blew out the candles. When she opened them again, her heart skipped a beat at the sight of Jonathan in the doorway.

"You're late."

Rosalind peered over her shoulder to where Valentina stood with a hand on her hip, her narrowed eyes fixed on her brother.

He sighed and ran a hand through his hair. "I know." Catching Rosalind's eyes, he added, "I'm sorry."

She opened her mouth to reply, but Valentina beat her to it.

"I do hope you have more to offer than a trite apology. A gift, perhaps?" She raised her brows expectantly. "And it'd better be a good one."

A sly smile tugged at the corner of Jonathan's lips. "Rest assured, dear sister. I aim to please."

The strangled noise that escaped Rosalind drew the attention of both Rashfords. Valentina eyed her with a puzzled expression while Jonathan had the audacity to look amused.

"Frog in my throat," she said with a shaky laugh.

Valentina considered her for a moment more, then held out her flute of champagne. "Here."

"Thanks," Rosalind murmured and took a generous sip before handing it back. Out of the corner of her eye, she saw Jonathan reach into his breast pocket and pull out a small box wrapped in brown paper. He extended it toward her.

"No ribbon, I'm afraid."

"Oh, th-thank you," she stammered as she took the gift from him. Rosalind hadn't expected him to get her anything, not when she had already asked so much of him.

She removed the paper and lifted the lid, revealing a pair of the most exquisite earrings she'd ever seen. Luminous pearls appeared as drops of moonlight suspended from delicate gold filigree.

"They're beautiful," she whispered.

"Well done, brother," Valentina exclaimed as she peered over Rosalind's shoulder. "You should put them on."

"Oh, I don't know," Rosalind started, her cheeks growing warm. "They seem fit for more formal occasions."

Valentina held out her hand. "Nonsense. Give me the ones you're wearing."

Rosalind acquiesced, removing the small silver earrings she wore and replacing them with the ones Jonathan had gifted her. Though she could feel him watching her, timidity gripped her, and she didn't dare meet his eye.

"Doesn't she look lovely?" Valentina cooed.

"Indeed she does."

Something about the softness in his voice made it impossible for her to look away any longer. Try as she might, she couldn't ignore the flutter of her heart when their gazes met.

"Now, who's up for some country dancing?"

Valentina's boisterous query and the subsequent round of cheers broke through the haze that surrounded Rosalind. She looked back to see Valentina chatting animatedly with Kemba and Charlene, likely to coordinate the dances. That left her alone with Jonathan.

"You didn't have to get me anything," she said quietly.

"I couldn't very well show up empty-handed. Val would've had my head if I had." Lowering his voice, he added, "Besides, I picked those out before you propositioned me."

Rosalind's eyes widened and she peered hastily around the room to assure herself no one had overheard him. To her relief, everyone seemed preoccupied with moving furniture to make space for the dancing.

"Jonathan, make yourself useful and give us a hand here, will you?" Valentina called out.

Minutes later, a lively melody filled the air. In the corner of the room sat Kemba, his fingers merrily traversing the keys of the pianoforte. On special occasions such as this, the seasoned groundskeeper would assume the role of maestro and bless the halls of the manor with joyful music. Once, Rosalind asked him how he had learned to play so well; he told her his grandmother had been an accomplished pianist and passed her love of music on to him.

A myriad of country dances and several bottles of champagne later, the evening drew to a close. Maria and Louis were the first to bid farewell, followed shortly by Franklin and Kemba. With half-lidded eyes and tiddly smiles, Charlene, Sylvia, and Colby said their goodbyes and meandered out of the room. Soon only Rosalind, Valentina, and Jonathan remained.

"I do believe I am"—Valentina hiccuped—"pleasantly sozzled." She hiccuped again.

Rosalind let out an amused hmm. "I'm inclined to agree."

"How is it *I* have had more to drink on *your* birthday?"

"Is it not tradition at this point?"

They glanced at one another and burst into a fit of giggles. After their laughs subsided, Valentina let out a long sigh.

"I think I'll call it a night." She rose unsteadily to her feet and asked, "How about you two?"

The question brought about a familiar flutter in Rosalind's chest, which had plagued her on and off throughout the evening. "Oh, yes, I-I suppose we should as well. The royal 'we,' I mean," she quickly clarified. "Really, I was referring to myself. I wouldn't presume to know what Jonathan wishes to—"

"Lead the way, Val," Jonathan said calmly as he motioned toward the staircase. Rosalind was relieved by his gentle interjection. In truth, she had started rambling, and she didn't know what might come out next.

Moments later, she followed Valentina out of the drawing room and up the stairs, with Jonathan trailing wordlessly behind. When they arrived outside her door, Valentina planted a kiss on Rosalind's cheek.

"Happy birthday," she murmured with a soft smile.

She turned to face Jonathan and patted his cheek with more gusto than perhaps was necessary. Then she wished them goodnight and slipped into her room.

The pair were left standing opposite one another, cast in near darkness. It was some time after midnight, and the lamps that lined the hallway offered only whispers of light. Against the quiet of the night, Rosalind could hear her heart beating louder and louder with each breath.

She was met with the enticing scent of amber and orange when Jonathan leaned forward, and she closed her eyes in eager anticipation. But to her surprise, he did not meet her lips. Instead, he leaned past her and turned the knob of her bedroom door. He pushed it open a few inches but made no move to enter. He pulled the door closed again and reached for her hand. With careful, quiet steps, he led her down the hallway to his bedroom.

She had entered the room on multiple occasions over the years, mainly at Maria's request, but she hadn't remembered it quite like this. In the light of day, it felt rather cold and uninviting. A heavy stillness filled the air. The imposing room had been without an occupant for nearly a decade. It was apparent Jonathan's return had breathed new life into it.

Golden flames flickered in the hearth at the far corner, draping the room in warmth and light. The soft glow illuminated the rich colors of the room she had never noticed before—the cherry tones of the towering mahogany posts that marked the edges of the bed; the intricate red-and-yellow patterns of the rug beneath it. And there were the traces of Jonathan, which could be seen throughout. Books lay strewn atop a desk. A decanter of brown liquor sat on the hand-carved wood mantel above the hearth. His glasses sat on a small table beside his bed.

"I figured my room was the wiser of our two options," Jonathan explained.

"Yes, I quite agree." Rosalind was acutely aware of how thin the wall she shared with Valentina was.

"It isn't too late, you know. Never is. If you've changed your mind," he continued slowly, "that is perfectly—"

"I haven't," she exclaimed. "Changed my mind, that is."

A small smile flitted across his face. "In any case," he said as he worked to unclasp the silver chain at his collar, "should you change your mind at any point, you need only say the word and we'll stop. Is that understood?"

The question, somehow tender and assertive at the same time, sent a shiver down Rosalind's spine. "Yes," she breathed.

She watched in quiet reverence as Jonathan continued to shed himself of his fineries. He relieved his wrists of their cufflinks and shrugged off his brown tweed jacket. He set them down on a nearby table before bringing his hands up to undo the top few buttons of his shirt, seemingly relishing the newfound freedom afforded to his neck. Then he made his way toward her.

He rested a finger under her chin and lifted it gently; he lowered his face until his lips were but a hair's breadth from hers. The eager anticipation she had felt outside her room coursed through her once again and propelled her forward onto her toes, closing the distance between them. She felt his lips curve into a smile as he returned her kiss with equal fervor.

Jonathan's hand dropped from her chin to skim lightly over her chest and down her stomach before coming to rest in the crook of her waist. He brought his other hand to her hip and, without breaking the kiss, guided her toward the bed. Moments later, Rosalind felt him pull away from the kiss, and when she opened her eyes, she found him seated on the edge of the mattress. With his hands at either side of her waist, Jonathan pulled her in between his legs.

At this angle, her eyes lowered to meet his, and what a sight he was to behold. His hair was free of its rigid coiffure and sat tousled atop his head. His lips looked exceptionally soft against the sharp, shadowed features of his face. And his gaze held what looked like ardor and admiration and yearning. Perhaps she was projecting her own feelings, but she hoped not.

Jonathan lowered his eyes to track the movement of his thumb, which trailed across her jaw and down her neck. Gooseflesh prickled her skin as he lightly skimmed the length of her collarbone. His thumb met her neckline and traced along the hem until it met the first in a line of buttons that cascaded down the center of her dress.

Rosalind couldn't tame her chest's quick rise and fall as she watched him unclasp the top button. With deft fingers, he undid the second and then the third. His hands stilled when he was halfway down the dress, and his gaze drew up to meet hers. He was, she realized, giving her the opportunity to change her mind. In answer, she lifted a hand to the top of her sleeve and pushed it off her shoulder. She did the same to the other side and the dress pooled at her feet.

It felt as if his gaze left a trail of burning embers as it roamed across her body. He leaned his head to one side and eyed her curiously, a playful smile on his lips.

Rosalind bit her lip. Damned undergarments. Initially, she had worried about what he'd think of them, but they were so comfortable she'd forgotten she was wearing them—until now. "They're... modern?"

"Indeed," he murmured as his fingers toyed with the silky fabric at her hip. "Never seen anything like them."

Nervously, she tucked a lock of hair behind her ear. "A bit much, aren't they?"

"No," he said softly. "No, I like them very much—so much that I'm almost sad to discard them. Almost."

His hands hovered over the gold clasps of the stay. "May I?"

Rosalind nodded.

With little effort, he flicked open the first clasp. And then the next, and the next after that. Once all the clasps were undone, the stay gave way to reveal the thin pale pink chemise underneath.

Jonathan's fingers danced along the delicate edge of the lace trim before trailing downward to caress the silk fabric. She sucked in a breath when the tips of his fingers grazed her nipple. He then hooked a finger under each of the delicate straps of the chemise and slowly drew them off her shoulders.

Rosalind stood before him, exposed from the waist up. She could feel his eyes on her and fought back every instinct to shy away and wrap her arms around herself. But whatever courage held her in place was not enough to brave a look at him.

Jonathan didn't let her stay that way for long. He brought a hand to her chin and gently guided her gaze down to meet his. Her breath caught in her throat at the way he looked at her. Like he wanted her. *Needed* her. She felt his hand settle behind her neck. And then he leaned forward and captured her lips.

His tongue delved into her mouth, and he kissed her like he were the desert and she was his oasis. He propelled himself off the bed causing her to stumble back a few steps, though the kiss did not break. Then he brought his free hand to rest at the small of her back and drew her closer. Something like a whimper escaped Rosalind as the bunching of his shirt brushed against her breasts.

"Bed," he murmured against her lips in a tone that toed the line between question and command.

Jonathan helped her onto the bed. Rosalind couldn't help but stare as he began to work the buttons of his shirt, revealing a long, lean torso. The mattress dipped as he climbed onto it and brought his lips to hers. He carefully lowered her onto her back and positioned himself over her. Their lips parted as he pulled back to look at her.

"Is this alright?" he asked as he shifted his weight onto one elbow, freeing one hand to brush a strand of hair from her face.

"Yes," she whispered. Even as her heart raced and adrenaline coursed through her, she felt a sort of serenity underneath him. She felt utterly surrounded by him, her senses attuned to him and only him.

Jonathan lowered his mouth to hers. Then he dipped his head to kiss the soft skin of her neck. She felt his fingertips skim up her arm leaving gooseflesh in their wake before embarking on an agonizingly slow descent. He swept the swell of her breast eliciting a small whimper from her before venturing further south, trailing lightly across her belly. His fingers stilled when he reached the waistband of her pale pink drawers.

He drew back to meet her half-lidded gaze. He didn't have to say a word for her to know what he wanted from her; she could read the question in his eyes. Rosalind lifted her head and answered him with a kiss.

Jonathan tugged at the drawstring of her drawers, loosening their hold around her. Rosalind gasped against his mouth as his hand disappeared under the silk fabric and slipped between her thighs.

His fingers moved in languid circles, sending pleasure skittering up her spine. Her back arched in response and Jonathan let out a low groan as her chest brushed against his. Moments later, Rosalind was met with another wave of pleasure as he gently pressed one finger into her.

He nipped at her lower lip before moving his mouth to her neck again. There he lavished her with delicate, little kisses, all the while his crooked finger beckoning her ecstasy closer. Having sought out the spot that drew soft moans from her, he now worked her with steady, deliberate movements. Rosalind's hips rocked in time with the rhythm he set as she chased her climax.

"Jonathan," she breathed. It was all she could manage as a crescendo of pleasure and a wave of euphoria crashed over her. When she regained her senses, she opened her eyes and met Jonathan's dark, heady stare. She let out a shaky laugh and offered a murmur of appreciation between breaths.

And though her immediate desire was satiated, a yearning still lingered. She wanted more. She wanted to feel the weight of him, wanted to see all of him. Still reveling in the afterglow of her climax, her typical reticence hadn't yet set in and so she wrapped her legs around him and pressed his hips to hers. In answer, Jonathan ground his hardness against her.

Rosalind's eyes trailed down to where their hips met, her hand following in its wake. Tentatively, she traced the band of his trousers.

"Are you certain?" Jonathan asked, his voice ragged.

"I am," she answered softly.

Jonathan nodded. "Let me grab something," he said, pushing himself off the bed. Reaching into his side table drawer, he pulled out a thin bronze ring and slid it onto his little finger.

Though Rosalind had never seen one in person before, she knew what it was. Valentina had informed her, as had several of the more explicit novels she had borrowed from said friend. It was known colloquially as a sheath ring. While the act of wielding magic was illegal in Sauvign, magic itself was not, and the laws regarding the use of magically imbued artifacts were vague.

In essence, a sheath ring acted as a condom might, but with two rather convenient upsides, three if you counted the trouble of acquiring condoms. For one, the owner of such a ring did not encounter any issues with fit, nor did they suffer any perceived loss of sensation since they needn't wear anything below. And two, magic made things less messy. It absorbed what would typically result from a satisfactory outcome.

After placing the ring on his fifth finger, Jonathan went about removing his trousers and remaining underthings. Rosalind found she was unable to tear her eyes away from his naked body.

"Your turn."

Rosalind flushed when she glanced up at him and saw the smirk on his face. Rather timidly, she shimmied out of her drawers and tossed them to the floor with the rest of her clothes. Her pulse thrummed as she felt his gaze rake across her.

"Now then, where were we," Jonathan murmured as he lowered himself over her once again. Eyeing her lips, he bent down to close the distance between them.

Settling between her legs, Jonathan rocked against her and the friction was like kindling to a flame; it set alight flames of pleasure in her lower belly.

He broke the kiss and met her gaze. "I'll be gentle."

The sincerity in his voice brought a soft smile to Rosalind's lips. "I know."

They held one another's gaze as he pushed into her slowly, carefully. Her grip tightened on his shoulder and back as she braced against the unfamiliar pressure between her legs. It wasn't painful per se, but it was uncomfortable and her body tensed, unsure of how else to react.

A low, stifled sound escaped Jonathan when his hips came flush with hers. He held himself still for a moment as if to recoup his composure before slowly drawing his hips back. "Breathe, Ros," he said in an unsteady voice.

She did as she was told and let out a long, shaky breath. With each measured breath that followed, her body began to relax a little more.

As promised, he was gentle with her. His pace was measured and attentive, and the tension in her body eased as she grew accustomed to the feel of him. When the pressure subsided and pleasure whirred within her once again, Rosalind's focus drifted to where their bodies met.

The soft gasp that slipped from her lips prompted Jonathan's restraint to falter. She felt it in the way he moved, how his pace quickened, and his rhythm became less refined. Still, he was careful never to overwhelm her.

He buried his face in the crook of her neck and lavished her with kisses, which grew fewer and farther between as his breath quickened. As his climax drew nearer, he slipped a hand under her back and pressed her closer to him. She responded in kind, her hands gripping his back, which was slick with sweat. Moments later, he shuddered, and Rosalind felt him pulse within her.

When his body slackened, she was met with the rapid rise and fall of his chest against her own. Rosalind shut her eyes and let herself commit to memory the weight of him and the sound of his ragged breath at her ear. How was it that, of everything she'd experienced tonight, it was this very moment that felt the most intimate?

Her eyes shot open and her breath hitched as Jonathan whispered in her ear. "Happy birthday."

11

CAPITAL ACQUAINTANCES

ROSALIND FANNED HERSELF WITH a hat as Valentina regaled her with a colorful account of an embarrassing incident at a garden party a few years back. They were returning from a walk around a small pond at the far end of the estate grounds. It was a beautiful day—the sun was bright, and a crisp, cool breeze danced along bare skin like a soft caress.

"And then he split his trousers—I swear it!"

Rosalind let out an incredulous gasp. "No!"

"Yes!" Valentina replied, matching Rosalind's tone.

Both broke into shrieks of laughter as they slipped through the rear entrance of the manor and headed through to the foyer. Rosalind had to wipe away the tears that pricked at the corner of her eyes.

"I thought I heard you two," came a familiar voice. "I daresay all of Proper might have."

Rosalind glanced up to see Jonathan eyeing them, arms crossed and the hint of a smirk on his lips.

"Oh, hush yourself," Valentina said with a dismissive wave in his direction. "It's called having a bit of fun. Ever heard of it?"

"Funny you should ask. I was just sharing laughs with a couple of friends visiting on their way back from the capital. Why don't you come and join us in the conservatory? They'd very much like to meet you both."

"What, now? You can't be serious."

"Why not?"

"Because," Valentina drawled, "look at us! We've just returned from the pond and doubtless reek of sweat. Not to mention the state of our attire." She pointed to the muddy hemline of her dress.

Jonathan's gaze flicked from Valentina to Rosalind. "I think you look quite well."

A light blush dusted Rosalind's cheeks. That is until she lifted a hand to her windswept hair and was met with tangled locks. She peered down at her slacks and spied flecks of mud at her ankles. There was little chance she looked as well as he made it seem.

"Who are they? These guests of yours." Valentina eyed her brother skeptically.

"Padraic and Ilora Mason. I met them in my first year and now count them amongst my closest friends."

"Mason," Valentina repeated thoughtfully. "As in..."

"The Chancellor of Meridian? Yes, he's their father."

Valentina nodded as if she were considering something. "Alright, I'll meet them."

Rosalind half expected her to elaborate, but she offered nothing more. Instead, she felt both Rashfords turn their attention to her.

"M-me as well?"

"He did say they'd like to meet the *both* of us."

"Ah, yes, well." Rosalind hesitated, absentmindedly touching her hair. "I suppose I should then."

She glanced over at Jonathan and offered him a small, somewhat reluctant smile. He flashed her a smile in return, making her heart skip a beat.

It had been four days since her birthday, and during that time, they had crossed each other's paths only twice, both instances brief and in the presence of others. Each time he was cordial and showed no hint of wariness or unease around her. In fact, he showed no signs of being affected at all. And while that was what she had asked for—that they would remain as they were before—Rosalind couldn't help but feel a pang of something that closely resembled disappointment.

What's more, she found herself unable to respond in kind. She fidgeted and fumbled her words more so than usual. He certainly noticed, and if she wasn't more careful, others might as well.

"But before we do," Valentina insisted, "we absolutely must change out of these clothes."

"Do know they don't have all day," he said dryly.

"Yes, yes. We'll be right down," she promised as she clasped Rosalind's hand and dragged her up the stairs.

A good deal longer than promised, Rosalind and Valentina descended the stairs. Both had changed into blue dresses, but unlike Rosalind, who threw on the first one she saw—a simple cotton frock—Valentina dressed to impress with an elegant brocade number, the color of sapphire. She had drawn up her hair into a loose chignon held in place by a gold hairpin. Rosalind was left to her own devices and, not capable of much else, wove her hair into twin plaits.

Valentina sashayed into the conservatory without bothering to wait for a lull in conversation. Rosalind slipped in silently after her. The pair were greeted with an arched brow from Jonathan and two sets of striking hazel eyes.

"About time," Jonathan muttered.

"Time is a construct, dear brother," Valentina said with a shrug.

"Hear, hear," cheered the sharp-dressed man to Jonathan's right, which prompted unimpressed glances from both Jonathan and the woman beside him.

"This, as you may have guessed, is my *delightful* sister, Lady Valentina Rashford. And accompanying her is our longtime friend, Miss Rosalind Carver."

"How do you do," Valentina responded with a tilt of her head.

Rosalind followed suit, lowering into a bow more pronounced than Valentina's. She was aware their guests were members of high society, which meant she was the only one in the room without a title.

"And these here are my dear friends, Lord Padraic Mason and his lovely sister, Lady Ilora Mason."

"Oh how dreadfully formal, Jonathan. Please, call me Padraic."

"Ilora," said his sister, offering Rosalind and Valentina a small smile.

"Padraic," Valentina began, "I take it you were in the law program with my brother?"

Padraic nodded. "You'd be right."

"You know," she went on, "he was rather insufferable during our shared lessons when we were younger. Knew all the answers, asked too many questions, and studied for far longer than was necessary—a real bootlicker. Ros can attest to it. Grandmum adored him for it, of course. Tell me, is he as insufferable as he was back then?"

Padraic chuckled. "Oh, undoubtedly, though I must admit it was to my great benefit. I wouldn't have passed my classes if he hadn't insisted I accompany him to the library. *On a weekend*. And him helping me with my dissertations on more than one occasion..."

"Let's not forget all the notes he let you borrow time and time again," Ilora added.

"Yes, alright," Padraic muttered with a roll of his eyes. "For those reasons, I can't tease him on such matters in good conscience. Now, if we were to speak of instances not pertaining to studies..." He trailed off and let a mischievous grin imply the rest.

Valentina's eyes lit up. "Do tell," she said excitedly as she approached the empty seat beside Padraic. The two began chatting animatedly with one another, luring Jonathan in on the conversation in a futile attempt to defend himself.

Left to fend for herself, Rosalind considered what reason she might give to excuse herself from the room.

"You're welcome to sit here."

She glanced up to find Ilora gesturing toward a nearby chair. With a murmur of appreciation, Rosalind sat down. Inclined to say something, she asked, "And how did you come to know Jonathan? Did you also attend university in the capital?"

"No, I attended university in our home region of Meridian as per my father's wishes, but I often traveled to the capital to visit Padraic. I met Jonathan on my second visit. He joined Padraic and I at a tavern late one evening." She peered over at Jonathan with a fond smile.

"I still remember, he'd spent the day cooped up in the Records Hall poring over international trade regulations, and he tried asking my brother a question or two. Our family is in trade, you see," she explained. "But Padraic doesn't much care about such matters. Lucky for Jonathan, though, I do have a bit of a penchant for legislation so I offered what insight I could, and the rest was history."

"What are you on about over there?" Head tilted, Jonathan looked from Ilora to Rosalind and back.

"Don't you fret. Unlike Padraic, I'm not keen to divulge your humiliations for fear you may respond in kind. I was simply telling her how we came to know one another."

Rosalind thought she saw his smile falter slightly at Ilora's assurance, but she was soon distracted by the sound of Maria entering with a cart of refreshments.

After freshly brewed tea and biscuits were passed around, the group settled into easy conversation. Valentina and Padraic did most of the talking, though Jonathan and Ilora were quick to jump in here and there. Rosalind laughed and nodded, content with sipping her tea and listening to the lively chatter.

It quickly became apparent how similar the siblings were to one another. For one, the Masons seemed to trade barbs as often as Valentina and Jonathan did. And just like the Rashfords, no genuine malice lay in wait behind their words.

Then there was the way they carried themselves; how all four displayed an abundance of confidence and composure. Jonathan's showed in the way he listened, like he had all the time in the world for each and every person in the room. For Valentina, it was how she spoke, with a fervor that commanded attention. Padraic's hands spoke as loud as his words, so much so that it made him impossible to ignore. And for Ilora, it was the way in which she held herself, calm and collected with her shoulders back and head held high.

But their most notable similarity was also the most discernible. Like Jonathan, Padraic wore an impeccable tailored suit, his even more ornate in texture and adornments. Underneath his midnight tartan jacket lay a white ruffled shirt with a large emerald brooch at his neck. He wore his short brown hair, which shone like bronze in the light, slicked to one side.

Ilora's hair, which held the same metallic glint, was twisted, pinned, and draped into an elaborate chignon. She wore a crimson corseted dress with fitted sleeves and a deep, rounded neckline. A similar shade of rouge tinted her full lips and dusted her defined cheekbones. Valentina would undoubtedly approve of her sophisticated ensemble.

"Rosalind, you must have your share of stories about Jonathan as well. You've called Brighthall your home for some time now, yes?"

She glanced up to see four sets of eyes on her. Focusing her attention on Ilora, who had been the one to speak, she nodded.

"Nearly sixteen years."

An astonished expression swept across Ilora's face. "Safe to say you know each other quite well then."

A strangled laugh bubbled up Rosalind's throat and she purposefully avoided Jonathan's gaze.

"You two must feel like brother and sister at this point," Padraic quipped.

Jonathan sputtered into his tea, prompting everyone to look at him.

"Are you alright?" Ilora asked, resting a hand gently on his arm.

He adjusted his collar and cleared his throat. "Had too much at once is all," he rasped. His eyes caught Rosalind's briefly before he turned to Ilora and offered her a reassuring smile.

"Speaking of," he went on, his voice having returned to normal, "tea's gone cold, hasn't it? Why don't I ask Maria to bring us something a little stronger? Any requests?"

Valentina and Ilora quickly offered suggestions, and Rosalind breathed a sigh of relief. She was glad Jonathan was so easily able to change the subject.

She glanced over at Padraic and was surprised to see he hadn't involved himself in the conversation at hand. Instead, he was studying Jonathan, who seemed none the wiser. Then his gaze flicked to her. A trickle of unease slid down Rosalind's spine as curious eyes surveyed her. Moments later, she watched in quiet horror as a small, almost imperceptible smile tugged at the corner of his lips.

"That's settled then," Rosalind heard Jonathan say. "I will ask Mari—"

"I'll go," Rosalind blurted, jumping to her feet. "You should stay with your guests. Besides, I have a good guess as to where she'll be right now. It's no bother at all."

"If you insist," he said slowly.

"I do," she replied a little too eagerly. Anything to escape Padraic's knowing gaze, she thought as she hurried out of the room.

Rosalind knew she'd spent much too long helping Maria prepare the drink cart, but she needed time to collect herself. She had to go back in there and act as if nothing was the matter because, for all intents and purposes, nothing *was* the matter. Whatever Padraic had concluded was merely conjecture, and she would make certain not to do anything to encourage it.

Such were her thoughts as she absentmindedly rounded the corner on her way out of the kitchen. She was heading back toward the conservatory when she collided with someone. Quick hands reached out to grasp her shoulders, steadying her.

"I'm so sorry," she said. "I wasn't looking at where I was going..." Her voice trailed off when she locked eyes with Jonathan.

"There you are."

"What are you doing here?" she asked.

"You'd been gone a while so I thought I'd check on things. Everything alright?"

"Oh, yes. I figured I might as well help Maria with—"

"I rather meant about earlier," he clarified. "You seemed more than a little eager to escape."

"Oh, that." She hesitated. "It's nothing. You know me, just a bit nervous around new people."

A part of her wanted to tell him the true reason why, but that would require her to mention the other night, and she didn't think she could manage it without sounding like a bumbling mess.

Based on the look on his face, Jonathan wasn't convinced. "Do you not like them?"

"No! I mean, yes," she said, her eyes wide. "I do like them. They seem very nice. It's just..."

"It's just..." he repeated.

She rubbed at the back of her neck. "Well, it's ridiculous, really, and probably all in my head. I get the feeling that"—she glanced around the corridor and lowered her voice—"he suspects something."

Jonathan inclined his head, bringing his ear closer to her mouth. "Come again?"

"I said I think he suspects something about..." She gestured between them.

"Do you mean Padraic?" He turned his head to meet her gaze, their faces mere inches apart. "What does he suspect?"

Rosalind eyed him incredulously. Had their night together been so trivial that he didn't know what she was referring to? She knew she shouldn't have tried to explain it. She looked away and shook her head. "Never mind."

When she dared a glance back up at him, she found him biting back a smile. A mixture of relief and frustration rushed her. "You *do* know what I was trying to say!"

"I do," he admitted, "but I quite enjoy watching you try to explain it to me. Your nose forms a charming little wrinkle when you're frustrated, did you know that?"

He held her eyes a moment longer then straightened himself. "What makes you think he suspects something about us?"

She shrugged. "I don't know... he just had a look about him." When she said it aloud, it didn't sound all that convincing. Perhaps it was all in her head. She sighed. "Let's just go back, shall we?"

"How about this: I'll keep an eye out," he promised. Then he held a hand out in front of her. "Ladies first."

She didn't miss the light press of his hand against her lower back as she preceded him along the corridor and back into the conservatory.

As soon as they entered the room, Rosalind looked to where Padraic stood, a sly smile playing on his lips.

"Dammit, he knows," Jonathan murmured under his breath.

Before anything could be done about it, Charlene entered the room wheeling a cart of sherry and accouterments, including ice, sugar, blackberries, and orange slices. Jonathan thanked her and set to work on the drinks.

"Let me help you with that," Ilora offered.

"Ilora, I'm perfectly capable of pouring some sugar into sherry."

"Are you now?" she teased as she swiped the bottle of sherry from his hand and moved him aside with a gentle nudge of her shoulder. "Last I recall, you're a bit heavy-handed."

They laughed amongst themselves as they went about preparing cobblers for the room.

"Those two seem comfortable with one another," Rosalind overheard Valentina say to Padraic as they approached.

"Ah, yes, two of a kind, they are," remarked Padraic. "Whenever she'd come to visit me at the capital, I'd lose sight of her only to find her hours later holed up in the corner of some seedy tavern with your brother."

Rosalind's chest tightened at the thought of Jonathan and Ilora nestled at a small table in a crowded, dimly lit room, exchanging quiet words and soft smiles.

"But that was some time ago," he went on as he sidled up next to Rosalind. "They haven't seen much of one another in the past year, what with Jonathan so focused on the chancellorship and all."

"Can't say we've seen all that much of him either," Valentina admitted. "He's been back a little over a month, and I've spent only a handful of days in his company. Probably for the best; I haven't felt the urge to tear his head off in ages."

Padraic chuckled. "Busy man, that one. Though I do hope he has some way of taking his mind off things every once in a while. He deserves a break."

Rosalind could feel his eyes on her and she had to fight the urge to shrink away. Hoping to get him to talk about something else—anything else—she asked, "What about you? Will you be succeeding your father as Chancellor of Meridian?"

"Not if it can be helped," Padraic muttered sardonically.

"You don't want to?"

"Truthfully, no," he replied. "Besides, our family will only retain the chancellorship for another six years. After that, it's for another family to contend with. My bet is on the Fowlers."

As in Denault, the Meridian Chancellorship changed families every seventy-seven years. The Masons were approaching the end of their decades-long tenure. Even so, their family would continue to hold a seat on the regional council.

"I'm of the mind that my father should see it through to the end," he continued. "Unfortunately, he doesn't share my opinion. He's adamant that I succeed him in the role, even if only for a few years. Having held the title will grant me more influence once I am but a humble member of the council, or so he says. As it stands, no one takes me seriously and I'm little more than a disappointment."

"Says who?" Valentina asked, visibly appalled.

"Says my father. Says a few of my old professors. Says that haughty, slippery little council member of yours."

Rosalind grimaced. "Lord DuPont?"

"That'll be the one. Always praising my father and offering his counsel on matters that don't concern him, be it Meridian or the family business. And for whatever reason, my father laps it all up. Jonathan has his work cut out for him where that awful man's concerned."

Padraic leaned in and dropped his voice so only Rosalind and Valentina could hear. "Ilora wouldn't like me saying this, but if Jonathan trusts you both, then I feel I can too. I have no intention of succeeding my father, and if things go according to plan, I won't have to."

Valentina looked about as surprised as Rosalind felt about the insinuation. "You have... a plan?"

"I do." Padraic grinned. "A very simple one I hope comes to fruition sooner than later."

"If you don't assume the council position, then who will?" Rosalind inquired.

"Ilora, ideally. She's much better suited to it than me. If only Father would entertain the idea..." Padraic trailed off, frowning.

"You three look to be conspiring over there. Anything I should be concerned about?" Jonathan's tone was light, but Rosalind didn't miss the slight twitch in his jaw.

He ventured over with a drink in each hand. He offered one to Valentina and the other to Rosalind. Ilora soon joined, sipping on one drink and handing another to Padraic.

"Are you not having one?" Rosalind asked.

"Sherry cobblers are a bit sweet for me," Jonathan said. "Luckily, Louis has set me up real nice in nearly every room." He made his way over to a small table in the corner and picked up a decanter of whiskey.

"So what's this I hear about you visiting the border?"

Jonathan stilled at Padraic's question and looked over to where Ilora stood.

"Sorry, it slipped out," she murmured. "Long carriage ride and all."

Jonathan took a long sip of his whiskey as if preparing for what came next. "It's something that's crossed my mind, yes."

"You? At the border?" Valentina eyed him incredulously. "Whatever for?"

"I think it's time. It's been twenty-five years since a Chancellor last visited."

Valentina scoffed. "Father was the last to visit? Something tells me that didn't go too well."

"Depends on who you ask," Jonathan said into his glass.

"I'll take that as a no then."

He remained silent.

Valentina crossed her arms and asked, "When do you leave?"

"Two weeks from now."

"And who is accompanying you?"

Jonathan didn't answer right away. When he did, Rosalind feared the mounting tension that coiled in the air might snap.

"No one. I'm going alone."

Valentina, still as a statue, eyed Jonathan for a long moment. When she finally moved, it was to bring her glass to her lips. She tipped her head back and didn't let up until it was empty. Setting the glass down on a nearby table, she clasped her hands in front of her and let out a slow breath. Then she smiled.

"Not anymore," she said in a calm, reserved tone. "Because I'm coming with you."

Jonathan huffed a laugh. "No. *No,*" he repeated more vehemently.

Valentina rested her hands on her hips. "Whyever not?"

Jonathan pinched the bridge of his nose. "Because, Val, this isn't some sort of holiday. Not a merry jaunt through the countryside. Odds are it's going to be a rather unpleasant trip, one I wouldn't wish to impose on anybody else. And you needn't concern yourself with my safety if that's what this is about," he went on. "I've been assured safe passage to and from the village. That said, I'm under no illusions about how I'll be received. There will be no welcome party; you know as well as I that father made certain of that. I only hope I can persuade the Keeper to hear me out."

"Hear you out, hmm? So this trip isn't only about showing face," Valentina remarked with one brow raised.

"It is," Jonathan answered before adding, "among other things."

"All the more reason for me to accompany you then. I'm quite adept at winning people over, am I not?" Valentina directed the last few words at Padraic, who offered Jonathan an apologetic smile as he nodded in agreement.

"Also, how do I put this delicately," she considered aloud, resting her chin on steepled fingers. "Are you being deliberately obtuse? Have you forgotten where our sweet Rosalind hails from? If anyone in this room has a remote chance of being welcomed at the border, it'll be Ros."

Rosalind stiffened as she felt three pairs of eyes fix on her. Only Jonathan averted his gaze, eyes trained on the floor at his feet. She knew then the thought had already crossed his mind. So why hadn't he asked her? Though, truthfully, she wasn't sure she would be of any real help. She'd spent most of her life in Denault Proper and still hadn't been accepted by high society. Surely, a place she called home for a mere six years would be even less inviting.

"She has a point."

It was Ilora who had spoken.

"Not about you being obtuse, of course," she continued, "but about leveraging every possible advantage you have at your disposal. Is that not advice you've bestowed upon me before? If Miss Carver here has a connection with the border, you should make use of it. Granted, nothing may come of it, but it won't hurt any. Moreover, knowing you weren't going alone would certainly ease my concerns about the trip. As I mentioned in my last letter, I'd be more than willing to accompany you if my father would allow it."

Rosalind felt her heart sink with the weight of Ilora's words. There was the notion of being reduced to something so impersonal as a *possible advantage at one's disposal*. If Jonathan had considered her company on this trip as she supposed he had, was it with a similar perspective? And then there was the disconcerting thought of Jonathan considering Ilora as his travel companion. Would she be but a possible advantage as well, or something more?

"I appreciate the concern from both of you," Jonathan said, his gaze shifting between Valentina and Ilora. "Ilora, we both know your father would not consent to such travel without protective personnel. And Val"—he let out a long sigh—"will you cease with the interrogation for now if I promise to consider your proposal? This is not me saying yes, mind you, but—"

"Works for me," Valentina interjected with a triumphant grin.

Jonathan drew his gaze to Rosalind. "Try as she might, Val doesn't speak on your behalf. I'll exclude you from any deliberations should you wish it."

"No, it's alright," Rosalind replied. "You may consider me as well if I may be useful." And she meant it. If there was even a remote chance she could be of help, she would. That's what friends were for, right?

"The more the merrier, I say," Padraic exclaimed. "Enzo's never had trouble at the border, but then again—"

"Padraic," Ilora warned quietly.

"Enzo?" Valentina inquired.

"My partner," he disclosed with a bright smile. "They"—Padraic shot Ilora a furtive glance—"grew up near the borderlands so they're more familiar with local customs and what have you. I could ask them for pointers if you'd like."

"Please do," Jonathan replied.

"I'm curious to hear about this Enzo of yours," Valentina said. "What are they like? How did you two meet?"

"They're absolutely lovely," Padraic said with a twinkle in his eye. "Gracious, thoughtful, and wise. They know something about everything and have endless patience, which works out quite well for me. They also have a deliciously dark sense of humor. Sometimes, I'm not altogether confident they don't mean what they say.

"In public and around people they aren't familiar with, they're very reserved," he went on, hardly pausing for breath. "So much so that when I first met them, I thought they didn't like me very much."

"That's because they didn't," Ilora offered. "They thought you talked too much. I daresay they still think that."

"Yes, well"—Padraic waved dismissively—"they're not the only person to feel that way about me at first. What matters is that I won them over in the end with my relentless charm."

"Wore them down is more like it," Jonathan quipped, joining in on Ilora's teasing.

Padraic lifted his chin. "You two are just jealous." Then he turned towards Valentina and Rosalind, adding, "Enzo is very handsome. Everybody thinks so."

"They are," Ilora affirmed.

Jonathan nodded. "Exceedingly so."

And with that, the tension in the room had dissipated, aided in part by a second round of drinks. Following a spirited debate around heavily patterned bowties, Rosalind and Valentina finally excused themselves to freshen up properly. They exchanged farewells with the Masons and made their way out of the room.

"I think I got on quite well with Padraic," Valentina remarked quietly as they ventured up the stairs.

"No, really?" Rosalind flashed her a wry grin.

"And Ilora seems nice enough, pretty and clever. Reminds me a bit of Jonathan, like a fairer-haired version of him with breasts. And less hubris, though that's more indicative of the society we live in than her character, I suspect. She certainly isn't shy about showing my brother affection, is she?"

"Not particularly," Rosalind mumbled, relying on her hushed tone to conceal the irritation in her voice.

"He seems comfortable around her, familiar. But I'm not convinced the feeling is mutual. Perhaps once, but..."

But what, Rosalind yearned to ask when Valentina did not elaborate further, having turned her thoughts inwards.

"You know what Grandmum once told me on her sickbed?"

The question caught Rosalind by surprise, seemingly unrelated to everything that had come before it. She must have given her an odd look because Valentina added, "I'm getting to it."

"She said Rashfords have a long history," she continued, "of marrying for purpose, not love, and that it was on me to change things. *Me*! Mind you, I must have been, what, fifteen when she imparted that lovely nugget of wisdom unto me. I thought, why is she telling me this? I have no intention to marry. Of course, I was careful to keep this bit to myself lest I wished to hasten her journey to the grave... But now, I realize she might have told me not for my sake, but for Jonathan's. She was always thinking about Jonathan," she explained and Rosalind could just make out the almost imperceptible tinge of hurt in her voice, though Valentina didn't linger in the thought for long. "All of this is to say I don't think I've ever seen Jonathan in love. Not yet, at least. Fancy, sure, but love? I should like to think I'll know it when I see it. Call it sisterly intuition," she said with a shrug.

Rosalind offered up an agreeable smile in lieu of words. Her thoughts were too all over the place to arrive at a coherent sentence. Valentina's musings had her contemplating one thing after another.

Had she meant to imply Jonathan did indeed fancy Ilora, but it had not yet manifested into love? And if she recognized when Jonathan showed interest in someone, did that mean she had noticed something between him and Rosalind? Or had he not even fancied her enough for Valentina to notice in the first place? Which scenario was worse, she wasn't sure.

Then, a bittersweet memory surfaced, one that distracted her from the small spiral of anxiety that had begun to whirl within her mind. It was born from Valentina's mention of her grandmother, the late Dowager Rashford, on her sickbed.

12

Eight Years Earlier

Rosalind stood at the rear window of the drawing room, her eyes tracing the outline of clouds that stretched across the seemingly endless blue sky. She turned at the sound of Jonathan's greeting.

"Dr. Ramirez," he said as he shook the hand of the gray-haired, bearded man who had entered the room. "How is she?"

A knot formed between the doctor's brows. "My lord, I'm afraid she isn't faring well."

Rosalind walked over to join the two, as did Valentina, who'd been sitting on the settee near the hearth.

The doctor hesitated. "I'm not sure these young ladies should be privy to what I have to say."

"Just get on with it," Jonathan urged, dismissing his concerns with a wave. "If they don't hear it from you now, they'll simply demand it of me after. Save me the time, will you?"

"If you insist," Dr. Ramirez replied somewhat reluctantly. "Her health continues to decline. There is liquid in her lungs now, which is causing the shortness of breath and fatigue."

"Is there nothing we can offer her to alleviate her troubles?" Jonathan asked. "Another tincture or imbued artifact perhaps? If you have any to recommend—any at all—I shall put in a request with one of our merchants and see if we can have something delivered from Erdesay."

Rosalind repressed a shiver at the mere mention of merchants, knowing he was likely referring to Lord DuPont of the DuPont

Trading Company. Though she hadn't many interactions with the man himself, the same could not be said of his nephew, Marcus. The young man was relentless in his pursuit to curry favor with Jonathan. Their friendship had never quite been the same after his callous treatment of Rosalind a few years back. And while he was all kind words and warm smiles in front of Jonathan, he made certain to disparage her every chance he got, be it a nasty remark as he nudged past her, or with cruel whispers murmured amongst his peers.

Dr. Ramirez shook his head. "I'm sorry, my lord, I don't believe the artifacts would arrive in time. But rest assured, there are two medicines I'll have my assistant deliver tomorrow morning that will make her more comfortable."

A hand took hold of Rosalind's. She looked over at Valentina, who observed the doctor with glassy eyes. Hoping to offer some semblance of solace, Rosalind gently squeezed her friend's hand.

Valentina's voice was barely above a whisper when she spoke. "How long does she have?"

Dr. Ramirez considered for a moment. Tentatively, he said, "I cannot say for certain, my lady. It depends on how well she takes to the medicine. It's crucial we do all we can to reduce the risk of infection and stave off any further complications."

Movement at the corner of her eye drew Rosalind's attention to Jonathan, who was now pacing the room. He had begun university in Denault earlier this year, forgoing an invitation to the prestigious Almorand University in the capital to remain close to home. Twice a week, he would travel two hours by carriage to visit Brighthall and check in on his grandmother. In addition to his classes, Jonathan had taken it upon himself to manage the estate. His only respite being that he had not yet assumed the chancellorship. In Jonathan's absence and his grandmother's ailing health, the affairs of the region were primarily overseen by the regional council.

Jonathan halted his steps and rubbed a hand over his mouth. His eyes were glazed and he appeared lost in thought. Though he remained in quiet contemplation, his inner turmoil manifested as frantic taps of his heel atop the wooden floorboards.

Hoping to alleviate his stress in some small way, Rosalind approached him. "Is there anything I can do to help? Perhaps—"

"No, Ros," he cut in, voice tight. "There's nothing more to be done right now."

Along with the dark circles that had taken up residence under his eyes, Jonathan had become more irritable in recent months. Rosalind couldn't blame him. So much responsibility weighed on his shoulders: too much for anyone, let alone a young man of only eighteen.

After a moment, Jonathan spoke again, his tone noticeably softer. "Keep Val company, will you? I don't have time to check in on her as often as I should. She'll say she's fine, but..."

"I know," Rosalind replied quietly.

Jonathan nodded his appreciation, then turned to the doctor. "Let me walk you out. I'd like to discuss any other recommendations you might have."

He and Dr. Ramirez spoke in hushed tones as they made their way out to the carriage, waiting beyond the entryway double doors.

The next day, Rosalind was seated beside Valentina in the conservatory, pricking her finger for the umpteenth time as she attempted to refine her embroidery skills.

"Rosalind, love."

She looked up to see Maria standing in the doorway. "Lady Rashford has asked to see you. While there, do you mind helping her take a spoonful of this tincture the doctor's assistant just dropped off?" The housekeeper held up a small glass vial.

Caught off guard by the request, Rosalind hopped to her feet and brushed out the wrinkles of her striped blouse and high-waisted trousers. She threw a questioning look at Valentina, who gave a small shrug without lifting her head from her sketchbook. Her friend sought the comfort of drawing when she was stressed and now was without doubt a stressful time.

Rosalind took the vial from Maria and made her way upstairs. She walked to the end of the long hall and gently knocked on the door before seeing herself in.

A bitter, tangy scent filled her nose as soon as she entered the room. Her gaze flicked to the countless vials scattered about on a nearby table, and she unconsciously tightened her grip on the one in her hand. Maybe this one will work, she thought.

Glancing around the rest of the room, Rosalind was relieved to see the curtains had been opened wide to welcome in the cool breeze and warm sunshine. And there, sitting upright in the massive bed opposite the door was Lady Rashford. At the sound of Rosalind entering, the older woman looked up and smiled, patting the empty space on the bed beside her.

Rosalind greeted her with as bright a smile as she could manage. "Maria asked me to give you some of this," she explained as she approached. Uncorking the vial, she carefully poured the molasses-like medicine onto a spoon.

Lady Rashford sighed. "Ah yes. Perhaps this one will taste bearable."

Slowly, so as not to spill it, Rosalind brought the spoon to the dowager's lips. A slight grimace crossed her features as she swallowed the medicine. "No," she croaked. "Tea, please."

Rosalind handed her the cup of tea beside the bed. "Much better," Lady Rashford said after a few sips.

Settling herself gently onto the bed, Rosalind spoke. "You asked to see me?"

"I did, my dear. I wanted to see how you were faring."

Though illness had weakened the older woman's constitution, it had not diminished her keen perception. Lady Rashford's gaze seemed to pierce the thin veil of composure Rosalind had fitted herself with upon entering the room. It felt as if her inner thoughts and feelings were now laid bare.

Still, she held on to the minuscule hope that she could persuade Lady Rashford and, if she were honest, herself, into believing she was alright. "I'm well enough, my lady," she answered quietly.

By Lady Rashford's knowing look, she hadn't been very convincing. But she didn't press, and Rosalind was thankful for it. She wanted so badly not to cry in front of her.

"I never did get you to break the habit of calling me lady," Lady Rashford said after a time. "Stubborn in that way, you are, like the pair of them. Far less pugnacious, though, for which I'm most grateful. Who would keep the peace in this house if not for you?"

Rosalind peered down at her hands, fidgeting in her lap as if of their own accord. "It's much quieter these days."

"Yes, I suppose so with Jonathan off at university." Lady Rashford was quiet for a moment. "How are they? Please," she said in a quiet plea. "They won't tell me anything."

It wasn't surprising to hear that Valentina and Jonathan had not divulged their true feelings to their grandmother. Rosalind knew from experience they preferred to keep their emotions, particularly those most vulnerable, close to their chest. And because both were charming and quick-witted, it was easy for them to deflect.

"They're not quite themselves," Rosalind admitted tentatively. "Valentina keeps to herself more than normal; spends most of her time drawing."

Lady Rashford nodded with a melancholic smile. "Yes, she has been sharing her sketches with me. Flowers and animals and sometimes even people. Says she will bring the world to me as I'm unable to leave my bed. So considerate, is she not?"

"Yes, try as she might to seem otherwise," Rosalind replied, with a breathy laugh.

"And Jonathan?"

Rosalind chewed at the inside of her lip, considering. "Jonathan's become rather elusive. He isn't around very often, and when he is, he is either tending to you or to affairs of the estate. I can't claim to know how he feels; I can only see he is tired. Exhausted, really."

A pained expression flitted across the dowager's face.

"I'm sorry, I shouldn't have said—"

"No, dear, there's no need to apologize," Lady Rashford insisted as she rested a frail hand atop Rosalind's. "I suspected as much and I appreciate your honesty. I only wish he hadn't had to take on so much at such a young age. He should be enjoying his first year of university, not fretting over me or Brighthall. I thought..." Her voice broke. When she spoke again, the words were little more than a whisper. "I thought I had more time."

Not knowing anything to say that could alleviate her sorrow, Rosalind shifted closer to Lady Rashford and leaned her head delicately against the older woman's shoulder.

"Oh, sweet child, I am so grateful to have you in my life. We all are."

Tears pricked the corners of Rosalind's eyes. "No, my lady, it is I who must be eternally grateful." She swallowed a sob before continuing. "You took me in, made me feel like one of your own. You've granted me privileges I never could have imagined, and I fear I'll never be able to return the favor." Rosalind curled in on herself.

"You already have, my dear. A thousand times over." Lady Rashford didn't elaborate. She simply sat quietly beside Rosalind, the sound of her slow breaths echoing around them. "Rosalind," she said after a moment, "you deserve to know something. The day you arrived, and I asked Maria to have you live with us in the home instead of with her and Louis in the cottage, it was not out of the kindness of my heart. I had a motive for doing so, one that has haunted me for years."

There was a wistfulness about her voice when Lady Rashford spoke again. "I loved my son, as did my husband, rest his soul. We disagreed about many things, but there was one thing we invariably agreed on—that our son, Arthur, deserved nothing but the very best."

Jonathan and Valentina's father. The siblings didn't speak of him often; when they did, the words weren't spoken with any particular warmth or fondness. It had surprised Rosalind at first, because she cherished every memory she had of her father and found every excuse to talk about him.

Over the years, she came to realize it was not a coldness on their part but on his. He hadn't provided them with fond memories to hold on to like her father had. Instead, praise of the late Lord Rashford was more often than not voiced by the upper echelon of high society—those whose wealth and power flourished during his time as Chancellor.

"We coddled him from the day he was born," she continued, "ensured he was afforded every privilege. In our view, he was next in line to serve as Chancellor, and as such, his safety and satisfaction were paramount, not only for his benefit but for the benefit of Denault's future.

"When he succeeded my husband as Chancellor, I couldn't have been more proud. He'd grown into such a smart, driven, and capable young man. Damn near every piece of legislation he wrote was enacted into law. There was little to no dissent from the regional council, and for good reason. High society was prospering, and people revered him for it. Even Chancellors in other regions began to follow suit."

A dry laugh escaped the older woman. "I felt vindicated in our decision to raise him as we had done. That Arthur wanting for nothing had allowed him to focus on what was important. But that was far from the truth. And by the time I realized it, it was already too late."

"The truth?" Rosalind asked meekly.

"Arthur had grown up with everything, and yet, it was never enough. He was never satisfied with what he had. He always wanted more and felt entitled to it. More power, more wealth, more adoration. That's what drove him. What blinded him."

Rosalind lifted her head from Lady Rashford's shoulder to peer up at her. There was a faraway look in the older woman's eyes. When the haze cleared, she spoke again.

"I didn't want to make the same mistake twice," Lady Rashford admitted quietly. "That said, I could not deprive my grandchildren of the privilege of their station. Then you came along, and I saw an opportunity. If Jonathan and Valentina were to have shared experiences with someone born of different circumstances, they might grow to be more compassionate and understanding. Perhaps then the sense of entitlement that ensnared my son would not have such a hold on them.

"The worst of it is, I knew full well what you would endure living amongst high society. That they would not welcome you as an equal. But I convinced myself that, by taking you in, I would be providing you with a better life than you would've had otherwise. Now"—her voice cracked—"I'm not so sure."

Rosalind lowered her head and fixed her eyes on the floral embroidery of the duvet. How different would her life have been if she'd lived in the cottage with Maria and Louis? If she grew up to serve high society instead of mingling amongst them? She would likely have worked alongside Charlene and Sylvia. Perhaps she would be the one to fix Valentina's bath and bring her tea. There would be no disparaging of her station as they would be equals, but there would still be the matter of her enchantment and the misgivings surrounding it.

"I'm so sorry, my dear Rosalind."

The wavering words pulled Rosalind from her ruminations. In the aftermath, a quiet whistle accompanied each breath the dowager took—echoing the labored breaths of her father from years ago. The sound, distinct and unforgettable, served as a stark reminder: Lady Rashford was sick, and she wasn't going to get better.

Sadness sat thick in Rosalind's throat. Whatever feelings the admission had stirred within her could wait. There would be plenty of time to contend with them later. Right now, she thought only of easing the older woman's suffering in whatever way she could. And so, she posed a question she already knew the answer to.

"Do you love me?"

With slight apprehension, Lady Rashford lifted a hand to stroke Rosalind's cheek. "Yes, my love. As if you were my own."

Rosalind forced herself to smile through the tears that clouded her vision. "Then that's all that matters."

13

ROAD LESS TRAVELED

TWO WEEKS LATER, ROSALIND found herself in what appeared to be the middle of nowhere. In every direction lay a seemingly never-ending field of tall, untamed grass that bowed to the whims of the cold wind as if waves on a golden sea.

Unsurprisingly, Valentina had gotten her way. She'd hounded Jonathan over and over until he relented, which is how all three ended up on a decaying wooden train platform near the northwestern border of Denault. From here, the trio would have to endure another three hours of travel until they arrived at Ashwind, a small border town that abutted the Endless Forest, a strip of neutral territory that separated Sauvign from its neighbor, Erdesay. That is if their transport ever arrived.

"I thought you said somebody would be waiting for us when we arrived."

"That's what I was told," Jonathan replied in the same clipped tone as his sister. Both stood with their arms crossed, staring down the desolate dirt road ahead.

Dressed in shades of gray, their tall, slender figures formed stark silhouettes against the bleak landscape. The weather was cold, and the sky was overcast. To combat the chill, Valentina wore a thick, buttoned-up houndstooth cape and matching riding skirt. Beside her, Jonathan kept warm with a wool herringbone coat, dark gray breeches, and black riding boots.

Rosalind had also come prepared for the cold, donning a thick, moss-colored sweater and a brown twill split skirt. It was a good thing they were all comfortable, seeing as they had little choice but to wait. She set her suitcase down on the platform and sat on it. The Rashfords soon followed suit, and there the trio sat for the unforeseeable future.

"Well," Valentina proclaimed aloud after a few minutes, "I'd say now is as good a time as any for you to tell us what this trip is *really* about, hmm?" She raised her brows at Jonathan expectantly.

He rolled his eyes in exasperation. "I've already explained it to you, Val—multiple times. A Chancellor hasn't visited the border in ages, and it's about time. I owe it to them to introduce myself and make known that they haven't been forgotten."

"And your council has no qualms about you visiting on your own? I'm surprised they didn't force a small army of protective personnel on you."

"They tried to," Jonathan admitted. "But I managed to convince them otherwise. Said I preferred to keep a low profile and that I wished to hand-select those who'd accompany me, to which they agreed." With a slight shrug, he added, "So I chose a few who looked like they needed a break, paid them double, and told them to make themselves scarce for a few days."

Valentina's hand flew to her chest, and she gasped. "My word, Jonathan. Have you any scruples?"

Jonathan huffed a laugh. "You're one to talk."

Rosalind watched him reach out to pick up a blade of grass that had blown onto the platform. He rested his elbows on his knees and turned it over in his hands. After a moment, he spoke.

"I noticed something curious while looking into the distribution of imports across Denault over the last few decades. On average, about an eighth of commodities imported into our region are dispatched to the borderlands. However, given the area's estimated population, that number should be closer to one-fifth."

Valentina scoffed. "What are you on about, Jonathan? You know damn well I've never been very good with numbers."

"Nor patience," he muttered before continuing. "What this means is that villages across the borderlands have been receiving significantly fewer rations than needed to supplement their food stores for quite some time now. And yet, there's been no notable indication of famine. We'd likely witness an increase in unrest or an exodus to nearby towns if there were."

If Rosalind understood him correctly, border villages were faring better than expected considering they hadn't received their allotted share of imported foods over the years. So, how were they compensating for the difference?

"You think they've found other means to sustain themselves?" she asked.

"I do."

Rosalind looked up to find Jonathan regarding her. The corner of his mouth quirked up in a faint smile. His gaze lingered on her a moment longer before returning to the blade of grass in his hand.

"Perhaps their harvests have been more bountiful," he suggested. "If that's the case, I'd like to know why that is. As Ashwind is the oldest and most prominent village in the borderlands, I don't doubt the Keeper will have answers. Whether or not she'll be willing to share them with me, I'm less certain."

The last few words were spoken in little more than a low murmur, nearly lost to the wind. It was the first time in a long while Rosalind had heard Jonathan sound unsure of himself.

"Looks like we might find out sooner than later," said Valentina, nodding her head in the direction of the gravel path. "It appears our ride has finally arrived."

In the distance, Rosalind saw what appeared to be three horses and a cart in tow. From the cart, a lanky arm waved at them wildly.

When the horses and cart came to a stop in front of them, an auburn-haired boy hopped out and rushed over to Jonathan.

"Mr. Rashford, sir," he said, lowering into a deep bow. Immediately upon straightening, he froze and his eyes grew round and wide. "I-I mean, Lord Rashford," he sputtered. "Wait, no... it's, er, Chancellor? Chancellor Rashford! That's it, right? I-it's an honor to meet you, sir." The boy hastily dropped into another bow.

"Any of those will do quite fine, but"—Jonathan leaned towards the boy conspiratorially—"between you and me, it's all a bit tedious, isn't it? I'd much rather you call me Jonathan if that's alright with you. What do you say?" He held out his hand.

The boy's face lit up. "Oh, yes! Yes, of course, Jonathan, sir," he exclaimed as he took Jonathan's hand and shook it vigorously.

"And what might I call you?"

"Tory, sir. Tory Darren."

"It's very nice to meet you, Tory."

The scene was not unlike the time Jonathan introduced himself to Albert. At least there was one in Ashwind they could count on their side.

"And this is my grandmother," Tory said, turning to the silver-haired woman seated on the small, wooden cart.

"Ah, yes, Ms. Hilde Darren," Jonathan acknowledged, bowing in her direction. "Thank you for traveling all this way. We're very grateful to have you as our guide."

Tory's grandmother regarded him with narrowed eyes. After an uneasy silence, she spoke in a clipped tone, her voice louder and gruffer than her petite frame suggested it would be. "Your luggage can go in the back."

"Right," Jonathan murmured. He went about setting his suitcase in the cart and then made his way over to Valentina. "What on earth have you packed in this bloody thing?" He dragged her suitcase over and hoisted it onto the cart with some effort.

Valentina shrugged. "One never knows what might come in handy."

"Miss, I can help you with that."

Rosalind jumped at the words. Her attention was on Jonathan and Valentina, and she hadn't noticed the boy approaching.

"Didn't mean to frighten you, miss. Just thought you could use a hand with your bag."

Up close, Troy looked even younger than Rosalind had initially thought. Though he was taller than her by several inches, she figured he couldn't be older than thirteen.

"Oh, that's very kind, thank you." She lifted the bag out toward him. When he reached out to take the handle, she found herself retreating slightly.

"My apologies," she said with a sheepish smile before holding the bag back out for Tory to take. Though it had been a little over two weeks since her birthday, she hadn't entirely broken the habit of shying away from interactions with the opposite sex. She breathed a small sigh of relief when their hands briefly met in the exchange, and no spark was to be seen.

"Forgive me," Jonathan said, addressing Tory and his grandmother once their belongings had been packed away, "I have yet to introduce you both to my companions, Lady Valentina Rashford and Miss Rosalind Carver."

A tingle at Rosalind's neck drew her attention to where Ms. Darren sat, who leveled her with a steely gaze. She did her best to offer the woman a small smile, though she had a feeling it ended up looking more like a grimace. She hurried over to join Valentina, Jonathan, and Tory, standing near a pair of chestnut horses.

"Esther here has a bit of a restless streak in her," Rosalind heard Tory explain as she approached the trio.

"Does she now?" Valentina purred as she gently stroked the mare's mane.

"Yes, ma'am. I recommend a more experienced rider take her reins."

"Happy to," she remarked. Leaving no room for objections, Valentina slipped a foot into the stirrup and swung a leg over, settling onto the mare's back with ease. Esther shifted beneath her and shook her head, whinnying. After a few soft pats and gentle murmurs, Valentina managed to soothe and steady her.

"Ros," Valentina said in a subdued tone so as not to rile the horse beneath her, "I think it best if you rode with Jonathan, don't you think?"

"Well, I..." Rosalind fell silent as no further words came to mind. In truth, the idea of joining Valentina atop the mare called Esther frightened the living daylights out of her. After being confined to a train carriage for four hours, her friend was no doubt itching for a spirited ride. Rosalind's stomach lurched at the thought. However, not going with Valentina meant riding with Jonathan. In close proximity. For several hours. It would be the first time they'd be alone together since...

She felt a familiar figure sidle up beside her. "Looks like you're stuck with me. But don't worry, I'll take it slow."

Not for a single moment did Rosalind consider the suggestiveness in his tone to be accidental. Any other time, it might have coaxed a slight blush from her, but not today. Today she was chock-full of anticipation and dread for the long ride ahead. She looked longingly at the cart where Ms. Darren sat, wishing she could ride with her. That is, until she met the curmudgeonly woman's narrowed stare. Suddenly riding alongside her no longer seemed all that enticing.

"I can accompany Miss Carver if you'd prefer to ride with my grandmother, sir," offered Tory from somewhere behind them.

"I think not," muttered Jonathan, seemingly sharing Rosalind's sentiments toward the older woman. He flashed Tory a bright smile. "Thank you, but I wouldn't wish to impose on Ms. Darren any more than we already have. I suspect she would much rather travel alongside her grandson."

Jonathan made his way over to Tory and the massive horse standing at his side. As easily as Valentina had, he swung himself up onto the horse's back and slid forward. "Your turn." He held out a hand.

Rosalind approached with trepidation. "Th-there's no saddle?" she asked meekly upon closer inspection.

"No, miss," Tory admitted apologetically. "Only had the one and gave it to Esther. But there are several blankets for cushioning."

As if having enough padding was her concern right at this very minute. No, she was more worried about getting on the horse—and then staying on it.

Tory knelt down and intertwined his fingers together, offering her an elevated step from which to push off. With more than a little help from him, Rosalind managed to hoist herself onto the horse's back. Once astride, Rosalind snaked her arms around Jonathan. She squeezed her eyes shut and held on for dear life.

"Ros," Jonathan rasped.

"Hmm?"

"Any chance you could loosen your hold a little?"

She shook her head. "Not likely."

"Seeing as this trip hinges on me being alive when we get to Ashwind, I think we should switch places."

Reluctantly, Rosalind let Tory help her as she, not so gracefully, slid down the side of the horse. Once off, Jonathan repositioned himself further back on the horse. "Let's try this again."

Again, Rosalind pressed a foot into Tory's hands and threw herself onto the horse, nearly kneeing Jonathan's unmentionables as she struggled to settle a leg on either side of its back. She couldn't help the squeal that escaped her as the horse shook its head and shuffled beneath her. A tightness gripped her belly, and for a brief moment, Rosalind worried she might be sick.

"It's alright, I've got you."

Jonathan's breath was warm against her hair, gently caressing the crest of her ear as he spoke. Rosalind was suddenly alarmingly aware of every inch of her body. The pounding of her heart. The raised hairs at the back of her neck. The heat of his body against hers. When she looked down, she realized the pressure she felt at her belly wasn't her roiling nerves but the press of his hand as he held her in place. He surrounded her, and as out of sorts as that made her, it also brought about a sense of comfort.

"Thank you," she whispered, willing her voice to remain steady even though she was anything but.

Rosalind watched Valentina's silhouette shrink in the distance as she rode ahead of the group. Every so often, she would circle back to update them on the endless sea of tarnished grass that awaited them. Closer in view were Ms. Darren and Tory. Their heads bobbed up and down in unison as the shabby cart rolled along the uneven, sand-coated road. It served as a reminder that Rosalind was riding down the same bumpy path on a giant, muscled beast with a mind of its own. She stiffened, her back already sore so early in the trip. How she wished they could be in the comfort of a warm, cushioned carriage.

"Ros, there are statues less rigid than you. Try to relax."

"Easier said than done, I'm afraid," she replied in a strained voice.

"Tell me, what's your favorite time of year?" Jonathan asked, seemingly out of nowhere.

"What?"

"For me, it's springtime," he explained. "I daresay many find it rather dreary, but I hold no such objection. The clouds hold the promise of rain. When confined all day in a dim room, I hear only my pen scratching and pages turning for hours on end. In those moments, I gladly welcome the sound of the rain. It's soothing. Shame it doesn't rain more often."

Now, Rosalind understood the reasoning behind his seemingly random question: he was trying to distract her. She smiled to herself before sharing why autumn was her favorite time of year.

For the next hour, the pair prattled on about a little bit of everything. One moment they were reminiscing over childhood memories, and the next they were discussing their favorites—books, activities, food, art. Rosalind felt the tension ease from her back and shoulders. That is until the horse let out an exceptionally loud and convulsive snort, which elicited a most unladylike squawk of surprise.

During a lull in conversation, the question that had been nagging at her for the past two weeks weaseled its way into the forefront of her mind. It became impossible to ignore, and she had no choice but to ask about it.

"Can I ask you something?"

"Certainly."

"If you thought I might be of help on this trip, why didn't you ask me yourself? Though I hardly think my ties to the border will account for much, it was apparent you'd already considered the idea when Val brought it up, and yet you said nothing." When Jonathan didn't immediately answer, Rosalind's nerves took hold of her tongue, and anxious words spilled from her mouth. "Is it because of... of what we did? Of what I asked of you? I promised it wouldn't change anything between us, but I fear it has. You've asked for my help in the past, but perhaps you no longer feel you can. I take it that's because of my awkward manner of late but—"

"That's not why. Not at all," Jonathan cut in.

She felt his chest press against her back as he took a long breath in and slowly exhaled.

"You're correct in knowing I had indeed considered what good-will or credibility my acquaintance with you might lend me on this trip," he explained. "Sauvign knows I could use all the help I can get. But I couldn't ask it of you, not again. Not when, only weeks prior, I requested your assistance at the council dinner. I took advantage of your background and circumstances then, to your detriment. To do so again seemed unfair because I knew you'd accept regardless of what position it might put you in. And I wouldn't wish for you to ever feel I was using you. Or worse still, that you might be inclined to do as I asked, not by choice but because you felt compelled to, because of who I am, what I represent. That's not what I want from you."

Though Rosalind was relieved to hear it wasn't as she'd feared, the weight on her chest didn't lessen. There was something melancholic about the latter half of his admission.

It was in the way he'd uttered the words more quietly than the rest, betraying a sense of uncertainty that Rosalind wasn't accustomed to hearing from him. It exposed a sliver of vulnerability that she wished she could soothe if only she understood it better. She was tempted to turn to him, to see if his expression revealed anything more. But she didn't. She hadn't the courage to face him; she'd already spent it all on asking the question in the first place.

"That was very thoughtful of you, thank you," she said in lieu of something more profound.

Hoping to ease his concerns and inject a bit of lightheartedness back into their conversation, she added, "You needn't worry. Not for one minute did I feel compelled to partake in this trip"—she inclined her head—"not by you at least. Your sister on the other hand..."

Jonathan let out a wry chuckle, and Rosalind couldn't help but be a little proud of herself. "That makes two of us. You know, I'd laud her for such remarkable tenacity were we not the poor sods relenting to it. As such, I can think of no better way to describe it than bloody annoying."

Rosalind laughed. She continued doing so as they exchanged anecdotes substantiating the younger Rashford's relentlessness. After a time, her sore cheeks and aching belly welcomed the relief of the companionable silence that followed.

We must be nearly there, Rosalind thought as she rubbed at her eyes. The ever-present gray and gold that tinted the edges of her bleary eyeline told her otherwise, and she groaned in dismay.

"So she awakens," said a voice from behind. She felt the words as much as she heard them, and it was then Rosalind realized she was leaning against Jonathan's chest.

"I'm sorry," she murmured as she hastily drew herself upright. "I didn't mean to fall asleep. Oh no." She gave a small gasp and pressed her fingers to her lips. "Did I... Was I, you know..."

"Snoring?" Jonathan offered. "I'm not sure I'd go as far as to say..."

"Talking," Rosalind quickly interjected. "Talking in my sleep was what I *actually* meant to get at. Mumbling, really. I don't snore... Do I?"

"Well..."

Rosalind covered her face with her hands. She could practically hear the smile on his lips. Before she could defend herself, Valentina called out to them. "I see a wall up a ways. Is that Ashwind?"

The wind whipped her hair about as Esther galloped toward them, having ventured ahead earlier.

"Yes, my lady," Tory exclaimed. "Granny and I gather we should arrive within the hour."

Rosalind perked up at the news. *Finally*, she thought. She couldn't wait to be on solid ground. Her neck hurt, her lower back was stiff, and her backside ached. Even her thighs were sore. And the news only seemed to amplify her body's craving for relief.

She shifted her weight to one side and reveled in the brief respite. She did the same for her other side, but the relief was frustratingly short-lived.

"Ros."

"Hmm?" she answered absentmindedly as she continued to shift in her seat, seeking a more comfortable position. Leaning forward in hopes of relieving some pressure from her backside, she pressed her hips back and arched her lower back as a cat might do.

"Ros," Jonathan bit out.

"Yes?" She responded in kind, mildly annoyed at his pestering while she was preoccupied with ensuring every fiber in her body didn't succumb to total and utter numbness.

A quiet whine escaped her as she readjusted once, twice more, to no avail, coming to terms with the sad realization that her efforts were futile. She would only be free from such wretched discomfort once she was off this dratted thing.

"Rosalind."

Firm hands gripped either side of her hips and held her in place. "*Please*," Jonathan rasped. "Please stop."

Alarmed, Rosalind craned her neck around to peer up at him. "What? Is something wrong? Are you alright?"

Jonathan's gaze didn't meet hers. Instead, she was met with his profile, his eyes fixed on something in the distance.

"Should be in a moment." A muscle in his jaw twitched as he spoke. "That is if you'd do me a favor and stop wriggling about as you are. Give me a chance to right myself."

Rosalind could have sworn she spied a subtle tinge of color on his cheeks. She took stock of their surroundings but didn't notice anything of concern. She cast her gaze back on Jonathan, her eyes scanning his face, neck, and chest for any signs of pain or injury. When she peered down to where their bodies met, it dawned on her. And she now *felt* his meaning. Blood boiling in her cheeks, she spun back around and stiffened in her seat. Even her breaths were stilted to prevent the slightest of movements.

She opened her mouth, closed it, then opened it again. "I... I..." The words stuck in her throat, and she had to force down a swallow to free them. "I-I am so sorry. I hadn't meant to. I hadn't even realized that might happen..."

Jonathan blew out a breath which quickly morphed into a low chuckle. The grip on her hips loosened, but his hands didn't leave her. Instead, they stilled atop each thigh. Gently, his forehead came to rest against the back of her head.

"It's I who should be apologizing. I thought I'd mastered such schoolboy inclinations years ago," he confessed wryly. "But it appears I have not."

His breath rustled her hair and brushed past her ear like a soft caress as he spoke, and mortification was no longer the overwhelming sensation rushing through Rosalind's mind and body. In its place, a warm tingling crept up her spine, skimming along her arms and leaving a trail of gooseflesh in its shadow.

"I don't imagine I'd make a good first impression by arriving with my breeches tented. Or worse..."

"Perish the thought, Jonathan!" Rosalind chided, nudging him gently in the torso with her elbow.

He let out a shallow grunt. "Alright, alright."

She bit back a smile. "If it did happen, Val would never let you live it down. Ever."

Jonathan laughed. "No, no she would not."

"Chancellor. I mean, Jonathan, sir."

Rosalind looked ahead. Tory was turned around in his seat in the cart that rode a little way in front of them, waving to get their attention.

"We're coming up on the outskirts of Ashwind now. Past the stone wall, it won't be very long until we arrive at the town square. That'll be where the Keeper will greet you. I reckon there'll be a few others there to see you as well, sir."

Behind her, Rosalind sensed Jonathan shifting, straightening himself. She felt further movement on her thigh and peered down to see Jonathan's third finger tapping against her. It was then she spied a thin gold band wrapped around it, one she hadn't noticed before. She knew of the signet he wore on his right thumb but none other unless she counted the ring he'd slipped on the night of her birthday. A small part of her was tempted to ask about it, but now wasn't the time.

14

ASHWIND

THEY PASSED THROUGH A gap in a crumbling stone wall and continued quietly along the dust-ridden path, which was now lined by a smattering of dilapidated cottages and farmhouses. Some appeared to be built of deadened wood logs and straw, others by handmade bricks and leaking mud. All were overrun by untamed vegetation, so overwhelming, it was as though they were on the verge of being swallowed whole by the ground beneath them.

Occasionally, a goat or rooster dotted the edge of the road. Each time Rosalind feared one would venture too close to the horses' hooves, she was relieved when they abruptly changed course and resettled a safe distance away. There they resumed their lazy grazing. It was as if an invisible fence lined the path, protecting them from a gruesome demise.

"Where is everyone?" Valentina questioned, a hint of wariness in her voice.

It was only then that Rosalind realized how quiet it was. Eerily so. She'd been so caught up in finally having new sights to take in that she hadn't considered these homes belonged to people—people who were nowhere to be seen. What's more, even the singsong of birds was absent, though she could have sworn she'd noticed a crow or two fly past them in the distance. Only the rare bleat from a meandering goat cut the crisp air. It was uncanny, to say the least. Like something wasn't quite right, but what, she wasn't sure.

"They're waiting at the square, my lady," Tory explained. "We don't get many visitors to these parts, you see."

"So earlier," Jonathan chimed in, "when you mentioned *a few others* might be awaiting our arrival, you were referring to the entire village?"

"Yes, sir," Tory replied, nodding eagerly.

"Lovely."

The small, almost indiscernible sigh following his sarcastic reply shed light on Jonathan's true sentiment.

"Jonathan," she said softly.

"Rosalind," he replied, mimicking her tone.

"It'll be alright."

Jonathan said nothing, and Rosalind had to admit the words seemed more encouraging in her head. Out loud, they sounded rather hollow.

"I have every faith in you," she started again, her voice wavering a little as she went, "as does Val. She wouldn't dare say it aloud but she's proud of you, you know. Keeps clippings about you from the papers in a hat box underneath her bed, which I discovered by accident. I wasn't snooping, I swear it. Oh, please don't tell her I told you," she added hastily. "She'd kill me just for knowing its existence. Then she'd bring me back to life only to kill me again for telling you about it."

Rosalind cursed her big, blabbering mouth. Could she not speak eloquently for just once in her life?

"Don't worry, I'll add it to our list of secrets," Jonathan said with a sly lilt. Then, in a tone so wonderfully gentle and earnest, he added, "Thank you, Ros."

And her heart skipped a beat.

After a time, the road beneath them shifted from dirt and sand to worn-down cobblestones. Soon after, buildings flanked them on either side, two or three stories in height. Made of blackened bricks and splintered wood, they fit snugly and unevenly against one another.

They passed a bookstore on their left. Embedded into the brick wall was a small, cracked window. Behind it sat a book splayed open for display, but it was so heavily coated in dust that she couldn't make out a lick of text. A few buildings down was another shop with its door ajar, though there wasn't enough light inside to see what was in it. Based on the lopsided sign that stood beside the door, it belonged to a grocer. Cabbage, onions, carrots, beets, and potatoes were listed in chalk, though all but the latter two were crossed out with jagged lines.

As they continued along the cobblestone road, they passed a shoemaker, a bakery, a woodworking shop, and a general store. Each and every shop looked like it had been heavily burdened by the blows of weather and time.

Again, there was little sound beyond that of their own making. Stranger still, though the buildings weren't particularly tall, they somehow managed to block out nearly all of the daylight. The sun hadn't been out, but the clouds in the sky were still a bright gray as if they carried the light within them. Not seeing any of this light in the street below was surprising. When Rosalind looked up, her eyes caught on a sliver of gold glimmer that shone atop the soot-stained wall of one of the buildings. Was that a reflection of the light? If so, it looked like nothing she'd seen before.

She was going to inquire about it when, suddenly, the horse came to a stop beneath her. Just beyond the heads of Tory and his grandmother, Rosalind eyed a large crowd of people.

"Well, shit."

"Valentina," Jonathan warned.

"Pardon my language," she muttered, directing an apologetic smile toward Tory and Ms. Darren.

Tory hopped off the cart and helped his grandmother down. Valentina followed suit and dismounted with ease. Rosalind felt Jonathan shift behind her. Moments later, she heard his boots hit the ground.

"Let me help you down. Swing your leg over and take hold of my shoulders."

Reluctantly, Rosalind did as she was told. So sore and exhausted from the ride, she didn't correctly judge how high to lift her leg when swinging it to the other side. Her heel bumped the horse's withers, and she lost her balance. She thought for certain she'd soon find herself face-first on the ground. To her relief, solid hands caught her at the waist and guided her down.

"Looks like we've both managed to arrive with our dignity intact," Jonathan said with a hint of a smile.

Rosalind grinned up at him. She thought she might have heard a faint voice in the distance, but her focus was too wrapped up in the dimple that showed on Jonathan's cheek and his hands still held firmly at her waist. The voice grew louder.

"Jonathan," Valentina hissed. The younger Rashford eyed her brother with a stare as sharp as daggers. "She's calling on you." She nodded her head to where Ms. Darren stood.

"Follow me. All of you." It was all the curmudgeonly woman said before venturing into the crowd.

Rosalind kept her eyes glued to the cobblestones beneath her feet as they moved through the narrow pathway made just for them by the parting crowd. Stares from dozens upon dozens of strangers bored into her. How much more Jonathan? And being the last one in line, she could feel the pathway falling away behind her, a wash of people filling the void to get a closer look. It was as if a large, slow-moving wave shadowed her, nipping at her heels.

Eventually, they came to a halt, and her curiosity won over. She looked up to see they had come to a large stone fountain that hadn't seen water in quite some time. In front of it stood a woman in a woolen blue dress, a gray-and-green plaid shawl draped around her shoulders. Her dark brown tresses were twisted behind her head, held in place by a black feather that was just visible, and loose locks framed her face. She eyed them, expressionless.

"Chancellor," she said in a crisp, cool tone.

Jonathan drew his hands behind his back and lowered into a deep bow. "Keeper Saintgarden, it's an honor to meet you."

The woman, who Rosalind understood was the Keeper, or leader, of the village, made no attempt to return the bow. After a prolonged silence, she spoke.

"You've come with no armed escorts."

"As promised," Jonathan replied.

Rosalind caught the Keeper's gaze darting over to where Tory and Ms. Darren stood. The petite, older woman gave a curt nod.

"And as I have promised, you'll be under my protection throughout your duration here—which I do not anticipate will be long. Rooms have been made up for you and your acquaintances at our inn. As you might have gathered on your way in, they are modest in nature."

"Thank you, Keeper. We appreciate the hospitality."

Keeper Saintgarden scoffed, then turned her attention in Rosalind and Valentina's direction. "Your acquaintances, as mentioned in your latest correspondence, I take it?"

"Yes. This is—"

She waved her hand, cutting him off. A brief look on Jonathan's face betrayed his surprise, but it quickly fell away, replaced by a practiced impassive expression. The Keeper approached Valentina and considered her.

"You must be his sister. Same eyes, same hair. Even your facial structure is not unlike that of your father."

"Looks alone are what we share in common with our father," Valentina assured as she met the Keeper's eyes.

"We'll see about that. And what of you? What might I call you?"

Rosalind didn't have to look up to know that Keeper Saintgarden was now watching her. The gooseflesh on the back of her neck indicated that.

"My name is Rosalind Carver, Keeper," she said with a hasty bow.

"Carver," the Keeper said, the name rolling around in her mouth as if she were tasting it. "That's a borderlands name."

Rosalind nodded. Low murmurs sounded around her, stilling her breath.

"I see. And who are you to them?"

"She's our friend. As much family as friend, in fact," Valentina chimed in. "Our grandmother took her in as a ward many years ago."

Warmth bloomed in Rosalind's chest, coaxing breath out of her once again. It was comforting to hear Valentina speak her affections so plainly, and she was thankful her friend came to her aid. She wasn't certain she would have been able to answer herself, under the weight of so many whispers.

The feeling disintegrated the moment Keeper Saintgarden leaned toward her and inhaled sharply.

"Intriguing perfume you wear, Miss Carver. A familiar scent not unlike that of..."

"Cloves," Jonathan murmured.

Several pairs of eyes, including Rosalind's own, glanced over to where he stood. Jonathan visibly stiffened at the attention, as if he hadn't expected his answer to be heard.

"I—well, I shared a horse with her for the past few hours. Had a lot of time to consider it," he explained rather hastily.

"Yes." Keeper Saintgarden's eyes shifted from Jonathan to settle heavily on Rosalind. "Quite unique. Might I ask where you acquired it?"

From beneath her lashes, Rosalind anxiously peered around at the crowd. What an odd question to ask of her now, in front of everyone, upon first meeting. She shook her head slowly. "I don't wear perfume, Keeper," she answered quietly.

If this was some sort of attempt at humiliating her, it was working. She felt her cheeks burn at the weight of attention.

The Keeper snapped her head up and called out to the crowd. "Where's Sylvan?"

"He's indisposed at the moment," someone called out from the crowd.

"Tell him to meet us at the tavern when he's fit to. Now," the Keeper continued, shifting her focus back to Jonathan, "how could I forget myself? You've come all this way to grace us with your company, and I have yet to ask the people to bow before you, my lord. My deepest apologies. I shall remedy that right aw—"

"No, no," Jonathan quickly cut in. "That won't be necessary. I expect no such thing."

"How gracious of you, Chancellor."

More than a few snickers sounded from the crowd.

"Already more gracious than his father was when he visited us five and twenty years ago," she continued.

"He stole from us," someone jeered. Others cried out in agreement.

"That he did," Jonathan exclaimed calmly, though a distinct thread of agitation was woven into his tone. The noise of the crowd ebbed at this.

"Have you come to return them?" The question was shouted from amongst the masses.

Rosalind understood they were referring to imbued artifacts the late Lord Rashford had seized during his visit to Ashwind. Under his command, security personnel charged into their homes and forcibly confiscated hundreds of items, some as small as a ring, others as large as a tapestry—anything they suspected of being suffused with magic. She knew this because Jonathan had informed her and Valentina of this when he agreed to let them accompany him to the border. Presumably, he thought to dissuade them from coming by underscoring how unfavorable they'd be viewed. It hadn't worked.

"No, I'm afraid not," Jonathan admitted. "Truthfully, the items taken from you were apportioned, destroyed, or sold off long ago. I'm sorry. I know an apology does little to atone for my father's actions, but I offer it all the same, and I promise from here on out to do all I can to regain your trust."

"Quite the rehearsed pronouncement, Chancellor," the Keeper remarked. "But how much weight does your promise hold, I wonder? Your like hasn't spared us a single thought in over two decades so I hope you can forgive my skepticism when I say I find it difficult to imagine why a young, newly inducted official such as yourself should be any different."

Several shouts of agreement erupted around them.

Jonathan nodded. "I understand. I wouldn't believe me either; I haven't given you any reason to. Not yet, at least. But I've come to seek your audience in the hopes that you'll hear me out all the same. I may yet convince you."

He and the Keeper looked at one another for a long moment, throughout which no one spoke. That is until a voice in the crowd called out. "Hornswoggler!"

"Oh shut up, Warren. And yes, I know it was you," Keeper Saintgarden chided. "Now, off you go. All of you," she added, waving away the mountain of people. "And don't forget what we discussed earlier."

She turned back to Jonathan, then to Rosalind and Valentina. "Come, let us continue this delightful conversation inside, shall we?"

Keeper Saintgarden pushed at a pair of thick, knotted, wooden doors, which opened into a dimly lit tavern. The smell of warm beer and smoked meats flooded Rosalind's senses as soon as she stepped inside. Beyond her lay rows of long tables and benches. As they proceeded to the end of one of the tables, she noticed a wall of shelves lined with large mugs and unlabeled bottles of liquor in varying shades of green, red, and brown. In front of the shelves stood a broad-shouldered man with a thick beard and bushy eyebrows. He was leaning on the bar, eyes narrowed and set on Jonathan.

"Leon," said the Keeper as she addressed the bearded man. "Can you prepare some plates for our guests? I'll take care of the drinks." She walked off without another word.

"I hate to be the bearer of bad news, dear brother, but she is not fond of you. Nor is anybody else for that matter," Valentina murmured as soon as the Keeper was out of earshot.

"Really? I hadn't noticed," Jonathan replied dryly as he settled onto the bench beside Rosalind.

His leg brushed against hers and stayed there. Since he made no attempt to move, neither did Rosalind.

Moments later, Keeper Saintgarden returned with mugs and a bottle of something brown. After filling each mug, she took a seat across from the trio.

Rosalind brought the mug to her lips and took a tentative sip. Sweet on the tongue, it was only after she swallowed that she noticed the burn left in its wake. She couldn't help the cough that escaped her lips.

"A little stronger than you get in Proper, yes?"

Nodding, Rosalind took another sip, intent on not coughing this time around.

The Keeper clasped her hands together atop the table. "Let's have it, then."

"Now?" Jonathan asked. "I rather expected a private audience."

"Leon has spent far too much time around noisy drunkards; you'd have to shout for him to hear anything. And his daughter is tucked away in the kitchen. I see no one else around." The Keeper made a show of looking about.

Jonathan glanced warily at her and Valentina. So it had been them he was referring to.

"Perhaps we should..." Rosalind started to move.

"No, it's alright," he said, placing a hand on her arm. "You should stay. It isn't anything I wouldn't have told you eventually." He drew his hand away, reached for his mug and took a long drink. Then he squared his shoulders and began.

"As you said yourself, Keeper, the council has neglected your people for the past twenty years, providing little in the way of support. But even before then, records indicate the well-being of borderlanders was little more than an afterthought. And now, I've come to find the council's neglect is not limited to the borderlands. The concerns of all those beyond the purview of high society are being blatantly disregarded."

Keeper Saintgarden's guarded expression didn't waver as Jonathan spoke.

"Things can't continue as they are," he went on. "People can hardly afford to feed their families, and the current solution fails to alleviate this. We need to come up with a way to make things more accessible to more people."

The Keeper's brows raised. "Ah, I see. So you've listened to the struggles of some poor farmers and witnessed children starving in the streets—all from the comfort of your private carriage, mind you—and now you believe you're fully versed in the plight of the less fortunate?"

"No, I wouldn't presume such a thing, but—"

"But you believe you can solve it? Be our savior," she exclaimed wryly. "And how do you expect to accomplish this? By taxing the wealthy? No, I doubt they'd be so willing to part with their hard-earned riches."

Jonathan winced. "That's not what I'm suggesting..."

"What then?" the Keeper retorted before he could say anything more. "Perhaps the problem lies within the sheer number of us to contend with. It'd surely be easier if you were to cast more of us out. Oh, and let's not forget, there's always the option to imprison us. It's not as if your lot hasn't done that before. Not everyone, of course—merely the peculiar ones. You know, the ones people tend to stay away from. Every town's got them, haven't they? Surely, no one would miss them."

A chill ran up Rosalind's spine. *She* was someone people stayed away from.

"No. Never," Jonathan said gravely. Under the table, Rosalind felt his hand grip her knee.

"This is ridiculous."

"Valentina," Jonathan grumbled.

"No, you will not *Valentina* me again, Jonathan."

Rosalind shrunk in on herself, wishing she could be anywhere other than wedged between the siblings. Valentina would say whatever she wanted, and no one could stop her. How everyone else would take it, however, remained to be seen.

"You permitted my brother to come here and vie for a chance to speak with you. He's doing just that, but you're not listening. You're merely berating him, and he's not going to do a thing about it because he's trying to show you respect. But why should he when you show him none in return? I think we can all agree our father was not a good man," she pressed on. "He was drunk on power and never missed an opportunity to use it. Eighteen years he's been gone, and he still manages to wield his influence from the grave. Don't you see? You're granting him power by undermining what might otherwise be a productive conversation if only you'd let it. Please, let him say his piece, or else Ros and I will have to listen to him piss and moan about what could've been all the way home."

Silence fell over the table. Only the occasional clanging of pots and pans resounded around them. Rosalind gaped at her friend. As startling and reckless as her outburst was, it was also magnificent. And damn convincing as far as she was concerned.

After considering Valentina for a short while, Keeper Saintgarden seemed to arrive at the same conclusion. "From here on out," she began slowly, "I'll refrain from any further rebukes, lest they be warranted."

When Rosalind turned to Jonathan, she found him smiling to himself. He eyed his drink for a moment, then spoke.

"I want to know the truth about wielding."

It took a moment for Rosalind to register what he'd said. Earlier, he'd mentioned inquiring about farming and food supplies. What had wielding to do with it? Is this why he'd been reluctant to include them in the conversation?

Keeper Saintgarden eyed him skeptically and opened her mouth to speak. Rosalind's best guess was that her promise to refrain from rebukes was about to be very short-lived.

"I have a theory," Jonathan said before she could get a word in. "One that speaks to why, year after year, our harvests continue to struggle."

He began to explain how, historically, agriculture in Denault had not always been a point of consternation. A handful of texts indicated that, for a time, it had flourished. Denault was once known for its abundant grain production, primarily wheat, rye, and barley. It's why the Chancellor's insignia consisted of wheat stalks.

The marked decline in harvest production began in the decade before the New Laws came into effect. Around this time, relations between wielders and non-wielders started to fracture, particularly within wealthier industrial towns and seaside villages throughout the country. This only intensified as the years went on, to the point that wielders began to go into hiding for fear of their safety.

From there, it wasn't long before those in power placed the onus of the country's persisting agricultural woes on wielders, claiming they had intentionally compromised the land in an attempt to undermine ruling parties. As many wielders had already fled the country or gone to ground, there weren't many to speak on their behalf. The New Laws were born shortly after, promising the end to civil strife and ushering in a new age free from the perils of magic.

"Now, I know, *I know* you are itching to ask me why I'm bothering to explain any of this." He shot a pointed look at Valentina. "It's so I can beg the question—what if wielders did indeed play a significant role in our agricultural downturn? But, not in the way the New Laws allege."

There was a sparkle in Jonathan's eyes as he spoke, one that hadn't been there earlier when doubt had shadowed his brows.

The Keeper, on the other hand, maintained a skeptical eye. However, the slight tilt of her head suggested she was intrigued.

"I don't believe wielders corrupted our lands. Quite the opposite. I believe they were largely responsible for making it viable in the first place, and the effects we're seeing now are a result of their absence."

"A bold claim," Keeper Saintgarden remarked. "And what evidence do you have of this?"

"Not much," Jonathan admitted. "Texts pertaining to wielding and magic were largely destroyed or heavily redacted when the New Laws came to be. That said, combing through thousands of texts would be an undoubtedly tedious job, likely imparted to low-level historians and students. Can't fault them for missing the occasional mention, especially those that were less explicit." The corner of Jonathan's mouth quirked upward. "I came across several accounts denoting the presence of rain whisperers and earth healers amongst farming communities," he explained. "Though my knowledge of magic is less than rudimentary, I do believe it has ties to the natural world, no? If that's the case, I'm inclined to believe these were wielders who worked alongside farmers to cultivate the land."

Jonathan met the Keeper's gaze. "Look, I'm aware this is largely conjecture. If what I've said is nothing more than inane musings, simply say the word and I shall pay it no mind any longer. But, if any of it rings true, I ask that you consider helping me uncover the truth about magic and wielding. I believe they could hold the key to overcoming our agricultural challenges. Imagine not having to rely so heavily on overpriced, imported commodities."

Keeper Saintgarden didn't answer right away. When she did, Rosalind thought she glimpsed a softness in her eyes. "Chancellor, you're a fool if you think wielding has any place in Sauvign."

"It did once; who's to say it can't happen again one day." Jonathan held up his hands in a conciliatory gesture. "Now, that's not to say I think wielding will be legal again anytime soon. I don't know enough about it to even be sure it should. But I do know magic isn't all bad, so perhaps wielding isn't either. And if it could help people put more food on the table, I'd say it's worth looking into."

Keeper Saintgarden sat back in her seat, arms crossed, regarding Jonathan. She looked on the verge of answering when her gaze flicked to something, or rather, someone over his shoulder.

"Ah, you've come. Good."

Rosalind followed Keeper Saintgarden's gaze to a man striding toward their table. He wore a billowing black shirt tucked into fitted brown trousers. Over his shirt, he wore a black suede vest that draped to his knees. Two brass buckles crossed one another atop his abdomen, securing the vest snugly around his broad chest. As he made his way over, he pushed back the hood he wore, revealing shoulder-length brown hair, the top half swept back in a knot.

Without a word, he settled onto the bench beside the Keeper, opposite Valentina. His eyes darted from her to Rosalind and then to Jonathan. After a moment, his eyes shifted back to Rosalind, which made her bristle. She chewed at her lip and stared down at her mug, avoiding his lingering gaze.

The Keeper made introductions, beginning with Jonathan. "And this is Sylvan Raynor," she said of the dark cloud beside her. "Sylvan here assists me in overseeing the cares and concerns of our village. And I daresay he knows the ins and outs of the borderlands better than I do."

Jonathan dipped his head. "Pleased to make your acquaintance, Mr. Raynor."

The man eyed him warily and scoffed. Rosalind half-expected him to offer up a snide remark, but instead, he turned his attention to her.

"Carver, hmm? Whereabouts the border is your family from?" he asked in a deeper voice than she had anticipated.

Rosalind shifted uncomfortably in her seat. "Somewhere east of here, I believe."

He cocked an eyebrow. "Does this village not have a name?"

She blinked. "Yes, of-of course," she stammered. "Only I... well, I-I can't recall it. I haven't lived there in quite some time." Under the table, she tugged anxiously at the sleeves of her sweater.

"It's not often our folk venture beyond the borderlands. Hard to make a living when so many think us a thieving, rebellious, and unrefined sort." He threw Jonathan a pointed look before returning his attention to Rosalind. "How is it that you found yourself in Proper, and, as it appears, in the good graces of high society?"

"I wouldn't go as far as to say all of high society," she murmured. "And to answer your question, I left because my father wasn't well. He could no longer take care of me and sent me to live with a relative."

"What of your mother?"

Rosalind shook her head. "It was only my father and I."

"Interesting. I'm curious why he chose to send you away. You see, we borderlanders take care of our own. I would have expected those in your village to come to your father's aid."

Rosalind squirmed under his scrutiny. "Well, had circumstances been different, then perhaps—"

"What's with the inquisition, Mr. Raynor?" Valentina interjected before she could finish. "You seem awfully concerned about my friend's upbringing." She leaned closer toward Rosalind as if to shield her. "Isn't my brother the one you should be interrogating? He's the bloody Chancellor after all. He's the reason why we're here."

"Your friend? I didn't know high society considered their servants as friends."

"That is a baseless assumption, sir. Rosalind is not our serv—"

Cutting Valentina off, Sylvan added, "And no, I don't care much for politics. I trust Serena has things covered where the Chancellor is concerned."

"Then why are you even here?" she bit back.

A smirk flitted across Sylvan's lips. "I could ask you the same thing, princess. What role does the Chancellor's sister play in such matters?"

Valentina's lip curled in disgust. "Princess? I see the patriarchy knows no bounds. Here I thought that a respite from the constraints of Proper high society would free me from the foolish assumptions and entitlement of men, but I can see now..."

The smile on Sylvan's face quickly faded. "Don't compare me to the likes of them," he said, nodding in Jonathan's direction.

"Then don't tempt me," Valentina replied icily.

"Alright, I think that's enough, Sylvan." Keeper Saintgarden let out a small sigh, giving Rosalind the sense it was not her first time saying as much to him.

"Quite," Jonathan said in a tight voice, his gaze fixed on Valentina.

"Quinn," the Keeper called out.

A young woman with tawny hair stuck her head out of the kitchen. "Yes, Serena?"

"When dinner is ready, please send the plates to their rooms. Our guests have traveled far and I rather suspect they'd like some time to themselves. And perhaps your father can bring up some hot water?"

She turned to Jonathan. "How does that sound?"

"Sounds perfect, thank you."

"I will think over your request this evening, Chancellor, and give you my answer tomorrow." The Keeper rose to her feet, and the rest of the table followed.

The young woman from the kitchen, whom the Keeper had referred to as Quinn, hurried over to them and dipped into a deep bow. She looked eagerly at the Keeper, who went about making introductions. Quinn was the daughter of Leon Stewart, the man with bushy eyebrows they had passed on their way in, and the owner of the establishment.

"My father and I are honored to have you staying at our inn. I'd be happy to show you to your rooms now."

"That would be lovely, thank you," Jonathan said with a warm smile. "We appreciate your hospitality. I'm very much looking forward to dinner; it smells wonderful."

Though the tavern was dimly lit, Rosalind could make out the broad grin and deep blush that swept across Quinn's cheeks.

"Let me show you to your rooms. We have one prepared for you and one for your sisters."

"Sister," Jonathan corrected as they made their way to the stairs at the back of the tavern. "Just the one. Ros and I are not related. Not even remotely so. We are"—he hesitated for the briefest of moments—"close friends. Have been for a very long time."

"Speak for yourself, brother. She's very much like a sister to me," Valentina said, reaching out to playfully pinch Rosalind's cheek.

Nose scrunched, Rosalind batted away Valentina's hand before nudging her to follow Jonathan and Quinn up the stairs. Following suit, Rosalind was just about to clear the first step when someone grabbed hold of her wrist. Glancing back, she was startled to discover Sylvan.

"Mr. Raynor?"

"Miss Carver, I—" he began, but before he could finish, his attention caught on where his hand gripped hers. A look of surprise flashed across his face, and whatever else he was going to say died on his tongue. He pushed her arm away and stumbled back a step, muttering to himself.

When he met her gaze, Rosalind saw his pupils were blown impossibly wide. His chest moved in quick, shallow bursts as if trying to catch his breath. Equal parts confused and concerned, she began to ask, "Are you alright—"

"I must go," he mumbled hastily. "Good evening."

And with that, Sylvan spun on his heel and walked away, leaving Rosalind to wonder what had just happened.

15

A Quiet Morning

A SLIVER OF LIGHT teased Rosalind's eyes open a fraction. She glared at the thin break in the heavy curtains of the small, solitary window in their second-story room. It had been a long and restless night, and the last thing she wanted was a reminder that morning had broken.

She couldn't stop thinking about her interaction with Sylvan at the bottom of the stairs. Once in the room, Rosalind had recounted it to Valentina, who agreed it was a strange encounter indeed. Perhaps he realized she was a border born, and like other dolts before him—Valentina's phrasing—he subscribed to unfounded rumors and fears. Or perhaps he was simply severely socially inept. Whatever it was, Valentina assured her they'd get to the bottom of it. She also assuaged Rosalind's concerns that her enchantment had returned. It hadn't because she had *felt* his touch.

Hoping to fall back into another hour or two of uneasy sleep, she slipped out of bed and made her way over to the window. Just as she was about to close the curtains, she spotted an impeccably coiffed head of black hair. Jonathan was seated on a wooden bench below, reading from a notebook in his lap.

Rosalind peered over her shoulder to where Valentina slept soundly in bed. She tiptoed past and dressed as quietly as she could. She pulled on her trousers from yesterday and then stuck her hand into the armoire and pulled out a white blouse with an oversized collar adorned with hand-stitched embroidery. Before heading out the door, she grabbed a knitted blanket from the back of a chair and threw it over her shoulders.

She went downstairs to find the tavern nearly empty, save for a man slumped over and snoring in the far corner. He was in for a tough morning.

When she pushed open the heavy tavern door, she was met with a rush of crisp morning air. She drew the blanket tighter around her as she made her way over to Jonathan.

"You're awake early. Even more so than usual," Rosalind said softly so as not to surprise him.

Jonathan lifted his head, and Rosalind watched as the deep lines of thought slowly faded from his face. Then, he smiled. "Looks like I'm not the only one. Care to join me?"

Rosalind nodded and sat down beside him. Around them echoed the sounds of shopkeepers setting up for the day.

"Doing a bit of light reading this morning?" she asked, peering down at the notebook in his lap.

"Ah, yes," he said as he casually flipped through the pages. "Just thought I'd go over my notes again. Though to be quite honest, the words are all a bit of a blur now, having spent the majority of the night poring over them." He sighed and ran a hand through his hair. "I want to make sure I'm as prepared as possible and have an answer to every question and concern, even though all of this could be in vain. Who knows if the Keeper will even give me a chance."

"I think she will."

Jonathan considered her for a long moment before leaning back and resting an arm over the back of the bench. "What makes you think so?"

"I will admit, at first, it seemed rather unlikely." She hesitated. "It's obvious the Keeper has harbored unfavorable assumptions about you for some time. That can be hard to shake." She knew that all too well.

"But," she continued slowly in an attempt to choose her words wisely, "I do think things shifted a little once we got to the tavern. She no longer had an audience and their expectations to uphold. You were honest in your reason for coming here and I thought you were rather compelling. It's obvious you've given the matter great thought. Then Val chimed in and"—she deliberated over the right word to use—"*encouraged* her to think twice. Somewhere in the midst of all that, I suspect she glimpsed the real you."

"The real me?"

"Not to say you aren't genuine as Chancellor," she said hastily, "merely more deliberate and reserved. That can make it harder to read you, which I gather is your intention. But when you take leave of such affectations, it's readily apparent how much care and effort you extend to things that concern you. Perhaps more than you mean to let on. Last night, for instance. When you explained your theory and how it came to be, you spoke with such ardor that I doubt anyone could deny how earnest you are—not even the Keeper."

Rosalind fell quiet, having said much more than she had initially intended. She picked at a loose thread of the blanket wrapped around her, unable to meet Jonathan's eye.

After a brief silence, he spoke. "Here I was, intent on spending the morning wallowing in self-pity and despair. Then you come along and give me no choice but to be hopeful. Rather miffed about it, if I'm being honest."

Rosalind eyed him incredulously. "You are?"

"Yes," he asserted as he leaned in closer, stretching an arm out toward her. "I spent all night building myself into a frenzy, and within minutes, you've quelled my fears. All that work for naught."

A light touch drew Rosalind's attention to her shoulder. There, she found Jonathan's fingers toying with a lock of her hair, and her heart squeezed a little at the sight of it. His hand was so near to her that, if she only leaned her head a little, she might feel the soft caress of his fingers against her cheek.

"Already, I hardly remember what had me so morose in the first place," he went on, eyes tracking the gentle twirls of her tresses. "You have a way of doing that, you know."

"Of doing what?" Rosalind breathed, leaning ever so slightly closer.

Jonathan's gaze met hers. "Making me forget what I was thinking about." A small smile tugged at his lips. "You're far more appealing than anything else rattling about in my head."

Rosalind's eyes fell to his mouth and traced the curve of his lips. Appealing indeed. If only he knew the singular thought that occupied her mind this very instant...

A clashing sound pierced the air, startling Rosalind and causing her to reel back in her seat. She looked over her shoulder and spotted the back half of a metal sign sticking out of a nearby shop window, shards of glass scattered on the cobblestones below.

She turned back to Jonathan whose arm had returned to its perch on the back of the bench, his brows raised in surprise.

"You bloody idiot!" someone shouted behind her. "How many times did I tell you a couple of strands of twine wouldn't be enough to hold up the damned sign? More than three times, bet my life on it, I do."

Rosalind met Jonathan's gaze and saw a twinkle of amusement in his eyes. It was enough to elicit a laugh from her, one she'd been trying to hold back. Before she knew it, Jonathan was laughing right alongside her.

16

Valentina's Confession

Valentina brought a steaming cup of coffee to her lips, pausing to inhale the tantalizing aroma of chocolate and bergamot before taking a sip. Coffee wasn't her typical choice for morning libations, but Quinn had informed her, somewhat regretfully, that the tavern didn't have tea on hand. To her pleasant surprise, the coffee tasted delightful—much better than anything she had tried back home.

It was much too early for her to be awake, but here she was wrapped up in an itchy blanket, bearing the morning chill. She peered out the dusty tavern window to the bench across the way. How did they do this every day?

The sound of slow and steady footsteps echoed in the space behind her. Valentina didn't have to look back to guess who the assured footfalls belonged to. "Keeper Saintgarden."

"Lady Valentina."

"Valentina, please," she implored as the Keeper came to rest beside her. "The honorific does me no favors here."

The other woman made no attempt to confirm or deny the sentiment; for a long moment, neither spoke.

"Do you make it a habit of spying on your acquaintances?"

Valentina huffed a laugh. "If the opportunity arises."

She looked to where Jonathan sat facing Rosalind, his arm outstretched toward her. They were looking at one another as if transfixed, lost to the rest of the world. Were she to tap on the window, she doubted they would notice.

"They think me oblivious, you know."

And what a ridiculous notion that was; to think that she—a sister to one and dearest friend to the other—wouldn't be privy to their poorly disguised affections for one another. Utter fools, the pair of them.

"Does that bother you?"

"Only my pride, really; that they think me daft enough not to catch on. And perhaps I was a smidge hurt at first, to know that Ros wasn't confiding in me. But she has her reasons. The fact that I'm divulging as much to you now probably has something to do with it."

"And why are you telling me this?"

Out of the corner of her eye, Valentina could see that the Keeper was observing her. She shrugged.

"I suppose it's because I've kept my mouth shut for this long—a feat in and of itself, honestly—and I relish the chance to tell some-body. Anybody. I like to think that this"—Valentina gestured to the scene playing out beyond the window—"wouldn't be possible without my machinations." Something she was rather proud of.

Her scheming began the very day Jonathan returned from the capital, inspired by the way the pair reacted to seeing each other after so many years apart. Her brother was hardly subtle in his appraisal of Rosalind. And unfortunately for poor, sweet Rosalind, her attempts to keep her wits about her were in vain.

From then on, Valentina took every opportunity she could to get them alone. Whatever happened when she was away, she couldn't know, but the progress was palpable. It was evident in Jonathan's lingering glances and Rosalind's betraying blushes. And then there was the evening of Rosalind's birthday. She hadn't wit-nessed it with her own eyes, but she could have sworn she'd heard two pairs of footsteps venture toward Jonathan's room down the hall that night.

Perhaps the most heavy-handed of her efforts was to insist she and Rosalind accompany Jonathan on his trip to Ashwind. It took quite a bit of convincing, but here she was standing beside the Keeper of the town, and there they were in their own little world.

"And to think," she mused, not bothering to temper the smug expression on her face, "up until a couple of weeks ago she hadn't felt the touch of a man. Now look at her—not a flinch in sight, though I endeavor not to think of how she came to be so comfortable with my brother..."

"Pardon?"

"Well, the thought of Jonathan being intimate in any way, shape, or form makes me physically ill—"

"No, not that," Keeper Saintgarden cut in. "It's your comment about Miss Carver that has me intrigued. You mentioned something about her not having touched a man before. Did you mean that figuratively or..."

"Ah." *Shit*. She'd said that aloud, hadn't she? Now what? It wasn't her place to tell Rosalind's truth, in the least, not any more than she already had. "You know," she began somewhat sheepishly, "I think perhaps I've run my mouth for long enough."

Keeper Saintgarden narrowed her eyes. "How old is Miss Carver?"

If the Keeper were asking such a question, it was likely because she had already inferred her meaning. Valentina blew out a defeated breath. "Two and twenty."

"So she's a border born," Keeper Saintgarden murmured. "That's why she—" She quieted, her lips forming a tight line.

"That's why *what*?"

Keeper Saintgarden met Valentina's gaze and studied her for a moment. She must have found whatever it was she was looking for because she answered. "I knew there was something about her, but I couldn't quite place it."

"Is that why your Mr. Raynor barraged her with questions last evening? That man is impertinent and lacks all manner of tact…"

The Keeper let out a dry laugh. "Yes, I'll admit Sylvan isn't known for his subtlety."

"Jonathan is right, isn't he? You, Mr. Raynor, perhaps the entire village. You know about magic. How it works, possibly even how to wield it."

Keeper Saintgarden didn't respond.

"Keeper," Valentina persisted, "I ask you once more. Hear him out, please. That man you see out there, that's my brother. That's who he truly is when no one else is around; when he can relax and drop the facade. He isn't like my father or the council members who think only of themselves. That's not to say he isn't a prick sometimes, but he's a good man. I wouldn't let him pursue Ros if he weren't. And while he isn't like them, he does know how to play their game. Humor him and you'll see for yourself. Who knows, you may even find an ally in him." Satisfied she had said everything she wanted, Valentina turned to leave.

"Serena."

Valentina looked back, head tilting in question.

"My name is Serena," the Keeper continued. "You've granted me the use of your name, free of honorifics. I'd like to do the same. Good day to you, Valentina."

17

REVELATIONS

A DAY LATER, ROSALIND sat across from Valentina at a rusted iron table outside the tavern with three cards in her hand. It was midday, though the sky gave no indication, gray and cloudy as it had been the day they arrived.

"I put," said Valentina.

Rosalind peered over at her friend with a critical eye. Valentina simply smiled back. Was she bluffing? There was only one way to find out. "I see it," she replied in her best attempt at a casual tone.

Valentina began by laying down the eight of diamonds, which Rosalind countered with the queen of spades. Queen beats eight; point to Rosalind.

Momentum on her side, Rosalind opted to reveal her highest card next—a two of diamonds. Valentina scoffed as she threw down a king of hearts. In this game, two surpassed any face card. Thus, another point to Rosalind.

With only a measly four of diamonds remaining, Rosalind knew she would lose the last hand. And indeed she did, as Valentina set down an ace of hearts. Point to Valentina. Still, because Rosalind had triumphed on two of the three hands, she won the game.

"I knew I should have played a different card first," Valentina grumbled. "Play again?"

Rosalind nodded as she brought a diminutive cup to her lips. She took a sip and smiled. It was sumptuous—warm, thick, and sweet with hints of bitterness and spice. Quinn referred to it as "drinking chocolate" and was eager to reveal its secret ingredient: cayenne pepper.

Everyone they'd encountered since arriving in Ashwind kept their distance. Everyone, that is, except for Quinn, the tavern-keeper's daughter. It was her hospitality that had coaxed Rosalind and Valentina out of their room, even as Jonathan was nowhere to be found.

The young woman spent nearly every free minute of her time talking with them, which wasn't that often given it was only her and her father managing the tavern and inn. When free, she was eager to learn more about life in Proper and the affairs of high society, confessing that she hoped to visit one day. In addition to entertaining them with conversation, Quinn also made certain they were never without something to eat or drink. Just this morning, they had enjoyed a hearty meal of porridge and sausages. She had also been the one to give them the deck of cards they were playing with now.

As the winner of the last game, Rosalind was to lay down the first card of the new hand. She was considering her options when she was interrupted by a gruff voice.

"You're a border born."

Rosalind looked up to find Sylvan Raynor staring at her, his arms crossed over his chest. She hadn't seen or heard him coming, and it took her a moment to register what he'd said.

"I am," she admitted warily. "How did you know?"

But he needn't have answered. She knew as soon as she glanced over at a rather rueful-looking Valentina. "Ah."

"But the enchantment has dispelled," Sylvan pressed on, his words more a statement than a question.

"You were able to touch her the other day, weren't you? When you grabbed her without permission," Valentina chimed in. "Not long after you threw a barrage of undue questions her way, might I add."

Sylvan frowned. "I admit my attempts to uncover the truth were rather indelicate," he conceded. After a brief pause, he added, "And for that, I apologize."

Rosalind's head drew back in surprise. A brief look at Valentina told her she wasn't alone. She opened her mouth to thank him but was stopped short.

"How many people know of the circumstances around your birth, Miss Carver?"

And here she'd thought the apology indicated he was done probing. Evidently not.

"About the enchantment? Well, I suppose you could say just about everyone in Proper knows. There are those who made sure of it."

"I see. I expect most didn't take kindly to such knowledge."

"Not particularly..."

"And what of border folk?" Valentina interjected. "Would they take kindly to someone like Ros?"

"Those more learned would be sympathetic. But..." He hesitated. "There are some who believe all enchantments, be they good or bad, attract misfortune. They'd rather not associate."

Valentina leaned back in her chair, crossed her arms, and considered Sylvan. "And which are you?"

"No need to fret, princess. I am of the former. Tall tales told by the fire don't sway my judgment, particularly when those tales were likely started by your lot to incite discord amongst us."

"I'm glad to hear your judgment is not susceptible to ghost stories. If only the same could be said for prejudices. I can only hope your Keeper's judgment is more resilient."

"Lucky for you," Sylvan bit back dryly, "it appears we'll soon find out."

Rosalind followed his gaze to see Keeper Saintgarden and Jonathan strolling side by side, heading in their direction. It was the first time she'd laid eyes on Jonathan since the morning prior. Not long after she had left him to brush up on his notes, Rosalind had heard word that the Keeper had agreed to speak with him. He was nowhere to be found the remainder of the day, though Quinn mentioned she had delivered their dinners to a back room the Keeper occasionally reserved for private meetings.

Jonathan looked more like himself than he had this entire trip thus far. Gone were the stiff shoulders and heavy brow that had plagued him since they'd arrived. He looked comfortable, relaxed even, with his hands tucked into his pockets as he walked alongside the Keeper. His jacket was undone, as were the first couple of buttons of his shirt. It was perhaps the most casual she had ever seen him in public as acting Chancellor.

"Ah, Sylvan, just the person I was hoping to find. We're not interrupting anything, are we?" Keeper Saintgarden glanced between Sylvan and Valentina.

"Not in the slightest, Serena. I take it things are going well?"

Rosalind was only mildly surprised to hear Valentina was on first-name terms with Keeper Saintgarden. She'd mentioned they had run into each other yesterday, and if anyone could build a rapport with someone in a single setting, it was Valentina.

Sylvan on the other hand appeared to have been completely caught off guard by it. And by the smug look on Valentina's face, she'd gotten the response she was hoping for.

"Yes, well enough to warrant more conversations. But to do that, I'm going to need to provide a bit of context." She directed her following words at Sylvan. "I would like to take our guests on a tour of Ashwind. A proper one. In the light of day."

Sylvan narrowed his eyes. "You're certain of this?"

"I am."

"What of the forest edge?"

"That, too." The Keeper nodded.

Sylvan held the Keeper's stare for a moment longer before offering a curt nod. "As you wish. I'll need to grab a few things first." He left without another word.

Keeper Saintgarden turned to Rosalind and Valentina. "I recommend changing into something comfortable. It'll be a bit of a walk."

Rosalind exited the tavern half an hour later with black trousers tucked into ankle boots and a navy wool coat Valentina insisted she wear. Because it was tailored to Valentina's form, the coat didn't quite button all the way up, so she threw on a gray scarf for added warmth.

Valentina followed closely behind, wearing a carefully crafted ensemble. She had packed an outfit for every occasion, she explained to Rosalind as they got dressed, hence the heavy suitcase. This specific outfit, consisting of a navy vest, matching trousers, knee-high riding boots, and a long burgundy tailcoat, was ideal for a brisk walk.

"You're overdressed."

Rosalind turned toward the voice and found Sylvan standing at the iron table they had been sitting at earlier, his foot resting atop one of the chairs. He appeared to be adjusting something on his leg. She worried he was referring to her. That is until he looked up and leveled a critical eye at Valentina.

"Am I? I'm not the one with daggers strapped at my thighs," Valentina replied, brow raised. "Are we to expect trouble?" She considered him a moment longer. "And what's with the case slung around your back? Is it a shovel? An axe? Tell me, Mr. Raynor, do you intend to murder us and dump our bodies in the forest?"

"Dunno," he said with a shrug. "Depends on how much you annoy me, princess."

Valentina rolled her eyes. "Will you ever cease with the 'princess' nonsense?"

"Does it bother you?"

"As a matter of fact, it does."

"Then, no."

"Pardon?" Valentina said, a hint of disbelief in her voice.

"No," he repeated. "I don't think I will stop." He flashed her a wry smile.

"Perhaps it'll be your body left in the forest," she grumbled.

Sylvan huffed a laugh. "I'd like to see you try, princess."

Just then, the tavern door flew open. "Oh good, you haven't left yet," said a relieved Quinn. She directed her following words at Sylvan. "Can I join, please? Father said you were going to—"

"Don't see why not," he said, cutting her off. He glanced toward the sky, then shouted over his shoulder. "Should be any minute now, Serena."

"Good. Let's be off then, shall we?" The Keeper said, ushering the group to follow her lead.

Not long after they'd started down the road, Rosalind tugged at her scarf to loosen its grip around her neck. Moments later, she felt the warm caress of sunlight on her cheek. It was a most welcome feeling, having spent the last two days trapped under the weight of a drab gray sky. The clouds seemed impenetrable until now, and the presence of sunshine was like a breath of fresh air. How fortunate it should happen now as they explored the village.

Glancing around, Rosalind was struck by how different everything appeared. It was as if the sun had brought with it a new visage that enveloped the entire street. The cobblestones beneath her feet seemed smoother than they had before. They passed a bookshop she had seen on the way in, though she recalled its brick walls being more cracked and worn than they were now. She also could have sworn its front window had been coated in grime. But she must have been mistaken, for she could see into the shop and spy its rows of books in various shapes, sizes, and colors tucked neatly into shelves lining the far wall.

The flash of blue caught her eye. Her gaze trailed up the wall of one of the nearby shop buildings and landed on a little bluebird chirping atop the roof. Was this the first bird she'd seen since they arrived? Thinking back to earlier that morning, she recalled opening the window to their room and hearing nothing like the sweet birdsong she listened to now.

Could it be she'd gone mad? How was it she'd perceived Ashwind in such a dreadful light when it appeared to be a perfectly charming place?

"Ros," Valentina murmured, leaning close. "Is it just me or..." Her words trailed off when Keeper Saintgarden brought the group to a halt.

"What you see now is Ashwind in its true form," the Keeper explained. "That is to say, without masking charms."

"You used magic to change the appearance of the entire village?" Jonathan asked. "Seems like quite an exhausting task."

"It can be, yes. Luckily, we have a few wielders on hand to aid in the process. Also, we didn't charm the whole of Ashwind, only parts you were likely to see. Had you entered any of our shops, you would've glimpsed them as they are now."

"Is this something you do often?"

"Every time an unfamiliar traveler ventures into Ashwind," replied Keeper Saintgarden. "We have lookouts near our wall who alert us of incoming visitors. That's when our wielders get to work. The less inviting a village appears, the less likely one is to overstay their welcome."

"It's certainly impressive," Jonathan said as he looked around. "I must admit, there are about a hundred questions racing around in my head at the moment."

"We can confer as we walk," the Keeper offered, gesturing forward. "I'll answer them as best I can."

As they continued down the main street, Rosalind could feel the stares of passing villagers boring down on them. Many of whom she locked eyes with maintained a look of skepticism, which was unnerving. However, she couldn't help but notice a growing number of curious expressions. Perhaps word had gotten around as to what their party was up to. It was certainly to their benefit that they were accompanied by the Keeper herself.

Rosalind and Valentina had been careful to follow Keeper Saintgarden and Jonathan at a respectable distance so as not to eavesdrop. They, however, were not offered the same courtesy, as Quinn and Sylvan trailed closely behind.

"The clouds, were they a masking charm as well?" Rosalind asked as she peered up at the blue sky.

"That was Sylvan's doing," said a cheery voice behind her.

"Quinn," grumbled another in response.

"Sorry, was I not supposed to say? I thought we were explaining things to them. Serena did." Without waiting for Sylvan to answer, Quinn went on. "It wasn't a masking charm. Those only work on inanimate objects. At least, I think that's how it works. He did something different. He called the clouds here and then suspended them in place."

Valentina turned on her heel and began walking backward without skipping a step. "You did that? Made it all somber and gray? Must have been hard for you, seeing as you're a beacon of sunshine."

To Rosalind's surprise, the comment garnered a chuckle from Sylvan.

"He's very good at weather-wielding," Quinn proclaimed enthusiastically. "Like his grandmother, rest her soul. My favorite is when he summons rain on a sunny day. Makes for a lovely rainbow."

"Tell them everything, why don't you," Sylvan huffed.

"How does one go about calling the clouds?" Valentina inquired. "A magic wand? A chant of some sort?"

"You'll just have to wait and see, princess."

Valentina frowned. She spun around so she faced forward again and slid her arm into Rosalind's. "I know," she declared louder than necessary. "I bet it's through dance. That's why we have to wait and *see*. Oh, I do hope it's dancing, preferably of the ballet variety."

Rosalind peered over her shoulder to find Sylvan scowling and muttering to himself.

A little while later, the party reached the end of the line of shops. The cobblestone road beneath them turned to gravel. Replacing the multi-story brick buildings of the main street were quaint cottages dotted along either side. They were quite fetching to look at. Some were adorned with colorful hand-painted porcelain tiles; others were covered in flowering ivy. All looked loved and lived in, unlike the homes they'd seen on their way in. Those, Rosalind realized now, must have been altered by masking charms.

The farther they walked along the gravel path, the more sparse the cottages became. Long grass of green and gold filled the spaces in between. Soon, there were no more homes in sight, only the grass, which grew thinner by the minute, and a grim tree line ahead.

As they neared the forest, a heavy mist settled in around them. Gone were the sunlight and birdsong. Ahead of them, skeletal tree trunks with long, spindly branches stretched out toward the sky and disappeared into the mist. Peering into the forest was like looking down a shark's mouth: rows and rows of sharp shapes fading into a black abyss. Rosalind shivered, but whether it was because of the damp chill or haunting silence, she couldn't say. What she did know was that she had no wish to stay.

Keeper Saintgarden halted. "This is where Ashwind ends and the Endless Forest begins. You wish to know about magic; this place is as good as any to start."

She turned to Sylvan and nodded. He knelt and began to undo the latches of the case he'd brought with him.

"Magic isn't born nor is it ever destroyed," the Keeper explained. "Instead, it ebbs and flows around us in rhythm with the tides of nature. And while magic is not tangible to most, it is to some. And to fewer who study and train, magic can be wielded."

As soon as the Keeper's voice stilled, the silence that loomed in its wake quickly descended over the group. Just when Rosalind thought she couldn't bear it any longer, a soft, unhurried melody pierced the oppressive quiet. She searched for its source and found it flowing out of a violin tucked under Sylvan's chin.

His body swayed gently back and forth as he coaxed out long, lingering notes that faded in and out, one after the other. They were so close to meeting yet always just out of reach—until they weren't. The notes began to touch, and slowly but surely, the melody gained pace. Soon, they wove in and out of one another as if they were dancing.

Rosalind didn't know when she'd closed her eyes, but they flew open when she heard Valentina gasp. The forest in front of them was changing. The thin, crooked branches of the ghoulish trees began to stretch out, filling in the empty spaces around them. Tiny fuchsia buds sprouted along the branches and began to multiply, spreading across the tree line like wildfire. To Rosalind's amazement, they were not small flowers but leaves that exploded to life. Soon, the forest was blanketed in a thick canopy of pink hues.

When Sylvan's bow stilled, the sound of birds chirping and leaves rustling in the warm breeze echoed from the forest's edge.

Rosalind inhaled a familiar scent that tickled her senses, though she couldn't quite put her finger on it. Was it that of mulled wine or perhaps freshly baked gingerbread?

"Incredible," she breathed.

Her eyes caught on gold specks that shimmered above one of the trees, not unlike the glimmer she saw on one of the buildings in Ashwind a couple of days back. The longer she stared at the forest, the more gold she saw. Soon, it was everywhere—it radiated from the treetops and rained down on the forest floor. How much more would she come to find within the forest itself?

It was then that a soft, low hum tickled the shell of her ears. There was something familiar about it, like the scent from earlier. Perhaps if she got closer, she could hear it better.

As she drew nearer, a warmth blossomed in her chest and radiated through her bones. The feeling was overwhelming and not enough at the same time.

In the distance, she thought she heard someone call her name.

"Rosalind," repeated the voice, louder this time.

A hand caught her wrist and jolted her out of the haze. She looked up at Jonathan, who was watching her with concern etched on his face. "What are you doing?"

Confused, Rosalind glanced around and found they were no longer with the rest of the group but on their own. An awning of fuchsia blotted out the sun not far from where they stood, steps away from the forest's edge.

"I... I don't know what happened. I think..." She paused, considering as she spoke. "I think I wanted to see the gold up close. And then there was the song."

"Song? There isn't any song, Ros. Mr. Raynor isn't playing anymore." Jonathan's voice was calm, but an undercurrent of worry shook the edges of his words. "And what gold are you referring to?"

Rosalind reached out and swept her fingers through specks of gold glimmer floating around them. "This gold, can't you see it?"

His brows furrowed, and his grip on her wrist tightened slightly. "No, Ros, I can't—"

Footsteps approaching from behind Jonathan got their attention. "Come on, let's head back," Sylvan suggested. "I can explain."

Rosalind's cheeks reddened as she returned to where Valentina, the Keeper, and Quinn stood waiting. They watched her, each with a different expression. Valentina wore a curious look, while Keeper Saintgarden appeared contemplative. Quinn's eyes were wide in surprise, but only for a moment. A shy smile appeared when her attention turned to Jonathan.

"As Serena alluded to earlier, magic exists everywhere in nature," Sylvan began. "That being said, there are places where it concentrates. We refer to these places as magic wells, and right now, we stand outside the oldest and largest known well on the continent. The Endless Forest is called such not because of its size but for the immense amount of magic it harbors. It's believed no amount of wielding could deplete it of all it contains."

"The magic is so abundant, it overflows and feeds into the nearby earth. It's why the borderlands are more fertile than elsewhere," the Keeper added, her words directed at Jonathan.

"Before the powers that be banned wielding in Sauvign"—Sylvan threw a pointed look at Jonathan—"wielders from all over would travel to the forest to draw on its magic to imbue artifacts and draft elixirs. On occasion, they would also use it to cast powerful enchantments, such as the one Miss Carver endured. It's an enchantment that has persisted for centuries and most know not to give birth within close proximity to the forest, but for whatever reason..."

"My mother fell ill and couldn't travel in time." Rosalind didn't elaborate beyond that. She couldn't even if she'd wanted to, because it was all she could recall her father telling her.

Sylvan nodded sympathetically. "And now, for the past twenty-two years, you've lived with this enchantment, and the magic from this forest has lived within you."

Rosalind gazed at the forest as she listened to Sylvan. Every word drew her closer to the realization that, deep down, she already understood.

"Once the enchantment ended, its precise magic dissipated," Sylvan explained. "But the magic had been a part of you for so long, your body adapted. So now, in its stead is a void. A void that is capable of housing quite a bit of magic." He met Rosalind's gaze. "Do you understand what I'm getting at?"

"I believe so," Rosalind replied as she rested a hand on her chest, recalling the warmth she'd felt when approaching the forest. "You're suggesting I'm like the forest, a well of some sort."

"A wandering well, yes," Sylvan confirmed. "One that is free to move about, the magic contained within you."

"The gold shimmer I see in the forest. Is that magic?"

"It is."

"Are you certain of this?" Jonathan asked. "Of Ros being a—a well for magic or what have you."

"I am. I knew she was as soon as I touched her that first night."

Jonathan straightened. "Pardon?"

Sylvan scoffed. "At ease, Chancellor. I was only trying to work out why she had magic about her. When I touched her hand, I felt it. Much more than you or I possess. And I reckon if I were to do it again now, there'd be much more."

Jonathan eyed him warily. "How do you mean?"

"When Miss Carver arrived at Ashwind, she would have had some amount of magic already dwelling in her, likely absorbed from the natural world. Now, here we are, just steps from the Endless Forest. Some of its magic has surely transferred to her. I suspect that's why the forest called to her. It recognized what she was and sought to share its magic with her."

"Why would it do that?" This time it was Valentina who spoke.

"Magic is," Sylvan considered for a moment, "well, it's not sentient, per se, but it is alive. And it doesn't like to sit still for too long if it can help it. It wants to be used, to move freely through the world. Without wielders to help it along, it gets"—he hesitated—"restless. Someone like Miss Carver offers a nice alternative."

"Can she use the magic?" Valentina asked.

"Wield it?" Sylvan clarified. "No, she cannot. She isn't a wielder, only a well, which is rare enough on its own. To be both would be exceedingly so."

"Is it dangerous? For her, I mean," Jonathan asked.

"No, magic on its own isn't dangerous," Sylvan began, "but..."

"Sylvan," the Keeper cut in. "Perhaps that's enough for now. You can explain more to Miss Carver later." She spoke gently, but her tone held command. "Wind carries."

"The forest has been revealed for too long as it is," Sylvan agreed. And with that, he lifted the bow to his violin, drawing out the somber melody from earlier. In front of their eyes, the forest's lush fuchsia leaves withered away, leaving a grave of wooden skeletons in its wake.

❧

Rosalind chewed the inside of her lip as she contemplated everything she'd just learned. She was growing accustomed to being free of the enchantment, free to finally live a normal life. Only, that would never be the case, not really. She was never going to be normal. Magic, it seemed, was destined to play a part in her life forever. At least with the enchantment, she knew what to expect, but now? What was Sylvan going to say before the Keeper stopped him? And why did she think it wasn't safe to discuss in the open?

Part of her was glad Keeper Saintgarden stepped in. She didn't think she could handle any more revelations today. They had witnessed so much in one afternoon, all of it wondrous. She wouldn't soon forget the transformative melody of Sylvan's violin or the Endless Forest in all its beauty. How she wished that was all she had come away with. Instead, she would also come away with the forest's magic dwelling within her. And while she was assured the magic itself was not harmful, Rosalind knew full well what people's perception of it could be. This, she feared, made her more of a liability to the Rashfords than her enchantment ever had.

If someone were to find out, she could be accused of wielding, and the Rashfords could be charged with harboring a wielder. It wasn't true, of course, but what proof could she offer to substantiate it? And even if they were somehow found innocent, the scandal of it all would be enough to ruin their reputation. The charges alone would be enough to warrant a call for Jonathan's dismissal from the regional council. Valentina's future, all that Jonathan had worked for, not to mention the livelihood of the Brighthall Manor household, would be at stake.

"Ros."

Rosalind glanced up absentmindedly, her mind still spiraling within. The thoughts dispersed as soon as she registered the tenderness and concern in Jonathan's gaze. A burning sensation raced along her lower lash line, and she had to look away before the tears surfaced.

The last she knew, she had been trailing the rest of the party on their way back to town. Sylvan accompanied the Keeper at the front while Quinn entertained Jonathan and Valentina with the latest gossip she'd overheard at the tavern. Rosalind wasn't sure when

Jonathan had fallen back to join her, but here he was, walking beside her with his hands clasped behind his back.

"You don't have to stay back with me. I'm fine. I'll be fine."

"I know."

When he didn't elaborate, Rosalind tried again, not wanting him to feel obligated to keep her company.

"Now that we've seen wielding first hand, aren't you eager to know how it's used in farming? That's what you came here for after all. You could be learning about it right this minute if you were up there with Mr. Raynor and the Keeper."

"I could," Jonathan admitted. "And I will. But it can wait. Right now, right here is precisely where I want to be."

A lump formed in Rosalind's throat, and his words made it all the harder for her to fight back tears that threatened to fall. Why was it always so difficult to rein in her emotions when people were kind to her? She was overwhelmed and didn't know what to think, let alone how to act. Hoping to distract from her emotions, she curled her hand into a fist and dug her nails into the palm of her hand.

"Do you want to talk about it?" he inquired.

"Not really," she said quietly so as not to risk a quiver in her voice.

"Alright."

Jonathan made no attempt to force the issue, and for a short while, the two walked together in companionable silence.

"What do we think? Does Val go out of her way to annoy Mr. Raynor because she despises him or because she's keen on him?"

"Huh?" Rosalind responded inelegantly, the question taking her by surprise.

Jonathan shrugged. "You know her better than I, but my bet's on the latter."

It took her longer to catch on to what he was doing than she cared to admit. "An astute observation," she said through a smile. "One I'm inclined to agree with."

Before long, Rosalind felt the gravel pathway give way to cobblestones. Up ahead, the buildings of Ashwind's main street were crowding in on either side. It had turned from day to dusk on their walk back and now the glow of streetlamps guided them toward the tavern.

Quinn shrieked, startling Rosalind and the rest of the party. Rosalind craned her head to see what had caused the young woman's reaction. The wooden door to the tavern was ajar. Bursts of shouts and laughter rang out from inside. A few patrons stood nearby smoking and chatting, drinks in hand, and by the looks of it, more were headed its way.

"Father's going to have my head," Quinn exclaimed as she hurried toward the tavern.

"Looks like the word's out," said Keeper Saintgarden. "I reckon Leon did the telling, knew it'd be good for business. Lots of curious folks will be wanting a piece of you tonight, Chancellor. I'd say we're in for a lively evening."

18

A LIVELY EVENING

NEVER COULD ROSALIND HAVE entered a place as crowded as the tavern was this evening had she still been enchanted. She and the rest of the party had to wrestle their way past a swarm of people just to enter the place, only to discover all the tables were filled. Lucky for them, just the sight of the Keeper approaching was enough to encourage a few children to move their game of knucklebones from the table to the floor.

Rosalind saw Sylvan mouth something to the group, but she couldn't hear what he said over the noise. He disappeared into the crowd soon after. Voices rang out all around her, a hundred or more people all talking at the same time. One had to shout to be heard, which only made things louder. Then there was the generous amount of booze circulating the room, which no doubt amplified the boisterous atmosphere.

She squeezed herself into a tight space on the bench, nestled between Valentina on her left and a rather busty blonde on her right.

"My, my, the whole damn village is in here tonight, and somehow, I'm the lucky one sat next to Denault's finest. Fancy that," said the woman, bemused. She was sitting so close Rosalind could smell the alcohol on her breath as she spoke.

"That's the bloody Chancellor there, that is!" shouted someone from further down the long table.

"No shit, Jack," the blonde shot back. "That's what I've been telling you. Pardon my language, hun," she said, looking back at

Rosalind. "Bet you don't hear that much back in Proper. Name's Rosie. Rosie Garner."

"Nice to meet you, Ms. Garner."

The other woman leaned closer. "What's that, hun?"

"It's nice to meet you, Ms. Garner," Rosalind repeated, louder this time.

"Just call me Rosie, dear."

"Rosie. Y-yes, of course. I'm Rosalind. Rosalind Carver."

"Well how about that," Rosie said with a grin. She turned and shouted down the table, "Hey boys, say hello to this one. Her name's Rosalind. A bit like Rosie, ay? Only more proper like."

Rosalind didn't bother to mention to her new acquaintance that she had also, in fact, been named in the borderlands.

Following Rosie's informal introduction, the man she had referred to as Jack raised his mug. "To our new friend, Rosalind," he bellowed, taking a swig.

"To Rosalind!" cheered others around him before knocking their mugs back.

Rosalind felt her cheeks burn at the loud and unexpected attention, glad the tavern was so dimly lit that no one else was likely to notice.

"Here," Rosie said as she slid a mug toward her. "They'll be waiting on you to reciprocate. A nice big gulp should do it."

Rosalind eyed the opaque liquid warily. What was it? She snuck a quick glance at the men down the table and saw they were indeed waiting on her. Groaning inwardly, she knew what she had to do. It would be rude of her to decline.

Hesitantly, she reached out and wrapped her hands around the mug. Before she could convince herself out of it, she brought the drink to her mouth and took two large gulps, one extra for good measure. The scent reminded her of mulled wine. And while the alcohol burned as it touched her tongue, it quickly gave way to a smooth and sweet finish.

Another round of cheers erupted from the table as she set the mug down. Seconds later, she hiccuped. Then she hiccuped again. And again. She covered a hand over her mouth in an attempt to smother them. Her eyes widened in surprise as she realized she could not feel her hand on her lips. They were numb.

Rosie laughed. "That'll go away in a minute, dear. It's the magic," she said with a wink.

Rosalind peered into the mug. Sure enough, a sheer gold sheen floated atop the liquid.

Valentina gave her a nudge. "Look at you, fitting in with the locals. Oh, what's this?" She reached for the mug in front of Rosalind and took a sip. "This is good," she said before taking another sip.

"Val," Rosalind hissed, "take it easy. There's magic in it."

Valentina eyed the drink. "Magic, you say?" She gave it a sniff, then tilted her head back and downed it. This garnered a round of cheers from Jack and the others down the way.

When Sylvan returned to the group, he brought a few bottles of liquor, and Quinn and Leon were in tow. They came with trayfuls of food—sweet and savory meatloaf, twice-baked potatoes, carrots in a honey garlic sauce, and black rice. Rosalind was grateful for the meal; she hadn't realized how hungry she was until she caught sight of it all. Looking around at everyone else's plates, she wasn't alone.

After they'd eaten and drunk their fill, they drank some more. Rosalind doubted she'd have been able to remain upright were it not for the liquors that glistened with gold. Though she didn't know precisely how they worked, she could *feel* them working. With every sip, she was relieved of the ails of too much drink; the spinning in her head stilled and the turning in her belly quelled. The only thing the imbued liquor did not recover were her inhibitions, but she was glad of this. She enjoyed laughing as freely as she did to all the amusing stories that passed around the table.

As the evening wore on, they were joined by several familiar faces. Tory and his grandmother, Ms. Darren, sat across the way, and while the broad grin on his face made it readily apparent the young man was enjoying himself, the same couldn't be said for the latter. The gray-haired woman wore the same stony expression she had when they'd arrived, and she hardly spoke. The only indication Rosalind had that she might not be miserable was the vigor with which she drank from her mug. When Ms. Darren glanced in her direction, Rosalind stiffened and hastily lowered her eyes to her own drink.

"Rumor is her face is stuck that way," Rosie murmured in her ear.

For the briefest of moments, Rosalind wondered if she was serious. Then the blonde offered her a wry wink. Rosalind responded by smiling and lifting the mug to her lips.

A short while later, Quinn and her father Leon settled onto the bench across from Jonathan. Dinner had wound down and there seemed to be an unspoken agreement between the tavernkeeper and his patrons regarding drinks. Whenever someone took a bottle from behind the bar, they tossed a coin into a little wooden box, freeing him and Quinn from refill duties.

Unlike Ms. Darren, Leon no longer wore the frown he had been sporting when the trio first arrived in Ashwind. Presently, he was red in the face, roaring with laughter at a story Jonathan had shared about a particularly riotous night in a public house at the capital, which ended with him and a classmate waking up in a water fountain at daybreak dressed in frilly gowns.

"Didn't think high society folks could hold their liquor," Leon exclaimed. "Now I know they can't!"

Rosalind didn't know how much time had passed when someone came by and slapped a hand on Sylvan's back. They leaned in and muttered something in his ear. Whatever was being asked of him took a bit of convincing, but eventually, he acquiesced.

Sylvan threw back the rest of his drink and pushed himself off the bench. Then he disappeared into the crowd. Minutes later, the entire tavern erupted in cheers as a festive tune began to play.

"Chancellor," Leon bellowed over the music. "What say you show my daughter how proper folk dance in high society?"

"Papa!" Quinn squealed.

Jonathan chuckled. His gaze rested on Rosalind's for the briefest of moments before he said, "I would be delighted, Mr. Stewart. Though I wish to apologize to Miss Stewart in advance, for as familiar as I am with the steps, my feet have a tendency to stray."

"He's a terrible dancer is what he means," Valentina explained.

Jonathan nodded in agreement before maneuvering himself to the other side of the table. Standing before Quinn, he inclined his head and held out his hand. "Miss Stewart, will you grant me the honor of your next dance?"

From where she sat, Rosalind had a full view of the far end of the tavern, which had been cleared of tables and benches and now served as a makeshift dance floor. She watched as Jonathan guided Quinn's hands to their proper positions and instructed her through the motions of a simple waltz step. Their measured steps were at odds with the lively tune they danced to, but they paid it no mind. Quinn was beaming with delight, and Jonathan, too, seemed to be enjoying himself, the dimples on his cheeks on full display. Every once in a while, one or both of them would stumble, but they merely shared a laugh and carried on.

Rosalind smiled to herself. She was happy to see Jonathan so at ease; it seemed a relatively rare occurrence these days. Nearly all of his waking moments were dedicated to the cares and concerns of others. As Chancellor, he was accountable for the lives of more than thirty thousand Denaultians. That was an exceptional amount of responsibility to place on any man, let alone one of only six and twenty.

It was easy to forget his age when he took such care to portray himself as older and wiser. His refined appearance and attire lent him a few years as did the confidence with which he carried himself. But it was doubtless a wearisome thing to maintain and in quiet moments, she saw as much.

But such was not the case now. Gone was any semblance of his practiced and polished facade. His tousled hair moved freely and revealed hints of its natural waves. He wore no jacket or glistening adornments. His starched shirt lay loose against his torso, his sleeves rolled past his forearms, and the hem only partially tucked into his trousers. There were specs of mud on his boots.

To see him as relaxed and unburdened as he was in this moment warmed her heart. But along with it came an unexpected ache.

They had been in Ashwind only three days and already he had revealed more of himself to a room full of near strangers than she'd ever seen him do in Proper. He could never be so forthright where high society was concerned. Doing so would leave him too exposed to the likes of Lord DuPont and Lord Armory. Because of this, Jonathan would always have to maintain the charade. Wouldn't that get lonely after a time? That thought hurt to imagine because it was the last thing she wanted for him.

"Ros, love," Valentina said, leaning into her, "let's dance, shall we?"

It took Rosalind a moment to register what she said, the fog of her gloomy thoughts slow to dissipate. But before she could answer,

Valentina had yanked her out of her seat and pulled her toward the dance floor.

"I needed to get out of there," Valentina explained as they waded through the crowd.

"I think one of Tory's little friends was working up the courage to ask me to dance. Jonathan might be willing to dole out dance lessons, but I most certainly am not. Especially not with a boy whose eyes look to be level with my chest." She grimaced.

The pair carved out a small space for dancing not far from where Sylvan sat atop a wine barrel playing the violin. He was accompanied by three others—a flutist, a guitarist, and a contrabassist. Together, the quartet was in the midst of another upbeat melody.

Though the liquor had undoubtedly helped to lower Rosalind's inhibitions, it hadn't obliterated them completely. She glanced around nervously. None of the dancing looked familiar.

"You think too much, Ros," said Valentina before grabbing her hand and whirling her around. "Imagine we're in my room, at home in Brighthall." She took both Rosalind's hands, pushing and pulling her around in time with the music. "How would you dance then?"

Rosalind took another look around and noticed no one was dancing in precisely the same manner as another. Instead, everyone seemed to move on a whim, smiling and laughing as they went. Tentatively, Rosalind followed suit, taking a cue from Valentina and dancing as she might on a random evening back home in Brighthall. She was stiff at first, but gradually her nerves relaxed, and soon, she found herself dancing and laughing freely through song after song.

More than once, she noted how Valentina's gaze would catch on something over her shoulder. Or rather, someone. When she looked back, she was unsurprised to see it was none other than a certain dark and stormy wielder.

The furtive glances were by no means one-sided. Once Rosalind caught on, she saw Sylvan too had a wandering gaze. She couldn't fault him for staring. The way Valentina danced was effortless. Her lithe body twirled and swayed to the rhythm as if the music moved through her.

"I'm parched," Valentina announced between breaths. "Let's go have ourselves another drink."

Rosalind didn't argue and followed her through the crowd. Having been on the dance floor for some time, she was eager to rest her feet. They had just breached the throng of dancers when they came to an unexpected halt.

"Val! Am I glad to run into you," Jonathan exclaimed with relief. "I seem to have gotten myself in a bit of a jam." With his head, he gestured over his shoulder.

Valentina was nearly as tall as Jonathan, so seeing what he was referring to wasn't difficult for her. Rosalind, on the other hand, had to strain her neck to get a good look.

Quinn and a handful of other young women stood near one of the tables. They were all glancing in Jonathan's direction and whispering excitedly to one another.

"When I finished with Miss Stewart, she asked if I would dance with a couple of her friends. I didn't realize there would be so many..."

Valentina snorted. "And what would you like me to do about it?"

"Help me, please. I've already danced with four of them. Not including Miss Stewart, mind you. I don't know how much more I have left in me."

Valentina considered him for a moment, then reached up and pinched his cheek. "Leave it to me, brother. But know this—you owe me. And you'll owe Ros too."

"Me?"

"Yes, you, love. We need to hide Jonathan away for a little. Out of sight, out of mind, and all that. So how about you take him back in there"—Valentina motioned to the crowd behind them—"for a bit of a whirl while I get to chatting."

"Sounds good to me," answered Jonathan, and before Rosalind could say anything on the matter, he'd taken hold of her hand and ventured into the crowd.

Right as Rosalind was about to be swallowed up by the mob of dancers, she glanced back at Valentina, who grinned and gave her a little wave. Was she imagining things or did her friend look a little too pleased with herself?

"I thought you hadn't much dancing left in you," she commented, once they'd settled into the eye of the crowd.

Jonathan drew nearer and lowered his head. "What's that?"

Rosalind raised her heels off the ground and leaned in to meet his ear. "I thought you hadn't much dancing left in you after all that waltzing," she repeated louder.

Their faces close, his warm breath ghosted along her ear and neck as he answered, "With the right partner, I can dance all night."

If Rosalind's cheeks weren't flushed before, they were now. Just then, someone bumped into her from behind, causing her to stumble forward into Jonathan. She was welcomed with the lingering citrus scent of his cologne and the warmth of his body against hers.

"Are you alright?" Jonathan asked as he helped to steady her, one hand on her arm, the other at her waist.

Rosalind nodded. She saw movement out of the corner of her eye and braced herself for another knock. But she didn't need to worry because Jonathan had observed it, too. He pulled her against him and held out an arm to shield her.

Not long after, the song that had been playing came to an end, and the jostling crowd subsided. There was a brief lull, and when the music started up again, a slower, gentler melody filled the air.

Glancing around, Rosalind noted how quickly those around them settled into pairs, gravitating toward one another like magnets. While no one pair's steps precisely matched another's, they all adopted a similar subdued sway about their dancing. Some conversed as they danced; others rested wordlessly against each other.

A delicate touch brought Rosalind back to herself. When she looked down, she found Jonathan had taken her hand and intertwined his fingers with hers. Suddenly, she found it difficult to hear the music over the sound of her pounding heart.

With his free hand on her back, he lifted their clasped hands as if readying for a waltz. But there wasn't room for that. As if in silent answer, he slid his hand to the small of her back and closed the distance between them. When she lifted her gaze, she met his and couldn't look away. Together, they fell into the same unhurried steps as those around them.

There was no mistaking this for a dance between mere friends. The way he held her and the tenderness in his eyes assured her as much. But what it was exactly, she didn't know. What she did know was she wanted to make the most of it. Rosalind hesitated only a moment before leaning in and resting her cheek against his chest. She shut her eyes at the feeling of Jonathan's fingers idly playing with the strands of her hair and let herself bask in his warmth and the contentment that accompanied it.

They remained like that, adrift in a sea of strangers, until the music stilled and calls for a round of drinks for the musicians rang out.

19

ONCE MORE

ROSALIND RESTED ON A worn velvet sofa, her head heavy against its tattered arm and legs tucked in close. A leatherbound book lay open beside her.

Though the tavern crowd waned as the night drew on, it was by no means empty when Rosalind decided to retire. As much as she had enjoyed the evening, she was eager to wipe off the sweat of the day and sober up next to the fire.

After washing up, Rosalind slipped into her nightgown, plaited her hair, and settled by the hearth. She had intended to read a few chapters from the book she recently borrowed from Valentina, but it wasn't long before the gentle crackling of burning wood lulled her into a half-sleep.

A knock at the door roused her. It seemed sleep had finally called to Valentina, who Rosalind had last seen engaged in a rather impassioned-sounding conversation with one of Quinn's friends.

"It's about time," she mumbled as she rubbed the sleep from her eyes. When her vision cleared, she was surprised to find it wasn't Valentina who had entered the room.

"Jonathan?"

The man in question offered her an apologetic smile. "I'm sorry to bother you at such a late hour, Ros."

"Is everything alright? Is Val alright?" she asked, slightly alarmed.

"Val's fine," he assured her. "But she is the reason for my being here."

Rosalind frowned slightly, unsure of what he meant.

"She's asleep in my room. Out cold. I tried to wake her, but she wasn't having it. Elbowed me so hard in the ribs, damn near cracked one."

"She must be well soused," remarked Rosalind. "At least she stumbled into your room and not a stranger's..."

"I suppose," Jonathan replied slowly, "though I don't recall her drinking much after you left. Perhaps she can't hold her liquor as well as I thought."

Rosalind was skeptical of this. She knew Valentina to be quite adept at drinking.

"In any case," Jonathan continued, "I came here to ask if you wouldn't mind joining her in the other room for the night? Seeing as she won't budge."

"Oh! Yes, of course. It's no trouble at all. I'll just collect a few things and be on my way."

Rosalind pushed herself off the sofa and set about the room. Mortified at Jonathan seeing the mess she'd made earlier, she hastily grabbed the clothes strewn across the floor and tossed them into the hamper. Then she gathered up Valentina's nightgown from the bed and glanced around for her comb. She would need to brush her hair in the morning and was certain Valentina would too, most desperately. Remembering she had left it atop the mantel, she made her way over to the fireplace.

Reaching out for the comb, she caught sight of her bare shoulder. It suddenly occurred to her that she wasn't wearing her robe. She hadn't needed it earlier, seated so close to the warm fire. Plus, she'd been alone. But she wasn't now, was she? Propriety dictated that she cover herself in front of company, especially when said company was of the male variety.

Rosalind peered down at her nightgown and groaned inwardly. Against the firelight, she could just make out the silhouette of her body through the thin cotton fabric. Taking hold of the comb, she turned slowly around. Perhaps he hadn't noticed. After all, propriety would have him turn his attention elsewhere to avoid witnessing her indecency.

But it seems propriety eluded them both. Rosalind waited with bated breath as his gaze made the agonizingly slow ascent of her body. When his eyes locked on hers, every thought she ever had escaped her, save for one.

"Jonathan," she breathed. "If you wished it, I could"—her eyes flitted briefly to the bed—"I could stay a while."

Jonathan said nothing, did nothing for what felt like an eternity. The brief flex of his jaw was the only indication he'd heard her. He simply stood there, staring back at her.

Rosalind fidgeted under his gaze, and she wasn't sure how much longer she could bear it. Had she so utterly misjudged his affection for her? Perhaps it was merely companionable fondness and she had mistaken it for more than it was.

When his gaze finally dropped from hers and drifted toward the doorway, she knew his decision was as good as made. She didn't need him to say anything aloud; she was almost appreciative he hadn't. Hoping to maintain what little dignity she had left, Rosalind turned her back to Jonathan and focused on the flames flickering in the hearth. Her eyes burned, but she'd wait until she heard the door shut to dab at them. Then she'd find her damned robe and retreat to the other room.

Rosalind started in surprise as an arm snaked around her waist.

"Had to make sure the door was locked," Jonathan whispered against her ear before pressing his lips to her neck.

Without hesitation, Rosalind melted into his warm embrace. She blinked away unshed tears as he lavished her with tender kisses.

Her breath quickened as the hand on her belly skimmed upward and cupped her breast over her nightgown. The fabric did little to dull the spark of pleasure that surged through her as his thumb swept across her nipple.

His hand continued its ascent, fingers tracing her jawline and guiding her face toward his. Their eyes met for the briefest of moments before his mouth was on hers. There was nothing tentative about the way he kissed her. Surprising herself, she met his voracity with a hunger of her own. Without breaking the kiss, she twisted around to face him and grabbed a handful of his shirt with one hand and the nape of his neck with the other.

Rosalind didn't realize they had moved until she felt the edge of the sofa's back press into her. In one swift motion, Jonathan hoisted her up onto it and settled between her legs, the shift in height bringing their faces nearly level with one another.

"Ros," he murmured between kisses, "there's something you should know."

"What is it?" she asked against his lips. Reluctantly, she pulled back to search his eyes. "Is it something dreadful?"

Jonathan let out a breathy laugh. "I don't think so, but you may feel otherwise."

Rosalind's brows shot up in surprise.

"I'd like to explain it to you properly, but to do that, I need my wits about me." His gaze fell to her mouth. "And right now, I don't think I do."

The words had hardly left his mouth before his lips were on hers again. Perhaps she should stop him and ask that he confide in her now—whatever it was seemed important. Then again, if he thought it could wait, so did she.

Her decision to leave it be was cemented as soon as she felt his hand slip beneath the fabric of her nightgown and work its way up her thigh. He stilled just before the crease of her hip, and she couldn't help but squirm as his thumb drew circles across the sensitive skin of her inner thigh.

"Hold on tight," he instructed as he moved to grip the backs of her thighs and proceeded to lift her off the sofa.

Reaching the bed, Jonathan laid her down gently and pulled off his shirt. He positioned himself over her and swept a strand of hair from her face before lowering his mouth to hers. Rosalind's hands made quick work of exploring the expanse of his back. She lifted one hand to run her fingers through his hair; she would be remiss if she didn't.

Jonathan teased her lower lip before trailing kisses across her jaw and down the crook of her neck. He continued lower and Rosalind sucked in a sharp breath at the feeling of his teeth nipping at the peak of her breast. Still reveling in the pleasure that lingered in the wake of his kisses, Rosalind didn't think to consider his trajectory. That is, until his mouth skimmed past her belly button.

Rosalind's eyes snapped open. "Jonathan..."

"Hmm," he replied, not bothering to break from his sensuous descent. Meanwhile, his fingers slowly coaxed the hem of her nightgown higher and higher up her thighs.

One of her hands darted out to clasp Jonathan's. "Really, you—you needn't do that."

He paused and glanced up at her. "I know," he replied softly, "but I'd like to if you'll let me."

If she were honest with herself, she *did* want him to, very much so. She had experienced it once before when Valentina convinced her to sneak out to a nearby tavern one night, and she knew just how spectacular it could be. But that was with a near stranger, a woman she shared no history with and would likely never encounter again. The situation couldn't be more opposite with Jonathan. Imagining him so closely acquainted with her most intimate bits flooded her mind with worst-case scenarios, most of which were born from her own insecurities.

"Ros."

The sound of her name brought her back to Jonathan. His eyes searched hers. "Do you trust me?"

"Yes." The answer came easily, and just like that, the torrent of misgivings within her came to a standstill. Without another word, Rosalind lifted her hand from his and laid back on the mattress. Her breaths came in rapid succession as she waited with anticipation.

She nearly choked on a breath at the first lap of his tongue. He wrapped his arms around her thighs to hold her in place and proceeded to stoke flames of icy-hot pleasure low in her belly with teasing, unhurried strokes. Every so often, he'd adjust the pattern or the pace of his movements as if to study her reactions. Once, Rosalind whined in protest when he drew back, only to cry out moments later when his hot mouth returned to suck at her most sensitive spot.

When she knew she was close, she scrambled for something to hold on to and wound up with fistfuls of bedsheets in hand. As her pleasure peaked, Rosalind's body bowed, and her thighs clenched around him. Breathy whimpers escaped her lips as she rode the waves of her climax.

Once her body relaxed and she came back to her senses, Rosalind dared a glance at Jonathan who looked back at her with a self-satisfied grin. To her mortification, his mouth glistened with what she knew to be evidence of her release. Unconsciously, she touched a hand to her mouth.

Jonathan pushed himself off the bed and picked up a nearby washcloth. "Nothing to fret over," he said assuredly as he patted his mouth dry.

When he didn't return to the bed right away, Rosalind asked, "Is something wrong?"

"I don't have the ring with me," he admitted. "Nor do I have anything else…"

Rosalind recalled the brass ring he slipped onto his little finger the evening of her birthday. Looking at his hands now, she saw only his signet ring and the thin gold band she'd first noticed on their journey into Ashwind.

"Oh, I see."

There was no hiding the dismay in her voice. She wasn't ready for it to end, not yet. It was selfish of her to feel this way. He'd given her so much already, and she still wanted more. To see him thoroughly undone and to be the reason for —that was what she truly yearned for. And perhaps it was her own greed now deceiving her, but she didn't think he was ready for it to end either.

"I do believe it's possible with a bit of finesse," Rosalind pointed out tentatively. She knew of such cases, having read her fair share of rather explicit stories over the years. "And if you've taken care in the past," she added hastily.

"It is," said Jonathan slowly. "And I have, but I'm very aware that it's a lot to ask of you to grant me so much of your trust over so few words."

"I trusted you earlier," she reminded him.

A smile tugged at his lips. "That you did."

Rosalind maneuvered off the bed and approached him. She placed her hand over his heart and lifted her gaze to meet his. "And I trust you now."

Jonathan threw the washcloth he'd been holding onto the bed and leaned in to capture her lips with his. Then, the pair shed their remaining clothes and fell back into the sheets.

Jonathan reached between her legs and Rosalind gasped into his mouth as he slid one finger into her, and then another. He kissed and nipped at her neck while he teased the spot that made her breath hitch. If he kept it up, it wouldn't be long before she climaxed for a second time, leaving her utterly spent.

She could chase such bliss anytime, but this moment wouldn't last forever and she wanted nothing more than to experience it with him. Boldly, she trailed a hand down his chest and stomach to take hold of him gently but firmly. "Please," she murmured against his ear, not caring how desperate she sounded.

Jonathan let out a ragged breath. "Anything for you," he uttered softly as he heeded her plea. He settled into position and held her gaze as he slowly pushed into her. Like their first night together, his every move was measured to give her time to adjust to the feel of him. Soon, Rosalind felt the tension in her muscles ease and her body relax. Her grip on his shoulders loosened and she lifted her head to bring her lips to his.

Gradually, Jonathan hastened his rhythm. Rosalind moved her hips in time with his and wrapped her legs around him, intensifying the dizzying friction between them. Their kisses grew more ardent and erratic as their breaths quickened. One of Jonathan's hands skimmed across her breast and down her side. Moments later, Rosalind felt his arm hook under her knee and spread her legs wider apart. At this angle, he pressed deeper into her, eliciting shuddered breaths from the both of them.

Jonathan's breaths quickly grew ragged. He leaned down to press a shaky kiss to her lips, then withdrew himself from her and sought out the washcloth from earlier. She watched his face as pleasure overwhelmed him and before he could catch his breath, she lifted her head up to steal another kiss.

After freshening up, Jonathan pulled Rosalind back into bed. "You've already been here a while and no one's noticed. What's a little longer?"

Rosalind woke up sometime later to the sound of steady breaths and the rise and fall of Jonathan's chest. There she remained for several minutes more, allowing herself to savor the feeling and commit it to memory. When it came time to leave, she reluctantly extricated herself from his warm embrace and slid out of bed as noiselessly as possible. She crept over to the window to confirm it wasn't yet dawn and set about gathering the things she needed.

Unable to resist, Rosalind looked back once more at Jonathan, who continued to sleep soundly, before slipping out of the room.

20

An Unexpected Visit

A LEATHERBOUND SKETCHBOOK SAT open in Rosalind's lap. Valentina had cajoled her into spending the early afternoon drawing in the town square. She looked up from her sketch to survey the scene around them.

Across the way, a woman stood selling colorful wildflowers and berries out of a small cart. When she wasn't assisting patrons, she was chatting with a man at the next cart, who had an assortment of engraved goblets, teapots, and other metal wares on display. More than a dozen carts were scattered about the square, selling various goods.

In the center stood the massive stone fountain, where a group of giddy children crowded around, taking turns racing handcrafted toy boats in the water—so different from the dried-up and eroded fountain of just a couple of days ago.

Every once in a while, Rosalind recognized one of Tory's friends from the night before weaving through the crowd with their hands full. Sometimes it was a bag of flour or a sack of potatoes; other times it was firewood. They appeared to be runners for nearby shops, helping with errands and gathering supplies.

Before yesterday, she would have shied away from sitting so out in the open, afraid of encountering distrustful glances. But there were none today; passersby merely smiled and went about their business.

Rosalind turned her attention back to her sketch. Truth be told, it wasn't very good. It was heavy-handed and disproportionate, among other things. Art had never been her forte; that was Valentina's area of expertise. She peered over at her friend's notebook, which confirmed as much.

Not only was Valentina's sketch impressive, but so was her whole demeanor. Not once today had she mentioned a sore head or queasy stomach. She had even woken up ahead of Rosalind this morning—a rare feat in itself—and she'd managed to straighten out her hair without help. Now, she sat beside Rosalind looking as refreshed as ever.

"I hadn't realized we've switched to drawing profiles," said Valentina, not looking up from her sketch.

"How is it bottle ache hasn't taken hold of you?"

Valentina shrugged. "Got lucky, I suppose."

"Lucky?" Rosalind eyed her incredulously. "Val, you were so cup-shot last night that you fell asleep *in the wrong room*. I've seen you suffer more with less."

"I admit that was rather silly of me. But it all worked out, did it not? I woke up this morning and there you were. Kind of you to let Jonathan have the other room. Imagine what sort of mischief he might have gotten into if you hadn't."

Rosalind bit back the nervous laugh rising in her throat. "Yes, well, I happened to still be awake when he came in and..." She swallowed. "H-he asked nicely."

Valentina smiled. "I'm sure he did."

A rush of guilt flooded Rosalind. She couldn't keep this up. She didn't want to do it anymore, and frankly, she wasn't very good at it. It wasn't just that she owed Valentina the truth; she also desperately wanted her friend's guidance on what to do next. She needed Valentina to tell her how foolish she'd been and to stop messing about. Surely Valentina would succeed in getting the point across to her—that this was nothing more than a dalliance, a fling. Something fun but fleeting for Jonathan that would surely end in hurt and humiliation on Rosalind's part. The longer she let herself indulge in whatever this was, the worse off she would be. If she didn't stop soon, she might risk her friendship with Jonathan in its entirety.

Another wave of guilt struck Rosalind. Again, she had gone from thinking about what was best for Valentina to thinking about herself. This had to end.

"Val," she started, unable to stop the trembling in her voice, "I need to tell you something."

"Can it wait?"

Rosalind blinked. "What? No, I think it's rather important—"

"Sorry," Valentina interjected, "but I think we might have more pressing matters at the moment." She nodded in the direction of the tavern.

Jonathan was pacing, hand running through his hair. He seemed to be explaining something rather frantically to Keeper Saintgarden, who stood nearby with a grave look on her face.

"I think we should go find out what's going on."

"What's the matter, Jonathan?" Valentina asked once they neared, not bothering with pleasantries. "And don't tell me it's nothing. I can see by the way you're acting that something is—"

"It's Padraic," Jonathan answered before she could finish. "He's taken ill and needs aid quite urgently. Ilora is on her way with him as we speak."

"They're coming here now?" Valentina asked. "Surely it isn't wise for him to travel when he's not feeling well."

Rosalind agreed it was an odd choice for the Masons to journey to Ashwind when there were plenty of esteemed physicians in Meridian. The trip would take some six hours by carriage.

"We suspect he'll need more than a physician," Jonathan explained.

Keeper Saintgarden nodded. "Based on what you've described, there is little doubt wielding is at play."

Rosalind and Valentina looked at one another in surprise.

"I will call on Constance to assist us," the Keeper said. "She is a healer—one of the best in the borderlands. I will also coordinate with Quinn and Leon to prepare a room for their arrival. When do you anticipate that might be?"

Jonathan rubbed anxiously at his forehead. "Sometime shortly after nightfall, I suspect."

"Is that how you two have been communicating?" the Keeper asked, eyeing his hand.

Jonathan hesitated for a brief moment, then nodded. He held out his hand to the Keeper, who reached out to examine the gold ring on his third finger.

"Thought it seemed a bit plain for someone of your stature." Peering more closely, she added, "I hadn't noticed the engravings before. Very intricate. Erdesian-made, I take it?"

"Yes."

"And your friend, he's the one who wears its twin?"

"Not Padraic, no. His sister, Ilora, is the one I share it with."

Rosalind didn't have a clear view of the ring from where she stood, but she knew which one they spoke of. And now she knew of its purpose, to enable Jonathan and Ilora to communicate with one another. He wore one and Ilora the other. Her throat tightened.

"Let us know if she sends you any further messages of note ahead of their arrival," the Keeper instructed. "In the meantime, I will ensure preparations are in order. Beyond that, there isn't much more we can do but wait." She placed a reassuring hand on Jonathan's shoulder and left.

The trio settled on a bench in the far corner of the tavern as they waited for nightfall. Rosalind and Valentina sat on either side of Jonathan as he filled them in on what he knew.

According to Ilora, Padraic had been growing increasingly erratic over the past fortnight. It began with sporadic remarks about how his partner, Enzo, had wronged him in one way or another. The remarks seemed at odds with all of the fond things he had to say about them in between. However, the critical remarks soon outweighed the fond ones.

Then came the lapses in memory. Ilora would comment about something Enzo had said or did and Padraic would have no recollection of it. At times, it seemed as if he had forgotten about Enzo entirely.

"Ilora fears for his sanity," Jonathan explained. "She says it's as if he has lost control over his own mind. And he's hardly slept or eaten, which has only made matters worse."

"I'm so sorry, Jonathan," Valentina said, sympathizing. "That is truly terrible. I can't imagine how frightening it is for Padraic and how difficult it must be for Ilora to see him like this. If I may, where is Enzo in all of this?"

"They are on their way, but..." He hesitated. "It isn't an easy trek for them. If it were, they would already be by Padraic's side with the help he needs."

Jonathan took in a deep breath and let it out slowly. "As it is, they will not arrive for another day or two and I'm not sure we can afford to wait until then." The heel of his boot began to tap furiously against the stone floor. "I just hope the healer will be able to remedy whatever has been done to him."

Any encouraging words that came to mind sounded trite in Rosalind's head. She doubted they would be enough to calm his nerves. Still, she couldn't bear to sit there and not console him. Tentatively, she reached out a hand and laid it atop his knee. Almost at once, the bouncing of his leg stilled. When he looked at her, she saw he sought relief in her eyes, and so Rosalind held his gaze, gentle and unwavering, until the lines on his face softened. Remembering they were not alone, she drew her hand away, not daring to look in Valentina's direction.

"I must admit my curiosity is piqued," Valentina said after a short while. "How exactly does that ring of yours work?"

"With regards to magic, I haven't a clue," Jonathan admitted. "But the mechanics are quite simple. When I want to convey a message, I turn the ring clockwise as I speak into it. The other person is then made aware of the message when their band turns cold. And I mean cold enough to notice. Burns a bit if I'm honest."

"Fascinating. And how do you go about listening to the message?"

"You simply hold it to your ear." He mimicked the gesture.

"Sounds quite useful. Had it for long?"

"No, not long at all. Ilora gave it to me when she and Padraic last visited Brighthall."

"So right before all of this began. Huh," Valentina remarked. "Apt timing, or was something like this anticipated?"

"A bit of both, I'd say. We knew something was bound to happen when the truth came out but didn't know when or how. And we certainly didn't expect him to be capable of this..."

Valentina opened her mouth to speak.

"Val," Jonathan cut in, "I know you have more questions, but it's not my place to answer them. I'm sorry."

She huffed a sigh but nodded in understanding.

"Oy, Chancellor," barked a familiar voice from across the room.

All three turned to where Sylvan stood, arms crossed. "Give me a hand, will you?" He nodded toward the kitchen door. "I could use some help moving things about in the back room. Nothing like a bit of hard labor to take your mind off things, eh?"

"Couldn't hurt," said Jonathan as he pushed himself off the bench and made his way over.

"You've been quiet, more so than usual," Valentina remarked as they watched Jonathan follow Sylvan into the kitchen. "Is everything alright?"

Aware of Valentina watching her, Rosalind answered hastily.

"Me? Oh, it's nothing. There simply wasn't much else to say that hadn't already been said."

And wasn't that the truth? Rosalind could think of nothing to say to console him, so she tried to show him, and any questions that came to mind, Valentina had voiced for the both of them.

"If you say so," Valentina replied, considering her a moment longer before turning her attention elsewhere in the room.

There was one question that hadn't been asked. One that had been eating away at Rosalind since discovering Jonathan's ring was one of a pair.

"Val," she began as casually as she could muster, "do you think the rings are meant solely for communication? Or might there be more to them than that?"

"More?" Valentina asked, confused. "Ah," she said moments later as understanding dawned on her. "No, I don't believe there is. For one, I think he'd have said something. Also, I don't think she's the one."

Rosalind eyed her friend skeptically. "You don't think the daughter of a neighboring Chancellor is an ideal match for him?"

"Oh, no, I agree she may be an ideal match, but that doesn't make her *the one*."

"What does then?"

Valentina shrugged. "That's on him to figure out."

Rosalind expected her to say more, but she didn't. And as tempting as it was to point out that she hadn't really answered the question, Rosalind didn't. She wasn't certain she wanted to know.

After long hours had passed, Tory burst into the tavern.

"They'll be here any minute," he gasped out.

Following behind him was a tall woman with silver hair trimmed close to her head. She wore a billowing emerald dress that draped to the floor and around her waist sat a gold chain. Dangling from the chain was a chatelaine, which held an assortment of tools—several spoons of varying sizes, a pair of scissors, tweezers, and two miniature flasks. Rosalind ventured to guess she was Constance, the healer Keeper Saintgarden had mentioned earlier.

No sooner had the room settled than the clamor of hooves and carriage wheels against cobblestone sounded outside. They came to an abrupt halt, and moments later, the heavy wooden door swung open.

Padraic didn't look as he had when Rosalind met him. He wore a linen shirt tucked haphazardly into his trousers with its collar hanging loosely around his neck as if it had been pulled at and stretched. His hair clung to his head and dark rings encircled his eyes. She distinctly remembered the set of his mouth, how it seemed to promise mirth and mischief. None of that was evident now. In its place was a deep and despairing frown.

Holding him upright was Ilora, whose weary eyes scanned the room. A flicker of relief crossed her face when she spotted Jonathan.

"Ilora, where are we?" Padraic asked, his gaze darting frantically about the tavern. "No, no, no," he muttered, "you've brought me to them, haven't you?" He turned to her, eyes wide. "How could you? I trusted you." He attempted to tear himself from Ilora's grasp.

"Padraic," Jonathan said gently as he slowly approached his friend. "You're in Denault, in a town called Ashwind. It's alright. Ilora brought you here at my behest. It's me, Jonathan. Your friend."

Padraic looked at Jonathan blankly for a moment before recognition lit up his eyes. "Jonathan," he said with a relieved smile. He started toward him, arms open in greeting, but he stilled partway. His smile fell away, and suspicion shadowed his features. "Why am I here? Why did you bring me here?" The suspicion faded and his face hardened. "They got to you too, didn't they? Where are they?"

Jonathan took a tentative step toward him. "They aren't here, Padraic. I promise you, Enzo is not here."

Padraic bared his teeth at the mention of Enzo. Then, his expression changed once again. The anger he wore only moments before dissolved away and his shoulders slumped. "Why aren't they here?" he asked quietly.

Resting a hand on Padraic's shoulder, Jonathan explained, "They're on their way, I can assure you. They want very much to be here with you, and they will be. We just need to give them a little more time. You know how it is."

Padraic nodded, eyes cast down at the floor in front of him. His head tilted slightly, and he seemed to brush at something on his shirt. He glanced up at Jonathan and blinked. "I apologize, my mind seems to have gone astray. What is it we were discussing?"

"We were speaking of Enzo," Jonathan said carefully.

"Enzo," Padraic repeated quietly. "Do I know them?"

A muffled cry escaped Ilora and she turned to Jonathan, her eyes pleading. Jonathan glanced over at Keeper Saintgarden, signaling it was time.

"Lord Mason, Lady Ilora," she began. "I understand you have come a long way to be here, and as it's getting late, I would not wish to delay proceedings any further. We have prepared a few things in anticipation of your arrival, so if you would please follow me."

She proceeded to introduce herself, Constance, and Sylvan as the group made its way beyond the kitchen double doors and through to what appeared to be a storage room. Inside was empty aside from a large metal basin, a small pile of blankets, and a serving cart topped with a tidy collection of unlabeled vials, pouches, and jars.

Quinn, who must have joined them as they passed through the kitchen, slipped in after Rosalind and closed the door behind her. As soon as she did, it became readily apparent the room wasn't meant to house nine people.

Rosalind pressed in close to Valentina and whispered, "Perhaps it best we offer them some privacy and wait outside."

"And miss out on this? Certainly not," Valentina muttered indignantly. "Keep quiet, and they won't even notice we're here." She grabbed Rosalind's wrist as if to hold her in place.

Constance approached the cart and picked out a few strands of thick straw from a canvas pouch. Wordlessly, she began to weave them into a long plait.

"You can't be serious." Padraic's tone was incredulous as he looked from Constance to Ilora. "A wielder?" He let out a wry laugh. "Is it not a wielder who put me in this situation in the first place? And now you expect me to put my trust in another? For all I know, she's conspiring with Enzo. Perhaps you all are," he added bitterly.

Constance did not react to his accusation, continuing to move about the room. She brought a vial to the metal basin and poured some sort of viscous purple liquid into it. Soon, the scent of lavender filled the air.

"You're familiar with wielding, I take it?" Sylvan inquired.

"Of course I'm familiar," Padraic snarled. "Hard not to be when Enzo is an Erd—"

"Padraic," Ilora cut in, her voice calm but strained, "I shouldn't think they need to be privy to such things."

"On the contrary," Sylvan replied. "I think it would do well for us to know who exactly we are dealing with."

"They are not at fault for this," she snapped.

"Your brother seems to think otherwise."

"My brother is not in his right mind," Ilora shot back. "Catch him in a moment of clarity, and Padraic will assure you that Enzo is not to blame for this."

Padraic threw his hands in the air. "Who is this Enzo we keep speaking of? And how should I know what they have or haven't done?"

Ilora squeezed her eyes shut as if teetering on the edge of a coin, one toss away from shouting or crying.

"It wasn't them," Jonathan affirmed.

Sylvan considered him. "If not them, then who?"

Jonathan said nothing. He only looked at Ilora, who let out a long breath. "Our father."

Rosalind's blood ran cold. The Chancellor of Meridian was a staunch anti-wielder, as vocal and ardent as Lords DuPont and Armory. To think that he illegally commissioned a wielder to enchant his son. To think a father could do such a thing. It was incomprehensible.

Sylvan nodded slowly. "Because this Enzo is a wielder... from Erdesay?"

Ilora didn't answer.

"Enzo isn't just any Erdesian wielder," Padraic threw out. Immediately after, he clamped his mouth shut as if realizing he said more than he should have.

Sylvan rubbed at his chin in quiet contemplation, then went over to Constance and gestured to her. They signed back and forth briefly in wordless conversation. When they'd finished, Constance approached Padraic and held out her hand expectantly.

He stared at her hand, motionless. "Fine," he said after a time, placing his hand in hers. "Do your worst, healer. It can't be any more grievous than whatever grips me now." Then his shoulders slumped and in a fragile whisper, he added, "I don't know how much more I can take."

Constance brought her other hand to rest against his temple. It wasn't long before she turned to Sylvan and nodded.

"She confirms his psyche is indeed enchanted," Sylvan relayed. "And by her measure, it's a powerful one."

Rosalind didn't miss Ilora's hand as it sought out Jonathan's.

"Does she know what it is?" Ilora asked. "Can she fix it?"

"She needs to call it to the surface to identify it. Lord Mason, if you will." Sylvan gestured toward the metal basin.

Padraic raised a brow. "You expect me to get in that?"

Constance nodded. They stared at one another, unwavering, until Padraic relented.

"Good thing I look like shit. You would never have convinced me otherwise."

For the first time that evening, Rosalind saw a glimpse of the Padraic she had met back at Brighthall.

Padraic stepped into the shallow basin and took a seat, wrapping his arms around his bent legs. Constance tied the ends of the plaited straw together and set it atop his head. She knelt beside the basin with a small tongue drum in her lap. She tapped at the drum, releasing a singular resonant note into the air. Before it faded into oblivion, she drummed another note. And then another. And another. It was as if the notes chased after each other, the former just barely beyond the grasp of the latter. Soon, threads of steam rose from the water, and beads of sweat formed across Padraic's forehead.

"What's happening?" Ilora asked, her voice tentative.

"She's warming the water, using heat to coax the magic inside him to the surface," Sylvan explained. "The aromatics help to make the magic more tangible, and the straw is there for it to bind to. From there, she can attempt to distinguish the enchantment from the natural magic that exists within him. They will have distinctive signatures. If she can harmonize with the enchantment, she can decipher which it is."

Using both hands, Constance tapped the drum in swift movements, drawing out multiple notes together and one after another in a brief melody. She let her hands hover over the drum as the sounds reverberated throughout the room. She did this several times, altering the cadence slightly each time.

After a time, she beckoned Sylvan over and the pair signed to one another for several minutes. Sylvan rubbed a hand over his mouth. A deep crease formed between his brows as his gaze flicked from the Keeper to Jonathan and then to Ilora. Rosalind hadn't seen him look so apprehensive before.

"It appears Lord Mason has been enchanted not just once but twice."

Ilora's hand flew to her chest as she let out a choked cry.

"Does she know which ones?" Jonathan asked.

Sylvan gave a curt nod. "One is bis memoria, or dual memory. In this case, the wielder attempted to offset every positive memory of this Enzo person with a false, adversarial one. The other is occulta memoria. It's when certain memories are concealed, hence why he experiences varied states of recollection."

He turned to Padraic. "I'm sorry. Memory modification is among the most challenging forms of wielding. It's said to take decades to master, and even then, the use of magic for such purposes is largely condemnable because of how dangerous it can be. Whoever did this to you knowingly put your life at immense risk, for they were neither adept at crafting the enchantments nor did they have enough magic to wield them effectively." He paused. "That being said, their inadequacy affords us better odds of disarming them."

"Will it hurt?" Padraic inquired.

"Disarming shouldn't hurt, no, but you'll experience a nasty headache in the coming days."

Padraic scoffed. "Can't imagine it'll be any worse than the bottle aches we endured back at the capital, eh, Jonathan?"

Jonathan managed a small smile. "Not likely."

"Let's get on with it, then," Padraic said, nodding at Constance.

The healer resumed the quick taps of her fingers and thumbs against the steel drum in her lap. A melody that charmed and unnerved Rosalind filled the room, the notes rising and falling as if traversing a jagged mountainside.

Constance's head lolled forward, though she did not cease her drumming. Sylvan was soon at her side, resting a hand on her bare forearm. His presence seemed to reinvigorate her, and she called forth the melody yet again. Rosalind felt herself growing overwhelmed by the sound that echoed around them and the faint reverberations that rippled across her skin when, suddenly, it stopped. For the briefest of moments, she thought she caught a glimpse of gold shimmer swirling above Padraic's head before it dispersed like dust in the wind.

Sylvan and Constance conferred with one another, solemn expressions on both of their faces. The healer shook her head, and it was difficult not to assume the worst. Moments later, she drew her head back, seemingly taken aback by something Sylvan had conveyed to her. Rosalind didn't miss the cursory look in her direction.

Pushing himself off the ground, Sylvan made his way over to Ilora and Jonathan. There was a sluggishness about his movements that hadn't been there earlier.

"Constance was able to disarm the enchantment that made him forget memories," he said.

A look of relief washed over Ilora's face. "That's terrific news. And what of the other? Is that next?"

Sylvan hesitated. "Dispelling occulta memoria is not wholly unlike lifting a cloth from over one's eyes. Because it's only meant to conceal memories, not remove them, the magic does not dwell deep within the psyche. Rather, it rests atop. Bis memoria is a more invasive enchantment, making it more difficult to disarm. It requires extricating false memories from real ones. Only after can the enchantment's magic attempt to be dispelled."

"What are you getting at?"

"As it stands, neither Constance nor I possess enough magic to first separate, then remove the second enchantment."

Tears welled in Ilora's eyes, and she threw herself into Jonathan's arms. She nestled her face into his chest, muffling the sob that escaped her. Jonathan wrapped his arm around her and held her.

A burning sensation gathered at the corners of Rosalind's eyes. She was sympathetic to Ilora's sorrow and hoped Padraic could soon be free of the treachery his mind endured. But something else toyed with her emotions. She felt it gnaw at her belly as she watched Jonathan's hand brush soothing touches across Ilora's shoulder. It was utterly shameful to feel such a way, here of all places.

Jonathan spoke. "Is there nothing we can do?" He considered a moment, then asked, "What of the forest? You mentioned wielders would seek it out for its magic in the days before the New Laws. Could you not acquire more there?"

"We could," Sylvan admitted, "but it's unwise to find oneself near the forest after nightfall. There are many who call it home and like magic itself..." He wavered briefly. "They tend to be more restless when nature sleeps."

"So our only option is to wait until daybreak?" Jonathan pressed.

Sylvan hesitated. "Not necessarily..."

The hairs on the back of Rosalind's neck rose as his attention fell to her.

"Do you recall what we discussed yesterday?" Sylvan asked.

Tentatively, she met his gaze. "I do."

"Well, wouldn't you know it," Sylvan said dryly, "an abundance of untapped magic would come in handy right about now."

"Now, hold on a minute," Jonathan started, but Valentina interjected before he could go on.

"But you said she couldn't wield the magic."

"I did," Sylvan affirmed. "And that still holds true. She is not a wielder. But just because she can't use the magic doesn't mean that nobody can."

Valentina eyed him skeptically. "How?"

"By siphoning the magic from her and redirecting it into whatever the wielder intends. In this case, I would draw the magic from Miss Carver and channel it into Constance so she can focus on disarming the enchantment."

Sylvan appealed to Rosalind directly. "It wouldn't require much on your end. A few minutes of your time now and a good long nap afterward is about all."

She looked over at Padraic, who sat slumped in the shallow basin, thoroughly disheveled and distraught. He was suffering, and it didn't look like he could take much more. Constance, too, appeared wearier than she had earlier.

"Will it hurt?" she asked in much the same way Padraic had, her voice even but not entirely free of trepidation.

"It shouldn't, but it will feel strange," Sylvan admitted. "The magic will be in a more excitable state as it's being siphoned. You'll feel it coursing through you as I draw it out, which I'll do by taking your hand. I suspect you'll lose consciousness not long after we begin, especially as it's your first time, but that should be the worst of it, and you'll be back on your feet after some rest."

That didn't seem all that bad in the grand scheme of things. She could endure a bit of discomfort for Padraic's sake. In the little time they had known one another, he'd been nothing but cordial and courteous toward her. And he was one of Jonathan's closest friends.

Besides, she couldn't very well stand by and watch him wait in agony when there was something she could do about it.

Rosalind opened her mouth to speak, but Jonathan beat her to it.

"You said that *should* be the worst of it, not *will* be. Tell me, Mr. Raynor, what precisely is the worst that could happen?"

Sylvan pursed his lips. "Nothing gets past you, does it, Chancellor?" His next words were slow to leave his mouth as if he were choosing his words carefully. "Like most everything, there are risks to siphoning. It isn't out of the realm of possibility to siphon too much magic from a person. In such a scenario, the result could prove fatal."

A deep chill ran through Rosalind.

"But I didn't think it necessary to bring up now because that's not a concern of ours here," he continued. "Miss Carver possesses far greater magic than one disarming enchantment requires. I would need to wield something of incredible magnitude to use it all at once, a feat well beyond my ability. Seeing as we don't know each other all that well, I can't blame you for not taking my word for it. So here, how about I offer extra assurance to allay your fears." He reached down the side of his leg and brandished a silver-hilted dagger. Then he beckoned Valentina over, grasped it by the blade, and held it out to her.

"And what do you expect me to do with this?" she asked incredulously.

"I give you permission to jab me with it if I don't release Miss Carver," replied Sylvan in a far too casual tone for the topic.

Valentina's face seemed to light up at the prospect, but just as she was about to grab hold of the hilt, Sylvan pulled it out of reach.

"Now, as tempting as it might be, princess, this is meant to be a last resort. To stop me from siphoning the magic, you need only to sever the connection. In this case, that'll be to separate our hands.

I kindly ask that you refrain from stabbing me unless absolutely necessary."

With mild reluctance, Sylvan proceeded to hand over the dagger. Then he turned to face Rosalind.

"It's up to you, Miss Carver. You're not obliged to help. We can wait until dawn to harness magic from the forest."

To say she had no reservations would be a lie. But as disquieting as Sylvan's admission had been, it hadn't changed her mind.

"I'll do it," she said with more confidence than she felt.

"I thought as much. Follow me," Sylvan instructed, not wasting any time. "You too, princess," he added, gesturing at Valentina to join them. "You'll want to stay close—not only in case you need to stop me from siphoning too much but also to catch Miss Carver when she faints."

Rosalind had just fallen in step behind Sylvan when Jonathan reached for her arm. She glanced down at his hand, then up at his face, where she met his intent stare.

"Ros, are you certain?"

Consternation shadowed the features of his face, and she was sorely tempted to reach out and smooth the furrow between his brows. But because that wouldn't do, not here, not now, she offered him a small smile instead.

"I am," she said softly.

He searched her eyes a moment longer before dropping his hand and returning her smile with a faint one of his own.

Sylvan knelt down next to Constance and asked Rosalind to do the same beside him. She did as she was told and felt Valentina settle behind her. It was comforting knowing her friend was close by.

"Are you ready?" Sylvan asked, holding his hand out in front of her.

"As I'll ever be," she answered, sliding her hand in his.

Rosalind braced herself as the first few notes sounded from Constance's drum, expecting to feel something right away. But they came and went, and she perceived nothing. No magic, no lightheadedness. She wiggled her fingers to confirm her hand was still clasped in Sylvan's. Perhaps the effects wouldn't be as drastic as he made them out to be. Wouldn't that be nice? Or what if he were mistaken and she didn't have the magic to siphon in the first place? Perhaps this whole wandering well business was a big misunderstanding.

And then she felt it. It was subtle in the beginning, nothing more than a tingling sensation in her hand. But before long, the tingling had worked its way up her arm and cascaded through the rest of her body. Suddenly, every inch of her was vibrating with unrestrained anticipation. Heat began to radiate from deep within her bones, and just when it verged on being too hot to bear, a rush of coolness washed over her—as if she had plunged headfirst into the waters of the far north in early spring. The relief was immediate but fleeting. Soon, she got the sense she was sinking. Black colored the edges of her vision, and the sound of Constance's melody grew more and more distant. She had a vague feeling she had lost something, but she couldn't say what. Then, darkness swallowed her whole.

21

WORDS LEFT UNSAID

ROSALIND WOKE TO THE sound of bickering.

"Be gentle, will you? Don't throw her over your shoulder like some sort of unmannered ogre."

"Wasn't planning on it."

"There's no need to play the hero, you know. We can ask someone else if you don't think you can manage. Someone with a bit more brute strength. Like Mr. Raynor perhaps."

"No need. I'm perfectly capable of carrying her up a few steps. I'd appreciate it if you could at least pretend to have a little faith in me."

"It's been a long and stressful day, brother, and if I'm being quite honest, you look knackered. I mean that in the most—"

"I think I can carry myself up," Rosalind mumbled as she attempted to push herself into a sitting position.

"Ros, darling, you're awake," Valentina said cheerily. "Not entirely coherent, but awake. How are you feeling?"

Rosalind groaned. "Like I've had far too much to drink." She rubbed at her eyes, trying to wipe away the haze. It wasn't working all that well.

"Do you feel ill?" Valentina asked, a little alarmed.

"No, just very tired. And a bit muddleheaded," Rosalind answered slowly, tongue heavy in her mouth. "And my arms feel like jelly."

Jonathan chuckled. It was such a pleasant sound. "How about your legs? Are they jelly as well?"

"More on the jammy side actually."

"Oh dear," he uttered, and Rosalind could almost hear the smile in his voice. "Shall we see what you're like on your feet?"

Carefully, Jonathan helped her to stand. She managed to find her footing, but not for long. Her legs buckled underneath her, but Jonathan was there to catch her.

"How about I carry you instead, hmm?"

"But everybody will see," she whispered, or at least she tried to.

"It's really only Val and perhaps one or two patrons, but I get the sense they won't remember much in the morning."

Too tired to truly care, Rosalind wrapped her arms around his neck, and before she knew it, he was cradling her in his arms.

"Mind her head around the corners," she heard Valentina call out from behind them as they made their way beyond the kitchen doors. Her head lolled against his chest as he carried her through the tavern and up the stairs. Warmth bloomed in her chest as she inhaled the familiar scent of amber and citrus that clung to Jonathan's clothes.

"You smell nice," Rosalind murmured.

She felt as much as heard his mirth. "I'm glad you think so. I'd hate to have to find a new one."

Once upstairs, they headed down the hall to what had previously been Jonathan's bedroom. Earlier that evening, Valentina had announced they'd be switching rooms, insisting his was larger and less drafty. Though Rosalind hadn't noticed much difference, she went along with it—as did Jonathan.

Jonathan approached the bed and gently lowered Rosalind onto it. He unclasped her arms from around his neck and rested her hands atop her stomach. One of his hands remained over hers while the other brushed a strand of hair from her face.

"How's Padraic?" she asked, recalling the reason for her grogginess.

"He's doing better, thanks in part to you. Recuperating in the other room as we speak," he said as he knelt beside the bed. "It was incredibly brave, what you did. We only learned the truth about wielding yesterday, and you've doubtless had proper time to come to terms with what you are. Taking part in something so unfamiliar would be daunting for anyone—yet you did it for someone you barely know."

"He's your friend." Though she could hardly think straight, Rosalind could still picture the sorrow and concern etched across his face when Padraic first entered the tavern. "You looked so unlike yourself, and I wanted to bring you back."

She wasn't sure she was making any sense. A throbbing in her temples was steadily growing more prominent, and the words she managed aloud didn't sound as coherent as they did in her head.

Jonathan smiled. "And you did. Thank you." His smile dimmed slightly. "Ros, there's something you should know. Something I should have told you last night, but..." He faltered. "But I didn't. I convinced myself it wasn't the right time and that it would be better to wait until things had settled down and we were back at Brighthall. But now, after everything that happened tonight, I don't know when I'll be home next."

Rosalind's chest tightened. "You won't be returning with us?"

Jonathan shook his head. "I'm afraid not. I need to help Padraic and Ilora contend with the repercussions of today."

It made sense, of course, for Jonathan to accompany the Masons to Meridian. If it were true that their father was to blame for what happened to Padraic, they would need all the help they could get. Rosalind understood this, but the knowledge did little to ease the constricting hold on her heart.

"I don't want us to part without you knowing," he continued. "Already, I fear my silence is little more than deceit, which is the last thing you deserve."

Without her knowing what? He'd mentioned this earlier, hadn't he? Admittedly, she'd been too preoccupied by the news he wouldn't be returning with them to pay it any mind.

Jonathan leaned closer to the bed and squeezed her hand. Rosalind watched his throat bob up and down before he spoke. "I realize now is most certainly not the right time to tell you. One could argue this may, in fact, be the worst possible time to do so, but I don't know how many more chances I'll have before I leave. And, honestly, who's to say when the right time will ever come? Does such a thing even exist? Besides, I doubt what I say will be all that surprising to you. It's not as if I've been particularly discreet, especially as of late..."

Rosalind stared up at him, perplexed. She fought to keep her brows from knitting together, fearing he might think she was upset. Contrary to what he believed, she hadn't a clue what he was talking about. It didn't help that her head was aching in earnest now, and he was speaking unusually fast. If she didn't know any better, she might think he was rambling.

A strangled noise escaped Jonathan as he ran a hand through his hair. "Somehow, I've arrived at a loss for words. Not in the literal sense, as evidenced by my inability to cease carrying on at this very moment. It's merely that I can't seem to find the right words to say, and I don't wish to say the wrong thing. You see, it's quite a delicate matter—one I'm sure you'll need time to consider. This brings me back to why I believe now is as good a time as any to tell you that I find myself inexorably en—"

"I should never have doubted you, dear brother," Valentina exclaimed as she burst into the room. "But I am not too proud to apologize for—" She stopped short when she saw them. "The interruption?"

"Val, give us another minute, will you? I'm kind of in the middle of something..."

Jonathan's voice trailed off as more figures stepped through the doorway. Rosalind squinted and slowly Quinn, Keeper Saintgarden, and Constance came into view. Each carried something with them—Quinn, a tray of tea; the Keeper, a wool blanket; and Constance, her instrument.

Head lowered and shoulders slumped, Jonathan let out a hollow laugh. "*So* close. Serves me right for prattling on like a fool," he murmured to himself before pushing to his feet. Rosalind shivered at the sudden loss of warmth as his hand slipped from hers.

Jonathan cleared his throat and made to straighten his jacket, only to realize he wasn't wearing one. "Come to take care of her, have you? Good. Very good," he voiced to no one in particular. "Well, seeing as my work here is done, I suppose I shall leave you ladies to it."

He glanced down at Rosalind once more. "Rest well, and I'll see you when you wake up." For the briefest of moments, it looked as if he might say something more. But instead, he bid the women farewell and excused himself from the room.

All four women quickly descended on Rosalind, not allowing her the time to fret over what Jonathan had been about to say. Quinn fed her tea, and Constance tended to her headache. Valentina and the Keeper rushed about adjusting the pillows and blankets to ensure she was comfortable. They helped her into her nightgown as she drifted in and out of consciousness and it wasn't long before she plunged into a deep sleep.

22

CAUTION

ROSALIND WOKE UP TO warm sunlight streaming onto her face. She blinked away the sleep from her eyes and glanced around to find herself alone in the bedroom.

The clock on the wall showed it was a little past eleven thirty. She couldn't recall the last time she had slept in so late, but there was no denying it had served her well, as she felt surprisingly refreshed.

After dressing, she made her way downstairs and spotted Valentina chatting with Quinn at a table at the far end of the tavern. A bright smile blossomed across Valentina's face as soon as she saw her.

"You're awake! I'm so glad to see you finally up and about. You must be famished. Come and sit." She patted a spot beside her on the bench.

As if on cue, Rosalind's stomach let out an audible grumble. "I could eat."

"I'll go and put something nice and filling together," Quinn said, hurrying to the kitchen. Shortly after, she returned with a coffee in one hand and a heaping plate of boiled eggs, fresh bread, sausages, and a generous serving of chocolate rice porridge.

At first glance, there seemed to be far too much food, but less than ten minutes later, Rosalind had finished nearly all of it, except for a slice of bread, so as not to appear gluttonous, of course. She offered a sheepish smile when met with Valentina's raised brows.

"I'm impressed," Valentina commented. "Though not surprised, seeing as it's been a while since you last ate."

"Yes, I daresay none of us had much to eat yesterday, what with everything going on. Hard to have an appetite when you're full of nerves."

Valentina and Quinn exchanged a look.

"Ros, love," Valentina began, "how long do you think you've been asleep?"

Rosalind shrugged. "A bit longer than usual, I suppose, seeing as it's nearly noon now." She didn't miss the uneasy smile that flitted across Quinn's face. "Am I mistaken?"

Valentina lightly patted the top of her hand. "It's been a bit longer than that... three days, to be precise."

"Three days?" Rosalind repeated incredulously. Her gaze darted back and forth between the two women, half expecting one of them to laugh as if it were a joke. But neither did.

"Don't worry, it's nothing to be alarmed by," Valentina explained. "Constance assured us it's not uncommon for people to require plenty of rest when they've had magic siphoned from them, particularly after their first time."

"I see..." Rosalind hoped she was being truthful and not merely saying so to make her feel better. Preferring not to dwell on it any longer, she shifted the focus to Valentina. "What have you gotten up to in my absence?"

"Nothing much, although Quinn here did show me how they make their blackberry brandy. I'm thinking of giving it a go when we return home."

Valentina's mention of home conjured up a string of words from recent memory. *I convinced myself it wasn't the right time and that it would be better to wait until things had settled down and we were back at Brighthall.*

Jonathan had said it to her the last time they spoke, but she never learned what he'd been referring to. Not yet, at least. Perhaps she would find out today. At that thought, Rosalind glanced about the tavern for any sign of him.

Valentina spoke. "He's not here. He left yesterday with the Masons."

"Oh?" Rosalind felt her throat constrict a little. "Padraic is doing well then, I take it?"

"He is. A bit frazzled still but in good spirits, all things considered."

Rosalind forced a smile. "That's good to hear."

She stared down at her plate, pushing crumbs around with her spoon. She was happy to hear Padraic was improving. Truly, she was. Yet, the feeling was muddled with disappointment; Jonathan had left without saying goodbye.

"He wanted to stay until you woke up," Valentina explained, "but whatever they intend to do couldn't be delayed any longer."

Rosalind nodded. "I understand," she said quietly. There was nothing more she could say without sounding insincere. Besides, it wasn't as if Valentina hadn't already seen right through her, as evidenced by the sympathy in her eyes.

The table had only just fallen silent when Valentina slapped both hands on it, making Rosalind and Quinn jump. "You know what? I think my brandy-making endeavors would greatly benefit from someone more proficient in the kitchen. Can you imagine me over a stove?" Leaning toward Quinn, she added, "Ros is quite skilled at baking, you know. It'd be good to let her in on the process." She looked at Rosalind. "What do you say?"

Rosalind knew what her friend was doing. She wanted to say no. She wanted to find a quiet corner and sulk for a while. But she knew Valentina wouldn't have it. If this didn't work, she'd try something else—and likely bring more people into it, which is the last thing

Rosalind wanted. Besides, it was Valentina's way of showing affection, and she didn't have the heart to deny it. And so, she acquiesced.

"I say, why not?"

"Lovely." Valentina beamed. "The first thing we must understand is what the end product should taste like. How else are we to know if we succeeded?"

Later that evening, hues of pink, orange, and purple colored the sky as Rosalind and Valentina ventured back to the tavern after an extended walk about town. Each carried with them an item purchased during their perusal of street vendors. For Valentina, it was an exquisite little hand-carved wooden jewelry box. For Rosalind, it was a pouch of anemone bulbs she thought would make a lovely addition to the courtyard garden.

As they approached, they noticed Sylvan leaning against the wall of the tavern. He appeared to be waiting for them.

"Miss Carver. Princess," he said in greeting as he pushed himself off the wall. "I was wondering if I could have a word with the two of you."

"We were just about to grab ourselves a drink. Care to join us?" Valentina asked.

Sylvan nodded and proceeded to hold the door open for them. "Away from the crowd, if you don't mind."

Valentina found a spot at the far end of an empty table. She was about to leave Rosalind to gather the drinks when Sylvan gestured for her to sit. He made his way to the bar, joining them a few minutes later with a bottle of wine and three glasses.

"You found glasses. I've only seen mugs here before," Valentina commented.

Sylvan shrugged. "Spied some underneath the bar and figured we'd put them to use. See what you're on about."

What she's on about? Rosalind glanced from Sylvan to Valentina, sensing there was something she was missing. As Sylvan poured their drinks, Rosalind noticed the hint of a smile flit across Valentina's lips. She was most definitely missing something.

"Right," Sylvan began as soon as he sat down, "there are some things you ought to know concerning your circumstances."

"Circumstances?" Rosalind repeated. "As in me being a—"

"Yes, that," he interjected. In a lowered voice, he went on. "I caution you to tread lightly when discussing such matters in public. You never know who may be listening."

Rosalind's eyes widened in alarm.

"Look, I don't mean to frighten you," he said. "Actually, yes I do. It's much more effective in terms of getting the point across."

"I can assure you it's working..." she muttered.

"Good, because it's imperative you understand what's at stake if the wrong person were to discover what you are."

"And that would be?" Valentina pressed.

"Her freedom," Sylvan said. "Possibly her life."

Rosalind swallowed the bile that rose in her throat.

"You are an untethered source of considerable magic," he explained. "With you by their side, a wielder could perform incredibly powerful enchantments whenever and wherever they pleased."

"And if she were to refuse? To deny them the magic?" Valentina inquired.

"It doesn't work like that, at least not in Miss Carver's case."

"What do you mean?"

"Without the ability to wield, she has no command over the magic within her. She can't withhold the magic just as she can't give it away freely. Only through siphoning can the magic be extracted and..." He hesitated. "That doesn't require her explicit consent."

"Let me get this straight," Valentina replied with an unmistakable edge to her voice. "Any wielder can take the magic from *within her body* and do with it whatever they wish? And on top of that, there is essentially nothing she can do about it?"

Sylvan didn't respond right away, but he didn't have to. The prolonged silence between them was answer enough. When he next spoke, it was to offer advice.

"Your safest bet is to prevent others from discovering what you are in the first place."

Rosalind recalled her first night in Ashwind when Sylvan took hold of her wrist. "All it takes is a touch?" she asked, in little more than a whisper, though she was quite certain she already knew the answer.

"If a wielder were to come in contact with your bare skin, yes, they would know."

Strangled laughter escaped Rosalind. The irony wasn't lost on her. Freed from a decades-long enchantment that prevented her from touching the opposite sex, only to discover she must now attempt to evade contact with everyone.

"Ros, I know what you're thinking, but it isn't the same." Valentina reached out to clasp her hand. "In this, you have control. You didn't before, but you do now."

Rosalind desperately wanted to believe what she was saying was true, but she struggled to think past how unfair it all seemed.

"I don't want this," she muttered. "I didn't ask for this. I don't—I don't deserve this." She looked up at Valentina. "Do I?"

"No, love, you don't," her friend replied softly. "Now, I think it only fair to let you have the rest of the evening to wallow in self-pity. But come tomorrow, we must begin preparations."

"Preparations?"

"No time to waste," Valentina avowed. "As soon as we return to Brighthall, we'll commission a new wardrobe for you. Dresses and shirts with sleeves. And gloves! Yes, gloves for all sorts of occasions. What else..." she muttered as she tapped a finger against her cheek in thought. "We'll need to inform Louis and Maria, of course. But I reckon it's best if we don't say anything to the rest of the household for now. You know Charlene, a bit of a chatterbox and a reliable gossip. Frankly, it's one of my favorite things about her, but I don't think it would serve us well in this case. Unfortunately, we'll have to wait to update Jonathan when he returns. I don't think it's wise to commit it to paper."

Rosalind couldn't help but smile as she listened to her friend think through other considerations aloud. Even in the darkest of times, she could never feel genuinely hopeless or alone with Valentina by her side.

Glancing over at Sylvan, she was surprised to find he also wore the beginnings of a smile. Was he amused by Valentina's ramblings or possibly even impressed? Once she could think past the unease that muddled her wits, Rosalind would set out to determine what precisely was going on between them.

Valentina turned to Sylvan. "Are there any tell-tale signs that could indicate whether or not someone is a wielder?"

"Magic has a particular scent of cloves and spices. That would be one indication, though it's easy enough to conceal with perfumes and such. Alternatively, Miss Carver might see the magic on their person if they'd wielded it recently. Then again, it could be that they're merely wearing an imbued artifact of some sort. More likely than not," Sylvan continued, "if a wielder is hiding amongst high society, living under the nose of New Law elitists, I suspect they'll have taken great pains to disguise themselves."

"Yes, good point," Valentina murmured. Then her face lit up. "You mentioned imbued artifacts—might there be some Ros could use to her benefit?"

"I should think so. I can confer with Constance and report back. Admittedly, I'm neither skilled nor well-versed in imbuement."

"That would be a great help, thank you."

Rosalind was tempted to pinch herself to make sure she was actually awake. It was just so odd watching how amiable they were being with one another.

"Speaking of skills you lack," Valentina said not a moment later, "I do think it couldn't hurt to learn how to divulge critical information with a bit more nuance. Don't get me wrong, your brevity is highly appreciated, but I do think it can be quite jarring to those with more delicate sensibilities." She nodded in Rosalind's direction.

That was more like it. It was the first slight she'd heard between them all evening. However, in this instance, the jibe wasn't exclusive to Sylvan. Delicate sensibilities, really?

"Nuance, ay?" Sylvan remarked with one brow raised. "When you told Miss Carver here that she was limited to a single night of woe after learning she'll have to spend the rest of her life watching her back—is that the 'bit more nuance' you speak of? If so, I think I can manage it."

The following day, Rosalind and Valentina packed their belongings and hauled them down the stairs. Quinn greeted them with a hearty breakfast, and after they'd eaten their fill, it was time to set off for the train station.

A small crowd gathered outside the tavern to see them off. Most were there to see Valentina. She had grown closer with many of them in the days Rosalind was recovering. Even Leon, Quinn's frowning father, beamed as she approached, wrapping his arms around her in a warm embrace.

In truth, Rosalind was glad to have only a few people to say farewell to. She was still raw from the conversation the night before and was hesitant to shake hands with anyone who didn't already know her secret. She said goodbye to Quinn and Constance, thanking them for their help and hospitality. Then, she shook hands with Keeper Saintgarden, who imparted choice words of wisdom.

"Take care of yourself, Miss Carver," she said with a knowing look. "Your circle may be small, but trust and loyalty lie deep. Don't be afraid to rely on them; it's clear they rely on you."

"We should be off soon, ladies," Tory called out. He was seated next to his grandmother on the same wooden cart they had followed on their way into Ashwind a week ago. Not far off stood Sylvan, who held the reins of the horse they were to travel on.

Valentina approached and gently stroked the horse's shoulder. "Esther," she said affectionately. "Hello, old friend."

She turned to Sylvan and held his gaze. They didn't speak, only stood there considering one another. As they did, Rosalind caught the twitch of Valentina's lips as if she were holding back a smile. Eventually, Valentina inclined her head and proffered her farewell in the form of a single word. "Sylvan."

Rosalind could hardly believe her ears when Sylvan inclined his head in answer and replied, "Valentina." Then he held out his hand.

Valentina glanced down at it before meeting his gaze once more. She took hold of his hand and lifted herself onto the horse. Rosalind knew full well her friend hadn't needed the help. Sylvan likely knew that as well and yet he still offered. And Valentina accepted. This was all the evidence Rosalind needed to confirm there was a newfound deference between them that hadn't been there before.

Rosalind required more than a little help from Sylvan as she gracelessly settled atop the horse and wrapped her arms around Valentina's waist.

"You're lucky I'm accustomed to corsets, or there'd be no way I could survive the ride with you holding on to me so tight."

And with that, they were on their way.

The train car felt more spacious with only the two of them in it this time around. Rosalind looked from the grassy plains visible through the window to where Valentina sat across the way. She wasn't sitting so much as lying across the bench, legs tucked in close. Her eyes were shut, and her breaths came slow and steady.

Rosalind was fiddling with a handkerchief in her lap when she decided she, too, should take a little nap. It'd help the time go by faster. She went to slip the handkerchief in her pocket when something brushed her hand. She pulled out a folded-up piece of paper. Opening it up, she noted the familiar scrawl. The blotchy periods indicated haste, but each letter remained neat and legible. Though the note lacked a signature, she didn't need one to know who penned it.

I'm sorry I couldn't stay. I promise to finish what I started when I return. Until then, please understand not everything is as it appears.

23

In the Papers

Rosalind sat in the corner of Valentina's room, her legs draped casually over the arm of an oversized red damask armchair. She was partway through one of her favorite novels, one she'd read at least half a dozen times. Throughout the past five days, she'd found comfort in stories she already knew the ending to. She had enough uncertainty on her mind; she hadn't the energy to contend with the uncertain fate of fictional characters as well.

As hard as she tried to distract herself since returning from Ashwind, memories of her last encounter with Jonathan wouldn't leave her be. Too often they stole her focus and left her with questions she didn't know the answers to. What had he been about to say? Why had he seemed so nervous? How much longer would she have to wait to speak with him? Did she even want to hear what he had to say?

I fear my silence is little more than deceit, which is the last thing you deserve. Though bits and pieces of their conversation were mottled, that was one of a few fragments that had shown crystal clear in her mind. What had he meant by it? There'd been something that had weighed on his conscience, some sort of explanation he'd felt he owed her. If he had felt guilty about it, it couldn't be anything good, could it?

A knock sounded from the doorway, interrupting her thoughts and the companionable silence in the room.

"I've come with fresh tea," Charlene announced as she entered with a tray in hand.

Valentina perked up at this. She pushed herself up from where she had been lying on the bed, sketching in her notebook.

The housemaid set about preparing their glasses. She poured hot tea into two delicate, gold-trimmed porcelain cups. In one, she added a splash of milk and one cube of sugar before offering it to an appreciative Valentina. To the other, she added only milk and handed it to Rosalind. The cup was warm against her hands and the delightful scent held notes of lemon and rose.

After gathering the old teapot and cups, Charlene paused and glanced shyly over at Valentina. "My lady, may I ask you something?"

"Of course. Anything for the bringer of life," Valentina replied as she smiled into her steaming cup of tea.

"Is it true?"

Valentina cocked her head. "Is what true, Charlene?"

"The Chancellor, is it true he's engaged?" The housemaid was almost giddy.

Valentina choked, a few drops of tea dribbling from the corners of her mouth.

To her credit, Rosalind didn't react as viscerally, though she felt as if someone had squeezed out all the air from her lungs. She set down her cup of tea, fearing it might slip from her unsteady hands.

"Everybody's talking about it," Charlene continued, seemingly oblivious to their shock. "Even the postman made a quip about it this morning. Not surprising, seeing as it's in the papers."

"The papers?" Valentina repeated incredulously. "What papers?"

"*The Great Vine*, my lady. I figured you'd read it already, but if not, I have a copy here." Charlene dug a hand into her apron and produced said paper.

Valentina quickly snatched it from the housemaid's grasp. "Yes, I read the paper this morning," she said as she skimmed the pages in hand, "but I skipped the society section seeing as I'm to meet up with a few ladies for luncheon tomorrow. I figured they'd fill me in on anything of note. With more tantalizing details to boot."

Valentina found the excerpt in question and began to read aloud. "*An engagement years in the making. The Denaultian Chancellor has been spotted sporting a ring matching that of Lady Ilora Mason, daughter of the illustrious Chancellor of Meridian, Lord Gerald Mason. Simple in nature, the rings are said to be placeholders until the engagement has been made public. For those close to both parties, the impending union doesn't come as much of a surprise.*"

"Sure comes as a surprise to me, *his sister*," she interjected dryly before reading on. "*The pair were linked to one another years prior, when Lord Rashford, the youngest Chancellor in Denaultian history, at six and twenty, was studying at the capital alongside Chancellor Mason's son, Lord Padraic Mason. To add fuel to the fire, a reliable source has confirmed the Chancellor of Denault's prevailing presence at the Mason estate. It looks as if they've rekindled their romance—anticipate a formal announcement in the coming days for what is sure to be an alliance for the ages.*"

Valentina scoffed before tossing the paper to the edge of the bed.

"Are you not thrilled, my lady?"

"There's nothing to be thrilled about," Valentina replied. "Because it reads like little more than conjecture to me."

Oh, how Rosalind hoped that was the case. She hoped it with every fiber of her being. Even so, no amount of optimism could quash the doubt that niggled at her. It dredged up memories she would have preferred to remain dormant.

In her mind's eye, she remembered the easy rapport between Jonathan and Ilora during the Masons' visit to Brighthall. It was followed by an image of Jonathan's hand gently stroking Ilora's back as she sought solace in him that night in Ashwind. Then, she recalled how she had felt upon learning that Jonathan and Ilora wore matching rings to confer with one another. Rosalind's throat tightened at the memory like it had at that moment.

"You don't think it's true then?" Charlene asked.

"No, I don't," Valentina snapped. "How could I? He hasn't said anything to me."

"Perhaps he says so here," Charlene exclaimed as she reached back into her apron and pulled out a letter. "Arrived this morning."

Again, Valentina was quick to snatch the letter from the housekeeper's hand. She tore open the letter and began to read. A frown settled over her features as her eyes darted back and forth across the page.

The frown deepened as she read the letter over again. She then held the paper up to the light as if looking for some hidden message. When it was apparent there was nothing more to the letter, she puffed out a breath and glanced over at Rosalind.

Something about the look in her eyes made Rosalind's heart seize. "Is it confirmed then?"

"No, not exactly..."

Valentina hesitated a moment, then cleared her throat and proceeded to voice the contents aloud. "*Dearest Valentina, I apologize for not writing to you sooner. I hope I have not caused you too much worry; I know how you can get while I'm away.*"

She made a face before continuing. "*Rest assured, I am well. Busy, but well. During the day, I am learning much from Chancellor Mason. His dedication to the role is truly remarkable. In the evenings, much of my time is spent with Padraic and Ilora. As you can well guess, we are never short on conversation.*

"Now, I am sure you are eager to learn when I will be returning to Brighthall. That day will be a week from Thursday, and" —Valentina faltered, a grim expression flitting across her face—*"I shall be accompanied by the Masons. I have written to Louis with instructions for we are to host a ball that evening. I recommended he consult with you on*

decor as I believe you to have exquisite taste. I look forward to seeing you then. Please give my regards to Rosalind and the rest of the household. Yours sincerely, Jonathan."

Rosalind had only ever witnessed one ball held at Brighthall, and that was back when Lady Tildawan Rashford was alive. To host another now suggested there was something significant to celebrate.

The timbre of Jonathan's voice rang out in Rosalind's head as another memory from the evening Padraic and Ilora came to Ashwind surfaced in her mind. She was lying in bed, looking up at him, and he was about to tell her something. *Now is as good a time as any to tell you that I find myself inexorably en—*

Before he could finish, Valentina had entered the room, and she never got to hear what he was about to say.

Ice-cold realization washed over her. What if, at that moment, he had been about to tell her he was engaged to Ilora?

Valentina carefully folded the letter in half and set it on the bed before her. Though she addressed the housekeeper, Valentina's gaze was trained on Rosalind. "Charlene, will you kindly leave us, please?"

The housekeeper nodded and hurried out of the room. In the silence that followed, Rosalind tried desperately to avoid squirming under her friend's watchful gaze, but it was no use.

Unable to meet Valentina's eye any longer, she looked away. "You know, don't you?"

"I do," Valentina said simply.

"How long have you known?"

"I've had my suspicions for a while now, but they were confirmed last week."

In Ashwind then. Rosalind quickly recounted the trip in her head, trying to determine what this confirmation was that Valentina had spoken of. Had she overheard them on the horse ride into the village? Perhaps she had witnessed them dancing? Or... A mix of horror and humiliation sent a trickle of dread down her spine as realization dawned on her.

Her mouth felt impossibly dry as she spoke. "That night, when you fell asleep in Jonathan's room by mistake..." Rosalind trailed off. She dared a glance at Valentina and regretted it immediately upon seeing the raised brow and sly smirk dancing on her lips.

"Ros, love, we've shared many a night drinking together, have we not? In all those instances, how often have I gone to bed without brushing my hair?"

"None," she murmured. And it was true. Valentina had always made a point of taking down her hair before bed. Brushed it every single night. She'd often reminded Rosalind to do the same on nights they drank, and had even helped her follow through with it on occasion.

"Precisely."

"Y-you did it on purpose," Rosalind stammered. "But why?"

Valentina shrugged. "As I said, I had my suspicions, and it wasn't as if you two were very forthcoming. So when the opportunity presented itself, I thought, why not?"

Rosalind buried her heated cheeks in her hands.

"I will admit," Valentina added, "I paid the price for it. Spent nearly an hour untangling the mess on top of my head the next morning."

"I'm sorry," Rosalind said, her face still in her hands. "I'm so sorry." She lifted her gaze to Valentina's. "I shouldn't have kept it from you. I'm sorry."

"I'm sure you had your reasons." This time it was Valentina who looked away. She straightened her shoulders and pressed on. "I know I'm not always the easiest person to confide in. I can be indelicate at times. I'm rather quick to judge and even quicker to act, and I'm aware that, on occasion, I'm liable to impose my opinions on others."

Guilt roiled in Rosalind's belly as she listened to her friend list out her perceived flaws in an attempt to reconcile why she hadn't confided in her. It wasn't for any of these reasons, and Valentina deserved to know that. She deserved to know the truth. Tentatively, Rosalind made her way over to the bed and sat down beside her.

"Val, me not being honest with you was through no fault of your own. You are the greatest friend anyone could ever wish to have, and there is no one I trust more in the entire world. Truth is, I don't have a good reason for why I didn't tell you. I suppose I was afraid; I still am."

Rosalind's breath shook as she went on. "I'm afraid to admit everything aloud because that makes it all the more real. I'm afraid you'll tell me it all meant nothing. I'm afraid"—she swallowed—"you'll lose your good opinion of me. That you'll think I was being opportunistic; that after all your family has provided me, I still wanted more. I'm afraid you'll be ashamed of me. And I'm afraid that—that you won't trust me anymore."

Valentina considered her for a long moment, her expression inscrutable. Then the lines of her face smoothed over and her eyes softened. She reached out and cupped Rosalind's cheek. "It's alright to be afraid, Ros, but avoiding the truth doesn't make it go away."

And so, Rosalind told Valentina everything. Her early morning encounters with Jonathan in the kitchen, when they'd spent a few minutes engaging in idle chatter. The welcome dinner, when she and Jonathan first discovered the enchantment was fading. The night they'd kissed after being left on their own, to which Valentina admitted she had retired early on purpose. Her birthday. Learning it was Rosalind who had propositioned Jonathan delighted Valentina immensely; she had assumed it was the other way around.

Rosalind went on to recount their interludes in Ashwind, during which she discovered the extent of Valentina's meddling. Her insistence that Rosalind accompany Jonathan on the trip was essentially to force them into spending time together. Then there was the horse ride, which was a lark more than anything else, and, of course, the evening she had not-so-accidentally slept in the wrong bed.

As she suspected, committing these moments to words made them feel more palpable, and in the light of day, she could no longer deny how they made her feel. How *he* made her feel. Though Rosalind had never been in love, she'd consumed her fair share of poems and plays to know the emotions it inspired in others. The longing when they were apart; the thrill when they were together, and all the push and pull in between. She had grown increasingly familiar with these feelings over the last month and a half, despite trying her damnedest to ignore them. But it was a fool's errand, simply prolonging the inevitable. She was falling in love with him and could ignore it no longer.

After detailing her last conversation with Jonathan, Rosalind rummaged through her pockets and revealed the note he'd left her.

"What a cryptic little bastard," remarked Valentina as she looked the note over. With her free hand, she felt around for something on the bed. Moments later, she brandished the letter from earlier.

As she scanned it again, she remarked, "Didn't you think his letter sounded a bit odd? *Dearest Valentina*—what was that about, hmm? He's never been so formal with me in his entire life. And then he goes on to compliment me about my exquisite taste? What utter nonsense. He'd never voluntarily commit kind words about me to paper. That, and he and I have very different views on what's fashionable and they don't overlap, save for a mutual respect for fine tailoring."

Valentina had a point. It did sound strange, though Rosalind hadn't noticed it the first time. She'd been preoccupied by the impending dread that plagued her as she waited for confirmation of a proposal.

"Something's up," Valentina concluded. "And I think this was his way of letting us know. Whatever it is, he can't say, and I reckon we'll have to wait until he returns to find out. Shame we don't have one of those nifty rings. Then we wouldn't have to wait for answers. I bet if we could ask him if he were engaged, he'd say no."

Rosalind's ears perked up at this. "What makes you say that?"

"Well for one, he didn't explicitly say so in his letter. A ball could be for any number of reasons. Secondly, he has feelings for you and was going to tell you as much had I not interrupted." Valentina shook her head and laughed. "After all my meddling, to think I was the one to ruin the moment!"

"You don't know that," said Rosalind, doing her best to temper the fluttering of her heart. "He may have been about to admit that he and Ilora were engaged. Sure sounded like the word 'engaged' was about to leave his mouth."

Rosalind threw herself back onto the bed and covered her eyes with her forearm. "I told you he hesitated the night before, didn't I? When I asked if he wanted me to stay, he froze, like he wasn't sure what to do. I was certain he was going to leave. Perhaps he had wanted to tell me then, but..."

"But your feminine wiles proved too tempting?" Valentina finished. She snorted. "You act as if you locked him in the room and threw away the key. You didn't. You offered him a choice, and he accepted. Besides, do you believe he's the type to bed someone while knowingly being engaged to someone else?"

Rosalind shook her head. "No."

"Ros, love, you seem to think you're the only fool in this situation, but you aren't. Jonathan knew full well what he was getting himself into when all of this began. You can't convince me he hadn't considered the ramifications. He's far too diligent for that, but don't tell him I said that," Valentina added quickly. "He'll take it as a compliment. What I'm trying to get at is that Jonathan is just as much of a fool as you. The wise decision would have been to say no the first time you asked. So why, then, did he say yes?"

Rosalind shrugged. "Because I... asked nicely?"

Valentina barked a laugh. "He's the bloody Chancellor. One of only four in the entire country. He's wealthy, he's powerful, and he's unmarried. People throw themselves at him all the time. He's more than capable of politely declining propositions such as the one you offered him. No, he said yes because he wanted to."

"That doesn't mean he—"

Rosalind squawked as Valentina thwacked her with a pillow.

"I don't want to hear it. I've seen the way he looks at you, how he seeks you out in a crowd. The feeling is mutual, and you can't tell me otherwise," Valentina insisted. "It just makes sense, you know? You balance each other out nicely. Plus, he's less obnoxious when you're around and I sincerely appreciate that. Want to know the most grievous part of all this?"

Rosalind eyed her warily. "What?"

Valentina let out a dramatic sigh. "That I won't get to hear about your foray into the world of men because the man you chose to jump in bed with is, in fact, my brother."

Rosalind stared incredulously at Valentina. "*That* is what you're most upset about?"

"Yes," Valentina hissed. "Had it been anybody else, I would insist you spare me no detail. Remember that night we snuck out? Think of the questions I asked you then. I'd ask you those same ones now and then some because you had sex with a man, Ros, and I want to know what it was like for you. You must've enjoyed it to have given it another go. But to ask you would be to learn far more about Jonathan than I ever wish to know." Her lip curled in disgust.

"So we'll be alright, you and I? Even after all you've learned. After I kept it from you for so long?" Rosalind ventured.

"Of course we will," Valentina replied. "Am I disappointed you didn't tell me sooner? Yes. I want you to feel as if you can tell me anything because you can. But it'd be hypocritical of me to expect you to confide everything in me when there are things I haven't told you."

Rosalind blinked. "There are things you haven't told me? But you're always so descriptive about everything..."

Valentina gave a wry smile. "I do like to tell a good story, but that doesn't mean I've told them all. I need to keep a bit of mystery about myself."

Remembering their departure from Ashwind, Rosalind's eyes grew wide. "Mr. Raynor!"

One of Valentina's shoulders lifted in a casual shrug. "Maybe I'll tell you about it someday."

24

Valentina's Interrogation

"Pardon, my lady, you asked me to inform you when Lord Rashford was approaching. Colby says his carriage and that belonging to the Mason family are venturing down the lane as we speak."

Valentina glanced over at her bedroom doorway to find one of the housemaids poking her head in. "Thank you, Charlene. Please let Louis know I shall join him shortly."

She added the last pin to her hair and swiped a tad more rouge on her cheeks before making her way downstairs to assume her place opposite Louis at the manor's entrance.

"As always, you look a vision of beauty, my dear. You were born to wear violet."

"You're too kind, Louis. And yes, I suppose I was," Valentina replied with a faint smile.

She knew she looked good in her evening gown. As Louis had pointed out, the color was the exact shade of Rashford violet that always complemented her skin tone so well. The neckline of her satin dress verged on indecent, saved only by the trail of beaded lace appliqué along its hem. That same appliqué wrapped around her waist and ran down the sides of her dress. Out from under the flowing Dolman sleeves that draped over the edge of her shoulders was again the appliqué, which ran down her arms like fitted sleeves, tapering at her wrists and looping around her middle fingers.

"What of Rosalind?" Louis asked. "Will she not be joining us?"

"No, I don't believe so. Probably off helping Maria with something or other. You know how she is."

Admittedly, Valentina wasn't sure where she was at the moment. She had expected Rosalind to join her in getting primped and preened for tonight's festivities, but she never came around. Before venturing downstairs, she peeked into her room only to find it empty. That wasn't altogether surprising, seeing as she had recommended that Rosalind keep herself occupied until the ball.

Even if Jonathan hadn't made a mess of things and left her in a tizzy, Rosalind was still in for an overwhelming evening. For one, tonight's ball marked the first high society event she would attend sans enchantment. Because nothing in Proper stayed secret for long, she was sure to encounter many a curious glance and possibly even an unbid advance or two. Rosalind never did like attention on her. Then there was her whole wandering well predicament to contend with, which would no doubt have her on edge.

This is why Valentina insisted she confront Jonathan first to get to the bottom of whatever was going on. Then, she could relay it back to Rosalind, allowing her a chance to process the information behind closed doors. If Valentina's suspicions were correct, she'd have nothing but good news to impart. She really hoped she was right.

"Ilora, Padraic, welcome," Valentina said with a smile as the Masons passed through the open doorway. "It's wonderful to have you both back here at Brighthall. I'm pleased to see you two looking so well. How was your trip? Pleasant, I hope."

"There were a few bumps along the way, but overall, I can't complain as I was in good company," Padraic answered cheerfully.

Valentina glanced between him and Ilora, barely holding back a grimace. The thought of spending an entire day traveling alone with Jonathan sounded like an absolute nightmare. To think the Masons actually enjoyed being around one another for so long was unimaginable. She considered asking them how they managed it, but she was interrupted.

"Afternoon, Val. You clean up well. Though admittedly, I'm a bit surprised to see you ready so soon."

Valentina looked over at Jonathan, who was standing in the doorway. The impressed look on his face only fueled her irritation toward him, though he was none the wiser. She didn't miss his eyes scanning the foyer, searching for something. Or, in his case, someone.

"Expecting a larger welcome party, were you? On a day we're to host the ball you announced on short notice? Sorry to disappoint, brother, but most everyone is preoccupied at the moment. Not to mention, you're cutting it quite close. Guests will be arriving in no time."

She knew her remark was uncalled for, especially in front of guests. Poor Louis was likely suffering from palpitations in the wake of her words; she would apologize to him later. She wanted Jonathan to know straight away how displeased she was with him. The uncomfortable shift in his stance suggested he'd received the message.

"Speaking of the ball," Valentina went on, flashing a bright smile at the Masons, "I'm sure you two are eager to freshen up for the evening."

"Oh, I don't know, I'd quite like to see what happens ne—"

Ilora nudged Padraic, silencing him. "Yes, very much so," she replied politely. "We had planned to arrive earlier, but unfortunately, we encountered a bit of a delay." Ilora glanced over at Jonathan, seeming uncertain as to whether she should elaborate.

"Let's not waste a moment longer then," Valentina exclaimed. Frankly, she had no interest in hearing why they were late; her mind was already set on confronting Jonathan.

She turned to where Charlene was hovering nearby. "Charlene, will you please coordinate with Colby to transport the Masons' things to their rooms as soon as possible? While he does that, can you prepare hot water for our guests and some light refreshments?" Valentina glanced around the foyer. "Where's Sylvia? I was thinking of having her show them to their rooms."

Charlene hesitated briefly. "She's indisposed at the moment, my lady. But I can check to see if she's faring better."

"No need," Jonathan chimed in. "I can show them to their rooms." He didn't dally, quickly whisking Ilora and Padraic up the stairs before Charlene or even Valentina could protest.

Valentina leaned against the desk in the study, her foot tapping against the patterned blue and gray rug that sat beneath. She stared at the door with her arms crossed, waiting. Jonathan was sorely mistaken if he thought he could evade her. And sure enough, it wasn't long before voices sounded beyond the door.

"...with the utmost discretion, please, Louis," she overheard Jonathan say as he entered the room.

Both he and Louis stilled upon seeing her standing inside. Valentina watched as Jonathan's expression shifted from bewilderment to wariness. "Val..."

"What exactly are you playing at, Jonathan?" she demanded.

At this, Louis raised a reproachful brow in Valentina's direction before wordlessly seeing himself out of the room.

Jonathan sighed. "Look, can we *please* do this later? I don't have time right now; I'm behind as it is. I'll gladly explain everything once this is over, but at present, I'm in need of assistance."

Nice try, but she wouldn't let him off the hook so easily. "Have something big planned for this evening, do you?"

"I do, but its success is contingent on everything going precisely to plan. I would greatly appreciate it if you could help ensure the right people are where they need to be at the right time. Will you do that for me?"

"It depends," she replied listlessly. "Seems like an awful lot of scheming for an engagement announcement if you ask me."

Jonathan pinched the bridge of his nose. "That's what you think this is about?"

She bit back a smug smile. He was so easy to irritate. She shrugged. "It's what you want everyone to believe, isn't it?"

"Sure, but I didn't think you'd fall for it."

"I didn't. I received your letter, and it was disconcerting, to say the least. Oddly formal, overly complimentary, and far too affectionate. I understood what it implied—that you were up to something but couldn't say."

Jonathan frowned. "Then why bring it up in the first place?"

"Because while I didn't fall for your gossip-fueled little ruse, I can't say the same for others."

Valentina made sure to emphasize the last word. She watched the puzzled expression on his face melt away as he realized who she was referring to.

"Surely, she can't think it true," Jonathan said, searching her eyes with an expression that suggested he half-expected her to declare it all a jest. When she remained silent, he pressed on. "Did you not show her the letter and convey your suspicions?"

Valentina stifled the urge to roll her eyes. If only it were that simple. "Of course I did. She wants to believe I'm right but still has reservations, and I can't blame her."

He rubbed at the furrow that had formed between his brows. "What of the note I left her? Did she not find it?"

"You mean the inscrutable scribble you stuffed into her pocket before you left? 'Not everything is as it appears,'" she recited in a mocking tone. "That note, Jonathan? Oh, yes, how very enlightening that was."

"I couldn't be forthright in case someone else discovered it," he explained. "We needed to be as discreet as possible until we grasped the full extent of Chancellor Mason's scheme and devised a plan; it wouldn't do to have him know we were onto him."

Jonathan scrubbed a hand down his face and leaned back against the door. "I never meant to hurt her or leave her guessing. To think, none of this would be an issue if I hadn't been such a bumbling ninny that night. I was *so* close to getting the words out too," he groaned, thumping his head against the door.

Dammit, he looked so miserable right now. Whether or not he had intended to make her sympathize with him, he had succeeded. "Perhaps you would have if I hadn't barged in on you two," she offered as an olive branch of sorts.

"Perhaps. But if I'm being honest, a small part of me is glad you did. I dread to think of the nonsense I was on the verge of saying..."

Curiosity peaked, Valentina leaned forward and asked, "Which was?"

"I don't know... We had just witnessed incredible, life-saving wielding before our eyes and, well, I suppose magic was much on my mind. When I tried to come up with what to say to her, the only words I could think of were..." He hesitated. "I find myself *inexorably enchanted by you.*"

Valentina snorted. How terribly ironic and unimaginative. Perhaps it was fortunate Rosalind endured a fortnight of torment instead. Going by the sour look on his face, Jonathan was thinking much the same.

"Please, *please* tell me you have something better prepared now?" She implored.

"I do," he said, patting at something in his pocket. "I had hoped to speak to her when I arrived, but she didn't show. I volunteered to take Padraic and Ilora upstairs thinking I might find her in her room, but she wasn't there. She wasn't in any of the common rooms, nor was she in the kitchen with Maria. And yes, before you ask, I did check the courtyard. She wasn't there either. Do you know where she might be?"

Valentina shook her head. She honestly hadn't a clue. Might it have been easier for him to locate Rosalind if Valentina hadn't encouraged her friend to effectively avoid him ahead of the ball? Perhaps, but she failed to see how admitting as much now would solve anything, so she didn't mention it.

"It wouldn't matter now anyway," Jonathan lamented. "I've run out of time to tell her properly, in the manner she rightly deserves. We should have been here hours ago, but Armory had to go and take his precious fucking time in making up his mind, and now we're in a rush to get things sorted."

"You met with Lord Armory today?" Valentina asked. She had figured tonight's true purpose was political in nature, but she didn't know to what extent. It was surprising to imagine there was anything Jonathan and Lord Armory might agree about. She couldn't help but be slightly intrigued, and Jonathan knew as much.

"I'll tell you why if you agree to help me," he offered.

"Fine," she grumbled. "I'll help."

"Thank you, Val," Jonathan said with a look of relief, though it didn't last long. Consternation loomed overhead and shadowed his brow. "I won't be able to speak with her privately until later this evening, which means she'll have to endure uncertainty for another few hours. Doubtless, she'll think me all the more indifferent for not seeking her out earlier."

Valentina pushed off the desk and approached him. She considered him briefly, then reached out to straighten his pocket square. "You'll just have to make it worth the wait, won't you? Lucky for you, you've fallen for someone who is exceedingly understanding."

Jonathan eyed her curiously. "You don't seem surprised about any of this. How did you find out? Did she tell you?"

Valentina raised a brow. "I have eyes, Jonathan. She didn't have to. That being said, she did confide in me once she learned I knew. Now, might I offer a bit of advice?" She poked him hard in the chest. "Don't fuck this up for us."

"Us?" he asked incredulously.

"Yes, I want this nearly as much as you do. If she's with you, she'll never have reason to leave Brighthall, and I shall never be without my dearest companion. It also saves me from having to feign niceties with whomever else you'd court in her stead. And really, she's as good as family, so you might as well make it official."

"Right." Jonathan drew the word out, then added dryly, "I shall be sure to heed your encouraging advice when the time comes."

Valentina smirked. He sounded less forlorn than he had moments ago—a small triumph in her book. Nothing like a little menace to shake him out of it.

"So, what's this you need my help with?"

25

A Moonlit Evening

This'll be the one to do it, Rosalind thought as she pushed another pin into the coiled hair at the back of her head. Tentatively, she moved her hands away, and for a minute, the upswept coiffure held. Unfortunately, it was short-lived as one by one, locks of hair fell loose.

She glanced over at the clock on the far wall and sighed. She was running out of time. If only Valentina were here to help. That had been the intended plan; she and Valentina were to prepare for the evening together, but the afternoon hadn't gone quite as anticipated.

After spending much of the day in the kitchen assisting Maria with last-minute food preparations, Rosalind offered to help Sylvia and Colby collect extra bottles of wine and champagne from the cellar. More guests had accepted invitations than initially anticipated, and they weren't convinced the amount they had ordered earlier in the week would be enough.

Rosalind was looking through a crate of cabernets when she heard a commotion behind her. She turned around to see a wide-eyed Sylvia clasping her hand, stained in red. Moments later, the housekeeper fell limp. Thankfully, Colby had been nearby and caught her before she dropped to the floor.

As Sylvia faded in and out of consciousness, Colby and Rosalind carried her up the stairs and to her quarters. There, Rosalind dressed the wound, which wasn't nearly as bad as it looked. Hands tended to bleed profusely, and poor Sylvia was inclined to faint at the sight of blood. Once Sylvia had regained color in her face, Rosalind returned to the cellar to clear things up. She found the crate containing the broken bottle that Sylvia had cut herself on and went about cleaning the small mess.

By the time she headed upstairs, dusk had fallen, and Valentina was no longer in her bedroom. Rosalind decided against seeking her out in case she accidentally bumped into someone else along the way. She knew Jonathan had arrived with the Masons because Louis had sought Colby out shortly after they brought Sylvia to her room.

So here she was, preparing for the ball on her own. She looked over at the door to her room, willing Valentina to appear before her. When nothing happened, Rosalind couldn't help but wonder if Valentina was with Jonathan at this very moment.

She knew it was cowardly of her to avoid him, but she didn't trust herself to maintain composure. Just the thought of him made her stomach churn. There was every chance she might cry, faint, purge, or smile at the mere sight of him. Whether out of dread or anticipation, she didn't know. So when Valentina suggested she make herself scarce until she could ascertain the truth and report back, Rosalind didn't argue.

Over the past week, Valentina upheld her conviction about Jonathan's affections. As persuasive as she could be, Rosalind refused to give in. She couldn't. Imagine if she did only to discover he didn't feel the same. It would be heartrending. No, it was in her best interest to maintain a healthy measure of skepticism.

However, that wasn't to say she didn't hold out hope that what Valentina believed was true. Every doubt she had regarding his affections for her was shadowed by the question: *but what if he does?* Though her memory of the last time they spoke was hazy, those that came before were vivid. How he looked at her that crisp, quiet morning in Ashwind. The way his hand interlaced with hers as they danced, the crowd falling away around them. The feeling of his arm wrapped around her as they drifted off to sleep. She had made a point of encasing those moments in amber.

She knew without a doubt he cared for her; she simply wasn't certain as to what extent. A friend or something more? What if her own emotions had colored those moments she held so dear? What if they showed her things that weren't true?

Rosalind shook her head and considered her reflection in the mirror. She needed to quit thinking about these things and focus on making herself presentable in a short amount of time. She eyed her unfinished hair. If she couldn't get it to stay up, she would just have to settle for half up, half down, and pray the wind would be kind to her.

After finessing her tresses into a style she was content with, she dabbed some rouge onto her cheeks and lips, then turned her attention to the dress on her bed. Sitting atop it was a brief note.

Can't ruin a dress with wine if it's already the color of merlot.

Rosalind smiled. Valentina was always looking out for her. Setting the note aside, she lifted up the first part of the dress. It was a strapless taffeta gown, corseted at the back. Once she loosened it enough to slip it over her hips, Rosalind was tasked with tightening it. Luckily, the laces were long and she was able to pull them taut and wrap them around her waist a few times to secure them in place.

On its own, the dress was far too revealing for Rosalind's comfort. The bodice was fitted, and the skirt hung around her legs in a column. Because the fabric had little stretch to it, a slit ran along the side of her right leg, cut unnecessarily high. Luckily it was only the first layer.

Carefully, she slipped her arms into the outer layer as she might a robe. Sheer silk crepe clung to her arms and wrapped around her torso, held in place by discreet buttons on either side of her waist. The bottom half cascaded to the floor, weighed down by delicate beading that appeared to drip down the skirt of her dress and pool at her feet.

Last but not least were the pair of gloves on the bed. They were made of the same silk crepe as the dress. She slid the first one onto her hand and fastened the buttons at her wrist. She attempted to do the same with the other but struggled to work the buttons as they kept slipping through the grasp of her gloved fingers.

"I'll just have to ask someone downstairs," she muttered.

Quietly, Rosalind opened her door and peered out to see if anyone was there. She sighed in relief when she found herself alone. She crept to the stairs and, again, stretched her head over the banister to see if anyone was at the bottom of the steps. With no one in sight, she rushed down the steps and hurried to the kitchen.

A familiar face was there to greet her. "Rosalind," Maria said warmly. "Don't you look lovely."

"You don't think it's too much?"

"Absolutely not." Leaning close, Maria murmured, "Wait until you see some of the guests. You'd think we invited royalty with all the tiaras and diamonds out there. I can't claim to know what is fashionable, but even I can see that money can't buy good taste."

"Maria!" Rosalind exclaimed before giving in to a laugh. Once she'd collected herself, she held out her hand. "Could you help me button this, please?"

"Of course." Maria threw the cloth she was holding over her shoulder and began to do up the buttons of Rosalind's glove. "There you go, dear."

Rosalind smiled in appreciation. Her smile faltered as she saw her gloved hand in Maria's. As beautiful as the gloves were, they weren't fashionable these days. Someone was bound to comment on them, to her face or otherwise. Unfortunately, she didn't have much of a choice. Though the risk of encountering a wielder in high society was low, it wasn't zero, and she had to do what she could to prevent anyone from discovering her secret. Plus, she had already anticipated facing a number of furtive glances and reproving whispers this evening. What were a few more?

Keeping her tone as casual as possible, Rosalind asked, "Is there anything I can help you with? I'm sure you're quite busy and could use an extra hand."

The squeeze of Maria's hand around hers indicated the older woman understood her intention.

"I'm sorry, love, but the answer's no," she said softly. "Your gown is far too nice. It deserves to be seen, and so do you."

"It was worth a try," Rosalind grumbled.

"Rosalind, if you don't go out there, you'll be giving them exactly what they want. You can't let them win, not after all you've endured. Show them how resilient you are, my love. You are free from the enchantment; they can no longer hold it over you. You belong here as much as anyone else. And if that's not reason enough for you to attend this evening, do so for Jonathan. Tonight is very important to him and he's worked hard to make it happen."

Rosalind eyed Maria questioningly. "You know what tonight is all about then? Is it what everybody—"

"I know he's had Louis rushing about doing all sorts of things," Maria interjected. "And that's all you're going to get from me. The rest I'll leave to Jonathan. But don't worry"—she patted Rosalind's gloved hand—"you'll find out soon enough. Until then, enjoy yourself as best you can. Valentina would be devastated if you didn't give that gown its proper due. She put a lot of thought into it, did she not?"

Rosalind groaned internally, displeased with Maria's non-answer, but there was no point in arguing as the housekeeper had already begun to shoo her toward the kitchen's back entrance. "Now, off you go."

Reluctantly, Rosalind stepped out into the night. The air was warm, but a cool breeze from the east promised relief. She was in no rush as she crept along the shadows cast by the manor's imposing form on her left. The hedges of the courtyard maze towered on her right. Eventually, the path in front of her gave way to light and sound and she found herself on the outskirts of the ball. She looked on in awe at the utter splendor of the evening.

Grand bouquets of blue, violet, and white flowers sat overflowing atop tall stone pillars scattered about the lawn. Draped between the pillars were handwoven garlands adorned with foliage and colored crepe paper. In the center of it all sat a spacious wooden floor constructed with an evening full of dancing in mind. At the far end sat a quintet of musicians whose festive and luscious melodies echoed into the night. And to ensure guests were never without refreshments, tables were strewn about, topped with an array of finger foods and what seemed like endless glasses of wine and champagne.

As impressive as the decorations were, perhaps the most remarkable display of the evening came courtesy of the night sky. Amid the cloudless starry expanse sat a bright, full moon, whose light bathed the grounds in an ethereal glow.

Rosalind nodded politely but largely avoided making eye contact with guests as she ventured over to one of the tables toward the rear of the soiree. She grabbed a glass of wine and downed it without pausing for breath. Then she picked up another and meandered to an unoccupied space nearby. She needed a bit of liquid courage to navigate the ball on her own for who knows how long. If she was lucky, she would simply wait here until Valentina found her. After all, she was accustomed to observing parties from afar.

As she sipped her wine, Rosalind surreptitiously scanned the scene in front of her. It wasn't long before her gaze landed on the double doors far across the way that led out from the manor and into the evening's festivities. She could just make out Jonathan's tall, lean profile as he stood outside, receiving each guest as was customary. Rosalind felt a pang in her heart as she noticed who stood beside him. Ilora Mason held out a hand as she greeted guests upon entry. Across from them were Valentina and Padraic, who rounded out the elite welcome party.

Though she was too far to see the expressions on their faces, Rosalind could easily imagine the slight curve of Jonathan's lips and the crinkle at the corner of his eyes as he warmly addressed the guests. If she closed her eyes, she could almost hear the rich timbre of his voice as he commented on their attire or inquired about their family.

"Beautiful night out, is it not?"

Rosalind jumped at the words spoken in a voice not half as pleasant as the one she'd been imagining. When she turned to see who had addressed her, she was at once surprised and dismayed. The man beside her had once seemed so imposing, but now he stood but a few inches taller than her. He wore a suit not unlike one Jonathan might own and styled his hair similarly, though none of it looked quite right on him. Perhaps it was the fit, a little too snug about his belly. Or perhaps it was the thin, dark mustache lining his upper lip that threw everything off.

"Mr. Trainor, good evening." She greeted him with a shallow bow.

"Oh, Rosalind, surely we are more acquainted than that. We have known one another for over ten years, have we not? Call me Marcus, I insist."

"Marcus," she muttered with a tight smile. He may have given her consent to use his first name, but she hadn't done the same, though that didn't seem to matter.

"I think this might be the most magnificent Brighthall's grounds have ever looked, don't you agree?" Marcus remarked. "Difficult to imagine this is the same place we used to run about as children all those years ago."

It was undoubtedly the most opulent it had ever looked, but Rosalind believed the grounds looked loveliest under the bright summer sun when the grass was at its greenest and all the flowers shone vibrantly. But perhaps Marcus couldn't recall this, as his attendance at Brighthall had been limited since he had been cruel to her *all those years ago*.

Besides Lord and Lady DuPont, Marcus Trainor was the last person Rosalind expected to approach her this evening. Not only was he Lord DuPont's nephew and so subscribed to the same spiteful notions about magic and those afflicted by it, but he'd also been especially sour toward her since being ousted from Jonathan's inner circle.

"Not children anymore though, are we?"

Rosalind had to stop herself from visibly gagging as she felt his leering gaze sweep the length of her body.

"Come to think of it," Marcus went on, "did you not recently celebrate a birthday? It was a rather significant one if I recall correctly."

She bristled, knowing what he was not-so-subtly alluding to. "I did, yes."

"And?"

The expectant look on his face irritated Rosalind, so she decided to feign ignorance. "And what?" she replied with a tilt of her head. The twitch of his brow indicated she had succeeded in irritating him in return.

"Is it gone?" he pressed. "Have you been freed of the curse?"

"Enchantment," she corrected. "And if you must know, yes, it has lifted."

"Brilliant. Then you must do me the honor of a dance."

Rosalind nearly choked on her own breath. "A dance? Oh, I don't know about that... I think you'd find me to be a dreadful partner. My dancing abilities are rudimentary at best, and I couldn't possibly subject you to such—"

"Nonsense," Marcus cut in.

Without another word, he plucked the wine glass from her hand and pressed a hand to the small of her back, ushering her forward. He set the glass down on the tray of a passing server. Panic rose in Rosalind's chest as the dance floor loomed closer and closer.

"Marcus, I mean it when I say I'm not well-versed in dancing. I'm really only familiar with a simple waltz, and even then, I have never attempted it in front of so many people..."

Marcus smiled and nodded at nearby guests as they swept through the crowd. Leaning in so only she could hear, he said, "Really, Rosalind, if I didn't know any better, I might think you were rejecting me. But you wouldn't do me the discourtesy, not when so many eyes are upon us now, would you?"

She glanced around at the handful of onlookers, who were watching them with a mixture of interest and surprise, and she couldn't think of a single word to say.

"Take my hand," Marcus instructed once they were opposite one another on the dance floor.

Rosalind stared down at his outstretched hand. She didn't want to do this, but her moment to deny him had come and gone. It was too late to say no now, not without giving high society another reason to ostracize her. Tentatively, she placed her hand in his. Why had he even asked her in the first place?

"That's it," he said approvingly. He waited until she put her other hand on his shoulder before settling a hand on her upper back. "Now, follow my lead."

Marcus stepped forward in time with the music and Rosalind obliged. Trying her best not to mess up, Rosalind focused on the movement of their feet. She mapped out the steps in her head as they went. *Right back, left sideways, together. Left forward, right sideways, together.*

"Stop looking down," Marcus snapped. "Look at me. Good."

Rosalind complied but didn't stop thinking through the steps. *Right back, left sideways, together.*

Marcus rolled his eyes. "I can see you thinking. And your movements are incredibly stiff. You'll need lessons, there's no doubt about that."

Rosalind didn't bother to answer. She just kept moving. *Left forward, right sideways, together.*

"And what's with the gloves?" Marcus went on. "Is there something wrong with your hands? Never mind, don't answer that. I don't wish to know. What I do know is they aren't fashionable. If you must wear them, we'll need to ensure everyone is too preoccupied looking elsewhere to notice them." His eyes lowered, and Rosalind could guess precisely where he was looking. "Tonight's dress is a good start."

She had to look away to avoid making a face at him. This dance had to end soon, right? She hoped it was any second now.

"Let's see, what else? You don't seem much for talking, which works out quite nicely as the last thing I want is an incessant twaddler on my arm," Marcus prattled on. Rosalind could hardly tell if he was speaking to her or aloud to himself. "Besides, when we're out in society, I should be the one speaking for the two of us. The exception, of course, is when we're with the Rashfords. You'll need to speak well of me when the opportunity arises."

The two of us? Suddenly what he was saying no longer sounded like supercilious chatter.

"I'm sorry," Rosalind said warily, "but I don't believe I follow..."

Marcus huffed. "I don't think it's too much to ask that you make a few changes. If I'm to take you as my wife, I expect you to look and act the part, at least until I have restored relations with Jonathan. Then I suppose you can slink off to whatever quaint country cottage I set aside for you."

Rosalind stumbled. Frankly, it was a miracle she didn't end up on the floor. Surely, she must have misheard him.

"Focus, Rosalind," Marcus bit out while his hand dropped to her waist. With a firm grip, he maneuvered her back into position. "I know this must come as a bit of a surprise, but I'm not keen to repeat myself, so listen up. This would be a marriage of convenience, of course. One that is mutually beneficial."

"How so?" Rosalind asked incredulously.

"As mentioned, I wish to repair my friendship with Jonathan. Being as you were the reason for my falling out of his good graces, you shall be the one to remedy it," he explained. "Your close relationship with him and his sister will be my way back in. Our union will show him I'm a changed man, that there is no longer a need for ill will between him and me. In return, I will offer you a secure and comfortable future."

Rosalind scrambled for something, anything to say. There's no way he was being serious. He despised her nearly as much as Lord DuPont did, which led her to the only thing she could think to ask at that moment. "What of your uncle? I can't imagine he would ever approve of such a thing."

"On the contrary, he was the one to suggest it."

His words rang in her ear so loud she hardly noticed the quieting melody. It was Marcus who stilled their dancing and stepped back. With unnecessary flourish, he brought her hand to his lips and kissed it. Then he tucked it into his arm and whisked her off the floor.

"You see," he explained in a low voice as they made their way through the crowd, "my uncle has no children to inherit his trade empire, so he must look to relatives. He has all but promised it to me, but before he can name me his successor, he has tasked me with re-establishing myself within Jonathan's inner circle. Seeing as he is to be Denault's Chancellor for the next twenty-odd years, it's crucial I foster close ties with him. The influence it would afford me would all but ensure the success of the business under my charge."

Rosalind couldn't care less about the future of the DuPont Trading Company. Marcus was a fool to think divulging his motivations would help to plead his case. Since approaching her, he had done nothing but insult and intimidate her, and she was beyond irritated now. What aggravated her most was how he assumed she would acquiesce.

As soon as they had cleared the crowd and returned to the same unoccupied spot they had met earlier, Rosalind yanked her arm from his. "What makes you possibly think I would accept?"

"Frankly, I don't think you have it in you to say no. We both know you've never been one for confrontation. But I see now you have a little more spirit than I remembered." Marcus took a step closer. "A quality I appreciate in *certain* situations," he added as his eyes raked over her lasciviously.

Rosalind took a step back, making no attempt to hide her contempt.

"Now, now, let's not make a scene," he remarked, taking another step toward her. "Consider your circumstances. Regardless of your newfound normalcy, your history will always precede you in Proper. No one here would deign to associate with you unless they were desperate. Lucky for you, I am *that* desperate. Besides, I daresay your time is running out, what with tonight's impending announcement and all," Marcus continued. "I can't imagine Lady Ilora will be in favor of having an unmarried woman of no relation sharing a home with her husband."

His words felt like a punch to her gut, and she struggled to catch her breath. Simply put, she hadn't thought that far ahead. She had been so preoccupied with uncovering the truth behind tonight's announcement that she hadn't even considered what might happen if the rumor proved true.

Her reaction had undoubtedly been palpable, as evidenced by the triumphant smirk on Marcus's face. But to her surprise, he didn't respond right away. Instead, he made his way over to the nearby refreshments table and picked up not one but two glasses of champagne. Then, with that peeving little smirk still plastered across his lips, he strolled back to her and held out a glass.

"So what do you say? Shall we cheers to it?"

Rosalind stared at the glass in Marcus's hand, wide-eyed and unmoving. Champagne had never looked so unappealing.

"Celebrating something, are we?" A voice said behind her.

"Certainly not," Rosalind remarked without a second thought. When she turned to see who had joined them, she was greeted by a familiar but unexpected face.

Marcus shot Rosalind a scathing look before dropping into an exaggerated bow. "Lady Ilora, what an honor." He wore an artificial smile as he straightened and added, "Your ears must have been burning as your timing is impeccable. We were just discussing the pleasure of being in your company this evening and how thrilled we are to be celebrating such a momentous occasion."

Ilora returned his smile. "As am I."

"I know I already mentioned as much during our earlier acquaintance, but you truly are a beacon of beauty this evening, my lady."

Rosalind may not have agreed with Marcus on most anything, but there was no denying he was right about this. Ilora looked as if she were born of the night sky itself. Her dress was the color of deep cerulean, matching that of the Mason crest. Panels of silver-embroidered velvet clasped high around her neck and cascaded down the front and back of her figure. Underneath was a layer of chiffon that rippled like waves as she moved, and a silver rope was tied snugly around her middle, emphasizing her narrow waist. Her hair was held up by delicate diamond-encrusted pins, which sparkled under the moonlight, and somehow, so did her skin.

Ilora nodded graciously. "That's very kind of you, thank you."

"You are most welcome. I realize you have spent much of the last hour greeting countless guests. Surely too many to remember all by name, so please allow me to re-introduce myself. I am—"

"No need," she interrupted. "I know who you are. You are Marcus Trainor, nephew to Lord Hamish DuPont, proprietor of the DuPont Trading Company, and the most senior member of Denault's regional council. If I recall correctly, you have long been acquainted with the Rashfords, though I must admit it curious as I have heard little mention of your name in passing conversations with Jonathan."

"Y-yes, you are correct," Marcus stammered, seemingly caught off guard by her forthright assessment. "Admittedly, I did not maintain correspondence as well as I should have while he was away. Now that he has returned to Denault, I have every intention of making up for lost time. In doing so, I also hope to better acquaint myself with you should I be so lucky."

To that, Ilora only smiled. Then her attention shifted to Rosalind. "Apologies for the interruption, but I was rather hoping I could have a word with you, Miss Carver." Her gaze darted back to Marcus as she added, "Privately."

"But of course," Marcus replied. "I'm certain you two have much to discuss."

His smug insinuation wasn't lost on Rosalind, and she had to walk away from him before she did something unbecoming or, worse still, cried.

"Shall we?" she asked Ilora, indicating the path that led far away from the despicable man.

The pair had only taken a few steps when Marcus's voice again grated on Rosalind's ears.

"Ros," he called out cheerily, "seek me out when you're done, won't you? Oh, and don't worry, I'll hold on to this for you until then."

Against her better judgment, she turned back to find Marcus raising the champagne glass she'd refused earlier in her direction. With a sly smile, he added, "I have a feeling you'll be wanting it after."

Rosalind stood frozen in place. He had called her Ros. *Ros*. The absolute nerve of him. There had only ever been three people to call her that—her father, Jonathan, and Valentina. The thought of adding Marcus to the cherished list made her want to retch. Never again did she wish to hear it from his lips.

She let out a steadying breath before politely asking, "My lady, will you pardon me for just a moment?"

"By all means," granted Ilora.

With that, Rosalind marched right up to Marcus. She couldn't quite meet his eye as she spoke aloud the single word that had been echoing in her mind over and over.

"No."

"No?" Marcus echoed in question.

"No," Rosalind reiterated. "That is my answer. I will not marry you."

"Let's not be hasty now," Marcus said with a slight edge to his voice. "You have yet to hear out Lady Ilora. Once you do, I suspect you'll be singing a different tune. Fortunately, I'm feeling quite amenable at the moment and am willing to disregard your senseless rejection." He leaned in close and added icily, "But I may not be so forgiving again, so think carefully before you answer me next."

Rosalind clenched her hands into fists to keep from shaking. With a resolve she didn't know she possessed, she spoke as steadily as she could so as not to attract the attention of nearby guests.

"Mr. Trainor, please understand this. I would sooner seek out the enchantment again than spend even a single day in abject misery at your side."

She turned to leave, not daring to give him a chance to respond.

26

Clarity

"Did you accomplish what you had hoped?" Ilora asked as she approached.

Rosalind nodded. A touch overdramatically, perhaps...

"That mustache is absolutely ghastly," Ilora commented as soon as Marcus was out of earshot.

"Befitting of his character if you ask me," Rosalind murmured grimly.

"So it seems. Valentina and Jonathan don't seem too fond of him either. Both were markedly displeased to witness you accompanying him on the dance floor. They were certain he was up to something."

They weren't wrong, Rosalind thought but decided against voicing it as she didn't want to have to go into details. So instead, she offered, "He knows I'm not an accomplished dancer and figured it'd make for some light entertainment. I'm pleased to say I managed to avoid embarrassing myself for the most part."

"Glad to hear it," Ilora replied. She glanced around before asking, "Is there somewhere quieter we can go? Somewhere we won't be overheard?"

Rosalind swallowed. "C-certainly. The courtyard should do."

She would be lying if she said Marcus's words hadn't gotten into her head. What was it Ilora wanted to say to her that couldn't be said here?

Her heart pounded in her chest as she and Ilora walked side by side toward the towering hedges. The ball's music and lively chatter faded into the distance as they walked along the stone steps toward the courtyard. She greeted Franklin, who was seated on a wooden chair partway along the path. He was getting on in years, so his primary duty for the evening was to ensure guests didn't venture beyond the perimeter of the ball. The courtyard was among the places closed off to guests, which guaranteed no one would be around to listen.

"Are you enjoying the evening so far?" Rosalind asked, unable to bear the silence any longer as they made their way along the hedge maze.

"I can't say I am, no," Ilora admitted, and Rosalind couldn't help but be surprised by her frankness. "It is undoubtedly a lovely venue and a beautiful night for a party, but welcoming guests is dreadfully tiresome. My mouth hurts from all the smiling. But perhaps I'll sing a different tune after we've made our announcement, and I can finally relax and enjoy a glass of wine."

"I haven't had to partake in a welcome procession myself, but Val tells me it's a 'soul-sucking affair' that takes years off her life every time."

Ilora chuckled. "Good to know I'm not the only one who isn't fond of them."

An assortment of divine floral scents filled the air as they entered the hidden courtyard. And though the night muted their vibrancy, the warm glow from lanterns scattered about the garden still illuminated the rich hues that blossomed around them. Lilacs, gardenias, sweet peas, and stargazer lilies were among the abundance of flowers that sat atop large stone planters encircling the quiet space.

After peering around to ensure they were alone, Rosalind steeled herself as best she could and turned to Ilora. Feigning an ease she didn't feel, she inquired, "What is it you wished to speak to me about?"

"Ah yes," Ilora began as she reached into a concealed pocket in her gown and pulled out a small velvet pouch. "Firstly, I wanted to give you this. From Padraic, Enzo, and I. It's a token of our gratitude for all your help in Ashwind."

"You needn't have troubled yourselves," Rosalind said as she took hold of the pouch. Gently, she tugged at the drawstrings, revealing what appeared to be matching bracelets. "They're beautiful," she breathed.

They were simple in nature, thin cuffs made from smooth, unblemished silver. The center of each curved into a chevron, reminiscent of the pattern birds made as they ventured south for the winter. Upon closer inspection, Rosalind noted detailed engravings along their insides.

"Erdesian-made, if you hadn't already guessed by the craftsmanship," Ilora explained. "When you wear them, they conceal the presence of magic in your hands. Enzo says they're common amongst the elite in Erdesay so as not to reveal the extent of one's wielding abilities."

Rosalind stared down at the bracelets she held in her glove-shrouded hands. It was perhaps the most thoughtful gift she'd ever received. Her voice wavered as she spoke. "This is incredibly kind of you. Thank you."

"Thank *you*, Miss Carver," said Ilora. "Do know Padraic wishes to offer his gratitude to you as well. I'm certain he and Enzo will seek you out later this evening."

Rosalind was intrigued to learn Padraic's partner was in attendance. The Masons had seemed reluctant to speak about them, and now they were here. It would be nice to put a face to the name finally.

"There's something else," Ilora said after a moment. "Something I'm not certain has been made clear to you yet."

Rosalind's shoulders stiffened. "Oh?"

She gripped the bracelets in her hand. Had these been given to her to help soften the blow of what was to come?

"There is no engagement. Never was one. It's nothing more than a rumor we fostered to account for Jonathan's extended stay in Meridian. He was certain you two would recognize it to be false, but judging by your absence upon our arrival and Lady Valentina's icy reception toward him, I take it that was not necessarily the case."

Rosalind let out the breath she was holding, and her heart began to race as the truth set in. Valentina had been right to believe it was a ruse. What else might she have been right about?

"In truth," Ilora continued, "we were sorting out what to do about my father. Once that was dealt with, we realized we had a unique opportunity on our hands, one we'd be remiss not to capitalize on. That is what delayed Jonathan's return to Brighthall."

"So it was true? Your father was responsible for what happened to Padraic?"

"He was," Ilora replied in a detached tone. "He learned of Padraic's intentions to elope with Enzo and renounce his succession to the Meridian council. Without Padraic to inherit his seat on the council, my father would have to elect a cousin or nephew to the position, something he wasn't keen to do. He thought to sully my brother's affections for Enzo in an attempt to change his mind."

"That's horrible."

"Isn't it? I want to say I never thought him capable of such a thing, but..." Ilora trailed off. "He's a proud and vain man, my father. I suspect he'd do just about anything to keep our family's name and position on the regional council."

Ilora spoke as though she felt nothing of his betrayal, but the glassy reflection of the lantern's light in her eyes suggested otherwise.

"Could he not name you the successor?" Rosalind asked, recalling how Ilora had mentioned an interest in diplomacy during their first meeting.

"He could, but he would never. Not of his own volition, at least. My family's seat on the council has only ever been held by men, and if it were up to him, it would remain that way." There was an edge of bitterness in Ilora's voice, but not nearly as much as was warranted.

"How terribly unfair. I'm sorry."

"I appreciate your sympathy, Miss Carver, but if anyone here is to apologize, it should be me."

"Apologize?" Rosalind repeated incredulously. "Whatever for?"

"I suspect my behavior in the brief time we've been acquainted is partially to blame for your belief in the rumor," Ilora explained. "You had cause to think it was true because, until recently, I had endeavored to make it so."

Rosalind's mouth went dry. "I see."

A part of her was relieved to hear it, to know she hadn't imagined things. The rest of her, however, was still wrapped up in a tangle of frayed nerves. Where was all of this headed?

"I've always thought us a suitable match," Ilora went on. "Common upbringing, similar passions and philosophies. We're both idealistic in nature yet pragmatic in our approach. We also get along quite well; if I couldn't involve myself in politics directly, I could at least marry into it. While it wouldn't be a love match per se, it would be an amicable one. I was certain Jonathan thought similarly, and perhaps he did until his return to Brighthall."

Ilora glanced around the courtyard. "Last time we were here, Padraic told me he suspected something had transpired between you and Jonathan. I paid little mind to it as it didn't change the fact that our union remained the most prudent choice. Besides, I figured it was little more than a dalliance, a consequence of two unattached persons residing under the same roof. But I was wrong, wasn't I?"

Rosalind didn't know how to answer. It had undoubtedly ended up being more than that to her, but she couldn't speak for Jonathan.

"You needn't say anything," Ilora continued. "I know Jonathan well enough to know the answer already."

It took a moment for Rosalind to grasp her meaning, but as soon as she did, there was no stemming the torrent of joy that rushed through her.

Ilora took hold of Rosalind's hand. "Please rest assured you have nothing to worry about where I'm concerned. I know that may be hard to believe, given only moments ago, I admitted to having hoped to marry Jonathan, but that was before everything came to light. He's a dear friend, and I would never dream of interfering with his happiness. Also..." Ilora dragged the word out, and the beginning of a smile tugged at the corner of her lips. "As of earlier this week, I no longer need to marry to get what I seek. Thanks in large part to Jonathan, things have worked out quite in my favor. Better than I ever could have imagined. Padraic as well." She was grinning in earnest now.

Though Rosalind hadn't known Ilora for long, she didn't doubt her assurance. Jonathan trusted her, which was enough for Rosalind to feel the same. Moreover, the gleam in Iloras's eyes as she spoke about her recent favorable development was so effusive that it left no room for uncertainty.

Admittedly, Rosalind was curious to learn more about whatever Ilora was alluding to, but before she could ask, a pronounced cough echoed throughout the courtyard. Both women whirled around to find Louis standing at the mouth of the hedge maze.

"Lady Ilora, Jonathan requests your presence," he said as he dipped into a low bow. He looked to Rosalind and smiled. "Yours as well, my dear."

27

LADIES AND GENTLEMEN

ROSALIND WORDLESSLY TRAILED BEHIND Ilora and Louis as they navigated through the crowd and into the manor. Louis paused outside the threshold to the dining room and held out a hand, ushering them inside. More than a dozen people were standing about the room, and as soon as Rosalind registered who they were, she turned to leave but the steward blocked her path.

"Louis, please let me by," she implored quietly. "You must have misheard. I don't belong here."

Behind her stood many of the same guests who'd attended Jonathan's welcome dinner—Lord and Lady Armory, Lord and Lady Sene, Lord Aston and Dr. Tremblay, and Lady Condry. Standing beside Lady Condry was a younger woman, who Rosalind guessed was the niece unable to attend last time. As it appeared to be some sort of council gathering, no doubt Lord DuPont and his wife would be joining shortly.

"Hearing's just fine, dear. Off you go," Louis said, making no attempt to move.

"There you are." Rosalind's shoulders relaxed slightly at the familiar voice.

"So sorry to have left you on your own for so long," Valentina remarked as she slid her arm into the crook of Rosalind's elbow and steered her to an empty space against the nearby wall. "I hoped to find you before welcome duties commenced, but I got held up elsewhere. This evening is turning out to be much more eventful than I anticipated."

"Why am I here, Val?" Rosalind muttered.

"Trust me, you don't want to miss this," Valentina replied. "And Jonathan would like you to know why he's been so evasive as of late." She leaned closer and whispered, "Plus, I think he wants to show off a little."

Rosalind felt her cheeks warm. While in the room, she had lowered her gaze to avoid catching the attention of others, but now she dared to glance at where Jonathan stood. He was joined by Ilora and Padraic behind the large dining table, which had been pushed back to allow for more space. Pieces of parchment, a fountain pen, and an inkwell were set out before him. His head was inclined as he exchanged hushed words with Ilora.

Seeming to sense her attention, Jonathan looked up, and when his eyes captured hers, it was as if the world had melted away. She could see only him and hear nothing but the thrumming of her heart. The moment was fleeting, however, as Rosalind was soon pulled back into the present by the world's most unpleasant sound.

"Yes, yes, I know it's this way," snapped a voice from beyond the doorway. "It isn't as if Brighthall is impressive enough to get lost in."

Seconds later, Lord DuPont strolled in alongside his wife. The unhurried demeanor with which he entered quickly evaporated once he realized the entirety of the Denaultian council was now in the room.

"What is the meaning of this?"

"Lord and Lady DuPont, how nice of you both to join us," Jonathan said as he flashed the pair a practiced smile. "Just a spot of business to attend to is all. Shouldn't take long, I promise."

"Last I checked, this was a ball, not a council session, my boy. Surely whatever it is can wait."

"Normally, I would agree," Jonathan said, "but tonight's proceedings go beyond the council's purview. Fortunately, those present here now will be able to assist us, which is why I must insist we carry on."

Lord DuPont's gaze narrowed. "And what is it you expect those not of our council to do?"

"Serve as witnesses."

"Witnesses?" Lord DuPont repeated incredulously. Then he eyed the papers on the table in front of Jonathan.

"Witnesses are only necessary if you intend to ratify an agreement that extends beyond our region." Glancing over to where Ilora and Padraic stood, Lord DuPont added, "And while we are certainly honored to have the young Lord Mason and the lovely Lady Ilora in attendance, only the Chancellor can represent Meridian in such an event."

"Right you are, which brings me to our first order of business," Jonathan said as he extended a hand in Ilora's direction. "It is my great pleasure to introduce the newly inducted Chancellor of Meridian, Lady Ilora Mason."

Murmurs of surprise reverberated throughout the room.

Things have worked out quite in my favor. Better than I ever could have imagined. So this was what Ilora had been referring to in the courtyard.

"W-what of your father?" Lord DuPont spluttered. Looking between Ilora and Padraic, he started again. "And why is it not his son who—"

"Father's health has suffered as of late," Padraic pointed out before the older man could finish. "After much deliberation, he made the difficult decision to step down. And, in an effort to focus solely on his recovery, he has also taken leave of his duties pertaining to the family's shipping enterprise."

"You can't be serious," cried Lord DuPont, visibly taken aback.

"Oh, but I am," Padraic replied. "I understand this news comes as quite a shock. We, too, were surprised by the unforeseen changes, but ultimately, we agree it's in the best interest of our dear father and the people of Meridian." He brought a hand to his heart, shut his eyes, and nodded solemnly as if deeply affected by it all, though Rosalind knew better.

"Knowing the amount of responsibility both roles require," he continued, "my father thought it wisest to divide them amongst the two of us. Considering my sister is prone to seasickness, and I can't name a single law passed in the last twenty years, we decided to delegate the affairs of the region to her and that of the high seas to me."

Rosalind didn't miss the unamused look Ilora leveled at her brother while his cheeky explanation garnered a few titters from the room. As if to appease her, Padraic added, "I jest, of course. In all seriousness, she is Chancellor because she's the best person for the job. You'll see soon enough."

For a moment, Lord DuPont appeared unconvinced. Then, slowly, the tension on his face eased and a thin smile spread across his lips. Lowering into a deep bow, he addressed Ilora.

"Chancellor Mason, if I may, I wish to extend the same offer I gave to Jonathan when he first stepped into the role. Should you need guidance, please do not hesitate to come to me. I have served Denault longer than you've been alive and have given counsel to both your father and the late Lord Rashford on many occasions. I am honored and humbled to have consulted on numerous laws that have contributed to the prosperity of our regions under their respective tutelages."

Rosalind bit the inside of her lip to keep from making a face. She didn't think anyone had ever sounded less humble and genuine than he did at this very moment.

"Thank you, Lord DuPont," Ilora replied. "I don't doubt the advice you might bestow upon me will prove as meaningful as that given to me by my father."

Lord DuPont puffed out his chest, pleased by her remark. If only he knew what she really meant.

Ilora looked at Jonathan. "Now that that has been settled, shall we continue with the next matter at hand?"

Jonathan nodded and peered down at the papers in front of him. After taking a moment to collect himself, he clasped his hands at his back and looked out at the group of expectant faces.

"As many of you are aware, I recently made the journey to our borderlands, to a town called Ashwind. Though brief, the visit was enlightening in more ways than one." His gaze flicked briefly to Rosalind. "Of all I discovered while there, two details stand out as pertinent to this evening's proceedings. Firstly, the import and export of goods in the area is minimal due to a lack of accessible trade routes. And second, the land near the border is more fertile, contributing to higher harvest yields. It's for this reason their demand for outsourced commodities remains low compared to other parts of the region."

Like a petulant child, Lord DuPont huffed, "What does any of this have to do with us?"

"As council members, we have a responsibility to serve our people—all of our people—to the best of our abilities, do we not? We have a burgeoning trade industry at our command, yet a significant portion of our population doesn't benefit from it. To remedy this, Chancellor Mason and I have put in motion efforts to expand trade routes in the borderlands and re-establish intercountry relations with our neighbors to the west."

Rosalind perked up at this. Had she heard Jonathan correctly? Judging by Lord DuPont's bulging eyes, she had.

"With Erdesay?" he shrieked. "Why would we even consider such a thing?"

"The expanded trade routes will only be effective if they're put to use," Jonathan replied calmly. He made no show of noticing Lord DuPont's alarm. "Currently, there is a stigma around the borderlands perpetuated by misinformation and its proximity to a magic-wielding nation. A conciliatory gesture like the one we propose would go a long way in helping to overcome it."

"This is preposterous," bellowed Lord DuPont, flecks of spit emanating from his mouth.

Jonathan cocked his head. "Is it?"

Rosalind suppressed a smile. He was goading Lord DuPont now, ever so slightly.

The older man glared at him and then looked around the room, expecting others to join him in voicing concern. "Does nobody else agree?"

Rosalind watched his eyes darken when he was met with nothing but averted gazes.

"It appears not," Jonathan spoke into the silence. "And because we are so certain it has potential, we have invited an emissary from Erdesay's southern court to join us this evening. They have reviewed the accord and agreed to convey it to King Philip personally."

He nodded at Padraic, who then disappeared into the adjacent conservatory. Moments later, he returned with someone who was surely not of this world. They looked as if they stepped out of a fairytale. Tall, but not too tall. Lean, with broad shoulders. Their hair was the color of the midday sun, sleek and sweeping with not a strand out of place as they came to rest beside Ilora. They had vibrant amber eyes framed by high cheekbones and full lips that lent a softness to their otherwise chiseled features.

To Rosalind, they were sunshine in human form. It was as if they glowed, though perhaps the offset of their attire made it seem this way. They wore a suit that was black as night, adorned with gold piping and two rows of buttons, which trailed down the length of their chest. Thick, gold embroidery embellished the collar and shoulders of their jacket and wrapped around the cuffs at their wrists and ankles.

"You're gawking, love," Valentina murmured in her ear.

Rosalind straightened and attempted to school her face into an expression that betrayed only mild fascination.

Valentina gently patted her forearm. "Don't worry, I was much the same way when I met them. I've been assured most everybody reacts as such. Well, with the exception of dreadful DuPont, that is."

Sure enough, when Rosalind peered over at Lord DuPont, she saw not an ounce of intrigue. It appeared their sunshine was no match for the putrid cloud of disdain that hovered over him.

"Please welcome Prince Innocenzo, child of King Philip, heir apparent of the southern realm of Erdesay," Ilora announced before bowing in their direction. "They join us this evening as acting emissary of the King himself."

Jonathan proceeded to bow, as did Padraic, and before long, the rest of the room followed suit. Except for the DuPonts, that is.

Something about the Prince's name sounded familiar to Rosalind. Realization dawned on her as she caught the coy grin on Padraic's face. Enzo was only a nickname. Prince Innocenzo was Padraic's elusive partner.

"Thank you, Chancellor Rashford, Chancellor Mason, for having me," said the Prince in a soft, honeyed tone. "It's an honor to have charge of delivering the accord to my father. Having looked it over myself, I am confident he will find it agreeable."

"If that's the case, let us not dally any longer." Jonathan turned to address the members of the council and their guests. "We ask that you all bear witness to the signing of this multilateral accord as proof that we do so under no un—"

Lord DuPont cleared his throat with unnecessary force.

"Is there something you'd like to say, Lord DuPont?" Jonathan asked without a hint of irritation in his tone. How he was able to keep his composure, Rosalind couldn't imagine.

Lord DuPont didn't rush to answer. Instead, he stifled a laugh with the back of his hand. When he was certain he had everyone's undivided attention, he spoke.

"I commend what you have endeavored to accomplish this evening, Jonathan, I really do. You are eager to prove yourself as a capable leader, and tonight, you had hoped to show us as much. However, regretfully, I must inform you that you've put the cart before the horse. Do not blame yourself for it; youth makes brazen men of us all."

He turned to address Prince Innocenzo. "I apologize, Your Highness, but I am afraid you have come all this way for nothing. A Sauvignian region cannot initiate formal negotiations with a foreign entity without first attaining majority approval within its council."

Rosalind's heart dropped at the implication. Meridian's council had seven members and Denault had six, including Ilora and Jonathan, respectively. If what he was saying was true, at least four from each region would need to be in agreement. Glancing around the room, she wasn't sure that was possible. Perhaps Jonathan could convince Lord Sene and Lord Aston to vote in line with him, but Lord Armory and Lady Condry? Needless to say, Lord DuPont was out of the question. And that was just within Denault. Rosalind wasn't familiar enough with the politics in Meridian to gather how likely it was for Ilora to win the favor of her council.

She looked to where Jonathan stood, hands still clasped behind his back. For someone who'd just been informed of an impediment to his plan, he didn't seem particularly bothered.

"I certainly had hoped for tonight to go well," Jonathan admitted, "which is why I made certain it would." He reached out and rested a hand atop one of the papers on the table. "Before drafting the accord, Chancellor Mason and I drafted a pact between our regions. In it, we outlined our intentions to expand trade routes in the borderlands, cooperate with farmers near the border to increase agricultural production, and formulate an accord with the southernmost realm of Erdesay."

Jonathan slid the parchment across the table in the direction of Lord DuPont. "You will note eight signatures at the bottom. Four from Denault and four from Meridian."

Rosalind gripped Valentina's hand in astonishment.

"Told you you wouldn't want to miss this," she murmured in response.

Lord DuPont rushed to the table and stared at the page before him. He squinted as he scanned the pact, and his expression reminded Rosalind of something Jonathan had once told her. Lord DuPont had advised him against wearing glasses in public because they were a sign of weakness. She wondered if the older man regretted following his own advice, seeing as he looked like he could use a pair right about now.

"You," he hissed as he spun on his heel and pointed a finger at Lady Condry. "After all I've done for you. Your husband left you near destitute, and if it weren't for me, you would have nothing. How *dare* you."

A wide-eyed Lady Condry held out her hands and shook her head wildly. "No, it wasn't—"

Before she could finish, Lord DuPont ground out, "We had a deal."

"I made a better one."

Rosalind followed the voice to where Lord Armory stood.

"I get the right of first refusal on all railroad construction for the newly proposed trade routes. That should keep business steady for the next ten to twenty years. No more having to pander to your whims to win contracts. As you're one to tout, it's business. Nothing personal."

Nothing was more satisfying than watching the color leech from Lord DuPont's face, though the pallid hue didn't remain for long. Soon, rage surged through his veins and flooded his face a dark crimson.

"So this is how you intend to run your council, Chancellor?" he said, seething. "By scheming in secret and excluding members from key decisions?"

"Is that not what you've done these past eight years? You simply aren't accustomed to being on the other end."

It took a moment for Rosalind to discern that Lord Sene had voiced the rebuttal. She hadn't heard him speak much at the welcome dinner. He seemed content to sit back and observe. Such was not the case tonight.

Lord DuPont shot Lord Sene a murderous glare before turning his attention back to Jonathan. "It appears you have indeed won their favor. Enjoy it while it lasts. And though the die may be cast regarding tonight's matters, don't think I will stand by and let this happen again. I shall not be caught unawares a second time."

"Nor would I expect you to," Jonathan acknowledged. "I also have no intention of making a habit of this. Moving forward, I am confident we'll find common ground, as it is in the best interest of Denault that we govern as a united front."

Lord DuPont scoffed. "We shall see about that. Now, if you don't mind, Mary and I shall take our leave. It is clear I am not needed here, and the shock and utter betrayal of this evening has no doubt been trying on her delicate constitution."

"Despiteful is more like it," Valentina remarked under her breath. Rosalind managed to stifle a laugh but she couldn't quite keep from smiling. Unfortunately, her amusement didn't go unnoticed.

Lord DuPont stopped dead in his tracks and leveled her with a gaze so cold it chilled her bones. "You had best wipe that smile off your face, you insolent, little wen—"

"Lord DuPont," Jonathan asserted, "you would be wise to consider your next words carefully."

"And what will you do if I don't?" The older man sneered.

Jonathan's face was void of emotion as he met Lord DuPont's steely gaze, his voice equally unaffected as he spoke. "Something brazen, I suspect."

Rosalind had never seen Jonathan look so intimidating before. She attributed it to the cool indifference he exuded now, unlike his typically charming and dynamic demeanor. And she wasn't the only one who felt this way. Though Lord DuPont looked as furious as ever, he did not counter. "We're leaving, Mary." He turned on his heel and exited the room.

Lady DuPont lingered in front of Rosalind a moment longer. "My nephew will put you in your place soon enough," she remarked under her breath.

Rosalind had half a mind to correct her, but she held her tongue and watched the older woman walk away. Better to let Marcus be the one to inform them of her refusal. She didn't imagine it would go over well. The thought made her smile.

"Well, that went about as well as could be expected," Jonathan announced wryly, easing the tension left in the DuPonts' wake. "If there are no other objections, what say we put pen to paper so we can return to the festivities?"

⁂

The council members and their guests began to filter out shortly after the ink dried. Soon, only a handful of people were left in the room, Rosalind and Valentina among them. They hadn't yet moved from their spot against the wall.

"What was Lady DuPont on about?" Valentina asked.

Rosalind grimaced. "I'm not certain you'll believe me. I can hardly believe it myself. As you said, it's been an eventful evening thus far."

"Color me intrigued. Very intrigued. But, wait, before you say anything, there's something I have to tell you." Valentina's expression turned grave. "I'm afraid you won't like it."

Suddenly, it felt as if the laces of Rosalind's corset had been pulled unbearably taut. Had she misunderstood Ilora? No, she couldn't have. Could she?

Valentina rested a hand on Rosalind's shoulder and bowed her head. "I know it hurts to hear this from me, but the truth is... I was right. I was so fucking right."

The tightness in Rosalind's chest gave way as soon as Valentina lifted her head. Gone was the solemn expression she wore moments before. In its place was a cheeky grin. "Should have known better than to doubt me. I know him, I certainly know you, and I know what's right. How did I know, you ask?" She shrugged. "Because I'm always right. And now you know that, too."

Rosalind scowled as she batted away Valentina's hand. "You know what? I could just about punch you right now."

"Oh, really? First Jonathan, and now you? My, my, what a fearsome match you two will make," Valentina teased. "But honestly"—she leaned in closer and whispered—"can you imagine if he'd actually swung at DuPont? I would gladly relinquish my title to witness that."

Rosalind laughed alongside Valentina, unable to feign outrage any longer. Once she'd regained composure, she risked a glance at where Jonathan stood with Ilora, Padraic, and the Prince, hoping they hadn't noticed them acting like children. But there Jonathan was, watching with an amused expression. He mentioned something to the others and started to make his way over.

"Oh, look, I think Padraic's calling for me," Valentina said before giving Rosalind's arm a reassuring squeeze and slipping away.

And then Jonathan was there, standing in front of her, looking as magnificent as ever.

"Evening, Ros."

The sound of her name on his tongue made her breath catch in her throat.

"Hello," she managed to say in return.

"I have to go out and make a few announcements now. But afterward, I was hoping we could talk. Will you meet me in the courtyard in, say, half an hour or so?"

Rosalind nodded. "H-half an hour."

The small smile he offered in response sent the butterflies in her stomach into a flurry. She really needed to get it together if she had any hope of saying more than a few words at a time.

28

Courtyard Rendezvous

Cheers erupted from beyond the hedges as Rosalind paced about the courtyard.

Jonathan cared for her as she cared for him. She was certain of that now. It was as she'd hoped, to the extent she had allowed herself to, that is. So why then did she still feel tethered to uncertainty? Why couldn't she shake the vestige of apprehension lurking in the shadows of her joy?

Because Jonathan wasn't just Jonathan; he was also Chancellor of Denault. He was, as Ilora pointed out, a pragmatic man after all. For him to entertain the possibility of her as anything more than a friend would be unwise. He held one of the most prominent positions in the country, and if tonight was any indication, he intended to upend the status quo. To do that, he would need a partner—an ally—by his side. Someone who could help him achieve all that he hoped to accomplish. The last thing he needed was someone who would complicate things. And she was undoubtedly a complicated thing. She was forever bound to magic, both in the literal sense and in the eyes of high society. Though she was no longer enchanted, those who knew her past would never forget what she was and treat her accordingly.

Thoughts of magic reminded Rosalind of the bracelets Ilora had gifted her. She was keen to try them on, but that meant removing her gloves. This proved next to impossible as the fussy buttons kept slipping from her gloved fingers before she could unclasp them. All manner of indecent curses spilled from her mouth as she attempted to undo them. She had half a mind to tear them right off when a voice spoke out.

"Would you like help with that?"

She looked up to see Jonathan across the way, standing at the edge of the towering hedges that opened up into the moonlit courtyard as if waiting for her to invite him inside.

"Yes, please."

She focused on steadying her breath as he approached. When he stopped in front of her, she held out her hand to him, her inner wrist facing upward to reveal a row of four delicate buttons.

Rosalind tried not to react to his fingers brushing against the thin fabric as he set to work. She watched as he finessed his way down the line of buttons, undoing one and then another.

Once he'd finished unclasping the buttons, he took hold of her wrist with one hand and tugged at the fingertips of her glove with the other. His thumb pressed lightly against the veins of her wrist, and Rosalind wondered if he could feel her pulse racing underneath.

Jonathan pulled off the first glove and tucked it into his breast pocket. Then he took her other hand and started on its buttons.

"I like when you wear your hair down," he said softly, drawing their shared silence to a close.

Rosalind's face warmed at the compliment. "Thank you. I hadn't intended to wear it down, but I'm absolutely hopeless when it comes to doing anything more than a simple plait. I usually ask Val for help, but, well, as you know, she was preoccupied. This is all I could manage on my own." The words escaped her in a hurried flurry. "Lucky for me, the weather's been kind and my hair has been cooperating. I doubt you'd be so kind if it was any more humid."

She shook her head. "I'm sorry, I can't seem to stop myself from prattling on."

"There's no need to apologize," Jonathan said. "I enjoy listening to the sound of your voice and watching the way your mouth moves when you speak. I like learning more about you, however trite you think the details may be. So, please say whatever comes to mind. Speak until you can no longer and know I'll delight in every word."

It was like she'd gotten the wind knocked out of her; she could hardly breathe. There was nothing she could say that could compare to such a lovely sentiment, and so she said nothing.

"There," he said as he pulled off her other glove and slipped it into his pocket to join the other. She hadn't even noticed him working on it.

Rosalind reached into her pocket, pulled out the bracelets Ilora had gifted her, and proceeded to cuff one onto each wrist. She peered down at her hands, half expecting to see some indication they were working. There was nothing. Ilora mentioned they would conceal the presence of magic within her, but exactly *how* she wasn't sure. What if they mimicked her enchantment? Acted as a sort of barrier against touch so no one could feel her and vice versa?

"What's wrong?"

She looked up at Jonathan to find him watching her. "It's nothing. It's only, I can't tell if they're working. I also can't help but wonder if..." Her voice dropped into a whisper. "What if they make it so I can't feel anything?"

"I can't be of much help with the whole magic bit, but I can aid in answering your question. May I?"

Rosalind nodded, and Jonathan took hold of her hand. Right away, she was relieved to feel the warmth of his hand against hers.

"Can you feel this?" he asked as he lifted her hand to his mouth and kissed it.

Rosalind's heart skipped a beat. She nodded—it was all she could do to answer him.

He turned her hand so that her palm faced upward and placed a tender kiss on her inner wrist. "And this?"

Rosalind swallowed. "Y-yes," she breathed.

"Good," he said softly, and for a long moment, silence lingered as they held each other's gaze.

"Jonathan, I—"

At the same time, Jonathan began, "Ros, let—"

Both quieted as soon as they heard the other speak.

"Ladies first," Jonathan offered.

Rosalind took a deep breath and tried again. "I wanted to apologize for avoiding you earlier this evening."

"You were avoiding me? I hadn't noticed." The knowing look in his eyes said otherwise.

Her hands bunched at the fabrics of her skirt as she pressed on. "It was cowardly of me, I know, but I wasn't certain how I'd react upon seeing you. I've never been very good at hiding how I feel…"

Jonathan let out the softest breath of a laugh. "No, I'm afraid not. Not in all the time I've known you."

"Yes, well then, as you may have gathered, I failed to keep the promise I made you—to want for nothing more between us. Truth be told, I'm not certain I ever really stood a chance," she admitted, her eyes avoiding his as she spoke.

She opened her mouth to continue, but her words were stilled by the lump of nerves caught in her throat. She shut her mouth, willed the nerves back down to the pit of her stomach, and tried again.

"When you're near, I can't help but feel drawn to you. I itch to be near you, to feel your warmth if only for a moment." Rosalind sucked in a shaky breath and kept on. "I want you to look at me that little while longer even though I can hardly bear it, let alone meet your eye. And I find myself wishing to be privy to all of your secrets, not only the one we shared. For every bit of hope I had that you might feel the same, I tempered it with reasons to doubt it could ever be true. Perhaps I mistook your kindness for affection. Or worse, I imagined more than was ever really there." She faltered. When rumors of your engagement spread, I feared I couldn't face you without betraying my true feelings. You are one of my dearest friends, and I wish only to celebrate your happiness in whatever form that takes. If she was the one you wished to marry, I wanted nothing more than to be happy for you. But I couldn't be sure my disappointment wouldn't show, so I thought it best to stay away."

Rosalind fell quiet. Right about now, she expected to feel a familiar twitch in her legs. The one that begged her to run. But it never came. As anxious as she was to hear what he had to say, there was nowhere else she'd rather be.

"I'm so sorry, Ros," Jonathan began. "I hadn't meant to leave you in limbo while I was away. To think this could have been avoided if I hadn't waited. If I had been honest with you that night in Ashwind. I knew I was in trouble the moment you asked if I wanted you to stay. I knew if I went through with it, that would be it. There would be no coming back—not for me."

Was that why he seemed hesitant? She remembered all too clearly the moment she thought he was going to walk out the door, only for him to embrace her seconds later.

"I should have said as much then," Jonathan said, "but I didn't have the words. That and, well"—he rubbed at the back of his neck, looking rather sheepish—"admittedly, my mouth had other priorities at the moment, talking not being one of them…"

He cleared his throat before starting again. "Please know I had every intention of respecting our bargain. Truly, I did. It's not as if I'm wholly unversed in the way of dalliances, and it sounded like a good idea at the time. You see, you'd taken up residence in my mind since the moment I returned to Brighthall. I believed one night with you would be sufficient to quell my curiosity."

Jonathan shook his head, smiling to himself. "But I was wrong. It only fueled my thoughts of you. I tried to ignore them by focusing on preparations for Ashwind. And I was successful, for a time. But then there you were. In Ashwind. With me. It was nearly impossible to get you off my mind with you right there, looking lovely as ever and soothing my ego with your sweet reassurances that all would be well. I tried to remain affable, but I only have so much self-discipline. I couldn't help but steal from you what I could—a smile, a glance, a touch. Anything to get by."

He pinched the bridge of his nose. "I sound like little more than a lecher, don't I? This is precisely why I thought it best to write things down."

Jonathan patted at various pockets on his person, then his hand slid beneath the lapel of his jacket and brandished a folded-up piece of paper.

"Are those notes?" Rosalind asked.

"Might be," he replied as his eyes scanned the page.

Curious to see what he'd written, she craned her neck to glimpse its contents. Before she could glean anything, Jonathan lifted it just out of reach above them. Rosalind narrowed her eyes at him, but her feigned ire cracked as soon as he flashed her a smug grin.

"I don't think so, love. I suppose you could try to jump for it, but I think we both know it'll be in vain. So how about I just tell you instead, hmm?"

Rosalind leaned back on her heels and waited with barely contained anticipation as he folded the paper back up and tucked it back into the inside pocket of his jacket. Then he reached out and took her hand, intertwining his fingers with hers, and held her gaze.

"From here on out, you will no longer be able to doubt my affections for you. I adore you, Rosalind. Not a day goes by when I don't think about you. Indeed, you consume my every spare thought, and I wouldn't have it any other way."

Rosalind's heart stuttered in her chest, and for a fleeting moment, she wasn't sure it'd start up again. Never had sweeter words been spoken to her.

"I've devoted so much of my life to the chancellorship, and I can't help but wonder if I'll lose myself to it entirely," Jonathan professed. "Sometimes I feel as if I might drown with the weight of it all—the expectations others have of me, of those I place upon myself. Worse still is the fear I might succumb to the motivations that have tempted so many before me. But I feel none of this when I am near you. Time spent with you is like wading into calm waters. All of the pressures and pretenses of the day wash away and I just get to be. My sole duty in those precious moments is to make you happy."

If ever Rosalind was inclined to swoon, it was now.

"I want more of that. More of you, Ros. I want to come home to you, to seek respite in your company. I want the privilege of falling asleep next to you in the evening and waking up beside you come morning."

Jonathan squeezed her hand, and she wasn't sure if it was for her sake or his. "I know it's selfish of me to ask this of you. To ask that you consider me, knowing full well a part of me is promised to another—to Denault. To choose me would mean subjecting yourself to my world and the people within it, good and bad. There would be no knowing who to trust. Prying eyes would follow your every move and you would never again know a moment of peace in public." He ran his hand through his hair. "I know I'm not the easy choice. But if you gave me a chance, I would do everything in my power to shield you from the worst of it. I would carve out a place just for us, and I promise I'd make it worth your time."

Jonathan lifted his hand to her cheek and brought his forehead to rest against hers. He released a shallow sigh, and then, in a voice so utterly raw it made her eyes burn, he confessed, "I'm yours if you'll have me. But if you wish only to remain friends, I shall readily oblige, for I would rather have some of you than none at all."

Rosalind shut her eyes to let her other senses take him in. The scent of his cologne confirmed he was close. The warmth of skin assured her she wasn't dreaming. And the sound of his breathing reminded her that all of this had been real.

He was right to think the idea of being with him terrified her. She had already faced her share of unbidden looks, courtesy of the enchantment; how much more if she walked out on his arm? No doubt, her days as a wallflower at society events would be a thing of the past. Then, of course, there would be the inevitable dissent of those like Lord and Lady DuPont to contend with.

But none of that terrified her as much as the thought of never knowing. Never knowing what it would be like to be his, to call him hers. That was a regret she couldn't live with.

"Jonathan, my answer is yes. I would weather it all for more of this. More of you."

At this, Jonathan drew back just enough to meet her gaze. He studied her face as if seeking some sort of confirmation.

"But," she intoned, a part of her reluctant to continue, "I'm not sure you've considered what associating with me in such a way might do to your reputation."

Jonathan didn't waste a second in answering. "Ros, we've known each other for, what, sixteen years? In that time, I've never shied away from associating with you, and my reputation is doing just fine. Besides, if anyone is going to put it at risk, it's DuPont, given what played out this evening. And that was a mess of my own making. One I'll be attempting to rectify for quite some time. But it was well worth it, as are you."

She eyed him skeptically. "Alright, but what about my"—her voice dropped into a whisper—"you know..." She eyed her hands and wriggled her fingers in demonstration.

"Your hands? Trust me, I've spent plenty of time thinking about them and what I'd like to do with—"

Rosalind swatted at his arm. "That's not what I meant!"

"Oh, you mean the bit about you being a potent source of magic," he replied, careful to keep his voice down. "Yes, well, I admit I was more than a little concerned when Sylvan explained it to me. But with help from him and Enzo, I intend to implement every precaution imaginable. Those bracelets, for starters. And it's not as if I'd let just anyone lay their hands on you." He crossed his arms. "Speaking of which, how is it you ended up dancing with Marcus Trainor, of all people this evening?"

"He didn't give me much of a choice..."

Jonathan's eyes narrowed. "He didn't try anything untoward, did he?"

"No, not exactly, but..."

"But what?"

She hesitated. "He sort of proposed to me."

Jonathan visibly stiffened. "I'm sorry, I must have misheard you," he said calmly, though the strain in his jaw suggested he was anything but. "I thought you said he proposed to you. As in—"

"Proposed is perhaps too generous a word," Rosalind hurried to explain. "More like he disparaged me and then strongly advised that I take his offer as it would be the best I could ever hope to receive. This is, of course, all in a desperate effort to get closer to you."

"I see. And you told him he could fuck right off, yes?"

Rosalind's brows shot up at his bluntness. "Well, actually... yes." It wasn't often she could say that.

The peevish expression on Jonathan's face was both amusing and endearing. Rosalind couldn't possibly pass up the opportunity to tease him; she so rarely had the chance.

She tapped a finger to her lips in mock contemplation. "But I wonder, might my decision have been too rash? His offer came with a cottage in the countryside, you know. Perhaps I should've given it a bit more thought..."

The corner of Jonathan's mouth quirked up. "I'll give you something to think about," he remarked in a tone so suggestive it made Rosalind's toes curl. Then he pulled her in close and captured her lips with his.

She clung to the lapels of his jacket as they kissed away the last remnants of longing. When their lungs could bear it no longer, their kisses slowed to stolen pecks between labored breaths.

"Let's sneak away," he murmured against her lips. "Leave the party to everyone else and lock ourselves in my room until morning."

"I think you'd be missed," Rosalind replied, though she was sorely tempted.

Jonathan sighed before reluctantly pulling away. "Fine. I suppose I can manage for a few more hours..." He straightened his attire and smoothed out his hair. Then he helped Rosalind do the same. When they were both ready, he held out his arm. "Shall we?"

Rosalind folded her arm in his, and the pair started toward the maze leading out of the courtyard. Her steps slowed as music and laughter sounded from beyond the imposing hedges. She told Jonathan she'd weather it all—the stares, the whispers, the aftermath that would surely follow—but did it have to be so soon?

"I don't know about you, but I'm in no rush to have others be privy to our personal matters," Jonathan explained. "Perhaps we could let it be our little secret for a while longer?"

Rosalind bit back a smile, knowing full well he was saying that for her sake. "I would like that very much. Thank you."

"Val will know, of course," he said as they started into the maze.

"Could say she knew the whole time."

Jonathan chuckled. "Quite right. There's also Ilora and Padraic. And Enzo, by extension."

"It could prove challenging to keep it from the rest of the household," Rosalind noted. "Charlene is a bit of a gossip."

"Louis and Maria should be able to help in that regard. If anyone can incentivize her to keep quiet, it'll be Maria. Oh, by the way, I'm fairly certain they know."

"What makes you think that?"

Jonathan shrugged. "Call it intuition. That and"—he reached into another one of his jacket pockets—"I found this tucked neatly into the drawer of my bedside table after Maria made up my room." From his fingers dangled a single luminescent pearl earring.

"I've been looking for that!"

"I've been holding onto it for safekeeping. I can't believe you misplaced my gift the very evening I gave it to you and said nothing of it."

Rosalind blushed. "Well, I wasn't ready to call it lost yet. I knew it had to be around here somewhere..."

"Ah, see, that's where we differ. I'm much quicker to declare something lost. For instance, I can say with near certainty that you'll lose something else in my room later this evening."

"What?"

He shot her a rakish grin. "That dress, for starters."

Reluctantly, at the end of the maze, Rosalind and Jonathan untangled their arms from one another. Not far ahead of their path stood Valentina, who made little attempt to conceal the fact that she had been waiting for them. She surveyed them briefly, and whatever she saw was enough to satisfy her. With a little clap of her hands, she hurried over to Rosalind's free side and latched on to her arm.

"So, are you two engaged then?" she asked excitedly.

"Come now, Val. I know better than to press my luck too far in one night."

Rosalind nearly tripped over her feet at the ease with which Jonathan replied as if the idea wasn't out of the realm of possibility.

"That and I refuse to be her second proposal of the evening," he added irritably.

Valentina gasped. "So *that's* what Lady DuPont was referring to?"

Rosalind nodded grimly.

"Oh, this I have to hear more about," said an all too eager Valentina.

"And I'll tell you, I promise. But I'll need a hefty glass of wine in my hand when I do."

"We can make that happen. But first, I have to introduce you to Enzo." She leaned in to whisper. "They're even more stunning up close."

Rosalind followed Valentina's gaze to where a small cluster of people stood not far away. She wasn't surprised to see Ilora, Padraic, and the Prince, but she hadn't expected to see the duo who accompanied them.

"I didn't know the Keeper and Mr. Raynor were here."

"Both have been advising us on how best to expand trade routes within the borderlands, so I thought it good to invite them," Jonathan explained. "Sylvan has also lent me a few texts on wielding. Understandably, he isn't keen to part with them, so I asked them to stay until I finished making notes."

"Between the Ashwinders, the Masons, and Prince Innocenzo, Brighthall has its hands full with houseguests for the next few days. As such, your room has been temporarily forfeited," Valentina told Rosalind. "Figured you wouldn't have much trouble finding somewhere else to sleep."

She must have been awfully confident things would work out the way they had, seeing as she'd offered up Rosalind's room before the evening transpired.

"Out of curiosity, who is taking my room?"

"Sylvan, I believe," Jonathan replied. He met Rosalind's gaze, and the two shared a knowing look.

As they approached the group, Rosalind noted Keeper Saint-garden's simple but sleek navy gown with black piping along the hem. Unsurprisingly, Sylvan was dressed in black from head to toe. His hair was tied back neatly, and upon closer inspection, she realized he was wearing a coat with tails. That, she hadn't expected.

"Mr. Raynor cleans up quite well," Rosalind observed, glancing sideways at her friend.

"Does he now? I hardly noticed," Valentina said a little too casually.

Rosalind bit back a laugh. If this was how she acted around Jonathan, it was little wonder those around her had read her like a book.

Rosalind sat atop the plush rug of the drawing room floor in the early hours of the morning. She leaned back against the bottom of the settee with her legs tucked underneath her, basking in the warmth of the hearth. Jonathan was beside her on the rug, one knee bent and the other extended in front of him, looking thoroughly at ease. At some point, he had removed his jacket and loosened the collar of his shirt. He was in the midst of a lively conversation with Padraic and Enzo, both of whom were seated on the settee behind them. As he spoke, his fingers danced with hers, their interlocked hands tucked between them, hidden from sight.

Rosalind glanced around. Louis, Maria, and the rest of the household staff had retired to their rooms as soon as the ball's last guest left the building, exhausted after the long day. Only a handful of people remained awake, and they were all in this very room.

Among them was Ilora, who had settled on the settee next to her brother. She was leaning forward, her chin resting on her hand as she listened intently to Keeper Saintgarden, who sat across from her in one of the paisley armchairs.

Valentina had also opted for a seat on the rug. She sat opposite Rosalind, and they spent much of the evening chatting with one another. Right now, however, Valentina's focus was on the man beside her, or rather, the sheathed dagger in his hand. One of Sylvan's arms rested on his knee as the other held out the dagger's hilt for Valentina to take. He yanked it out of reach just before she got a hand on it, not unlike he had done that night in Ashwind, the last time everyone in this room was together. Though Rosalind couldn't hear exactly what was being said, she guessed he was warning her to be careful. The rolling of Valentina's eyes confirmed as much. Sylvan was right to be cautious— Valentina with a weapon was equally fearsome and terrifying.

Rosalind smiled to herself. Never in her wildest dreams could she have imagined a moment like this. It was absurd, really. Unexpected, to say the least. Here she was, watching her dearest friend flirt with a wielder in a room full of not one but two Chancellors, a borderlands Keeper, and an Erdesian Prince. Perhaps most incredible of all was how at ease she felt among them. There was no urge to slink away, no notion that she didn't belong. She didn't have to conceal what she was or pretend to be something she wasn't.

A gentle squeeze of her hand turned her attention to Jonathan. His eyes searched hers in silent inquiry. She assured him all was well with an almost imperceptible nod. He raised her hand to his mouth and pressed a tender, unabashed kiss to the top of it. All the magic in the world couldn't temper the unbridled smile that unfurled across Rosalind's lips. She hadn't known it was possible to be so thoroughly, indisputably, and wondrously content.

Epilogue

Eyes glued to the book she held up in her hand, Rosalind felt for her cup of tea on the side table and brought it to her lips. She had reached a thrilling part in the story. Only when the weight in her lap shifted did she tear her eyes away.

She peered down and found Jonathan staring up at her, a smile on his face. "What?"

"You've gotten to the confrontation scene, haven't you? In the throne room?" he asked. "I can see it on your face."

She raised a brow. "Aren't you meant to be reading Laithan's Treatise on the Law of Taxation in the Naetali Lands?"

He sighed. "I am, but it's painfully dull. I keep having to read sentences over again because I lose focus halfway through. The man writes like he's being paid by the word. I'd much rather look at you."

Rosalind chewed her lip. She should probably let him get back to reading since he aimed to finish it by the end of the week and looked to be only a few chapters in, but her excitement got the best of her. "They have arrived at the throne room, and Okoro has just drawn his sword. Eva's acting surprised as if she hadn't expected them to come, but I think she knew they would. She did know, didn't she?"

Jonathan shrugged. "You'll just have to read on to find out."

She rolled her eyes, but before she could answer, a knock sounded on the door.

"Come in," Jonathan called out. He lifted his head from Rosalind's lap and righted himself on the settee.

Valentina swept into the study, followed closely behind by Charlene. She skipped pleasantries and instead ushered the housekeeper forward, saying, "Go on, tell them what you heard."

Charlene shifted uncomfortably, looking from Jonathan to Rosalind, then back at Valentina, before returning her attention to Jonathan. "My friend Archie—she's training to be a housekeeper at the Hanover Estate, you know, the one with the fountain featuring a buxom mermaid—well, she was telling me that she heard from another housekeeper who works for Lady Condry's sister that their footman saw you and Miss Rosalind being"—Charlene lowered her voice—"intimate with one another. He insists he saw you two holding hands near the pond a few days back."

"The pond that sits within our property?" Jonathan asked pointedly. "How would he have seen us there? Unless—"

"I asked the very same, I did," Charlene exclaimed. "The footman claims he was out searching for truffles and didn't realize he'd ventured onto the estate."

"Right," Jonathan said, though he didn't sound convinced. "Well, I appreciate you bringing this to my attention, Charlene. I can always count on you to have an ear on the ground. Thank you. I'll take care of things from here."

The housemaid beamed. "Yes, my lord." She offered a bow to everyone in the room and left.

Rosalind recalled their most recent turn about the pond. It had been a lovely morning, with the sun peeking through the clouds and a sheer blanket of mist that felt ethereal in the quiet calm. After sharing their daily cup of coffee in the kitchen, Jonathan asked if she wanted to accompany him on a stroll. He said he knew he'd be stuck inside for the remainder of the day and wanted an opportunity to stretch his legs before then. They held hands as they walked beside the pickerel weeds and cardinal flowers in companionable silence.

In the four months since the ball, they'd managed to enjoy each other's company, with society being none the wiser. It was easy enough to do as Rosalind had little reason to accompany Jonathan in public. If she did, which was a rarity, Valentina was right there beside her. As far as most in Proper were concerned, Rosalind was little more than Valentina's peculiar companion.

And then there was Brighthall—their safe haven. Every member of the household was aware of their courtship and maintained the utmost discretion, even Charlene. That meant the pair were essentially free to do as they pleased within the grounds. Or so they thought.

"So, what's the plan here?" Valentina asked, a hand on her hip.

"That depends on how Ros feels about it." Jonathan looked to her for an answer.

"I don't know," she admitted, hands wringing as she tried to make sense of how she was feeling. "I suppose I feel a little exposed. I feel like something was taken from us without our permission. Still, I don't think I'm as perturbed as I ought to be. I think..." She paused. "I think a small part of me feels relieved."

Jonathan didn't answer right away. He was studying her, and it was evident by the slightly unfocused look in his eyes that he was contemplating something. When he made his mind up about whatever it was he was thinking through, he looked to Valentina.

"Would you mind giving us a moment?"

Valentina pursed her lips, leveling a scrutinizing gaze on Jonathan. She was every bit as inscrutable as her brother amid her silent deliberation. Such instances revealed how alike the siblings were despite their insistence to the contrary.

"Oh," Valentina murmured. "*Oh.*"

Rosalind waited for her to say more, to protest her dismissal, but to her surprise, Valentina did no such thing. Instead, Valentina rushed over to where Rosalind stood and began to fuss with her hair and dress. "Val, what are you—" she began, but before she could finish, Valentina reached out and pinched her cheeks.

"Ow!" Rosalind exclaimed, quickly batting her friend's hands away. She frowned as she rubbed at the tender skin.

"You'll thank me later," Valentina said before throwing Jonathan one last look and hurrying out of the room.

Jonathan shook his head as he watched Valentina close the door behind her. When they were alone, he beckoned for Rosalind to follow him. "There's something I want to show you."

Jonathan opened a drawer at his desk and pulled out a sheet of parchment paper. "The sooner we get ahead of this, the better. As such, I prepared a statement in advance for the press should such a scenario arise. Before I submit it, I would like your approval."

"Y-yes, of course."

Rosalind was a bit taken aback. She had thought they might discuss things first—consider their options together. Obviously, something had to be done; the word would get out soon enough. But did they need to act this very instant?

She approached Jonathan and peered down at the paper in front of them. Printed at the top was the seal of the Chancellor of Denault. Below it was a brief handwritten statement. A few sentences at most, written in the most impressive handwriting. Smooth, distinct lines with not a hint of indecision in any stroke.

Of late, rumors have been circulating concerning an alleged personal liaison between Chancellor Rashford and Miss Rosalind Carver of Brighthall Manor. While he typically refrains from addressing such allegations, he does so now in the name of respect and amity. Chancellor Rashford would like to reiterate that he and Miss Carver are longtime acquaintances and remain only as such. His focus at this time lies solely with the responsibilities of his office and to the people of Denault.

Rosalind felt a wave of nausea wash over her. It was a perfectly sound statement, and she could find no fault with it. The wording was respectful yet straightforward, and there would be no doubting its meaning. She was certain it would prove successful in dispelling the rumors, for a little while longer at least. That being said, she didn't care for it. It felt *wrong*. She knew it wasn't true, but seeing it written out like that still stung. What if committing this to ink would somehow make it true? She knew it was a foolish thing to think, but that didn't stop her from thinking it.

"It's... well, it's..." She trailed off, unable to get the words out.

"I did draft an alternate version in case this one didn't quite hit the mark. Care to read that one as well?"

Not particularly, she wanted to say. If it were anything like the first one, she wouldn't like it any better.

"Yes, alright," she mumbled.

Again, Jonathan reached into the desk drawer and pulled out another sheet of paper. Like the former, it was hardly more than a few sentences. However, this statement was markedly different in tone.

It is with great pleasure that the Chancellor of Denault announces his engagement to Miss Rosalind Carver of Brighthall Manor. Chancellor Rashford holds her in the highest regard and looks forward to their future together. He also kindly requests that the public extend the same respect and goodwill bestowed upon him to the future Lady Rashford. As always, the Chancellor remains steadfastly committed to the responsibilities of his office and is honored to continue to do so with such a remarkable partner as Miss Carver by his side. Details to be announced in due course.

Rosalind read it over again and again, her heart beating as fast as a herd of horses galloping through open pastures. Surely Jonathan heard it, possibly even felt it, as he came up behind her and wrapped his arms around her waist.

"For this version to go to print, there's something I need to ask you," he said as he set a velvet blue box in front of her.

Hands shaking slightly, Rosalind picked up the box and opened it. Inside sat two gold bands. They looked unassuming at first glance, but a closer look revealed delicate engravings inside each band. These were no ordinary rings.

"Rosalind Carver," he said softly against her ear, "will you do me the honor of becoming my wife?"

The words set her soul alight with incandescent joy. She hadn't known one could be so happy. And while she couldn't claim to be fearless, she wasn't nearly as terrified of what would come next as she once was. The future held too much promise for that.

Though she could hardly feel her legs, Rosalind managed to turn herself around to face Jonathan. She reached up to take his face in her hands and smiled. When he smiled back, she couldn't help but press her thumb to that lovely little dimple of his.

"Yes, Jonathan, I will. Forevermore, I am yours. I love you."

Rosalind lifted herself onto her toes and kissed him.

"I love you, Ros, and I look forward to spending the rest of our lives showing you just how much."

Just then, the door to the study swung open, and Valentina tumbled inside. She showed no hint of regret for having blatantly eavesdropped on the proposal as she cheered, "Congratulations!"

Evidently, she had also wasted no time informing others as the rest of the household trickled in shortly after her, glasses and bottles of champagne in hand to toast the joyous occasion.

Rosalind glanced up at Jonathan, and the pair shared a quiet laugh. It looked as though Laithan's Treatise and the much-anticipated throne room confrontation would have to wait.

Author's Note

If you made it to the end of this story, it would mean the world to me if you could take a minute to leave a review on websites like Amazon or Goodreads or on social media. It helps to get the word out!

I wrote this book for people like myself who find comfort in reading stories they more or less know the ending to. Real life can be stressful and overwhelming, and sometimes, it's nice to have an easy read to fall back on. One you can scarf down in one sitting or nibble at a few pages at a time.

This story is for those who want something understated and less trying on the heart. A gentle romance, if you will, but with a bit of spice baked in for the thrills. Just enough to make you look over your shoulder while reading it in public.

Psst...want a little more of Rosalind and Jonathan? I wrote an extra scene (of the intimate kind) that sadly didn't make the cut. If you'd like to read it, please visit alriverswrites.com.

ACKNOWLEDGMENTS

IT HAS TAKEN ME nearly four years to complete this book. There were plenty of times I wanted to quit, but here we are. I wouldn't have been able to do it without the support of those around me.

I'd like to begin by thanking my sister for helping me every step of the way. She read every draft and offered feedback in a way that didn't make me cry. She advised me on how to improve my cover design. She also introduced me to people who know a thing or two about writing and design—thank you, Nicole, Clare, and Nate. Perhaps most importantly, she hyped me up whenever I was in doubt and gave me the courage to finish the book.

I would like to thank my parents for their unwavering support in everything I do. They have always made it known how much they believe in me, which has empowered me to believe in myself. When I told them I wanted to write a book, they were excited for me. Because of them, I am fortunate to know what it's like to grow up in a home filled with love.

I have a list of amazing friends to thank as well: Cassie, for being one of the first people I told about my writing aspirations and for responding with genuine enthusiasm and encouragement. And the consonants of GLAM, for addressing all of my very important and often explicit research inquiries, and for listening to me drone on about writing this book like it was my job and not judging me for it.

On the professional side of the house, I would like to thank Sharon Rutland for her invaluable copyedits. She provided constructive feedback without making me want to throw the whole thing out. Her insight not only enhanced this story but also helped me grow as a writer. If the opportunity arises, I would very much like to work with her again.

Last but not least, I'm grateful to my husband for his endless patience and support. He spent countless evenings listening to me talk through storylines and vent about my writing struggles. He always made sure I had time to write, and never once did he make me feel foolish for taking this hobby as seriously as I did (and still do). He's a good person who makes me feel wonderfully loved, and if I can convey even a fraction of that feeling to readers, I would consider it a success.

Oh, and I can't forget to thank my doggo for being my constant writing companion.

About the Author

A.L. Rivers lives in California with her dog and her husband. She's a tech marketer by trade but is trying to figure out if that's where she sees herself in ten years. When she's not writing or second-guessing her word choice, she's likely eating, laughing, snuggling, or sleeping. After her family and friends, she loves food, wine, sunshine, cozy things, and Keanu Reeves (ordering may change on any given day).